A Rebellious Bride

Though she tried, she could not ignore the persistent flutter in her midsection that began when Lord Marcus touched her face—so sensuously!—and only intensified when he handed her down from his phaeton. Her feelings toward him careened wildly from one extreme to the other. All the more reason to extricate herself from their betrothal without delay!

She needed time to think, to compose herself. She would not allow her future to be bartered like too much cotton—her fortune for Marcus's name. She had more pride than that.

Then she heard her father call out for her to join him. "How was your drive?" he asked. "Was Lord Marcus . . . pleasant?"

"I'm not sure 'pleasant' is the term I would use. Let us say it was . . . enlightening."

Other AVON ROMANCES

Coming Soon

And Don't Miss These
ROMANTIC TREASURES
from Avon Books

BRENDA HIATT

A Rebellious Bride

AVON BOOKS

An Imprint of HarperCollinsPublishers

AVON BOOKS
An Imprint of HarperCollins*Publishers*
10 East 53rd Street
New York, New York 10022-5299

Copyright © 2002 by Brenda Hiatt Barber
ISBN 0-380-81779-9
www.avonromance.com

First Avon Books paperback printing: April 2002

Avon Trademark Reg. U.S. Pat. Off. and in Other Countries, Marca Registrada, Hecho en U.S.A.
HarperCollins® is a registered trademark of HarperCollins Publishers Inc.

Printed in the U.S.A.

10 9 8 7 6 5 4 3 2 1

Prologue

Oakshire, England
June, 1816

"**H**ow long before we'll see you in London again?" Lord Marcus Northrup, fifth son of the Duke of Marland, asked his good friend, Lord Hardwyck. "I imagine you'll have a stronger inducement than ever to stay tucked away in your own world now." He nodded toward Luke's new bride, Lady Pearl Moreston—now Lady Hardwyck—where she stood chatting with her father, the Duke of Oakshire, near the doors of the great hall of the Duke's imposing country manor.

"I will indeed," Luke replied, smiling in Pearl's direction with a degree of besottedness that made Marcus pity him. If he also felt a faint twinge of envy, he refused to acknowledge it.

Not about to dampen his friend's spirits on his wedding day, Marcus broadened his smile. "Then

1

I'll see you when I see you. The tour of your northern estates will doubtless take months, in any event. But I can't deny I'll miss you."

During Luke's past few weeks in London, Marcus had become closer than ever to his old school chum. He had discovered remarkable things about Luke, including the fact that for years he had been living a double life.

Society knew Luke as a gentleman of fashion, recently elevated to the title of Lord Hardwyck, but he had also, secretly, acted as the Saint of Seven Dials, the legendary thief who stole from the rich to give to the poor.

Being in on the secret had added welcome excitement to Marcus's dissipated existence. But now the coming months stretched ahead with little promise of diversion beyond the stale pleasures of Town he had pursued for years.

As though sensing his melancholy, Luke clapped Marcus on the shoulder. "I'll be back, never fear. In the meantime, I don't doubt you'll find ample ways to fill your time." He punctuated his words with a wink.

Marcus almost asked him what he meant, but just then a clamor arose, and Luke hurried to join his bride near the massive front doors. With smiles and farewells, the couple was swept out onto the broad front drive toward the waiting carriage that would bear them northward on the first leg of their wedding trip, to Lady Hardwyck's own estate of Fairbourne.

Unwise as it seemed to Marcus to give a woman, even such a one as the redoubtable Lady Pearl, control of land and wealth, he knew Luke had felt it necessary. Shaking his head, he turned back to the house as the carriage dwindled from sight.

The day was growing warm, and he pulled out a handkerchief to mop his brow. From the corner of his eye, he saw something flutter to the ground. Curious, he bent to retrieve it, but examination only deepened his puzzlement.

Heedless of the merrymakers streaming back into the great hall, Marcus stood on the front steps, staring at a decidedly odd calling card. No name was inscribed upon it. Instead, it sported only a black numeral seven, surmounted by an oval—a halo?—in gold ink.

Understanding broke upon him and he grinned, recognizing the distinctive device of the Saint of Seven Dials. So that's what Luke had meant! He must have used his legendary skill to slip the card into Marcus's pocket while they were chatting earlier. Though he had intended to stay the night, he abruptly decided to start back to London immediately.

If he was going to take up Luke's mantle and become the next Saint of Seven Dials, he had work to do.

Chapter 1

London
July, 1816

Ladylike pursuits were vastly overrated, Quinn Peverill decided, throwing down her pitiful attempt at embroidery in disgust. How could something be simultaneously so frustrating and so boring? Her father insisted that all Society ladies embroidered, but after several hours' trial, Quinn took leave to doubt it.

Rising, she restlessly moved to the window of the sumptuous parlor of the hotel suite, kicking at her pale pink skirts as she walked. What did she care whether she impressed her mother's relatives or the stuffy young men her father wanted her to meet? English Society would never accept her as one of their own. Nor did she wish them to.

It hadn't been her idea to come here, after all. Her father had overridden her protests, insisting that she accompany him to England for the sake of the business—and to meet her late mother's estranged family, the very people who had cast her mother off some twenty-five years earlier. It seemed almost disloyal to her mother's memory to care what *they* thought of her.

Quinn thought longingly of Baltimore, an ocean away. Would her brother, Charles, be able to handle her role in the family shipping business? He knew far less than she about the most competitive routes to China and Europe, or the best suppliers, as he'd been away at college for the past few years. What if he botched everything? And who would catch the clerks in their inevitable errors, without Quinn there to oversee them?

With an impatient sigh, she turned from the window just as her father entered the parlor, a broad smile on his handsome, weathered face.

"Quinn," he exclaimed in obvious delight, "I have the most wonderful news."

His ebullience was infectious, and she couldn't help returning his smile, pushing her worries about the business momentarily aside. "What news, Papa?"

"Look!" He waved a letter at her. "We've actually been invited to stay with your uncle and aunt, Lord and Lady Claridge, at their town house. I feared they might have gone down to the country or to the seaside by now. Your mother used to tell me London is all but deserted from July till October."

Quinn glanced over her shoulder at the activity outside, on the fashionable corner of Albemarle

Street and Picadilly. "Clearly not, though I confess it does seem tame compared to the bustle of the docks at home."

"Oh, the docks here in London are every bit as busy—even more so. Don't you recall the confusion when we landed?"

She did. The London shipping district put American ports to shame, in volume if not efficiency. "So we are to remove to their house?" she asked without enthusiasm. "When?"

"Tomorrow. Lord Claridge himself sent this letter, offering to send a coach to move us and our things to Mount Street. Wasn't that handsome of him?"

"Indeed." Sometimes Quinn couldn't understand her father. Eminently capable in business and all things nautical, he took orders from no one but himself—yet he seemed to hold the British nobility in a respect amounting to awe. It was an awe Quinn did not share. "I suppose it will be more interesting than staying here, in any event."

Her father's brow crinkled apologetically. "You will enjoy London once I have a chance to show you about, my dear. I know you miss home, but—"

"But this is an admirable chance to expand my horizons," she finished, repeating what he had told her numerous times. "You're right, of course, Papa. I'll have that new French maid of mine pack up my things."

The worry disappeared from her father's brow. "That's my girl! When I return from my meeting, I'll pack as well."

"Another meeting? Can't I come this time? I have

a proposal about the tobacco trade, and some thoughts about the cotton warehouses that—"

He cut her off, as he'd done whenever she raised such subjects lately. "Not today. I'll pass along your ideas, and if there are any developments, I'll inform you when I get back."

Though Quinn sighed, she did not protest, knowing it would do no good. When he left, she headed to her bedchamber where, instead of her maid, she found only a hotel chambermaid—a young redheaded girl of perhaps twelve. At Quinn's entrance she snatched up her dust cloth, ducked her head, and hurried to the door.

"Excuse me," said Quinn, halting her flight. She had meant to ask the girl to fetch her maid, but a glimpse of her frightened face halted her. The girl's eyes were red with weeping, and a large bruise was purpling across one cheek.

"What on earth . . . ? Who did this to you?" Quinn demanded.

The girl shook her head violently. "Nobody, mum. I . . . I fell, is all." She headed for the door again, but Quinn put a hand on her shoulder, stopping her.

"Please, don't be afraid. Did someone here at the hotel strike you?"

Another quick shake of the head. "No, mum. I'll . . . I'll be fine."

"What is your name?" If she could get the girl talking, she might be able to get at the truth.

"Polly."

"And have you worked here at Grillon's long?"

That question, unaccountably, seemed to increase the girl's alarm. Ducking away from Quinn's restraining hand, she darted for the door, but before she could reach it, a heavy, enameled box slipped from beneath her apron to bounce on the thick carpeting. The girl froze, lifting horrified eyes to Quinn's.

"My jewel case. You were . . . stealing it?" Quinn could scarcely believe it. The girl was a mere child!

Polly's reserve broke, shattered by fear. "Oh, please, mum, don't tell no one! I ain't never stole nothing before, I swear! I only did it for my little brother. His master beats him if he don't bring nothing back, but if he's caught again, they'll hang him, sure."

Now Quinn was confused. "Your brother's master makes him steal? Is he the one who struck you?"

She nodded. "I tried to keep him from beating Gobby yesterday, so he walloped me, and said I could just bring in Gobby's share instead. But Gobby, he's that stubborn, he wants to do his own work, for all he's only nine." The girl began to cry.

"Shh, Polly, it's all right. I won't turn you in, and in fact I'd like to help you. Will you take me to your brother's master? I should like to have a few words with the man." What kind of monster forced children to steal for him?

"Oh, no, mum! He might hurt you—and me, too."

"To your brother, then? Perhaps together we can persuade him to a more honest way of life." A nine-year-old boy could scarcely be a hardened criminal, after all.

Now Polly's thin face brightened. "Oh, would you, mum? That might work. Likely he'd listen to a real lady like you. But—it might not be safe for a lady to go there. It's a rough area."

"I won't go as a lady, then."

Opening her trunk, Quinn dug to the bottom to retrieve an old outfit of her brother's, which she'd occasionally worn at home when climbing trees or riding astride. She wasn't quite sure why she had packed it, but now she was glad she had.

Tomorrow she would be trapped in her stuffy English relatives' house, unable to do anything but play the proper lady. She snatched at this opportunity to do something worthwhile—and exciting—while she still could.

Polly helped her undo her gown, then watched, wide-eyed, as Quinn donned Charles's shirt and breeches. Glancing into the pier glass as she tucked the last strand of her curly dark hair beneath Charles's cap, she decided she made a fairly credible boy.

"There. I should be safe enough like this. Let's go."

Lord Marcus stared sightlessly through White's famous bow window, letting Lord Fernworth's idle chatter wash over him. Peter was right. The fellow was a complete nodcock.

In fact, most of his friends were nodcocks, with the notable exception of Luke, who was by now several counties away, more than a week into his wedding trip. Why hadn't he noticed it before?

Peter often warned him that he was frittering his

life away on wine, women, and cards. He had always credited that to his older brother's propensity to coddle him, as the youngest of their large family. But maybe he *could* do something more worthwhile with his life. He idly fingered the now-tattered card in his pocket.

"And then Scottsdale tied her garters to the front gate of Beck House, just to show her he knew what she had done, and with whom!" Fernworth concluded his tale with a laugh. "The scandal sheets are having rare fun with that, as you can imagine."

Marcus managed a smile, but his heart wasn't in it. Why had he come here? He rose. "Sorry, Ferny, but I've just recalled an appointment with my tailor. Think you can finish the bottle without me?"

Fernworth snorted at the foolish question. "You've been a dashed dull dog lately, Marcus. What say we take in that do at Madame Sophy's tonight? All her best girls will be at their finest, I doubt not."

A month ago, Marcus would have jumped at the chance to attend a party at the most fashionable bordello in London, but now it held little appeal. He wondered why.

"Perhaps I'll meet up with you there," he replied evasively, then took his leave.

Outside, he glanced across St. James's Street at the Guards' Club, where Peter and his friends tended to gather. He'd once thought to make his mark in the Army, had even tried to run away and enlist when his father refused to buy him a commission. Then Robert, his oldest brother, had played tale-bearer, his father had hauled him back home in disgrace, and his last chance was gone.

He shrugged off the old bitterness that had led him to his life of dissipation. Regret was pointless, and the war was now over. There were other paths to heroism and adventure. Luke had shown him one.

Done with shilly-shallying, he turned his steps east, toward Covent Garden and Seven Dials. Thievery might be beyond him, but he could carry on with the help Luke had given to the people there. He headed down Piccadilly, then Coventry Street to Cranborn, finally turning north on St. Martin's Lane.

He passed from wide, gracious avenues through narrow but still respectable working-class areas and finally to the squalid alleyways of the rookeries. He'd been there before, in the company of other young bucks out on the town looking for amusement. Alone, however, he was glad the July days were long and the afternoon still early.

Looking around him with interest, his enthusiasm for his project revived. There must be dozens, nay, hundreds of people here who needed his help. He spotted a one-legged beggar in a filthy infantry uniform and walked over to him.

"Ahoy there, my good man," he said jovially, dropping a few coins into his extended cup. "What do you call yourself?"

Suspicion flared in the beggar's rheumy eyes. "What's it to you, guv? I've a right to sit here if I likes."

"Of course you have," Marcus agreed, taking a

step back, both to reassure the man and to distance himself a bit from his reek. "I mean to do you good, not harm. If you'll tell me what you need to make your way in the world, I'll try to provide it."

Now a cunning gleam warred with the suspicion. "Will you, then? A case or two of daffy would make my world a better one, I'm thinking."

Marcus clung to his smile. "Surely there's something you want more than gin? Some new clothes, perhaps? A position somewhere?"

The suspicion returned. "One of them do-gooders, are ye? Spare me your temperance yammering." The man spat with disgust. "And here I thought you was wanting to help."

Against his better judgment, Marcus tossed another coin into the beggar's cup, knowing it would likely go for nothing more constructive than drink. Perhaps these people were already beyond whatever help he could give.

Turning, he nearly bumped into a boy of perhaps nine or ten who had sidled up behind him while he spoke to the old soldier.

"Hey there, my lad, what are you doing?" he asked, quickly reassuring himself that his purse was still in his pocket. His handkerchief, however, was clutched in the boy's grubby fist. With a yelp, the lad turned and ran.

"Wait! I won't harm you," Marcus called. "You can keep—Oh, bother it." Hoping the boy might be someone more able to benefit by his assistance, he trotted after him.

Though clearly underfed, the lad was quick and

knew the area far better than Marcus did. He was able to keep the boy in sight for two or three twists and turns, but then lost him heading back west on crowded Monmouth Street.

He continued along the street, alert for a scrawny lad in a tattered blue cap, but without success. Still, there were plenty of other unfortunates about. That girl there, at the corner of Church Street—no more than thirteen or fourteen, and apparently driven to prostitution.

Pricked by sudden compassion, he took a step or two in her direction, then stopped, realizing how his offer of help might be interpreted. No, he'd do better to limit his assistance to the boys on the streets, at least until he knew their world better.

Reaching Gordon Square, he saw a small knot of ragamuffins clustered near a house that likely belonged to a wealthy merchant, as this was still east of the ultrafashionable Mayfair area. Looking closer, he spotted a blue cap, as well as a general air of furtiveness among the boys. Cautiously, he moved closer.

"Garn, Stilt, he'll still be at his shops, and the household taking it easy, like. Safer now than at night, if you ask me," a redheaded strip of a lad was saying to the tallest of the boys.

"Gobby's right," agreed the blue-capped lad who had absconded with Marcus's handkerchief. "We can nip in and out with none the wiser, and cop enough for a grand dinner with enough left over to satisfy old Twitchell. Look at all them open windows!"

A mutter of agreement among the others elicited a reluctant nod from the tall boy, Stilt. "If we're goin' to do it, then, we'd best get to it," he said. "Gobby, you're the smallest."

"Aye," agreed Gobby. "I can fit through that window a treat. And if I'm spotted, I'll just say I got lost."

The group moved toward the house and Marcus abruptly realized he had to act. Here, surely, was the chance he'd been waiting for. Using the hedge for cover, he sidled closer while the boys were focused on the house. Then, as Stilt was whispering final instructions to his cohorts, Marcus burst upon them, grabbing Gobby and the blue-capped lad each by one arm.

For an instant, all of the boys froze, then began to scatter. Tightening his grip on the two he'd caught, Marcus called out, "Wait! If you care about your comrades, you'll listen to me."

Stilt paused, worry and defiance playing across his thin, grimy face, and one of the others slowly returned as well, but the others kept running. "Let 'em go, guv," Stilt said. "We didn't mean no harm, none of us."

"I rather doubt that," Marcus replied, ignoring the struggles of the three boys he held. "But I'm not here to turn you over to the authorities. I want to help you. This doesn't seem like the best spot for a chat, however. Follow me." He guided his captives out into the lane.

"Gobby! No!" came a feminine cry. Turning, Marcus saw a redheaded girl and a boy in a brown cap approaching, the girl's eyes wide with alarm.

"You two come along as well, if you care about these lads," Marcus called to them. The two hesitated, but then the boy whispered something to the girl, and she turned and ran. The boy, however, came slowly forward, his eyes narrowed speculatively.

There was no way Marcus could pursue the girl, so he focused on the boy. "I won't hurt you or turn you in, I promise. Come on, then." Rather to Marcus's surprise, the lad shrugged and followed along with the others.

They must look an odd group, Marcus thought with a spurt of amusement as they turned onto Grosvenor Street a few minutes later. Reaching the house he shared with two of his older brothers, he was just as glad neither would be home just now. Marcus led the motley group of boys around back, to the small kitchen garden, where he released the two he held, latched the back gate securely, then turned to face all four of them.

"You may not realize it yet," he began, "but you're all very fortunate that it was I, and no one else, who happened upon you—and that I did so before you could commit your intended crime."

The boys looked skeptical and sullen, and he couldn't blame them. Even to his own ears, he sounded pompous. He tried again.

"I assume you're all in dire financial straits. Do any of you even have parents?"

Most of them shook their heads.

"Though it may seem the quickest way out of your difficulties, thievery is not the answer. It's far too risky, for one thing. You can't possibly realize the consequences if you were arrested."

The blue-capped lad sniffed. "Transportation or

the gibbet," he said carelessly. "We know, guv. But you got no proof."

"No?" Before the boy realized what he was about, Marcus reached out and snatched his own handkerchief from the lad's pocket. "Perhaps you've forgotten this?"

The boy blanched, but before Marcus could reassure him that he would not involve the authorities, he saw the brown-capped lad, the last one he'd rounded up, inching back toward the gate.

"All of you, into the house," he said, herding them like so many skittish lambs through the back door and down into the kitchen. Heedless of the staring servants, he turned first to the brown-capped boy.

"You, lad, what's your name?" He had to somehow establish a rapport with these boys, if he was to help them.

"I'd rather not say, if you don't mind," came the reply.

Marcus stared, for the voice was undeniably feminine—and cultured, as well, though with an accent he couldn't place.

The other boys were staring, too, clearly as surprised as he. With a deep sense of foreboding, Marcus pulled off the brown cap. As he'd feared, a mass of dark curls tumbled down to dance around the girl's shoulders.

"You . . . you're not a part of this group, are you?"

Four heads shook back and forth.

"May I go now?" she asked, her gold-flecked green eyes holding more than a hint of amusement.

"Not just yet," replied Marcus, feeling both foolish and irritated, all too aware of an interested audience of servants. "You three, stay here. You—come with me," he said to the girl.

Whispering quick instructions to the startled cook that she was to feed the boys all they could hold, he led the girl out of the kitchen and up the stairs to the front hall. "Now, perhaps you'd care to tell me who you are and why you were wandering about London in breeches?"

"Not particularly," she replied. "Your bullying tactics may work on those poor boys, but they won't intimidate me."

He blinked. Short and slight as she was, he'd taken her for maybe fourteen years old. Now he revised his estimate upward.

"I wasn't trying to intimidate you," he said, nettled. "Do your parents know you are out on the streets dressed like that?" Her clothing was probably borrowed from a brother, as it was clearly too large for her. "I thought not," he continued, when she colored instead of replying. "I'll escort you back to them."

"Escort—? Now that would present a pretty picture, wouldn't it, with me in breeches?" She still seemed more amused than concerned, which irritated Marcus further.

"One of the maids can lend you a skirt." He glanced in the direction of the kitchen. He didn't want to leave that gang of young thieves under the cook's supervision for long.

She clearly understood his concern. "You can't

very well leave them here while you take me home," she pointed out.

He ignored her, instead motioning to a passing housemaid. "Millie, have you or one of the others a skirt this young lady can borrow? Quickly, please."

The maid nodded and scurried upstairs, and he turned back to the girl. "I can have a footman take you home—or even send you in a carriage, if you prefer it."

"I'll walk—by myself, thank you. It isn't far."

That meant she lived in or near the West End. Perhaps she feared a scolding, or worse, if her ramblings were discovered. Certainly she deserved it! He didn't think much of parents who left a mischief-prone girl like this to her own devices.

"Very well," he said at last, "but you must promise me to be careful—and never to go out on your own like this again. You haven't lived in London long, have you?"

After a slight hesitation, she shook her head. "I've been in England only two days."

He finally placed her elusive accent. "American?" She nodded.

"A piece of advice: London is larger and more wicked than your towns back home. You're lucky you didn't end up in a brothel."

Her eyes widened, making him feel oddly protective. She was a pretty little thing, under the male garments. He was about to elaborate, but just then Millie returned with the requested skirt.

"Here, fasten this on over your breeches. Otherwise, you'll have to carry them, which would look odd." It also meant she wouldn't have to remove them, and he felt awkward enough having an apparently gently bred girl in his house.

She pulled the skirt on, tucking it into the waistband of her breeches when it proved both too long and too big around the waist. "Will that do?" She was still mocking him.

"I suppose it will have to." He tried not to think about what she would look like in proper attire. She was surely too young for—"Are you sure you don't want a footman to—?"

"No! I'll be fine."

Mindful of the boys waiting in the kitchen, Marcus decided to take her at her word. It was still full daylight, and no one was likely to accost her in the heart of Mayfair. He led her to the front door, as that seemed more fitting than the back.

He opened the door and she stepped through, then paused on the broad top step to sweep him an absurdly formal curtsy. "My thanks for your assistance, kind sir."

Marcus started to reply in the same vein, then glanced beyond her. Two or three Society matrons were strolling past, clearly enjoying the fine weather, and had paused to witness the unusual tableau on his doorstep. Worse, one of them was Lady Mountheath, possibly the biggest gossip in Town.

Mindful of their stares, Marcus raised the girl from her curtsy, then planted a light kiss on the back of her hand. "Be careful," he repeated, reinforcing his warning with an earnest look, directly into her remarkable eyes.

She flashed him a grin that lit up her face quite remarkably, then hurried down the steps and away. He gazed after her for a moment, then turned to face the ladies, who were still watching him with varying degrees of disapproval. Doubtless they thought he was bidding farewell to a lightskirt whose favors he had just enjoyed. The notion both amused and disturbed him.

He bowed to the matrons, at which they seemed to realize the impropriety of staring, and continued along their way. Lady Mountheath, he noticed, was already whispering something to one of the others. But what did it matter? If the girl was merely in London for a visit, they could do her reputation no lasting harm.

With that reassuring thought, he headed back to the kitchen to begin the task of getting his group of street urchins to trust him—something he didn't think he'd accomplished with the girl. It was just as well he was unlikely ever to see her again.

Chapter 2

Quinn hurried along Grosvenor Street, her heart hammering at the nearness of her escape—and at her reaction to that final, searching gaze from those outrageously gorgeous blue eyes. No man had a right to be that handsome!

Walking quickly, she shook her head over the encounter. She hadn't helped Polly as she'd promised—hadn't had a chance to talk to Gobby at all. There was no knowing what that self-righteous Englishman meant to do to those poor boys. Probably send them to some horrible workhouse somewhere, just to get them off the streets. At least he hadn't turned out to be their monstrous "master," as she'd assumed when she first followed him home.

Then she chuckled. Handsome as he was, he was also insufferably pompous, and the expression on his face when he realized she was female had been positively priceless.

Still, his interference meant she'd be late returning, and if her father discovered what she'd done,
she'd have quite a bit of explaining to do. Though
generally affable with family, he was capable of
stern discipline, as she'd seen on the Baltimore
docks. She preferred not to have that side of him
turned toward herself.

Squinting up at the westering sun to get her bearings, she headed south. Unfortunately, her route
was less than direct and it took her another forty-
five minutes before she finally arrived back at the
hotel.

Even more unfortunately, her father was waiting
for her.

"Where on earth have you been—and *what* are
you wearing?" he demanded, in the voice she recognized all too well from his ship-captaining days.

"I was just . . . exploring." Mentioning Polly might
bring her father's wrath down on that poor girl, too.

"Inside." He waited for her to precede him
through the front door and up the wide stairs to
their second-floor suite before continuing. "Do you
have any idea how dangerous it was for you to wan-
der the streets of London alone?"

He sounded remarkably like that insufferable
English gentleman. The similarity irked her enough
that she found her voice and spirit again. "I came to
no harm. I was careful."

"Careful?" Her father snorted. "This is not Baltimore, where everyone knows you—and knows that
you are my daughter. Perhaps you don't realize
what protection that confers."

Quinn swallowed. She hadn't thought of it that way, but he was doubtless right. Captain Peverill had a formidable reputation throughout Baltimore and up and down the American coastline.

"London is a far bigger—and older—city, with corresponding dangers," he continued. "I've even read of young women kidnapped off the streets and sold into prostitution."

She started as he again echoed the gentleman who had sent her home. Was such a thing really so common? She'd had no idea. "Surely, here in the West End—"

"Less likely, I'll grant you, but not impossible. And what of your reputation? I've told you that English Society requires much stricter standards of behavior in young ladies than you've been used to at home. Did my words make no impression on you at all?"

"Of course, Papa. I simply thought—"

"No, I don't believe you thought at all." But now his tone softened slightly. "Quinn, you frightened me half to death, disappearing like that. Promise me you'll do nothing of the sort again. If you wish to walk outdoors, take your maid—and have her dress you properly. Where did you get those clothes, anyway?"

Relaxing slightly, she dared to meet his eye. "They were Charles's—well, except for the skirt." She kicked at it, briefly revealing the breeches underneath. "That belongs to a maid." She saw no point in mentioning where that maid was employed.

"I'm glad you had the presence of mind to add the

skirt, at least. Running about in breeches at home is one thing, but merely being seen in them here would make you—us—unreceivable. You need to consider consequences before you act, Quinn."

"I know. And I'm sorry. I won't do it again. I know how important it is that we be accepted by English Society—for the sake of the business." That did matter to her, even if she didn't share her father's social aspirations. "I'll, ah, go change now."

"Excellent idea," he agreed. "And don't forget to choose an outfit for your introduction to Lord and Lady Claridge tomorrow. I'd like you to look your best for that."

Quinn hurried to her own chamber, grateful to have escaped so lightly. Papa and that stuffy young gentleman—much as she hated to admit it—were right. She'd been so glad of a chance to escape, if only briefly, she hadn't thought through the possible consequences before agreeing to help poor Polly.

Still, she did wish she could have done something for the girl and her young brother. With a sigh, she realized there were probably hundreds of children in such straits in a city this size. There was no way she could make a difference in all of their lives. The longer she stayed in England, the more that knowledge would gnaw at her.

Better that she return as soon as possible to Baltimore and the business, where she *could* make a difference.

On descending to the kitchens, Marcus discovered that generous helpings of Mrs. MacKay's excellent Yorkshire pudding and mutton collops had already predisposed the three street urchins more kindly toward him. The boys were making serious inroads into two large mince pies by the time he joined them.

"You're a right 'un, guv, and no mistake," declared Stilt. Nods and mumbled assents implied that he spoke for the group. "I got to wonder, though, what you'll be wanting for all this."

Sending the servants out of the room, Marcus seated himself across from Stilt at the kitchen table, ignoring the stares of the other boys. "I can't blame you for being cautious," he said. "And in truth, I do want something, but I hope it's something you'll be only too happy to share."

The tall lad set down his fork to regard Marcus suspiciously. "Eh? And what's that?"

"Information."

Stilt shook his head quickly and started to stand. "Sorry, guv. C'mon, lads!"

"Wait!" Marcus started to grab the lanky boy's sleeve, but stopped himself. He would never win their trust by force. "I mean the sort of information that has allowed the Saint of Seven Dials to help you and others like you."

Now he had the boys' full attention. "What do you know about the Saint?" demanded Gobby, the diminutive redheaded boy.

"Probably more than you do," Marcus replied calmly. "He's one of my closest friends."

A startled silence was followed by a gust of whispers as the boys debated the likelihood of such a claim. Marcus waited until he had their attention again before continuing.

"The Saint has had to change the way he does things a bit, due to altered circumstances," he said carefully, not wanting to implicate Luke too clearly in case these boys couldn't be trusted. "In fact, he is gone from London entirely for the time being."

The blue-capped lad chuckled. "No wonder the Runners have been asking so many questions. I figured he was lying low somewhere. Fair frustrated them that has. Bet they won't never catch him now." Then he turned serious eyes back to Marcus. "But where does that leave us, guv? And where do you come into it?"

Marcus hadn't realized that the authorities were still seeking Luke, but he had no time now to dwell on that. "The Saint hasn't forgotten you. He, ah, has asked me to be his go-between for the time being, as his primary informant has gone with him. I also want to make certain the Runners can never touch him, whatever he may do in the future. But I'll need your help."

The boys exchanged glances, then Stilt spoke up. "We have a friend or two what owe their lives to the Saint. We'll help him—and you, sir—any way we can."

The Claridge house on Mount Street was every bit as imposing as Quinn had expected. As they mounted the broad steps to the front door, she noticed that her father seemed almost nervous—

something she had never observed in him before. She smoothed her skirts as he plied the ornate brass knocker, telling herself again that she cared not a whit what these people thought of her.

The captain gave their names to the supercilious butler, who then conducted them up a flight of stairs and into an exquisitely furnished drawing room. "Captain and Miss Peverill," he announced tonelessly before fading back into the hallway.

A thin gentleman of about forty, who Quinn realized must be the marquess, rose to greet them. "Captain Peverill. It has been a . . . a long time, has it not?" he said with an uncertain smile, glancing over his shoulder at a pair of opulently dressed ladies whose handsomely patrician similarity of features declared them mother and daughter.

"My wife, Lady Claridge, and our daughter, Lady Constance Throckwaite," the marquess said, indicating each in turn. The ladies each acknowledged the captain's deep bows in their direction with chilly nods. "We are all delighted to have you here, are we not ladies?"

"Assuredly." Lady Claridge's stiff formality belied her response, while Lady Constance declined comment. Lord Claridge, however, had already turned back to his guests.

"And Miss Peverill. Quinn—my dear mother's family name. I must say I am delighted to make your acquaintance. You are . . . very like your mother, you know." Sorrow clouded his expression briefly, but then he smiled again.

Despite herself, Quinn found herself warming to this tentative man with her mother's eyes, who seemed so eager to please everyone—and so unlikely to succeed.

"You resemble her as well, my lord," she replied with a curtsy. "My mother spoke fondly of you." That was an exaggeration, as Glynna Peverill had rarely spoken of her English family at all, though Quinn did recall her once mentioning her younger brother. In any event, it pleased the marquess.

"Did she?" he exclaimed. "She and I were very close, you know. Poor, dear Glynna."

The captain stepped forward with another bow. "It's true, my lord. She even named our firstborn Charles, after you. It was her dearest, almost her dying wish that Quinn come to you, for she much regretted the breach between our families."

Quinn stared at her father, appalled that he would utter such a falsehood. Certainly, her mother had never expressed any such wish in *her* hearing, nor any regrets, either.

Lord Claridge, however, was profoundly affected, tears starting to his hazel eyes. "Then it is in my power to honor Glynna's memory by welcoming you both back into the bosom of the family. We are to attend a rout at Lord and Lady Trumball's this very evening, a perfect opportunity to introduce Quinn to Society. Will it not be, my dear?" He glanced at his wife again.

"To be sure," she said in frigid tones. "I fear, however, that though you may have forgotten the scandal your sister once brought upon this family, others will yet remember it."

"But . . . but that was nigh on twenty-five years ago," the marquess said uncertainly. "Surely, by now—"

Lady Claridge sniffed. "I suppose we must hope you are right." She then turned to Quinn and the captain with a tight, unpleasant smile. "In any event, as it will be known you are both staying here, it will look odd if you do not accompany us."

To Quinn's vexation her father bowed yet again, rather than refuse the ungracious invitation. "You are too kind, my lady. Of course we will be most honored. It will be just the thing for Quinn. Perhaps your daughter can introduce her to other young people, as they appear to be much of an age."

A quick glance at Lady Constance showed Quinn's lovely cousin scarcely more eager to embrace her American relatives than her mother was. In fact, she was regarding Quinn as she might a zoological curiosity.

"Of course," Lady Claridge said blandly. "And pray rest assured that I will not demand the same standard of behavior from Miss Peverill that I expect from my own daughter. I am prepared to make allowances for her upbringing."

"Too kind," murmured the captain uncertainly, but Quinn seethed at the insult, which was directed as much at her parents as herself—and particularly at her mother.

The marquess attempted to smooth over the awkwardness of the moment. "Now, my dear, I'm certain Quinn is fully versed in the proprieties and will fit in here famously."

Quinn took leave to doubt that very much. Judging by her pinched expression, that was one matter on which she and Lady Claridge were in complete agreement. Not trusting herself to speak civilly, Quinn remained silent, listening with resignation when the marquess ordered their trunks carried up to their chambers.

"Now I'm certain you will both wish to settle in," Lord Claridge declared once the last of their possessions had been transferred. "William will show you to your rooms. It will be famous having you here. Simply famous!"

As they mounted the stairs, Quinn wished she could share even a modicum of her uncle's enthusiasm. "Father, *must* we?" she asked, once the footman left them in the upper hallway.

"Tut, tut, Quinnling, it will be perfect! I know Lady Claridge seems a bit off-putting now, but she will warm to you in no time, just as everyone does. Pray don't be nervous about it."

His use of her old nickname mollified her only slightly. "I'm not nervous, precisely, but I begin to think I've experienced quite as much of England as I care to."

"Now, now." He patted her shoulder awkwardly. "You've scarcely seen London yet, much less England. It's a change from home, I'll grant you, but everything is bound to be fair sailing from here on out."

Quinn opened the door to her new bedchamber—more elegant than any she had ever occupied—and sighed. She hoped he might be right, but she felt the odds were against it.

The Trumball house was one of the grandest Quinn had yet seen in London—even more impressive than the Claridge house, and certainly finer than that gentleman's house yesterday. Looking around at the flowers and greenery decorating the large reception hall, she idly wondered whether that gentleman was married.

Not that it concerned her in any way, of course. Should she see him again, she had determined that she would pretend not to recognize him. That would spare them both embarrassment—something he would surely desire, with his obvious concern for propriety.

Still, it might be amusing to see his expression if he spotted her dressed like this. She glanced down at her exquisite jonquil-satin gown, embroidered with tiny green leaves.

She was pulled from her complacent regard of her attire by the sound of Lord Claridge introducing her to their hosts. ". . . and this is my niece, Miss Quinn Peverill."

Her mother had instructed her at a young age in all of the social forms, so she was able to drop a curtsy of the proper depth to Viscount and Lady Trumball, conscious of Lady Claridge's critical eye. "I am honored, my lord, my lady. So kind of you to welcome us, newcomers to Town as we are."

"I am delighted that you were able to attend, my dear," replied Lady Trumball. "Town is so thin of company at this season, I nearly despaired of having enough people in attendance to make my little party worthwhile."

Quinn murmured something about the lady's hospitality and followed the Claridge party into the hall. "This is a 'little party'?" she whispered to her father. "There must be close to a hundred people present!"

"I told you London Society operated on a larger scale than that of Baltimore, didn't I?" he responded.

Sensing a reference to yesterday's lecture on her behavior, Quinn dropped the subject. She was about to comment on the music, provided by a small orchestra in one corner, when a green-turbaned matron who seemed vaguely familiar accosted them.

"Captain Peverill, as I live and breathe!" she exclaimed. "I was so delighted when I heard you were come to Town. I declare, it's been an age! Never say this is little Quinn?"

The captain bowed. "I am delighted to see you, Mrs. Kennard. Is Captain Kennard here this evening?"

"He is indeed, and will love to talk over dull nautical topics with you, I doubt not. Come, he can make you known to some of the other naval captains, as well." She paused to pinch Quinn's cheek, which she bore stoically, now recalling a visit this woman had paid them in Baltimore six or seven years ago.

"I declare, you were but a child when I saw you last. You've become quite the little lady."

"Yes, ma'am. Thank you," responded Quinn with a mechanical smile. Not until the woman had turned away did she surreptitiously rub her assaulted cheek.

Her father had not motioned her to follow, so she remained where she was, having no desire for more of Mrs. Kennard's reminiscing. The Claridges had already moved on, so she found herself momentarily alone.

Though she knew it was improper to stand about unchaperoned, Quinn welcomed the chance to take stock of her surroundings. She watched the shifting throng with interest, the ladies like butterflies in their summer gowns and the gentlemen providing a sober counterpoint in black, brown, or dark blue.

One more brightly clad gentleman caught her eye, not only for his lilac waistcoat, but because he rather reminded her of the man who had plucked her off the streets yesterday, though he was not so handsome. A relation, perhaps?

Glancing around just then, he caught her watching him and came toward her with a smile. "I know it's not at all the thing for me to speak to you without an introduction, but you seem rather at a loss, Miss—?"

"Peverill," she replied, touched by his kindness. "Quinn Peverill."

He swept her a bow. "Lord Peter Northrup, at your service. Quinn Peverill, eh? An unusual name, but familiar somehow. New to Town, are you?"

"Yes, we arrived just a few days ago. My father is Captain Palmer Peverill, out of Baltimore," she offered helpfully. "He's over there." She motioned toward a group of a half dozen gentlemen engaged in spirited conversation.

Lord Peter's brow furrowed for a moment, then cleared. "Ah! Now I have it. Your mother would be Lady Glynna Throckwaite, daughter to Lady Adela Quinn and the late Lord Claridge. That makes you niece to the current marquess, does it not? I see the Claridges over there. Shall I restore you to them?"

"No, I thank you," Quinn said, amazed at his knowledge of her family history. "That is, I . . . I will rejoin them presently." Her aunt would doubtless make another nasty comment about her upbringing if a gentlemen to whom she had not been properly introduced were to escort her across the room.

"Certainly, certainly," he said, clearly perceiving her reluctance. "Meanwhile, there are others here who would be delighted to make your acquaintance, I'm sure. My brother Marcus, for one, as well as various of the younger ladies attending. London is a dull place without friends."

He extended an arm, and she gingerly took it, torn between gratitude and embarrassment. Did she appear a charity case, or did Lord Peter simply have a penchant for helping ladies in perceived distress?

"Marcus, ladies, I'd like to present Miss Quinn Peverill, but recently arrived in England. Miss Peverill, my brother, Lord Marcus Northrup." He went on to name the three ladies standing there, but Quinn barely heard him.

Instead she stared, speechless, at her sanctimonious "rescuer" from the day before!

Marcus turned with a smile at his brother's words, only to pause in astonishment upon facing again the pretty young hoyden he had plucked off the streets only yesterday. Quickly schooling his features, he bowed, hoping no one had noticed his hesitation.

"Delighted to make your acquaintance, Miss Peverill." He tried to keep any trace of mockery from his voice, but the amusement in her eyes told him he did not succeed. He hoped the silly chit would not refer to their unorthodox meeting.

She did not. "Lord Marcus," she said coolly, inclining her head quite properly, though her eyes now sparkled with mischief. She then turned to greet the others in his group. Miss Chalmers asked her about life in America, giving him a chance to rein in the conflicting emotions that assailed him at the sight of her.

After spending much of last evening puzzling about her, he had decided she must be the daughter of some American merchant—well-to-do, perhaps, but beyond the social pale. Clearly, he had guessed wrong if she was at a gathering like this one.

What startled him even more was the flash of pleasure he'd felt on facing her again. Oh, she was comely enough, especially dressed as she was tonight, but too young for his taste and clearly deficient in manners, judging by their encounter yesterday and her evident lack of remorse.

"So you have no Indian savages living near

you?" Miss Chalmers was asking her, in evident disappointment.

"No, Baltimore is hardly a wilderness, but one of America's major port cities," Miss Peverill replied. "Far smaller than London, of course, but more than twenty thousand people live there, all told."

"Goodness! I had no idea," exclaimed Miss Chalmers. The other ladies agreed, and continued to pelt her with questions.

"You seem rather struck by Miss Peverill," Peter murmured to Marcus while the ladies were thus engaged. "A taking little thing, I admit, and with impeccable connections on her mother's side."

Marcus frowned, then attempted to look bored. "Oh?"

Peter nodded. "Granddaughter to the fourth Lord Claridge and cousin to the beauteous Lady Constance."

That did surprise Marcus, but he only said, "A new face is always a novelty, of course, especially so late in the Season. But that can scarcely compensate for a lack of sensibility."

Now Peter looked surprised. "You find Miss Peverill lacking in sensibility? In what way?"

But Marcus had no intention of relating yesterday's events to his brother. Miss Peverill's reputation didn't concern him unduly, as she had been clearly in the wrong, but he had no mind to explain his encounter with the street urchins—or his plans to help them, to which Peter would certainly object.

"American girls have always struck me as rather hoydenish," he finally responded. "I doubt Miss

Peverill is any different. It comes of being raised
without regard for the proprieties our English ladies
take for granted."

He realized belatedly that he had spoken a shade
too loudly, and that the conversation of the ladies
had ceased. A quick glance showed that Miss Peverill, at least, had heard him. Her unusual green-gold
eyes flashed with resentment, though she said nothing. Hastily, he turned back to Peter, who was now
frowning.

"There certainly seems to be *one* person present
who has an incomplete grasp of the proprieties," Peter said severely, and at the same volume, that Miss
Peverill might hear his rebuke.

Then he lowered his voice. "You're a fine one to
preach propriety, in any event, Marcus. I'd like to
think this indicates a desire to mend your ways, but
I suspect it is merely evidence of the hypocrisy all
too common to rakes and wastrels."

Peter moved away then to greet some other acquaintances, and Marcus was just as glad to see him
go. He was no longer a lad, to be scolded by his older
brothers for his shortcomings.

His relief was short-lived, however, for across the
room he spotted Lady Mountheath and one of the
other matrons who had seen Miss Peverill leaving
his house yesterday. Would they recognize her in her
current guise? Surely not.

Still, he cudgeled his brain for a plausible explanation for her presence there, just in case. Nothing
came to mind.

"Lord Marcus, did not you say that you intended

to visit the Americas someday?" Miss Augusta Melks asked then, drawing him into the ladies' renewed conversation. Clearly, she had not heard him earlier. "You must hear what Miss Peverill says of it!"

"Yes, I suppose I must," he replied, trying to appear both polite and disinterested at once. "Baltimore, you were saying, Miss Peverill? That is in Maryland, is it not?"

She nodded, regarding him warily. No doubt she feared he meant to reveal her foolish escapade, after his earlier comment. "Yes, just north of Washington—you know, the city the English tried to burn down a few years ago," she added with a raised brow. "There is much worth seeing in that part of the world, as I have been telling the others."

"So I have heard," he replied, trying to reassure her with his smile. He thought she relaxed marginally, though her eyes were still unforgiving. Then, looking past him, she stiffened again.

"I see you are making friends, Quinn," came a booming voice from behind Marcus. "Excellent! Excellent!"

Turning, he found the voice to belong to a tall, broad-shouldered, older man whose weathered face bespoke years at sea. Though impeccably dressed, he seemed out of place at such a tame gathering, like an eagle in a cage full of canaries.

"Papa, let me introduce you to my new acquaintances." Marcus thought Miss Peverill spoke hastily, as though to prevent her father making further comments. "Miss Chalmers, Miss Melks, and Miss Augusta Melks. And Lord Marcus Northrup," she added, almost as an afterthought. "My father, Captain Peverill."

Marcus looked sharply at her, wondering if the almost-insult had been deliberate, but she returned his glance blandly.

"Charmed, ladies," responded the captain with a sweeping bow that set them all simpering. Then he turned to Marcus. "Northrup. That would make you a connection of the Duke of Marland, would it not, my lord?"

"Yes, sir. The Duke is my father."

Captain Peverill's brows rose, and he shot a quick grin at his daughter. "Then I am particularly pleased to make your acquaintance, my lord. I trust my daughter has been behaving herself?"

Marcus blinked. Had she told him about—?

But Miss Peverill's anguished whisper of "Papa!" implied she had not. However, yesterday's escapade was most likely in character for her father to ask such a question.

"Perfectly, sir," he felt obliged to say. The grateful glance the girl shot him was further evidence her father did not know.

Marcus began to wonder whether Captain Peverill was a fit parent. Surely he had allowed his daughter's release from the schoolroom at far too young an age. She could not be more than sixteen or seventeen, which explained her impulsiveness and lack of judgment. What was the captain's excuse?

Before he could wonder why any of this should matter to him, a voice he had been particularly dreading broke into the conversation.

"My dear Lord Marcus," exclaimed Lady Mountheath, fairly oozing insincere affability. Her substantial form swathed in amethyst silk, she inserted herself into their growing circle as though by right. "What a delight to see you again so soon."

His heart sank at this oblique reference to the day before, but he merely smiled and bowed. "A pleasure indeed, my lady." Unable to think of any way to politely avoid it, he reluctantly turned to make introductions. "Lady Mountheath, let me present to you two newcomers to London, Captain and Miss Peverill."

She returned the captain's bow with a regal inclination of her head, then turned to his daughter, only to give an exaggerated start of obviously feigned surprise. As Marcus had feared, this had clearly been her purpose in joining them.

"Why, Miss Peverill!" she exclaimed. "I had hoped I was mistaken, but I see now that I was not. I confess myself amazed that you have the courage to show your face at a respectable gathering such as this one."

A murmur of protests broke out among the ladies at the blatant insult, and Captain Peverill's heavy brows drew down ominously. "I beg your pardon, my lady! What can you mean, to speak to my daughter like that?"

Lady Mountheath turned pitying eyes upon him, though her mouth twitched with triumph. Marcus stood rooted to the spot, wishing he were anywhere else.

"My dear sir, I regret to inform you that your

daughter has so far overstepped the bounds of propriety as to . . ."

She hesitated, as though reluctant to continue, though Marcus knew it was merely for dramatic effect. ". . . to visit a gentleman's residence *alone*, without so much as a maid in attendance. I saw her leaving his house myself."

A collective gasp greeted her words, and the captain's frown was now turned on his daughter.

Compelled to do something, Marcus spoke, though having no idea what he was going to say. "There is a perfectly reasonable explanation, my lady. You see, the truth is that Miss Peverill—that she and I—"

"Are betrothed," finished Captain Peverill smoothly. Marcus gaped, as did Miss Peverill.

"Betrothed?" Lady Mountheath looked extremely skeptical.

The captain nodded vigorously. "We intended to wait to make the announcement until her brother in Baltimore could be informed, but given the impetuosity of the young, it appears the delay was perhaps unwise."

Lady Mountheath rounded on Marcus. "My lord, is this true?"

From the corner of his eye he could see Miss Peverill shaking her head and mouthing something at him, but he realized that mattered not a whit. Squarely meeting Lady Mountheath's eye, Marcus said the only thing he could, in honor, say.

"Of course it is true, my lady. Why else would she have been visiting me yesterday?"

Chapter 3

Momentarily speechless from outrage, Quinn found her voice at last. "Betrothed!" The word came out as a strangled whisper. Before she could say anything further—or more audibly—her father seized her arm in an iron grip that was unexpected enough to startle her back to silence.

"Yes, we are all delighted," he said rather too loudly. "It was a bit sudden, of course, but you know how these things go with young people. Love at first sight and all that."

"But—" Her father's grip tightened to the point of pain, and she stopped again to stare at him, tears starting to her eyes. He had never hurt her. What—?

He met her look with one that held both a warning and a plea—but it was the plea that finally penetrated. Swallowing, she turned to look at Lord Marcus, but his face seemed chiseled in stone, completely expressionless. Finally, she faced Lady Mountheath with the brightest smile she could muster.

"It was such a foolish thing, really," she said, hating her own simpering tone. "Lord Marcus offered to take me walking about Mayfair, but before returning home I insisted on stopping for a sip of something, as it was so warm. He did warn me that it was not precisely proper for me to step into his house, but as it was only for a moment, I fear I paid him no mind."

Her father chuckled indulgently. "Quinn can be rather stubborn at times, too often to her own undoing. Isn't that right, Lord Marcus?"

Thus applied to, the gentleman nodded, though his face was still expressionless, Quinn noticed. "Yes indeed. Dear, impulsive Quinn." Though his words sounded almost mechanical, they seemed to have the desired effect.

Lady Mountheath's overeager smile vanished, to be replaced by an expression that reminded Quinn forcibly of a dog deprived of a coveted bone.

"You gentlemen would do well to instruct the young lady in proper *English* behavior," she said severely, her eyes still darting suspiciously to each of their faces in turn. "What might be permissible in the wilds of America can destroy a lady's reputation here, I assure you."

"Yes, my lady, I am just coming to realize that," said Quinn meekly, though she seethed inwardly at the denigration of her homeland. "I will certainly be more circumspect in future."

Lady Mountheath sniffed, plainly still disbelieving but thwarted by their united front. "I hope so, for your sake, my dear. A reputation is such a fragile thing, after all."

On that unmistakable note of warning, she left them, to Quinn's vast relief. She had no time for reflection, however, for now Miss Chalmers and the Misses Melks closed in, wanting to know every detail of the fictitious betrothal.

"Love at first sight," sighed Miss Augusta. "How very romantic! And you sly things, pretending that you had only just met. Wasn't that sly, Lucinda?"

Her sister agreed, with a look that told Quinn that she was the more perceptive of the two. "Indeed. Did you really believe you could keep it a secret? How long will it take for the news to reach your brother in America?"

Quinn glanced at her father and saw that he was unprepared to elaborate on the story he had himself put forward. "Not for a month or more, I fear," she said quickly, before any hesitation could be noticed. "The shipping schedules must be taken into account, as well as the weather."

Captain Peverill belatedly agreed with this assessment, sending Quinn a grateful glance. With scant assistance from Lord Marcus, who still appeared stunned by the turn of events, she and her father managed to answer or deflect the volley of questions that ensued.

Finally, the three ladies made their excuses, no doubt to spread the word among their other acquaintances. Captain Peverill seized the opportunity to speak briefly to Lord Marcus.

"Thank you, my lord, for doing the honorable

thing. I realize a betrothal is not what you had planned."

The gentleman regarded him warily. "Er, not precisely, no," he admitted. "That is—"

"Well of course not," exclaimed Quinn. "I cannot believe you told everyone such a thing, Papa! Now we will look even more foolish when it becomes known that there was never any betrothal at all." Still, the idea of being betrothed to the handsome Lord Marcus caused an odd flutter in her midsection. Foolishness!

"Moderate your tone," her father said sternly. "Perhaps if you had told me the full tale of your *adventure* yesterday, I'd have had time to think of a different tale. But now we are stuck with this one."

"Stuck?" Lord Marcus echoed the word just as Quinn did, and she thought he sounded as horrified as she.

Captain Peverill nodded. "We cannot recant now without irrevocably ruining Quinn's reputation—and perhaps your own, my lord. You heard what Lady Mountheath said."

"That odious woman!" But Quinn's anger was not directed only at Lady Mountheath. "I refuse to let her—or anyone—direct my actions by threat of gossip. What can she do, really?"

It was Lord Marcus who answered. "Quite a lot, I fear," he said heavily. "She has the ear of everyone who matters in Society and delights in using her influence to shred reputations. I have seen her destroy more than one—"

He was interrupted by the arrival of Lady Claridge, her husband and daughter in tow. "I understand congratulations are in order?" She glanced from Quinn to Lord Marcus and back. Behind her, Lady Constance watched, wide-eyed with curiosity, and Lord Claridge smiled, though he looked uncertain.

Quinn met her aunt's critical gaze as defiantly as she could, considering her inner turmoil, but before she could deny or her father confirm the news, Lord Marcus spoke.

"Yes, Lady Claridge, Miss Peverill has done me the very great honor of agreeing to become my wife."

Quinn stared at him in disbelief, and he responded with a barely perceptible shrug that made her suddenly aware of the width of the shoulders beneath his superbly fitted coat.

"It's quite amazing how quickly the news has spread," he continued, holding her eye for a moment before turning back to Lady Claridge. "Especially considering that there has been no formal announcement as yet."

That allowed Captain Peverill to launch into his explanation of how they had thought to delay publicizing the match until Charles could be notified. If anything, Quinn thought Lady Claridge's expression grew even more pinched and suspicious.

"One might have expected that her uncle would have been informed, as he has opened his home to her," she said frostily. "That would have prevented our learning her news through other channels." She frowned in the direction of Lady Mountheath, who was now talking animatedly to yet another group.

"I do apologize, my lady," the captain responded, even as Lord Claridge made soothing noises. "You are correct, of course, particularly as it is our hope that Quinn might be married from your home in a few months' time. While I cannot remain in England so long, I will try to return for the wedding, of course."

Months? Quinn had absolutely no intention of remaining in England for months! Indeed, it was more imperative than ever that she return home without delay, before this absurd, fictitious betrothal could somehow become a real one.

"Papa, I'm certain we needn't impose—" Quinn began hastily, but Lord Claridge cut her off.

"Nonsense, my dear, nonsense. You are family. It's quite right and proper that you should stay with us until the happy event takes place." He appeared genuinely delighted at the prospect.

Her father heartily agreed, and Quinn subsided, contenting herself with an apologetic glance at her aunt and cousin, coldly returned. Once they were alone, she would convince her father of the folly of continuing this fiction—as well as of the necessity of allowing her to return with him to Baltimore on the next available vessel.

The next few hours allowed no opportunity for Quinn to speak privately to either her father or Lord Marcus, however. They were continually accosted by people congratulating them. Quinn sent her father many a speaking glance, all of which he blithely ignored. It was a relief when they finally took their leave.

Lord Marcus bowed over her hand, his expression still stiff, though something that might have been amusement lurked in his vivid blue eyes. If anything, that irritated her further. She took her leave of him coolly, ignoring an urge to probe his true feelings. Surely he must see that they faced possible disaster?

Captain Peverill, however, appeared to consider the whole affair an unqualified success. "I couldn't have planned it better if I'd tried," he whispered to her as they waited with the Claridges for their carriage a short time later. "Betrothed to the son of a Duke! Not bad for our first evening in Society, eh?"

Quinn stared at him. "Not bad?" she whispered back fiercely. "How can you say so? The world believing me betrothed when I am no such thing! If you *had* planned it, I would think you quite mad."

Now he looked a shade uncomfortable. "Yes, well. Lord Marcus has agreed to call upon me tomorrow. I'm sure everything will be worked out then to the satisfaction of all."

Quinn breathed a sigh of relief. "Thank heaven for that. It's clear he has no more desire to be trapped into a match than I do."

She refused to acknowledge the tiny pang that observation cost her. After all, he knew no more of her than she knew of him, and she certainly had no desire to be bound to the man. Why ever should she expect him to feel differently? If he did, it would only show a want of sensibility—and sense.

The carriage arrived then, ending conversation, though not Quinn's reflections. Though reassured by her father's assurance that all would be settled on the morrow, she couldn't help reliving the embarrassments of the evening during the short drive, or as she prepared for bed afterward.

As she drifted off to sleep, however, it was Lord Marcus's blue eyes and deep voice that lingered to color her dreams.

"I told you, it's all a mistake." Marcus was becoming irritated at his brother's unwillingness to drop the subject. "Tomorrow I'm to call upon the Peverills, and we'll no doubt find a way to extricate ourselves from this coil with a minimum of fuss."

Peter regarded him with that maddeningly knowing expression of his. "A mistake, no doubt—but whose? I can't believe you were forced to declare yourself betrothed simply because that busybody Lady Mountheath threatened to stir up a bit of scandal. She does that almost weekly, and when has scandal ever bothered you?"

Stripping off coat and gloves, Marcus handed them to Clarence and waited for his valet to leave the library before replying. "I didn't do the declaring. Captain Peverill did. Had the scandal concerned only me, I'd have denied it on the spot. But that harpy threatened to ruin Miss Peverill as well, which you would no more have allowed than I did."

"I? Of course not. What you did would have been completely in character for *me*, which is what makes this so very amusing." Peter went to the sideboard and poured himself a judicious measure of brandy. "In fact, I feel inclined to celebrate."

Marcus glared at him. "Well I certainly do not,

though some of that brandy would not go amiss. Pour me some, will you?"

Peter complied, watching in silence as Marcus took a sip, then another. On his third, more relaxed sip, Peter spoke again. "Perhaps it is fate."

The brandy caught in Marcus's throat, making him cough and sputter. "Fate?" he rasped after a moment. Clearing his throat, he continued more audibly. "You ascribe the ill-judged romp of a young girl and Lady Mountheath's evil tongue to fate? What fate?"

"Yours, of course. Fate uses whatever tools are to hand. I have often observed it."

"Easy enough to say after the fact," Marcus pointed out. "I, however, prefer to believe I am the captain of my own destiny—and a wife has no part in it. Especially one who should still be in the schoolroom, and who has no more desire to wed than I have."

"Is Miss Peverill as young as all that, then? After speaking with her, I rather thought—"

"I don't know her exact age," Marcus admitted. "But you did not see her yesterday, tricked out in her brother's clothes. She may speak intelligently, but her judgment is clearly not that of an adult—which is how we find ourselves in this predicament."

Still, he couldn't help remembering that surge of protectiveness he'd felt yesterday—or the seductive innocence of Miss Peverill's lovely green-gold eyes. What if—?

But Peter was now watching him again with that disconcerting shrewdness. "Predicament? I suppose time will tell."

"Time will not be an issue," Marcus informed

him, thrusting away such inappropriate memories. "By midday tomorrow, I'm confident this will all be behind me. Captain Peverill doesn't seem the type who would force his daughter into a match repugnant to her."

He was careful to conceal his irritation at being considered repugnant by Miss Peverill. The last thing Peter needed was more ammunition for his meddling.

It was with some trepidation that Marcus presented himself at the Claridge house the next morning. There had been no opportunity last night for a private word with Miss Peverill, so he still had no idea what she had told her father about their encounter two days since. What should he himself reveal, if anything? He would take his cue from her, he decided.

But when the butler ushered him into an elegant drawing room a few minutes later, Captain Peverill alone awaited him. "Good morning, Lord Marcus, good morning," he boomed jovially. "Delighted you could come."

Instead of putting him at his ease, Marcus found the man's cheerfulness rather oppressive. "Good morning, Captain Peverill. It would seem we have, ah, business to discuss."

"Business. Yes, hm. Business." The word seemed to sober the captain, to Marcus's relief. "I suppose we'd best get to it, then. It appears that between you, you and my daughter have stirred up quite a scandal, my lord."

Marcus swallowed, realizing that he could hardly state the truth—that any scandal was purely Miss Peverill's fault. "Surely, sir, the scandal is not so great? Lady Mountheath is known for blowing minor social infractions all out of proportion."

"So I have been told. However, the potential damage to my daughter's good name is not inconsiderable, given the venue Lady Mountheath chose for her, ah, disclosure last night." His look now was questioning.

With a mental shrug, Marcus answered the implied question. "It is true that Miss Peverill was at my house, though only for a few minutes. It was quite an accident, however—the result of an unfortunate misunderstanding."

Captain Peverill said nothing, so Marcus hurried on, trying not to dither. "She was dressed as a boy, you see—her brother's clothing, she said. I took her as such, at first, but sent her on her way as soon as I discovered my mistake."

Now the captain was frowning. "She was wearing a skirt when she returned."

"Oh! Yes. I, ah, insisted she borrow one from one of my housemaids, as it was clearly not fitting that she walk about in breeches." The room was beginning to feel uncomfortably warm.

"It was clearly not fitting that she be walking about London unescorted at all," Captain Peverill pointed out. "I would never have allowed it, had I known her intentions. I confess myself a trifle disappointed that you did, my lord."

Marcus tugged at his cravat, wondering why

Clarence had tied it so much more tightly than usual. "I tried to insist she allow one of my footmen to accompany her, but she refused. Your daughter seems to have rather a strong will, sir, if you will forgive me."

To his relief, the captain nodded. "She does indeed. I have warned her repeatedly that her impulsiveness would land her in trouble one day, though I confess I had not envisioned anything of this sort. But now the damage is done, however innocent the actual circumstances. I must ask, my lord, whether you mean to abide by your given word and marry my daughter?"

Caught off guard by the suddenness of the question, Marcus answered automatically, "Of course, sir, I have no intention of going back on my word. However, I had the impression last night that Miss Peverill was less than amenable to the idea?"

"Tut, tut." The captain waved a dismissive—and very large—hand. "She was merely startled. Once she had a chance to consider the advantages of such a match, I assure you she became quite enthusiastic. Her main concern seemed to be that you might disavow the promise you made last night."

Why, that conniving little jade . . . ! Trapped, Marcus said stiffly, "To do so would be dishonorable in the extreme, Captain Peverill. Pray assure your daughter that I intend to do my duty by her, if that is her wish."

At once the captain was all smiles again. "Excellent! Excellent! She will be relieved beyond measure, I know. And I must say it is very good of you, my lord, as it was Quinn's foolishness that created the scandal in the first place. I have no doubt that you will be able to train such tendencies out of her, in time."

Marcus felt a cold weight settle in his stomach at the finality implied by that last statement. "Of . . . of course."

"I presume you'll wish to set a future meeting to discuss settlements and such?" the captain continued. "You'll have had no time to give thought to such things yet, any more than I have."

He rose and extended his hand. Automatically, Marcus did likewise, his mind still numb. "Another meeting. Yes."

Pumping his hand and beaming, Captain Peverill declared, "I'm sure you and Quinn will deal admirably together. She's a bright little thing, and nearly as pretty as her mother was. Just send a message round when you're ready to discuss the particulars."

Before he knew what he was about, Marcus found himself descending to Mount Street alone. He was just as glad he'd not taken the carriage, feeling the need to walk so that he could better sort through what had just happened.

He was well and truly betrothed now, and there seemed no honorable way to get out of it. Miss Peverill had grasped opportunity with both hands, no doubt about it! But she would not find him so easy to manipulate as her father, he was determined.

Not until he reached Grosvenor Street did it occur to him that it was a trifle odd that Captain Peverill had ushered him out of the house without allowing him so much as a glimpse of his bride-to-be.

*   *   *

Quinn watched Lord Marcus's departure from the window of her bedchamber, where her father had insisted she wait while the gentlemen worked out their problem. Now that he was gone, however, she wasted no time in hurrying down to the drawing room.

"Well?" she demanded, when her father only looked up affably at her sudden entrance. "Were you two able to figure a way out of this mess? Is everything settled?"

The captain rose, smiling, to take both of her hands in his. "Indeed it is, my dear, settled quite famously. Let me be the first to congratulate you!" He dropped a quick kiss on her cheek.

Quinn pulled back to regard him suspiciously. "You *are* congratulating me on my escape, are you not, Papa?"

"Your escape from scandal, most assuredly," he said, though his smile now held a hint of wariness. "Lord Marcus was only too eager to make certain you would not suffer from your lamentable lack of judgment."

"Was he?" She narrowed her eyes, her sense of foreboding growing. "And how does he mean to ensure that?"

Her father's surprise was almost certainly feigned. "Why, by marrying you, of course, just as he promised last night."

"Marrying me! Papa, you assured me you would find another way out of this," she reminded him severely.

The captain looked the slightest bit uncomfortable, refusing to meet her eye. "Now, my dear, that is not precisely what I said. If you will recall—"

But Quinn was having have none of it. "You know full well I have no intention of marrying Lord Marcus. I will sail for Baltimore at once rather than do so. Nor can I believe he has any particular wish to wed me."

"On the contrary, he seemed more than ready to do the proper thing. I imagine he is considering his own reputation among the *ton* as well as yours. Not that we can blame him for that."

Quinn could more readily believe that Lord Marcus would marry her to salvage his reputation than her own, but she refused to believe her little foray required such an extreme remedy.

"Once it is known that he has offered, surely his honor will be safe from scrutiny. Then I can cry off and leave England, and no scandal can possibly attach to him." She sat down in the overstuffed chair near the window and smiled up at her father, quite pleased with her own solution to the problem.

"But scandal would then attach to *you*, Quinn, or rather to us, and we cannot have that," he said, clearly alarmed. "Think of the business! And of Lord and Lady Claridge. Whatever reflects upon us will reflect upon them as well. Surely you would not repay their hospitality so shabbily?"

She barely restrained a snort. "Hospitality! Reluctant duty, rather. Lady Claridge, at least, will be happy enough to see me out of England."

"Do not forget the marquess," her father said.

"He seems most pleased to have you here. He said so again last night."

Since Quinn could not dispute that, she said, "Surely you are relying too much on what Society may or may not think, Papa. Who am I that they will notice my actions at all, except in passing?"

"Why, you are the daughter of Lady Glynna, granddaughter to the Marquess of Claridge. You have connections among the highest in the land." He strode back and forth as he spoke, gesturing grandly, but then he stopped. "Will you disregard your mother's dying wish? Would you besmirch her memory, and prove Lady Claridge's predictions true?"

Quinn felt trapped, torn again by guilt that she had been busy at the warehouses rather than at her mother's bedside during her final hours, as her father had been. As out of character as this supposed last wish seemed, how could she question it now?

"I will try not to do anything to tarnish our family name," she said at last. "I will even attempt a true reconciliation with the Claridges."

Her father began to smile again, so she held up a hand. "However," she continued, "I make no promise to mortgage my future happiness for the sake of appearances, or even for the business. Nor can I believe Mother would have wanted me to do so. I will continue to seek an honorable way out of this betrothal."

And if she could not find one, Quinn fully intended to take ship for Baltimore, by herself if necessary!

Chapter 4

Marcus returned home to find Peter entertaining his friend Harry Thatcher in the library. Mr. Thatcher always had tales to tell about the war and his other, more colorful exploits, and normally Marcus looked forward to hearing them, but just now he preferred solitude. That was not to be an option, however.

"There he is now," Peter exclaimed before Marcus could back out of the library. "Come, tell us how things stand. I was just bringing Harry up to speed on your latest scrape."

Reluctantly, Marcus advanced into the room and flung himself into one of the deep leather chairs. "You make it sound as though I was caught in a neighbor's orchard," he said sourly. "This is a bit more serious."

Harry Thatcher chuckled. "Sounds as though the consequences may be dire indeed. You should have been more careful, lad." He nodded sententiously before draining his wineglass.

"You're a fine one to talk," exclaimed Peter with a laugh, refilling Harry's empty glass with claret. "Don't forget, Marcus has heard the story of how you really lost that arm." He nodded toward his friend's empty left sleeve.

Harry shrugged, taking another generous sip of his wine. "Better an arm than my freedom," he said. "When it comes to women—ladies of quality, at any rate—I'm remarkably careful."

"I did nothing wrong," Marcus informed them both. "Miss Peverill was the one at fault, gadding about town without an escort." They were enjoying his predicament far too much, and they hadn't even heard the worst of it yet.

"Then she admitted her fault and her father released you from your obligation?" Peter sighed. "Pity. Marriage would have had a steadying effect upon you."

A snort from Harry echoed Marcus's own opinion. "That's what you said about Jack, if you recall," Harry said to Peter. "Yet he stirred up quite a scandal with his wife, from what we heard on returning from Vienna. Took becoming a father to turn him into a proper stick-in-the-mud."

"Ah, but you can't deny he's blissfully happy," Peter retorted. They were referring, Marcus knew, to their mutual friend, Lord Foxhaven, who had married nearly two years since.

"But Foxhaven made his choice himself," Marcus pointed out. "A woman with a reputation completely opposite to his own. Miss Peverill will hardly have the same effect upon me, given what I have seen of her so far."

Peter sat up straighter. "Then you intend to marry her after all? Why did you not say so at once?"

Marcus shifted uncomfortably in his chair. "Didn't want to give you the satisfaction. But she and her father have trapped me nicely between them. It appears I won't be allowed to back out."

"Captain Peverill struck me last night as a rather formidable man," said Peter, showing his first sign of sympathy. "Unwilling to admit his daughter's fault, was he?"

"Oh, he admitted it readily enough. Expects me to train the wildness out of her, in fact." Despite his irritation at the entire situation, Marcus couldn't keep his lips from twitching at the absurdity of such an idea.

As for Peter and Harry, they fairly exploded with laughter, which restored Marcus's foul humor quite efficiently. "You!" Peter gasped after a moment. "Train the wildness—! Oh, that's too rich for words."

Abruptly, Marcus rose. "Your felicitations leave something to be desired. You will excuse me, I know. I have matters to attend to." Stiffly, trying to maintain at least a shred of dignity in the face of the others' hilarity, he left the library.

"You there, James," he said to the nearest footman upon regaining the hallway. "Nip around the corner to Marland House and tell Mr. Fairley to expect me within the hour."

The footman bowed and left.

The Duke's man of business would be able to advise him with respect to marriage settlements and other such matters. He might as well get that over with—that, and confronting his father with the news. Whether the Duke of Marland was angry or as pleased as Peter was, Marcus knew he himself would find little pleasure in that interview.

An hour later, Marcus was shown into his father's study, a room he'd always disliked. Now he glanced around at the dark, heavy furnishings and brown-velvet drapes, remembering the innumerable occasions throughout his youth when he'd been called to account for some misdemeanor in these somber surroundings.

As always, the Duke awaited him at the far end of the room, enthroned upon his vast mahogany chair, separated from lesser mortals by the polished expanse of his claw-footed mahogany desk. Marcus reminded himself that he was now an adult, and that he had not been summoned here. He had nothing for which to apologize.

"I presume you have come to inform me of your ill-considered betrothal?" the Duke asked dryly before Marcus reached the desk. "I am delighted not to be the last one to know."

Marcus felt all the old, defensive feelings welling up, adult or no. "When are you ever the last to know anything, Your Grace? As my betrothal was finalized less than two hours ago, it appears you had earlier intelligence of it than I."

The Duke of Marland's thin, aquiline countenance displayed the merest trace of curiosity. "Yet those present at Lord and Lady Trumball's last night were told that it was an accomplished fact. Would you care to enlighten me as to the details?"

Not particularly, Marcus thought, but aloud he said, "The interference of gossips threatened to transform into scandal what began as a simple misunderstanding. I therefore offered Miss Peverill the protection of my name."

"How very noble." The Duke infused those three words with a wealth of scathing commentary upon Marcus's past, as well as his present judgment—or lack thereof.

"Miss Peverill is quite agreeable, actually," Marcus lied, nettled. "I don't doubt we will deal comfortably together." Quinn Peverill might be many things, but agreeable and comfortable were not among them.

Though he was nearing seventy, the Duke's pale gray eyes had lost none of their sharpness. "Peverill. That would make her granddaughter to the third Marquess of Claridge?"

Marcus nodded, impressed in spite of himself at his father's deductive abilities. It must be where Peter came by that gift.

"A grasping man, whose pride overshadowed his wisdom on more than one occasion. And the current marquess is an ineffectual milksop. Still, the mother's family is old and respectable. What of the father? American? A sea captain or some such thing?" His thin lips pressed together with disapproval.

"He heads up a large shipping concern out of Baltimore." It felt strange to defend the Peverills, whom he himself regarded as crass opportunists. "He is in England to expand upon that concern. A man of some substance, I believe."

"Hm. We must hope so, as you've little enough of your own."

Marcus was never allowed to forget who held his purse strings, and this reminder galled him more than usual. "I'll try to hold out for a handsome dowry, then." He attempted to match his father's tone for dryness.

The Duke appeared not to notice. "Still, you'll have to settle something on her. One hundred pounds per annum should suffice."

"One hundred—!" Marcus stared. It was an absurdly small sum. His sister-in-law, Lady Bagstead, received five times that amount, not to mention the household funds to which she had access whenever planning an entertainment. Of course, she would be Duchess when Robert inherited, but—

"As a colonist, I imagine Miss Peverill is used to living simply. If her father balks, you are authorized to offer as much as one hundred fifty. Work out the details with Mr. Fairley."

It was clearly a dismissal, so Marcus bowed and left, relieved, even through his irritation, to have the interview over.

The next two hours were tedious in the extreme, but he left Marland House with a better understanding of his own finances than he'd ever had before. It was not an encouraging picture. Despite the extent of the Marland holdings, with five sons, the portion set aside for the youngest was extremely modest. No wonder his mother had once pressed him to consider a calling in the Church.

Returning home, he handed his hat to a footman. Turning to go upstairs, however, he caught sight of a coarse scrap of folded paper among the hot-pressed calling cards in the tray on the hall table. Snatching it up, he found it contained just a few scribbled words: "Gobby. Garden. Sundown."

The boys must have information for him, then—which led to another problem. How was he to play the Saint if he was married—or even betrothed? Well, he should have some weeks to work out that conundrum.

He checked his watch. The July days were long—the sun wouldn't set for hours. This would be as good a time as any for him to become better acquainted with his bride-to-be. With more resignation than enthusiasm, he ordered up his phaeton and set out for Mount Street to invite Miss Peverill for a drive.

Becoming a Saint was turning out to be more trouble than he'd bargained for, on all fronts.

Quinn's stomach was growling by the time she was summoned downstairs, only to discover a disappointingly light afternoon tea of cakes and tiny sandwiches instead of dinner. She would never get used to London hours! The conversation, however, diminished her appetite considerably.

". . . and of course you will have to take Miss Peverill with you to the modiste tomorrow," Lady Claridge was saying to her daughter. "I had Hortense examine her wardrobe and she tells me it is quite hopeless."

"Of course, Mother," agreed Lady Constance, looking bland and beautiful in pristine white muslin. "Madame Fanchot will be able to rectify the problem, I doubt not, as her taste is impeccable."

"I suppose I'd best stay close in my room until you can dress me properly." Quinn tried to speak lightly, unwilling to give them the satisfaction of knowing they'd nettled her. "I wouldn't wish to embarrass you."

Lady Claridge sniffed. "Clothing alone will not prevent that, but it is a start. Still, it will look odd if you do not accompany us to our evening engagements. Perhaps Madame Fanchot will have something she can pin up for you at once, or Hortense might be able to make some of your existing gowns presentable."

Quinn thought about the pains she had gone to in Baltimore, having several dresses made up in the latest fashions. Her new French maid, Monette, had not implied that they were in any way substandard, which she had no doubt she would have done, were it true. She opened her mouth to say so, then caught her father's eye across the little enameled table and closed it again.

"Whatever you think best, of course, my lady," she said instead, seething inwardly.

Lady Claridge regarded her suspiciously, but before she could speak, the butler entered to announce Lord Marcus Northrup.

Any distraction was welcome just now, but when Quinn saw the wooden expression on Lord Marcus's handsome face, her spirits fell as quickly as they had risen.

"Good afternoon, my lord," she murmured coolly, when he turned to her after greeting his hostesses.

"I had hoped to persuade you to drive out with me, Miss Peverill," he said stiffly once the amenities were past. His attitude, however, seemed to belie such a hope.

Much as she wished to escape the oppressive presence of her relatives, Quinn had no desire to be obligated for that escape to his clearly unwilling gallantry. "I'm sorry, my lord, but I fear that would not be proper."

"Oh, nonsense!" her father exclaimed. "You are betrothed to the fellow, after all. And besides, young ladies drive out with their admirers all the time, do they not, Lady Claridge?"

Quinn looked to her aunt, but even she seemed to have no reservations—or perhaps she simply wished to be rid of her for a time. "You may go without concern, Miss Peverill, though you may take your maid if you are at all nervous."

Unwilling to be thought the least bit nervous, Quinn said, "No, no, I merely wished to be certain of the proprieties—for *your* sake, my lady. I will fetch my parasol."

She took her time upstairs, first selecting a pale yellow parasol that matched the trim of her spring green gown, then having Monette put some finishing touches to her hair. Examining herself critically in the glass, she decided the color of the gown, at least, flattered her, emphasizing the green of her eyes. Was she really so unfashionable as all that?

No! She refused to care. Head high, she headed back downstairs, where Lord Marcus awaited her, still looking as though he'd rather be anywhere else.

"Shall we go, my lord?" She made no particular effort to appear cheerful, as he seemed anything but.

Silently, he extended his arm and escorted her out to his waiting phaeton. She placed her gloved fingertips on his sleeve, resolutely ignoring the tiny shiver of excitement that went through her at the contact.

"I thought perhaps a turn in Hyde Park," he said when they reached his phaeton, helping her up into the high-sprung vehicle.

Quinn tried to suppress another instinctive lightening of her mood at the prospect of riding in such a conveyance. She had seen phaetons and curricles tooling about the London streets and thought it would be great fun to ride in one. If only her companion were as agreeable as he was handsome!

"Hyde Park will be fine, my lord. I don't wish to put you out, however."

Lord Marcus's mouth twisted in a cynical mockery of a smile. "It's a bit late for that, isn't it, Miss Peverill? A drive in the Park is no inconvenience by comparison, I assure you."

"How reassuring," she said icily. No matter where she turned, it seemed people were determined to disapprove of her. Well, let them! She would be gone from England and away from them all as soon as she could contrive it.

He set the matched pair of grays into a trot, and Quinn couldn't help admiring his skill as he took the corner from Mount Street onto Park Lane, neatly skirting a ponderous delivery cart and its enormous draft horse.

As they rode in silence, she had time to wonder why he had come to call when he apparently had no more desire to spend time in her company than she had in his. Clearly her father had overstated his "eagerness" for the match—or perhaps he was only eager for her inheritance?

That unpleasant thought finally spurred her to speech. "I confess myself surprised that you felt obliged to follow through on the impulsive claim you made last night," she said as they turned into the Park gates. "I can't believe it was necessary."

He looked sidelong at her, and in spite of herself—and his frown—she noticed again how classically handsome his profile was. What a pity it was wasted on such a stick-in-the-mud!

"Perhaps the concepts of duty and honor are foreign to Americans, but I assure you we English take them very seriously." His words only served to irritate her further.

"I have noticed that the English elevate propriety and appearances to the level of a sacred trust, my lord," she said, lifting her chin to face him defiantly. "Where I come from, duty and honor are reserved for more important things."

He blinked, and she felt a small satisfaction in seeing that she had startled him. "As you are the beneficiary of what you seem to consider a misplaced sense of duty, it ill behooves you to criticize my motives, Miss Peverill," he said dampeningly.

"Oh, I have no doubt that your motives are as pure as *gold*, my lord," she retorted with a knowing smile.

His brilliant blue eyes narrowed, and he seemed about to deliver another attempt at a set-down—one that Quinn felt quite eager to turn back upon him—when a feminine voice accosted them.

"Lord Marcus! Such rumors are flying about Town. Can they be true?" Turning, Quinn saw a plump, pretty blonde driving a smart blue phaeton, holding the reins herself.

"Good afternoon, Lady Regina," Lord Marcus responded. "You are looking particularly lovely today."

With a pang, Quinn realized he had made no similar comment on her own appearance. But then, she could scarcely compete with this vision of femininity in lavender ruffles.

The lady gave a sweet trill of laughter at the compliment, but her eyes, resting now on Quinn, were speculative. "You are too kind, my lord. But the rumors? Do you really mean to tie parson's knot and devastate half the women in London?"

"I have no doubt they will recover," he responded lightly, though Quinn could hear an underlying edge to his voice. "But yes, it's true. Let me introduce Miss Peverill, my bride-to-be."

The blonde's smile was as false as any Lady Claridge might produce. "How very delightful!" she exclaimed. "I understand you are American, Miss Peverill?"

Quinn assented. "From Baltimore. I am pleased to make your acquaintance, Lady—"

But the woman cut her off. "How quaint. Well, I promised to tell my sister as soon as I knew the truth, so I'll be on my way. I trust marriage won't change you *too* much, my lord."

With a saucy wink that bothered Quinn more than she cared to admit, the woman whipped up her horses and trotted off.

"Pray don't mind Regina," said Lord Marcus as soon as she was gone. "She's high-spirited, but she means no harm."

Quinn refused to meet his eye. "Mind? Why should anything she said—anything anyone says— matter to me, my lord? It is not as though this is to be a love match, after all."

For the first time, she allowed herself to imagine what it might be like to actually be married to Lord Marcus, to interact with him daily, to share a house with him, perhaps even a bed—the idea was thoroughly disturbing.

"I find I have rather lost my enthusiasm for a drive, my lord," she said abruptly. "Perhaps you would be kind enough to take me back."

"We'll have to finish this circuit, as I can't safely turn here, but then I'll take you home if you wish," Marcus replied, stifling a sigh. He was fairly certain he couldn't have handled things more clumsily if he had tried.

He'd been in a foul mood when he'd arrived in Mount Street, after his interviews with the Duke and his man of business. Still, there was no reason to take it all out on the girl, even if she had been the original instigator of his current woes. It wasn't as though she'd done it intentionally, and it was clear that she was nowhere near as keen for the match as her father had implied, which was to her credit.

So why did that knowledge dampen his spirits further?

"I know I haven't been particularly pleasant today, and I apologize," he said as they neared the end of the loop. "My ill humor is nothing to do with you—or very little, anyway," honesty forced him to add.

"How reassuring to know that you are generally bad-tempered, and that I need not take it personally."

What a tongue the girl had on her! But even as he thought it, Marcus detected a quaver in her voice. This had to be at least as difficult for her as it was for him, he realized. Why had he not considered that before?

"I am not generally bad-tempered," he replied with a gentleness that came surprisingly easily. "This has been rather a trying day, however."

She finally looked at him, only to turn away again—but not before he saw the glitter of unshed tears in her wide green eyes. A totally unexpected wave of protectiveness assailed him. Protectiveness and something else. He transferred the reins to one hand, reaching for her averted face with the other.

"I'm sorry to have been yet one more trial then, my lord. If you wish me to cry off, I will be only too happy to do so."

"No, of course not," he said automatically, then paused, startled. "That is—" With one gloved finger, he stroked her cheek, trying to comfort her. At least, he thought that was what he was trying to do.

She frowned up at him, clearly startled, the threat of tears gone. "Do you mean that you actually *want* to marry me? Why?"

For the first time, he really saw her—not as an irksome child, not as a scheming social-climber, but as a young woman, unsure of her place in a world that was strange to her. A young woman whose combination of spirit and vulnerability struck him as decidedly attractive, in fact.

"Why not?" He traced the curve of her jaw with his finger, and she did not flinch away. "It's quite possible we will deal quite comfortably together." The words seemed less unlikely than when he had said them to his father. "Certainly, I could do worse things with my life, and I'll likely marry someday anyway."

As soon as the words were out, he realized they were the wrong ones—even before she withdrew from him again.

"Then you would do better to wait until you can make your own choice in the matter and not have one thrust upon you," she said stiffly. Not that he could blame her. What a nodcock he was!

They had reached the Park gates, and for a moment he debated taking another circuit. No, with more time with her, he would no doubt only make things worse. "But I might never make a choice," he pointed out, leaving the Park. "Then where would I be?"

She looked up at him suspiciously. "Single and carefree?" she suggested.

"Or bored and lonely." It occurred to him that one thing Quinn Peverill was unlikely ever to do was to bore him. A definite point in her favor. That, and those remarkable sparkling eyes.

"I'm sure that is possible even within a marriage," she said, "though it seems more a risk for women than for men, who frequently manage to alleviate those conditions elsewhere."

Marcus stifled a grin. "I am shocked, Miss Peverill, that a proper young miss like yourself should have knowledge of such things." No, definitely not boring!

"You are easily shocked, I have noticed. That is yet another reason we should not suit."

Now where on earth had she gotten that idea? Easily shocked? Him? How Peter would laugh at *that* notion! Perhaps it was time he showed her otherwise. "I was jesting, Miss Peverill," he began, reaching for her again, but she cut him off.

"No, pray do not feel you must adjust your sensibilities to my unorthodox ways. It is clear I shall never fit into English Society properly. I intend to take ship for America as soon as may be, relieving you of a burdensome responsibility—and relieving Lord and Lady Claridge, as well. It becomes increasingly clear that will be best for all concerned."

They reached the Claridge house on Mount Street then, so Marcus handed her down from the phaeton, enjoying despite himself the feel of her hand in his. "You must do what you think best, of course, Miss Peverill," he said, and wondered if he imagined the quick flash of disappointment in her eyes. Probably.

Still, as he drove away after seeing her to the door, he realized that he was not at all sure he wanted to be relieved of this particular burdensome responsibility. How very strange.

Though she tried, Quinn could not ignore the persistent flutter in her midsection that had begun when Lord Marcus had touched her face—so sensuously!—and had only intensified when he handed her down from his phaeton. Her feelings toward him careened wildly from one extreme to the other. All the more reason to extricate herself from this betrothal without delay, before she could embarrass herself and everyone connected with her.

She needed time to think, to compose herself, but as she passed the drawing room on her way to her chamber, her father called out for her to join him. At least he was alone.

"I'll just go up and put off my bonnet, then return," she said as an excuse for at least a slight delay, determined that her father not sense any sign of her inner turmoil.

"Nonsense," the captain responded. "That's what servants are for, after all. You there!" he called to a housemaid who was polishing a pair of brass candlesticks on the landing. "Take my daughter's bonnet up to her chamber, there's a good lass."

With a sigh, Quinn handed bonnet and parasol

to the maid and took a seat in the parlor, commanding herself to calmness. She might as well let her father know at once of her intention to return to Baltimore with him, unwed. He wouldn't like it, of course, but—

"How was your drive?" he asked as she seated herself. "Was Lord Marcus . . . pleasant?" He looked wary, Quinn thought, and no wonder. If he had exaggerated Lord Marcus's enthusiasm to her, he had very likely done the same in reverse.

"I'm not certain 'pleasant' is the term I would use. Let us say it was enlightening." She enjoyed watching her father's expression change from wary to alarmed.

"Enlightening? What—that is, I presume you mean that you and Lord Marcus feel better acquainted now? That is just what I had hoped, of course."

She smiled, but her father knew her too well to be put at ease by it. "Certainly we are better acquainted with each other's feelings about this match. We have agreed that we will not suit."

The captain surged to his feet. "Will not suit! Do you mean he now refuses to do his duty by you? I won't have it! I'll call the blackguard out! Do you want his blood—or mine—on your head?"

Though fairly certain her father was exaggerating, Quinn couldn't quash her sudden alarm at the idea of him fighting Lord Marcus. "No, he didn't refuse," she said quickly. "I offered to cry off, and he made no particular objection to my doing so."

That wasn't quite true, she realized, thinking back

over their conversation, but his objections had been vague. He must surely admit that she was right, once he thought it through.

Her father pounced on her words. "He didn't refuse? Then he *is* still willing to marry you, if you don't cry off?"

Though she'd have preferred not to answer, Quinn was forced to admit it. "I suppose so. However, it is obvious—"

"Well, then, all is not lost—not lost at all, though you gave me rather a start. Now, let's have no more missishness about the business."

"Missishness! Papa, you are *forcing* me to marry against my will, as though you are some feudal lord consolidating estates. I thought we were living in more enlightened times than that."

For a moment she thought her words had had the desired effect, as he regarded her with a worried frown. But then he said, "Quinn, dear, you must trust me to know what's best. I've made inquiries, and Lord Marcus is fine young man, with no notable vices and a long, illustrious pedigree. You could do no better in a husband if you waited to be wooed by dozens of young men."

"Which is scarcely likely now," she said dryly. "At least not here in England. That is why I'd prefer to return home when you do. Surely you can see that would be best?"

His chin jutted out stubbornly. "I don't see that at all. There is no one in Baltimore you wish to wed, is there?"

Quinn had to shake her head. In truth, one reason

she had come to England was to escape the increasingly insistent attentions of an earnest young clerk employed by the family business.

"There you are, then. You'll have to wed someday, so it may as well be to Lord Marcus. Certainly, you could do far worse. We'll get him for you yet, my dear."

"Buy him for me, you mean." Quinn felt a sick weight settle in her stomach at his words, so similar to the insulting ones Lord Marcus had spoken. Though she had come close to accusing Lord Marcus of marrying her for her money during their drive, she had not really believed it—until now.

The captain waved a hand, as though to dispell her concerns. "Tut, tut. Any man must see that you are a prize, money or no."

She noticed, however, that he did not deny her charge. Before the prickling behind her eyes could manifest into tears, she excused herself.

Mounting the stairs to her bedchamber, she burned with shame and fury. She would *not* allow her future to be bartered like so much cotton or tobacco—her fortune for Lord Marcus's name. No, it was imperative that she free herself—and Lord Marcus—without delay, before this mockery of a betrothal could become a cold, mercenary marriage.

Dashing a salty drop from her cheek, she hurried upstairs to plan.

Chapter 5

⟨ᴄⁱᴏ⟩

The last rays of the sun had long disappeared. Marcus pulled out his watch to check it by the light spilling from the dining-room windows. Nearly ten. Clearly, the boy wasn't coming. With a shrug, he turned to leave the garden, when he heard a rustling amid the beanpoles.

"Psst! Guv'nor, are you there?"

Turning back, he saw the pale oval of a face topped by a shock of red hair peering through the broad leaves of the bean plants. "Yes, I'm here," he whispered. "What do you have?"

Gobby disentangled himself from the poles and vines to come forward cautiously. "A couple of things, guv, and we're hoping you can get word to the Saint. First, Mrs. Plank and her two little 'uns will be out in the street tomorrow if they don't pay their rent. He'd want to know about that, we're thinking."

Marcus vaguely remembered the name. Luke had mentioned something about Lady Pearl curing one of the children after the little girl had taken poison. "What else?"

"Second thing's about the Saint himself. Stilt heard the Runners have brought in someone special to catch him. They're saying's how the fact he ain't done a napping lately proves who he must be. You might should warn him they're on to him, so's he can be careful when he comes back."

Marcus nodded slowly. "I'll make sure no harm comes to the Saint, and I'll let him know about Mrs. Plank, as well."

The boy grinned through the dimness and tugged his forelock. "You're a right 'un, guv. Later, then." As quickly as he had appeared, he was gone, leaving Marcus to walk slowly toward the house.

So, it appeared that Bow Street had been suspicious about Luke, and saw the cessation of the Saint's activities while he was away as proof of his identity. There was only one way to solve that problem—and with luck, it would take care of Mrs. Plank's insolvency, as well.

It was time for Marcus to assume the mantle of the Saint of Seven Dials.

With a grim smile, his heart beating faster at the prospect of an exciting night ahead, Marcus entered the house, only to be greeted by a footman, who handed him a message that had come while he was outdoors.

To his surprise, Captain Peverill wished him to call tomorrow at the Claridges' to discuss settlements.

What had his daughter told him? Clearly not the same thing she had told Marcus himself. But there would be time enough in the morning to puzzle out that mystery. At the moment, he had work to do.

Two hours later, Marcus paused just inside the deserted dining room of Hightower House to get his bearings. Getting into the house itself had been absurdly easy. With the family in the country for the summer, the few servants had retired early. He was pleased to discover he hadn't lost his touch for stealth—a talent Luke had often praised back in their school days at Oxford.

Now, what to take? He held no particular animosity toward Lord Hightower, except that he shared his father's politics, and he was out of charity with his father at the moment. But the man was wealthy enough that a few pieces of plate would scarcely be missed, much less cause him any hardship.

Yet they could be the difference between life and death to Mrs. Plank and her children.

Still, it was necessary for his purposes that whatever he stole *was* missed, and that the theft be credited to the Saint of Seven Dials, so he turned away from the sideboard to consider the more prominent valuables in the room. Ah! The silver candelabrum on the table would do nicely, though carrying it would be awkward. That, along with the matching silver sconces on the walls, should pay the Planks' rent for two or three years, at least.

His decision made, he first removed the sconces. Using his penknife, he was able to unfasten them from the walls with a minimum of noise and effort.

Setting them aside, he plucked the candles from the candelabrum on the table, then bundled them all into the sack he had brought for the purpose. They clanked, and he realized he should have brought extra cloth to wrap them in. Next time he would come better prepared.

Turning to go, he suddenly stopped. He'd nearly forgotten! Pulling a card from his pocket, he laid it carefully in the exact center of the dining-room table. Then, smiling to himself, he hefted his bundle of silver and headed for the French doors leading to the gardens at the back of the house.

Slipping back through the doors and latching them behind him, using the trick he'd perfected in his school days, he couldn't help thinking that the new Saint of Seven Dials was off to an admirable start.

Quinn woke later than she had intended, for she had hoped to slip away before the rest of the household was astir. Her plan was risky, with no guarantee of success, but she could see no other sure way out of her predicament. Therefore, she was anxious to embark on it at once, before she could lose her nerve. Now, however, she would likely have to manufacture a pretext for leaving the house.

Dressing quickly, she descended to the breakfast chamber, only to find it deserted. A good meal might sharpen her wits, she reasoned, serving herself from the sideboard. Besides, if her plan was successful, it might be her last chance for eggs and fresh milk for some time.

She was halfway through her meal when she

heard the captain in the hall, bidding someone farewell. Before she could decide whether to alert him to her presence, he entered the room.

"Ah, you are up already, my dear! Excellent." He appeared exceedingly pleased with himself, which immediately aroused her suspicions.

"Who were you speaking with just now, Papa?" she asked, fearing she already knew the answer.

"Why, your bridegroom, of course. He wished to work out the settlements at once, and most generous he was, too, I must say."

Quinn stared. "Settlements? Marriage settlements?"

"Certainly, my pet. What other sort would I mean?" The captain signaled to the hovering footman to fill his plate with ham and kippered herring.

"You say *he* was anxious to have things settled?" She'd made it clear to Lord Marcus that he wouldn't be required to marry her after all. What could he be thinking? Nor had she had the impression that he was in a position to be making generous settlements. Rather the opposite, in fact.

"Yes, yes, of course. Why do you look so surprised? I told you he was eager for the match, did I not?"

"*You* told me that. He did not. And you knew full well—you both knew—that I have no desire to marry him. I don't understand either of you."

The captain laid down his fork and covered her hand with his own enormous one. "Now, Quinn, pray do not fret. The more I see of Lord Marcus, the more I like him. He will make you an excellent husband, truly he will. You'll see I was right, in time."

Though he spoke soothingly, there was a hint of

steel underlying her father's voice that told her he would brook no argument on the matter. He honestly seemed to believe he was doing the right thing for her—or for the business, at any rate. Abruptly, Quinn pushed back her chair.

"I suppose time will tell, then. But now, I pray you will excuse me, Papa. I have correspondence to attend to, then a visit or two to pay, and I must hurry if I am to be finished before Lady Claridge's proposed shopping expedition."

Her father quirked an eyebrow suspiciously. "Visits? Visits to whom? You are not to go out alone again, Quinn."

"Alone? Of course not." She managed to trill a laugh, which unfortunately seemed to deepen her father's suspicion. Struck by sudden inspiration, she added, "Why, Lord Marcus is to accompany me. I am surprised he did not mention it to you this morning."

At once the captain relaxed. "He was rather distracted—that is, he probably assumed I already knew. Well, well, that will be fine, then. You go on upstairs and get yourself ready. Give Lord Marcus my regards when he returns. I am due at the Exchange myself, so must hurry off to Threadneedle Street."

Quinn escaped upstairs, her heart pounding. What luck that her father was leaving again! Now her path was clear—and she'd best take it while she could. She had no other choice.

Dismissing her maid, she pulled out the valise she had packed last night. She waited until she heard her father leave the house, then quietly left her room, taking the servants' stairs at the rear of the house to the ground floor. A housemaid was dusting the mantelpiece of the library, but she was able to tiptoe past to the open back door without being noticed.

Once outside, she made her way through the mews and out to the street. A few stableboys stared as she passed, but she didn't care, as they were unlikely to raise any alarm. She set off at a brisk walk, waiting until she was well away from Mount Street to hail a passing hackney. Climbing inside, she directed the driver to take her to the London Docks at Wapping.

Looking out of the hackney window as they passed the Tower and continued on to the East End of London, Quinn began to have her first misgivings about her plan. The area around the docks seemed dirtier and more crowded than she remembered, somehow.

"This be the London Dock, ma'am," the jarvey called down through the trapdoor in the roof of the cab as he pulled to a halt by a hulking warehouse. "Someone meeting you here?"

"Ah, yes," she lied, afraid the man might refuse to leave her otherwise. "Thank you." She paid her fare and allowed him to help her to the slick pavement, trying not to wrinkle her nose at the odors assailing it.

"Want me to wait till he gets here?" The driver, a kindly-looking older man, seemed genuinely concerned.

"No, but thank you. I'm to meet him . . . inside

this warehouse. I'm sure he's here already." Quinn turned and walked toward the indicated building, refusing to look back until she heard the hackney coach drive away.

Only then did she realize how foolish it was to let the jarvey leave. What if she could not get passage for days? But surely she could hail another hackney if necessary—even if none were in sight at the moment.

Veering away from the warehouse, she headed for the docks, scanning the berthed ships for one that might bear her home. The welter of bobbing masts made it difficult to focus, but she spotted a packet off to the right flying an American flag. She would inquire of its captain, she decided, heading that way.

A group of sailors approached her, jostling her rudely as they passed on their way into Town. "Hoy there, missie!" one called. "Come wi' us, and we'll make it worth your time."

Quinn averted her eyes and hurried on, acutely conscious of how out of place she was there, in her pale yellow gown with its rows of flounces. Glancing nervously about, she noticed that the few women she could see were dressed in dingy workdresses, helping the men and boys who were carrying cargo to and from the ships—except for one.

Lounging under a tavern sign that declared it the Scarlet Hawk, a woman in a red, low-cut dress engaged the group of sailors in raucous conversation. As Quinn watched, horrified, the woman lifted her skirts above the knee, presumably to show off her

fine legs. With a chorus of cheers, the sailors followed her inside.

Hastily, Quinn looked away before anyone noticed her watching and quickened her pace.

" 'Ere now!" exclaimed a rough voice.

She turned too late, bumping headlong into a
burly man who grabbed her by the shoulders to
steady her. "I . . . I beg your pardon, sir," she stammered, and tried to back away.

To her dismay, he did not release his grip on her
shoulders, but paused to examine her. "Now, what
'ave we 'ere, then? I ain't seen you about 'ere before,
missie. New, are ye?"

He was dressed like a gentleman in coat, waistcoat, and breeches that might once have been well
tailored and expensive, but were now overdue for a
cleaning. A dirty red cloth was knotted about his
neck in lieu of a cravat.

"No! That is, I am here to speak to the captain of
that ship." She pointed toward the American flag,
which now seemed impossibly far away.

"A choosy one, are ye? Special for the captains?
Too bad for them I saw ye first." He grinned, revealing an inadequate number of yellowing teeth.

Quinn tried to pull away from him, but he only
tightened his grip. "You don't understand." She
tried to sound commanding, as her father might, but
could not control the quaver in her voice. "I am to set
sail on that ship as a paying passenger."

The man's eyes only brightened further, and she
realized that had been a stupid thing to say. "Paying,
are ye? Well, let's see yer purse, then." Before she

could prevent him, he snatched the reticule dangling from her wrist, breaking the strings.

"No!" she cried. "Stop it, you thief!"

Anger giving her sudden strength, she swung her valise up toward his head, but he was too quick for her. Sliding one hand from her shoulder to her arm, he used the other, the one holding her reticule, to deflect the blow and send the valise flying, to land in the mud several yards away.

"Now, missie, none o' that," he admonished, though without heat. If anything, he seemed amused by her show of resistance. "Mick! To me! I need a bit of assistance 'ere," he called to another grubby man lounging by the side of the Scarlet Hawk.

Wildly, Quinn looked around for anyone who might be able to help her, but all she saw were dockworkers going about their business. Another knot of sailors wandered far down the docks, and a couple of street urchins shoved each other in a friendly altercation, all seemingly blind to her situation. Oh, why had she told the hackney driver to leave?

"Looks like ye've copped a prime 'un, Tom," said the aforementioned Mick, sauntering over. Casually, he imprisoned both of Quinn's arms behind her in a powerful grip, freeing his confederate to empty her reticule. "Gor! Look at all that!"

In despair, Quinn watched as Tom pocketed the money for her passage—some sixty pounds. "Please!" She tried again. "I need that to get home to America."

Both men laughed. "And we need it to get through the next month or two," said Mick. "You'll bring us even more, though, unless I miss my guess."

"What do you mean?" she asked, though she was afraid she already knew. Hadn't her father and Lord Marcus both warned her? Why hadn't she listened?

"An innocent, eh?" said her original captor with a chuckle. "That's all to the good, wouldn't ye say, Mick?"

"Aye. Sally pays extra for virgins. Let's take her in and start our dickering."

Though Quinn struggled desperately, her strength was no match for Mick's—and even if she were to break free, Tom was there to seize her again. In moments they had forced her through the entrance of the Scarlet Hawk, into a boisterous taproom lit only by two windows grimed with the smoke that hung heavy in the air. Quinn coughed.

"You there! Bill! We got summat for Sally. She upstairs?" Mick called to a burly man behind the bar.

Before he could respond, Quinn shouted out to the assembled patrons, "Please! Won't someone here help me? These men are holding me against my will!" Surely *someone* in all this crowd must have a modicum of decency!

But though many of them stared at her with varying degrees of interest, none came forward to help. One tall, thin lad who looked vaguely familiar stared longer than the others, giving her a moment's hope, but then he frowned and disappeared through a rear doorway. "Someone! Please!" she cried again.

Mick shook her roughly. "Enough o' that. What's that, Bill?"

"I said Sally's upstairs. You can take the wench up to her."

Quinn had never felt so helpless or humiliated in her life, as her captors dragged her through that sea of stares to the steps on the opposite side of the room. It was almost a relief when they reached the landing and she was no longer exposed to all of those taunting eyes.

But now new anxieties assailed her. The upper passage was dimly lit by a pair of guttering candles in a wall sconce. From a closed door on her right came gasps and moans of a most disturbing nature. Before she could even speculate at what might be occurring within, a buxom woman in a too-tight gown of bright pink satin emerged from another door farther along the passage.

"What's all the commotion, then? I heard shouting downstairs." The woman confronted them, hands on plump hips, her improbably black hair spilling over her bare shoulders to partially conceal her ample cleavage with fat ringlets.

"Look what we brung ye, Sally," said Tom triumphantly, as Mick thrust Quinn forward. "Worth a nice sum, don't ye think?"

The woman's eyes narrowed speculatively as she surveyed Quinn from head to toe. "A bit young," she commented.

Quinn opened her mouth to protest as she always did when people assumed she was younger than her years, then closed it, hoping the misconception might work to her advantage.

But then Mick said, "Garn! You know that only ups the price. Ain't she a pretty piece?"

Sally took her time answering, circling around to examine Quinn closely in the wavering candlelight. "Pretty enough, I suppose. What are you two cheats wanting for her?"

"Cheats! Well, I like that!" exclaimed Tom. "Only a fair price, as always, Sally."

Quinn gasped with indignation—and horror. "I am no piece of property to be bought or sold! Please, ma'am, if you'll see me returned to my father—a shipowner and captain—I'll make certain you are well rewarded."

"Ship captain?" Sally frowned at the two men. "That increases my risk, if it's true."

"It is true, I swear it!" said Quinn eagerly. "You can ask about it on the docks. My father is Captain Palmer Peverill."

But Sally didn't so much as glance at her. "Two pounds off the price for the extra risk," she said to the men. "I'll give you thirty-eight for her, and another half-crown for the dress."

"Thirty-eight! You'll have twice that out of her in a week," Mick protested.

They fell to dickering then, while Quinn continued to struggle, scarlet with humiliation. To think she'd been running away because she objected to being "sold." A marriage settlement was nothing to this!

The men pointed out her youth, health, and fine teeth, while Sally countered that the chance of rescue or escape threatened her profit. When they finally settled on forty-two pounds, ten shillings, Tom clasped Sally's plump hand to seal the bargain.

"Bring her in here, then." Sally indicated the room she had just vacated. "It has a strong lock, and a grate on the window."

Mick shoved Quinn into the small, heavily perfumed chamber, then stood guard at the door while Sally counted out their money. Then, tipping his cap at Quinn with an unpleasant smile, he and Tom left. Quinn took a step toward the door but Sally quickly shut and locked it, then put her back against it, to face her.

"You needn't look so scared, dearie. I'll make sure your first isn't too rough." Her words and tone were no doubt intended to be reassuring, but had quite the opposite effect.

"You don't understand," Quinn pleaded, tears of anger and hopelessness tightening her throat. "I don't belong here. My . . . my father will come looking for me."

"Then we'll have to make you a mite less recognizable, won't we?" said Sally reasonably. "First, that frock. Those louts had no idea, but it's worth everything I paid them, if we don't sully it. Off with it, now."

"Wh . . . what?" Quinn backed away from the woman, her arms instinctively coming up to shield her breasts.

"Come on, then. You don't want me to call Bill up from the bar to help, do you? He'd be only too happy, I know."

Remembering the burly bartender, Quinn shuddered. "But what shall I wear instead?" she asked, still trying to delay what was beginning to appear inevitable. She refused to think further ahead than a change of clothing.

"This'll do, I think." Sally held up a garish red-and-black-striped dress. "Should suit your coloring, too."

Quinn stared at the hideous garment in horror, but when Sally made an impatient movement as though to call for help, she reluctantly agreed, and with trembling fingers began to undo the fastenings of her gown.

"With me? Why would they think Miss Peverill is with me?" Marcus asked the Claridge-liveried footman in bewilderment.

The man shifted uncomfortably from one foot to the other on the top step outside Marcus's front door. "I don't rightly know, my lord. I was told to come here and inquire for her. Seems she's late for an appointment to go shopping with Lady Constance."

"And she is presumed to be here? Or are they merely checking every possibility?" It appeared his reluctant bride-to-be had escaped her relatives' care—again. Marcus wasn't sure whether to be worried or amused.

The footman furrowed his brow. "Captain Peverill said she was out driving with you, my lord. I don't think he expected me to find you home, but wanted me to leave word for her to return at once, as she is late. Lady Claridge is in a fair fury, she is."

"Thank you, my good man. You may consider your message delivered. Should I see Miss Peverill, I will convey it at once."

With a nod and bow, the footman departed. Marcus closed the door slowly, thinking hard. What sort of scrape might Miss Peverill be getting herself into this time? And why?

Surely, her father wouldn't have told her the details of the settlements they'd agreed upon? If she discovered what an enormous sum Captain Peverill had offered as dowry, she might well believe that Marcus was only marrying her for her fortune. Of course—

"Who was that?" Peter asked from the stairs, interrupting his thoughts.

"No one," replied Marcus automatically. Then, concern overcoming reticence, he replied, "Actually, it was a footman asking for Miss Peverill. It seems she has disappeared."

Peter joined him by the door. "Disappeared? Run away, do you mean?"

"No one seems certain, but that would be my guess." He thought back over his conversation with her yesterday. Would she actually be so foolish—? "I need to go out," he said abruptly.

"Yes, you must bring her back, of course. Do you know where to find her? If you'll give me a moment to dress, I'll join you."

Marcus shook his head. He knew from long experience that Peter could no more dress in a moment than he could fly. "You can follow me, if you like. I'm headed for the docks."

"Very well. The docks are no place for her—or you—to be wandering alone."

"I can handle myself." He stifled his irritation at Peter's protectiveness.

"Of course," Peter replied, clearly unconvinced. "Go on, then. I'll follow as soon as I may. Which docks?"

"Captain Peverill mentioned that his own ships use the new London Docks, so I'll start there." Now that he'd made up his mind, he was anxious to be away.

Peter seemed to sense it, so caused no further delay, but went back upstairs to change out of his dressing gown. Marcus called for his horse, as it would be faster. If he found Quinn—rather, Miss Peverill—he could always hire a hackney to carry them back to Mayfair.

Five minutes later he was headed east, hoping against hope that his guess had been wrong.

Chapter 6

Marcus clattered along the cobbles of East Smithfield Street, already beginning to feel more than a bit foolish about his sudden burst of heroics. Most likely the girl was safe at home by now. Besides, how was he to search the docks for her without publicizing her name?

He had to try, however. If Miss Peverill was really impulsive enough to attempt sailing on her own, there was no knowing what sort of trouble she might be courting. She deserved it, of course, but that didn't mean he was capable of leaving her to her fate. In fact, the idea of Quinn in danger constricted his vitals in a most disturbing manner. He rode faster.

Entering the London Docks district, he first surveyed the ships at anchor, then the surrounding streets and buildings. Where to begin? With a ship bound for America, presumably. Two of those anchored appeared to be flying American flags, but that was no guarantee that country would be their next port of call. Still, it was a place to start.

Dismounting, he tied his horse at the edge of the wharf nearest one of the American ships and hurried down the quay to ask questions of its crewmen. As he'd feared, the ship was bound for Spain, then points south, before it would head back to its home port of New York—nor were any passengers booked for its departure a week hence.

More certain than ever that he was on a fool's errand, Marcus headed toward the other American ship, inconveniently located at nearly the opposite end of the docks. As he drew near the warehouses midway, however, he was startled by a tug at his sleeve. Turning, he discovered the tall street urchin, Stilt, from the group he had befriended.

"Beg pardon, m'lord," the boy stammered nervously. "B-but I'm that glad to see you here. I think someone you know may be in a spot o' trouble."

Quinn stared at her reflection in the looking glass with revulsion and shame. The gaudy red-and-black dress was scandalously low-cut. Her inadequate bosom, shockingly enhanced by the corset Sally had insisted she wear, was almost completely exposed. Below, only a flimsy red petticoat concealed her legs, as the skirt was split from the waist down.

"Now, a touch of rouge and you'll pass for a lusty fifteen-year-old," Sally declared, applying the cosmetic herself to Quinn's already flaming cheeks. "What are you really—seventeen?"

"Twenty," Quinn whispered. What would her father say if he saw her like this? She tried not to think of Lord Marcus, though in comparison with what she surely faced, marriage to him would have been paradise.

For a moment she allowed herself to imagine it again—chatting with him across the dinner table, perhaps an occasional touch of the hand, bidding each other a pleasant good night with a kiss, or perhaps more . . . No chance of that now.

"Twenty? I never would have guessed it. Mind you don't tell anyone. No one will believe you're still virgin at twenty."

Quinn glared at her, a spurt of anger reviving her courage. "Why should I cooperate with you in any way? I'll claim to be thirty, and spit in the face of any man who comes near me."

Sally merely shrugged, her ample bosom rippling with the motion. "Some gents like that kind of spirit—mostly the ones what like it rough. I can always save you for them."

Her courage dissipating as quickly as it had revived, Quinn turned away—only to catch sight of herself in the mirror again. She looked every bit as frightened as she felt. She simply *had* to escape somehow, before the worst happened.

"That's better," said Sally, when Quinn remained silent. "Now, I'll go down and do a bit of advertising. Want I should bring you back something to eat?"

Quinn shook her head. She hadn't eaten since breakfast, but the thought of food made her nauseous. With another shrug, Sally left her. Quinn heard the key turn once the door closed, but she tried to turn the handle anyway. Locked.

Frantically, she gazed about the room. The window, true to Sally's words, was covered by an iron grating, impossible to climb through. Perhaps, though, she could summon help from it?

The casement was stiff, and it was difficult to push against it through the close-set bars of the grate, but finally Quinn managed to open the window. Looking down, however, she saw only a drunken group of sailors emerging from the tavern below. No, she didn't want *their* attention.

Scanning the street as best she could from the deep-set window, she saw what might be a gentleman's horse tethered nearby, judging by its clean lines and rich harness. If only its owner would come back, perhaps—

Heavy footsteps sounded in the hallway. Quickly, she pulled the window closed again, though she didn't latch it. Could Sally have found a . . . customer already? The tiny chamber offered no place to hide. In unthinking panic, she threw herself flat on the floor and tried to squeeze beneath the bed, just as a male voice rumbled outside the door, the words indistinguishable.

"Yes, I'm sure," came Sally's voice in response to whatever the man had asked. She sounded irritated. Quinn hoped that didn't mean she'd had to settle for one of the rougher "gents."

Frantically, she wriggled farther under the bed, then stuck, a button catching on a loose floorboard. The door creaked open.

"What trick is this? Where is she?" demanded a voice that Quinn recognized with a shock. She swiveled her head painfully, to see Lord Marcus gazing angrily around the room—and Sally staring straight at her.

Turning quickly away, Sally said, "I must have been mistaken, my lord. Perhaps she's in the next room along." They moved back through the door.

"No! No, wait!" Quinn cried, scrambling out from under the bed. "I'm here!" Almost weeping with relief, scraping her knees and elbows, she crawled forward, then stood up. Sally uttered an extremely unladylike curse.

"Miss Peverill! Thank God I found you," Marcus exclaimed, striding forward. Then he stopped, suddenly awkward, gazing fixedly at a point over her head.

Glancing down, Quinn saw that one breast had sprung free from the low neckline of the awful dress. With a gasp, she turned away to rectify the problem, noticing as she did so that her chest and arms were filthy from scrambling about on the floor. "Might I have my own dress back?" she asked Sally, turning back to face them.

"Hmph. Your fine gentleman ought to pay me the fifty pounds I'm out, plus extra for my trouble. If he won't, I'll have to keep the fancy frock to offset my losses." The procuress looked up at Lord Marcus hopefully.

"Don't pay her a penny!" exclaimed Quinn before he could answer. "It would only encourage her in her disgusting trade."

"No fear," replied Marcus, stepping toward her again now that she was as decent as the garish dress allowed. "She'll be lucky if I don't use my influence to have this place burned around her ears and her clapped in irons."

Sally glared at them both. "Big talk, when there's nowt but the two of you, and me with a houseful of friends. Threaten me, and I'll not let you leave after all."

Quinn shrank toward Lord Marcus at the woman's venom, but he never flinched. "I rather doubt you or your confederates could prevent it. Though if you'd care to try—" He took a step toward her, smiling dangerously. Quinn blinked, not having seen this side of him before.

"Go on, then," snapped Sally sullenly. She backed through the door, then turned away with a flounce.

"There, I thought you'd see wisdom. And just as well, as my brother and an army of servants will be here momentarily. Miss Peverill, if you are ready to depart?" He turned back to Quinn.

"Oh, yes, *please!*" But then she paused, glancing about for a shawl or anything else she might use to conceal her bosom.

"Here." As though reading her mind, Marcus stripped off his coat and placed it around her shoulders.

She shot him a timid, grateful smile, and pulled it tighter. "Thank you. And now, let's leave this place before anything else dreadful can happen."

One hand at her waist, he led her back to the staircase, keeping himself between her and the crowd in the taproom when they reached the bottom. His touch was both comforting and distracting. She wanted to ask whether he'd been bluffing about his brother and the army of servants, but didn't dare while they might be overheard.

"How did you find me?" she asked instead.

He escorted her out of the building before answering. "Someone saw you being forced into the Scarlet Hawk. A few inquiries yielded your exact whereabouts."

Stopping, he gazed down at her, his expression showing some strong emotion held in check. "You're certain you are all right?"

She nodded, suddenly shy. "I was never more relieved in my life than when you appeared. It was like an answer to prayer—a miracle. I told no one I was coming here, so I thought—" To her horror, she felt tears welling up in her eyes.

"Shh! It's all right." He folded her against him, and she gratefully pressed her face to his shirtfront, hiding her tears. They stopped almost as soon as they began, so novel was the sensation of being held against a man's hard chest.

"When I heard you were missing," he continued, "I recalled what you had said yesterday in the Park. This seemed a logical place to look." His voice vibrated through his chest, against her cheek, making her even more aware of his body, his masculinity. Hastily, she backed away.

"How are we to get back?" she asked, not meeting his eyes.

He released her at once, leaving her slightly

shaky—but it was what she had wanted, wasn't it? She sneaked a glance at him, but he was gazing up and down the street.

"That's my horse, but we can scarcely go riding double through London, with—"

"With me dressed like this," she finished, a fresh wave of mortification making her flush.

"Er, yes. But hackneys seem scarce hereabouts. Perhaps we could—" he broke off, staring.

Following his gaze, she saw an elegant crested carriage coming their way. Mindful of her appearance, she shrank back, trying to hide behind her rescuer. To her dismay, however, he strode forward and waved.

"That will be Peter," he said reassuringly, though she felt anything but reassured. "Our difficulties are solved."

The carriage pulled to a halt before them and not one, but two men climbed out. Lord Peter Quinn she recognized from the evening at the Trumballs' but the other gentleman, dressed just as impeccably, was a stranger to her. Glancing quickly up at Lord Marcus, Quinn was startled to see annoyance, even anger, on his face, though it was quickly concealed.

"Miss Peverill, may I present two of my brothers," he said then. "Lord Peter, whom you have already met, and Robert, Lord Bagstead, my eldest brother."

Lord Bagstead looked down at Quinn as he might at a grubby child in danger of sullying his boots. "Miss Peverill." He inclined his head very, very slightly. "I understand that felicitations are in order."

Quinn swallowed. "Thank you, my lords. May . . . may we go?"

Lord Peter stepped forward, shooting a glance of disgust at his elder brother. "You mustn't mind Robert, Miss Peverill. He's insufferably high in the instep, already fancying himself a duke. Only brought him along because his carriage was ready. Marcus, help her into it, there's a good lad. I'm sure this has been a most unsettling experience for the lady."

With a warm rush of gratitude and relief, Quinn smiled at Lord Peter, then extended her hand to Lord Marcus. When he took it without a word to help her into the carriage, she glanced up at him. His lips were pressed tightly together, as though in barely suppressed fury, and he avoided her eye. He hadn't seemed angry at her earlier. Was it something she'd said?

Peter climbed in next, then, after instructing the coachman to tie Marcus's horse behind the carriage, Lord Bagstead joined them, sitting beside Peter on the backward-facing seat. Quinn felt uncomfortable in the extreme under his supercilious regard, so looked again to Peter, who suddenly seemed her only ally in the group.

"I . . . I don't know how to thank you—all of you. I've never been so frightened in my life."

"There, my dear, pray try not to regard it," Peter responded with a paternal smile. "It's all over, and you'll shortly be restored to the bosom of your family."

His choice of words was unfortunate, reminding

Quinn of the scandalous nature of her present attire. But though she felt herself reddening again, she said nothing. Apologies would only make things worse.

Peter, seemingly unaware, chattered lightly about the latest social and political news for the duration of the drive. Though his brothers appeared bored by such trivia, Quinn was grateful, for it distracted her from her situation and the reception she was likely to face at the Claridges' house.

It could not distract her, however, from Marcus's nearness, his thigh nearly brushing hers. As the carriage turned one corner they did touch, and the contact made her whole body flare into gooseflesh, a tautness she could feel to the tips of her breasts.

He seemed completely unaware, however, and she was careful to allow no hint of her response to show in her expression. What was the matter with her? It seemed her frightening experience had completely overset her wits. With an effort, she focused again on Peter's continuing monologue of small talk.

When they turned onto Mount Street, Quinn felt both trepidation and relief. Finally rousing from his brooding silence, Marcus turned to her. "Come, I'll take you inside and help you to make your explanations."

"Good man, Marcus," said Peter. "We'll leave your horse and see you at home. See if you can't distract Lady Claridge while Miss Peverill runs up to her room—that would probably be best."

Quinn thanked the brothers again, then followed Marcus from the carriage, pulling his coat even more tightly across her exposed chest. Perhaps no one would be home. Perhaps they were all out looking for her, or visiting—

The door opened to Marcus's knock, and Quinn was dismayed to hear the hum of numerous voices from the parlor. Taking a deep breath, she stepped forward, determined to brazen it through somehow—unless she could indeed slip up to her room unnoticed.

For a moment she thought it might be possible, as they neared the parlor door and she saw that it was partially closed. "I'll just—" she began, turning to Marcus, but then the door was flung wide to reveal her father.

"Quinn!" he exclaimed. "You're safe! Look, everyone, she's here—Lord Marcus has found her!"

To her mortification, the captain pulled her into the parlor, where no fewer than six other people were assembled—her aunt and uncle, Lady Constance, Lady Mountheath of all people, and two others she did not recognize.

Behind her, Marcus cleared his throat. "Yes, sir, she is safe, but she has had quite a fright. I imagine she would like nothing more than a hot bath and a lie-down, in fact."

Quinn heartily agreed, but Lady Claridge was staring at her in horrified outrage—as were most of the others. "*What* are you wearing, Miss Peverill?" she demanded. Then, to Marcus, "My lord, I had thought better of you than this. Indeed—"

To Quinn's relief, her father waved a quelling hand, then pushed Quinn back into the passageway, closing the parlor door behind him. "Never mind her right now. You go on up for that bath, Quinnling. Lord Marcus and I need to discuss your wedding—which I think now had better occur without further delay."

Captain Peverill waited until his daughter had disappeared upstairs before turning to Marcus. "I would be most interested, my lord, in an explanation of what occurred today and how Quinn came to be wearing such, ah, odd attire. But that can wait. Surely you will agree that a quick marriage is an absolute necessity now?"

After only the barest moment's hesitation, Marcus nodded. "Yes sir, I believe it is."

"Come, then. Let's go down to the library to discuss the most expeditious means of achieving it."

By the time Miss Peverill ventured downstairs an hour later, clean and properly clad in a flattering but discreet gown of cream muslin, all had been arranged. The captain was waiting for her at the foot of the stairs, Marcus hovering uncomfortably behind him. The Claridges, thankfully, had gone upstairs to change for dinner.

"My dear, you look much recovered from your experience," boomed the captain as she reached them. "Lord Marcus has told me all about it."

She darted a quick look at Marcus, who gave a quick shake of his head to reassure her that he had not told her father *everything*. "If I might have a few moments with Miss Peverill?" he asked, preferring that she hear the news from him.

"Of course, of course!" exclaimed Captain Peverill with irritating joviality. "You'll want to discuss the wedding, your wedding trip, and other such things. A special license, my love!" he then said joyfully to his daughter, dashing Marcus's hopes. "With that, you can marry at once. Isn't England grand?"

He kissed her cheek, and, with a jaunty wave of his hand, headed up the stairs, whistling a sea chantey.

"At once?" she echoed, looking up at Marcus doubtfully, her green eyes wide and dark.

"Come, let's step into the parlor to discuss it." The sight of her brought back everything he had felt upon finding her at the docks. Overwhelming relief, an inclination to shake her, and—desire. The way she had felt in his arms. That perfect, pert breast, peeking above that garishly seductive gown . . .

He forced the image away as she preceded him into the room, then chose a straight-backed chair as far from any of the others as possible. With an inward sigh, he pulled another chair over so that he could speak to her without raising his voice.

"My father said at once?" she asked again, and he thought he heard a hint of a quaver in her voice. "How? I'm afraid I don't—"

"Not today, obviously. We agreed on Saturday, day after tomorrow. A private ceremony, with a discreet announcement in the papers after the fact. Your father thought that would be best."

"My father? I'd have thought he'd want to trumpet it from the rooftops." Now her voice was wry.

Marcus felt a grin tugging at the corner of his mouth, despite the seriousness of the situation and his own wildly conflicting feelings about it. "I was able to persuade him that such fanfare might draw unwelcome gossip. He seems eager enough for the match that he was willing to be reasonable on that head."

She dropped her eyes, all trace of amusement gone. "And now I've made that match inevitable. I'm sorry, my lord. My intent was quite the opposite."

"Yes, I know. I realize you intended to return to America to avoid our marriage. I'm sorry the prospect is so repugnant to you, given our present circumstances."

For the first time, he admitted to himself how galling it was that she would risk her life rather than marry him. He hoped she would deny that, but she did not.

"In that case, why did you agree to wed me?" she asked, raising her eyes to his again. "Why not convince my father to allow me to return home instead? No scandal would follow me to Baltimore."

Her intelligence combined with her courage stirred him again, but he commanded his body to behave. This was not the time. "I did point out to him that you seemed unwilling to marry, and even to suggest that as a possible solution, but in the face of his insistence—"

"You quickly capitulated," she said accusingly.

Frustrated desire, her clear rejection of him, and his brothers' interference in his affairs all combined to provoke Marcus's own temper. "If I'd refused, he'd have been well within his rights to call me out. I am not willing to sacrifice my honor to keep you from reaping the consequences of your own foolishness."

"Your honor again," she retorted. "Clearly keeping that precious commodity intact matters more to you than my happiness."

"Your own honor is in a more precarious position than mine," he felt obliged to point out.

When she would have spoken again, he held up his hand. "Yes, I know you think you can simply flee England and leave all problems behind you, but it is not so simple as that. Your father informs me that no ship will be taking passengers to Baltimore for weeks. Nor can you travel alone. Surely your experience today has shown you that?"

Her eyes glittered with anger—and with unshed tears. He fought the urge to take her in his arms again, to kiss those tears away. She would not welcome his touch, that was clear.

"I am aware that without your help or my father's, I can do nothing but accede to your wishes. But whatever he is paying you to go through with this marriage, I can assure you, my lord, that you will not find it a bargain."

With that threat hanging in the air, she rose and left the room, to head back upstairs. Marcus made no move to stop her, realizing that she was still more distraught over the day's events than he had at first perceived. Still, her final words augured ill for any chance of a happy marriage.

Leaving the parlor, he asked a passing footman to inform Lord and Lady Claridge that he would not be staying to dinner after all. Then, still trying to see any way he might have handled matters differently, he made his way out of the house.

Riding back to Grosvenor Street, he decided that he had nothing to feel guilty about, unless it was his increasingly strong physical attraction to Quinn—something he had not at all expected. If she was to be his wife, however, surely even that was no bad thing?

Turning the corner, the sight of a ragamuffin street sweeper suddenly reminded him of last night's foray and the future ones he had planned—plans that might now have to be altered. He urged his horse to a quicker pace. If he was to marry in two days' time—and it appeared he was, whatever his or Miss Peverill's feelings on the matter—he had much to do first.

Chapter 7

The next day and a half were almost unbearable to someone so used to constant employment as Quinn had been. Her father and aunt both suggested she keep to her room until the wedding, and she had agreed, having no desire to face anyone.

Unfortunately, her enforced inaction gave her ample time to regret her final words to Marcus. She *had* behaved foolishly, and was largely to blame for her predicament, she had to admit. She couldn't help feeling, however, that Marcus had been far too ready to take advantage of her situation.

Still, however mercenary his motives, she couldn't deny he had saved her from a horrible fate. And she had responded by flinging accusations in his face. Deserved or not, he must now think her the most ungrateful wretch in nature.

Would he really care, though, as long as her fortune was at his disposal?

"Thank you, Madame Fanchot, that will be all," she snapped impatiently at the modiste, induced by a fabulous sum to attend her here. The woman had lived up to her reputation, Quinn reluctantly admitted, turning a partially made-up gown into one fit for a wedding in less than a day's time.

"Of course, mademoiselle," responded the modiste with a respectful bob of her head. "You'll not worry about disgracing your relatives now, *oui*?"

Quinn grimaced, wishing she hadn't been so frank with the woman. Loneliness had led her into indiscreet chatter. It was a tendency she'd have to curb, as loneliness was likely to be a way of life from now on. A tear tickled the corner of her eye, but she dashed it away.

"No, I certainly won't. You've done a magnificent job, and I do thank you."

The older woman smiled. "It was a pleasure, mademoiselle, indeed. I'll be seeing you again after your wedding?"

Though she winced at the reminder of that event, now scarcely two hours away, Quinn nodded. "You certainly shall, Madame. You have earned both my gratitude and my future business."

In a protracted argument with her father the night of her return from the docks, Quinn had forced him to admit that marriage to her would indeed make Lord Marcus's fortune. She might as well do her part in spending it.

With a final bob, Madame Fanchot gathered up her pins, scissors, and two assistants and left. Alone at last, Quinn turned again to the tall pier glass. The ivory silk was richly trimmed with Mechlin lace—an ethereal confection more suited to a fairy princess than a down-to-earth girl like herself. A girl who couldn't seem to go two days without landing herself in trouble.

She sighed. Though she couldn't quite suppress a thrill of feminine satisfaction at her appearance, the dress was just one more attempt to force her into an unnatural mold and tie her irrevocably to this alien land. Fashionable gowns would never make her fit into English Society.

Though she'd thought she wanted time alone, she was actually relieved when a tap at the door interrupted her dismal thoughts, even when it opened to admit her aunt and cousin, as well as the captain.

"Oh, my Quinnling!" he exclaimed, stopping with one hand on his heart. "You're every bit as lovely as your mother. Who would have thought—" He broke off with a misty smile of such paternal pride that Quinn nearly forgave him.

"It's a lovely dress, cousin," Lady Constance said then, the admiration—and a glint of jealousy—in her fine blue eyes proving her sincerity.

"Of course it is," her mother snapped. "Madame Fanchot would never risk her reputation by putting her in anything shabby. Are you nearly ready? I've arranged to have the coach at the door in an hour."

Quinn nodded. "Monette still has to pin up my hair, but that is all. I'll be ready." She steadfastly tried to ignore the sudden trembling in her stomach. Everything was happening so quickly, and she felt powerless to stop it.

"I'll send her to you at once, then. And pray remember that even at a private, family ceremony, gossip has eyes and ears everywhere. Society would love to see the daughter of Lady Glynna create another scandal for their amusement. Pray try not to give them the satisfaction."

With that admonition, Lady Claridge swept the others from the room before Quinn could formulate any sort of response. When Monette entered a moment later, she was still seething.

"Did you decide upon the ringlets we discussed, miss?" the maid asked, picking up a brush as Quinn seated herself at the dressing table.

"Ringlets, curlicues, frizz—I don't care. Do what you will," she said shortly, determined that no one, not even her maid, would see her cry. "It won't matter anyway."

No one but the captain had the spirits for conversation during the brief carriage ride. Lady Claridge and Lady Constance rode in censorious silence, and Lord Claridge appeared more nervous than ever, alternately patting Quinn's hand and shooting worried glances at his wife, while nodding at the captain's pleasantries.

"Another fine, fair day," Captain Peverill declared, as they turned into Grosvenor Square. "A good omen for your marriage, my dear. A very good omen indeed."

Quinn found his cheerfulness oppressive. She felt as though a cage was closing about her, inescapable and inexorable. Once married, she would never be able to return to America, to the home and work she loved. Despite her best efforts, a tear slipped down her cheek. If anyone in the carriage noticed, they ignored it.

They pulled to a stop and stepped to the pavement, one by one. Quinn was last. She stared up at the Marland ducal mansion in mingled awe and terror. She could not go through with this. She could not!

As though sensing her urge to flee, her father placed a large, firm hand upon her elbow, guiding her up the broad marble steps to the imposing double doors, held wide by a pair of bewigged and liveried footmen. Quinn proceeded, each step more reluctant than the one before.

A soberly clad retainer led the party to a small chapel at the rear of the house, where the ceremony was to take place. Frantically, Quinn's chaotic thoughts beat against her skull, seeking a way of escape. She could refuse to say the vows. This was 1816, not the Dark Ages. No one could force her to marry against her will . . .

The chapel seemed filled with people, dozens of eyes turning to condemn her upon her entrance. Wasn't this supposed to be a private ceremony? she wondered wildly. Then, forcing herself to a degree of calmness, she was able to focus upon those present.

That elderly, autocratic-looking man must be the Duke, Marcus's father, and the lady beside him the Duchess. Robert, Lord Bagstead, looked as disapproving as he had two days earlier, and his plump wife appeared to share his sentiments. The two unfamiliar gentlemen were presumably Marcus's other brothers, and she was relieved to see that they, and the lady she presumed was the wife of one of them, looked more curious than condemning.

Lord Peter grinned when she caught his eye, and winked encouragingly, bolstering her courage somewhat. Finally, she looked at Marcus, waiting at the far end of the chapel, next to the clergyman who stood ready to perform the sacred rite.

Dressed in a dark blue coat that mirrored his eyes and tight-fitting buff breeches, Marcus looked more handsome than she had yet seen him—and impossibly remote. The idea of being the wife of such a fine gentleman seemed suddenly ludicrous to Quinn. He turned slightly, and their gazes met.

For a moment, Quinn thought she might be about to faint. Why else would she feel so light-headed? Before she could analyze the odd warmth in her midsection, her father pressed her elbow again, leading her down the center of the room toward the small altar at the far end. Toward Marcus.

Quinn moved forward mechanically, her gaze still locked with Marcus's. When he turned back to the clergyman, she felt as though a prop had been withdrawn. Desperately, she glanced about, catching Peter's eye again. Even he looked somber now, though he nodded encouragement.

On reaching the altar, her father released her arm, removing her last vestige of support. Gone were her rebellious plans to refuse to speak the vows. Before the unified dignity of the entire Northrup family, she could do nothing but what was expected of her, however much she might regret it later. When the clergyman asked her to repeat the words that would seal her fate, she did so without a quaver, her head held high.

Marcus spoke his vows steadily as well, his voice giving no hint of conflict or regret. Not until they were pronounced husband and wife did Quinn look at him again. To her surprise, he appeared as stunned as she felt.

Married? How in blazes can I be married? Marcus wondered dazedly. The whole ceremony had seemed surreal, more like a dream than reality. Especially the part when Miss Peverill—now Lady Marcus—had first entered the chapel and their eyes had met.

For a confusing instant he'd felt as though he'd known her for years, instead of just five brief days, despite the fact that she appeared more mature and, yes, lovely, than he'd ever seen her before. It was as though something within him had been waiting for her, coiled tight, releasing only when she arrived.

But now that moment was long past, or seemed so, though in truth it was only a few minutes ago. Now she was a stranger again, young, scared, but also headstrong and American. And she was his wife. The families converged to offer good wishes with varying degrees of sincerity, and he had no more time for reflection.

"Well done," exclaimed Peter, a welcome relief after his parents' frosty felicitations. "Well done indeed, both of you." He dropped a quick kiss on Quinn's cheek, reminding Marcus that he had yet to kiss his new bride himself. This did not seem the time, however.

"Quinn—may I call you Quinn?" Peter asked. At her shy nod, he continued. "Marcus may not have had time to tell you, but Anthony and I have vacated, so that you two can have the house to yourselves. Don't know if you planned any sort of wedding trip—" he looked questioningly at Marcus.

"Ah, no," he responded. "Not just yet, at any rate." He glanced at Quinn, to find her looking more frightened than ever. "We scarcely know each other, after all. No need to rush things."

She relaxed visibly, and he was startled to feel a pinprick of hurt. That's why he'd phrased it that way, after all, to reassure her that he didn't mean to force unwanted attentions upon her. She turned her green gaze up to him, but before he could decipher the expression there, she withdrew it again.

"No, no need at all," she echoed to his brother. "You've been very kind, Lord Peter, and I thank you."

Captain Peverill descended upon them then, and his joviality more than made up for the reserve of some of the others. "Short but sweet—just the kind of wedding I like to see," he boomed. "You've snagged yourself a rare treasure here, Lord Marcus. Mind you treat her like one."

To Marcus's surprise, the gruff captain's eyes glistened with the threat of tears. "I will, sir. That's a promise," he said. Though the words were automatic, forced from him by the older man's emotion, he discovered he meant them. He would do all in his power to keep Quinn from being unhappy in her unwanted marriage.

They were summoned then to the lavish wedding

breakfast the Duke had ordered for the occasion. Though the food was excellent, the conversation was strained, and Marcus was relieved when it finally ended. Bidding polite farewells to the company, he prepared to take Quinn home.

His bride's farewells were equally polite, and even more aloof, though she listened patiently to some parting admonitions from her father.

"Mind you behave yourself, Quinnling," the captain said at last, enfolding her in a bear hug. "You'll do your family proud, I don't doubt."

"Of course, Papa," she responded quietly. It appeared she had not yet forgiven him for forcing her to this step. Marcus wasn't sure he had, either, come to think of it.

Peter was the last to bid them good-bye. "I expect you to treat this little lady properly, Marcus," he said, serious behind his grin. "You tell me if he doesn't, Quinn, and I'll thrash him for you."

To Marcus's surprise, she dimpled up at his brother. "It relieves me to have such a champion, Lord Peter. Thank you." Standing on tiptoe, she kissed him on the cheek, then turned to Marcus, her smile quickly fading. "Shall we go, my lord?"

An absurd wave of jealousy washed through him. Would she ever look to him with the trust and friendship she had just shown his brother? He recalled her relief Thursday, when he'd rescued her from the docks, the softness of her against his chest, and again, that perky little breast, sprung free from her dress . . .

"Yes, let's go," he said, more brusquely than he'd

intended. Peter frowned at his tone, but Quinn did not react at all. Placing her fingertips on his sleeve, she allowed him to lead her through the house, out the front door, and down to the waiting carriage that was to bear them around the corner.

"Silly to ride such a short distance on such a lovely morning," he commented, as a footman lowered the carriage steps. "Would you care to walk instead?"

"Whatever you wish, my lord." Her voice held no emotion.

Dismissing the carriage with a nod, Marcus turned his steps to the left, toward Grosvenor Street. "Well, for good or ill, we've done it," he said, once they were out of earshot of the servants. "Now it's up to both of us to make the best of it." It was a mere platitude, something to break the awkward silence, but she stiffened beside him.

"I consider this marriage my just punishment for exhibiting such poor judgment on two occasions, my lord. Making the best of it would seem to undermine my repentance."

He swallowed, ignoring the sting of her words. "Your father had no mind to punish you, as I'm sure you know. Nor have I."

They turned the corner and headed east, already halfway to his—their—house. Marcus realized they were both walking quickly, as though doing so would shorten the awkward moment, when of course it would do no such thing.

"Intentional or not, I am prepared to accept the consequences of my actions."

Nettled by her determination to play the martyr,

he said nothing more until they reached the steps to his town house.

"Your dungeon, my lady." With a mocking bow, he motioned for her to precede him to the door.

The glance she shot him held alarm, but also a trace of something that might have been amusement. Head held high, she marched up the steps and through the door, which was flung open by a footman as she approached it. Marcus was glad he'd asked the servants to refrain from the traditional assemblage at the front door. It was a distraction he didn't need just now.

Halfway down the front hall, Quinn stopped her haughty procession, clearly at a loss as to which way she should go.

"Your abigail can show you to your rooms when you are ready. She has already put away your things, I believe. But perhaps you will join me in the drawing room for a glass of sherry first?"

Quinn glanced up the stairs, where her maid hovered, then back at Marcus, her small frame quivering with tension, indecision plain on her face. Finally, she gave a slight nod. "Very well, my lord. For . . . a moment."

Despite the elegant wedding gown and the elaborate, upswept hair, she suddenly looked absurdly young, like a girl playing dress-up. She turned toward the door he indicated and one long, dark ringlet bounced against her cheek.

Marcus felt an almost irresistible urge to touch that ringlet, that soft cheek, to soothe the fear and worry from her brow. Instead, he turned to the hovering footman and directed him to bring the sherry decanter and two glasses to the formal drawing room—a room he rarely used. When he turned back to Quinn, she was perched on the edge of a chair, as though ready to flee at the slightest provocation.

Cautiously, he moved to the chair opposite. "I thought we might talk for a bit—get to know each other," he began. She tensed again, and he sighed.

"No, this isn't a seduction, if that's what you're thinking. But incredible as it seems, the fact is that we met for the first time only five days ago and have had but one or two opportunities for private conversation since. Hardly a basis upon which to build a marriage."

"I suppose not," she agreed, watching him warily.

The footman appeared then with the sherry. Marcus took the tray and dismissed him, then poured out two glasses. "I thought this might help us to relax a bit," he said, handing her a glass.

Though she still looked suspicious, she took a sip. "It . . . burns."

"Only at first," he assured her, his mind wandering to other things than sherry. "Once you become used to it, I'm sure you'll find it quite pleasant."

Frowning, though seemingly oblivious to his double entendre, she took another sip. "It is sweeter than I expected. What did you wish to discuss, my lord?"

"As we have clearly progressed past the point of casual acquaintances, perhaps you can call me Marcus? 'My lord' is so impersonal."

She swallowed visibly. "Impersonal, but . . . safer. Very well, however, if you insist."

"No, of course I don't insist. It's just that—" He stopped, running a hand through his hair in frustration—frustration of more than one sort. "Never mind. Call me whatever you wish. May I call you Quinn?"

"That is your prerogative, obviously. But yes, I prefer my own name to 'Lady Marcus.' What odd customs you English have. I see now why we Americans abolished titles."

Though her assumption of colonial superiority irked him, he had to smile. "That particular convention may be one of our strangest, but it's a time-honored one for wives of younger sons, nonetheless. I trust you will grow accustomed to it in time."

She set down her glass with a sharp click. "I doubt I will ever grow accustomed to any of this. I wish I could wake up to discover this was all a dream, and I had never left Baltimore at all!"

Marcus felt he had been more than patient, but now that patience suddenly gave way. "Would that I could grant your wish! I was perfectly happy with my life before this complication, I assure you."

Quinn stood. "And I can assure you that I never intended to be a *complication*, my lord—even one that has been extremely profitable for you."

That stung, for it was quite true that this marriage had improved Marcus's financial situation substantially—so much so that he would be able to buy his own estate, a dream that had previously been out of reach. He wondered now whether it would be too dearly bought.

"In that case, it would have been well if you had behaved more circumspectly," he snapped. "I certainly never went looking for profit."

"Yet you found it. Had I known what would ensue, I would have run for my very life when first I saw you. And I may yet!" She took a step toward the door.

Marcus surged to his feet. "You'll do no such thing. Like it or not, you are Lady Marcus now, and hold my reputation and that of my family in your hands. I will not permit you to sully it in any way. I was jesting before when I called this house a dungeon, but if I have to lock you up to shield you from your own foolishness, I'll do just that."

Though she trembled, her green eyes blazed up at him in fury. "How dare you? I thought you were only stodgy and grasping, but now I see that you are also cruel, tyrannical, and an insufferable bully. If this is how Englishmen treat their wives, it is no wonder my mother contrived to escape this country. And if she managed it, then so can I!"

With that, she fled the room, Marcus close behind her. Reaching the hallway, she hesitated, and he quickly placed himself between her and the front door. She glared at him for a moment, then, with a strangled sob, turned and ran up the stairs.

Chapter 8

Quinn reached the upper hall, half-blinded by tears, with no plan in mind. She did not even know which room was hers. A door on her left opened then, and Monette emerged.

"My lady?" she said, in evident surprise at Quinn's distress.

"I . . . I wish to be alone," said Quinn as steadily as she could, pushing past her maid into the chamber she assumed must be hers and closing the door behind her.

She stopped then and looked around, momentarily distracted from her anguish. The room was certainly sumptuous, with rich fabrics at the windows and bed frame and a thick, springy carpet underfoot, but it was also masculine. Definitely masculine. Dark woodwork, deep green and brown draperies and upholstery, even a hunting scene on one wall. Had she shut herself into her husband's room by mistake?

Hurriedly, she reached for the door handle, but then paused, relaxing slightly. There would have been no time for any sort of redecorating on her behalf, of course. Most likely, this chamber had been occupied by Lord Peter or Lord Anthony until yesterday.

Not for the first time, she wished it had been Lord Peter who had come to her rescue twice this week rather than his brother. Peter seemed so much kinder, gentler . . . so much more *manageable*. All good qualities in a husband, surely? She had to admit, however, that Peter had never caused that same tendril of warmth to curl through her that Marcus did, nor that something more she had felt at the docks two days since.

Not that that mattered now.

Her troubles came rushing back, and she threw herself onto the brown counterpane of the four-poster to resume her interrupted cry. What hateful things Marcus had said to her! And now she was a prisoner, with no hope of parole, her jailer a man who, in the eyes of the law, had complete authority over her person.

For nearly half an hour she wallowed in the wretchedness of her lot, weeping until no more tears would come.

Finally, she sat up, feeling far more clearheaded after the catharsis of a good cry. Self-pity would solve nothing. What she needed was a plan, and the means to implement it.

She went to the window and looked out. Unfortunately, it faced the street, so there were no trees nearby—nor did the wall look particularly scalable. And even if she did escape, say, through the kitchens, what then? She had no place to go in London. Not the Claridges, and certainly not the docks again, not if the next ship for Baltimore wouldn't be sailing for weeks.

No, at the moment her choices were severely limited—but she was determined to change that.

Suddenly, her gaze sharpened. On the street below, directly across from the house, a boy and girl stood talking—and the girl was almost certainly Polly, from Grillon's Hotel. The boy must be her brother, Gobby . . . short, red-haired, yes, he was one of the urchins Marcus had been bullying the day Quinn met him.

Perhaps she couldn't escape just yet, but Quinn *could* do something worthwhile until an opportunity presented itself. Somehow, she would find a way to help children like Polly and Gobby, to give *them* a chance at a better life—but she would have to do it without Marcus's knowledge. She was sure such a project would never meet with his overdeveloped sense of propriety.

The very idea of rebelling by doing something useful, perhaps even noble, but of which Marcus was sure to disapprove, made her feel better immediately.

Marcus finished a third glass before deciding he'd never cared for sherry in the first place and switching to Madeira. As often as he'd railed against his older brothers for sticking their noses into his business, just now he would have welcomed Peter and his sage advice.

Well, perhaps not Peter. Quinn seemed to like Peter better than she did himself. Not that he could blame her. There was no denying he'd made a total botch of things today. Hell, he'd botched everything since meeting her!

Stodgy?

"Damnation," he said aloud to the fireless grate. It wasn't the first time she'd called him that. It galled him, considering that he was anything but. Perhaps he should just go upstairs and prove to her that—

"Excuse me, my lord."

Turning, he saw the head footman hovering in the doorway. "Yes, what is it?"

"A, er, young man is asking for you at the kitchen door. Cook would have sent him away, but recalled that you had invited him in earlier this week, so sent me to ask you first."

Marcus rose, welcoming the distraction, though he itched to prove Quinn wrong. "Thank you, George. I'll go see what he wants."

The footman bowed and disappeared as Marcus made his way to the kitchen to find Gobby waiting for him just inside the door to the garden.

"Ah, yes, I did promise you a shilling to bring me a bouquet for my new bride," he improvised. "Come, let's go out into the garden to discuss what flowers would be best." Marcus generally trusted the staff, but there was no point in being careless.

Once outside in the flowerless kitchen garden, he

turned to his small cohort. "I trust you were able to put those candlesticks to good use?" he asked.

The redheaded lad nodded, though Marcus thought he looked worried. "Aye, m'lord. The Planks be set up in new digs now, rent paid out a year in advance—and enough left over for me and the lads to satisfy old Twitchell, too. Hope you don't mind."

"No, no, you're entitled to a cut for doing the leg-work for me. But what's wrong? Is this Twitchell still requiring you to steal?" Marcus had difficulty imagining how anyone could be evil enough to live off the criminal proceeds of children.

"Oh, he don't much care, long as we bring in the brass regular-like," said Gobby with a shrug. "Tig, though, he's always been one for taking chances for a lark, and now he's landed in trouble for it."

Tig, Marcus recalled, was the lad who had stolen his handkerchief and unwittingly led him to this group of boys in the first place. "What sort of trouble?" he asked. "What did he do?"

"Picked a gent's pocket," Gobby replied. "Thinks he's real slick at it, but he ain't. Didn't you catch him at it yourself? Well, he got caught again, but this bloke don't want to help him none."

Marcus frowned. "So he's been arrested?"

"Nah, that wouldn't worry us much. We're all pretty good at talking our way 'round the Charleys, and Twitchell pays 'em to let us go. This gent is run-ning his own game, crimping. Plans to sell Tig to some ship captain, and he don't want to go."

"I can't say that I blame him." Marcus had heard of crimps kidnapping or bribing young men into forced labor upon the ships, short of crew after the recent wars. He'd had no idea they took boys as young as Tig, however. "This is a gentleman, you say?"

Gobby shrugged again. "Don't rightly know, but he was dressed like one, and lives hereabouts, where the other swells live."

"Here in Mayfair?" This was a surprise. Marcus had assumed such activites were confined to areas near the docks. "Can you show me which house?"

His answer was a wide grin. "I knowed you'd help, sir. Told the others you would. I can take you there now."

Quinn was rather surprised when more than an hour passed without a summons from Marcus or any attempt at communication whatsoever. Her self-imposed isolation had given her ample time for reflection—too much time, in fact. After running over their last conversation in her mind several times, she was more than a little ashamed of some of the things she'd said—again.

Not that it altered her resolve to leave England at the first opportunity. This marriage was clearly doomed. Among other things, she had thrown Marcus's relative poverty in his face. Surely no man could forgive such a blow to his pride—not that she *wanted* his forgiveness, of course!

Still, it might be as well if she apologized. At the very least, it might lull him into trusting her, which would make her eventual escape easier. If there was any other reason she wanted to lessen the antagonism between them, Quinn refused to admit it to herself.

Trying the door, she discovered it unlocked—not that she'd heard anyone lock it, now that she thought about it. Monette appeared almost magically the moment it opened.

"My lady? Will you be wanting to change for dinner?"

The abigail's eyes were wide with sympathy—and curiosity. Quinn supposed she had been behaving oddly for a new bride, but then her circumstances were odd in the extreme.

"Yes, Monette. Yes, I would, thank you." She could hardly go wandering about in her wedding dress, she realized. Selecting a simple lilac muslin, she allowed the maid to help her change into it, then to unpin her hair and brush it into a simpler style, with a small knot at the back and the rest of her curls falling about her shoulders. She nodded at her reflection in the glass, feeling more like herself.

"Thank you, Monette. If you'll ask one of the maids to bring a pot of tea to the drawing room, I'll go downstairs now."

Almost fearfully, she descended the staircase, unsure of her reception. She saw only a footman in the front hall, at his post by the door, and wondered whether he'd been given orders to prevent her from leaving, should she try. Marcus was not in the drawing room, so she peeked into the other rooms. Library, dining room, morning room, all were empty. Had Marcus gone out?

Frowning, she returned to the drawing room just as an older woman, the housekeeper, judging by the large ring of keys she wore, approached with the tea tray. "Bring it in here please, Mrs.—?"

"Walsh, my lady. And let me take this opportunity to offer my congratulations and welcome you to the family. This house has needed a woman's touch, and it's glad I am that you're here to provide it."

Tears actually pricked at Quinn's eyes again at such a warm show of support. "Thank you, Mrs. Walsh."

Preceding the housekeeper into the drawing room, she watched the woman place the tray on a low table between two chairs. Then, oddly unwilling to be left alone, she said, "I hope Lord Anthony and Lord Peter were not terribly inconvenienced by my arrival?"

Mrs. Walsh's smile was positively motherly. "Oh, no, my lady! Lord Anthony was almost never here anyway, spending most of his time at his hunting lodge up in Leicestershire. And Lord Peter has been talking of finding his own place for two years now. This was just the push he needed."

"This house, then—it belongs to the Duke?" Everything had happened so quickly, there had been no time for questions and explanations—and when she did have the chance, she'd thrown accusations at Marcus instead.

"Aye, it's been in the family for two or three generations. It was the present Duke's grandfather's main London residence, before big mansions on the squares became all the thing. Every one of his sons has lived here at one time or another."

"Oh, so it's a sort of temporary residence for them?"

Mrs. Walsh nodded. "As Lord Marcus is the youngest, likely it would have stood empty soon enough, so it's that glad I am that you've come along, my lady. Lord Bagstead's sons won't be old enough to be wanting this place for years and years."

Quinn poured herself a cup of tea, one source of anxiety gone, if a minor one. "Thank you, Mrs. Walsh. I'm very pleased to know I haven't deprived anyone of their home."

"Nay, you make it *your* home, my lady. I hope you and Lord Marcus will be happy here, for many a long year." With that, she bobbed a curtsy and left Quinn to her tea—and her thoughts.

Where *was* Marcus? Surely it was not usual for a man to go wandering about London on his wedding day. He couldn't have taken a carriage, or she'd have seen it from her window upstairs—unless it was while she was indulging herself in tears.

Setting down her cup, she decided to attempt a small test. Leaving the drawing room, she went to the front door, where the footman still stood guard. "I believe I'll take a breath of air," she said, expecting him to bar her way, or at least issue a protest.

Instead, he merely bowed and opened the door for her. Nonplussed, she just stood there for a moment, then stepped outside and down the stairs to the pavement. Glancing up and down the street with no idea what to do next, she saw the girl Polly across the street again, though two houses farther away. It took her a moment to catch the girl's eye without attracting the attention of passersby, but finally Polly turned and saw her.

At Quinn's discreet gesture, she eagerly moved forward. Glancing back at the house, Quinn saw that the footman had closed the front door again. Still, he might be watching her through the long windows flanking it, so she walked partway down the block, where she would be out of his line of sight.

"Afternoon, mum," said Polly as she drew near. "I'm pleased to see you're all right. You didn't get in no trouble for trying to help me and Gobby before, did you?"

Quinn considered all that had befallen her as a result of that impetuous bit of charity, but she shook her head. "No, no trouble to speak of. But what are you doing here now? Not stealing again, I hope."

"Oh, no, mum! I won't never do that again. I was just keeping an eye on Gobby, so to speak." Quinn noticed that the bruise on her cheek was fading.

"To keep him from stealing, you mean?" Quinn asked her. "Is his master still forcing him to do so?" The same anger she'd felt before, nearly forgotten during the turmoil of the intervening days, came rushing back.

Polly hesitated, then shrugged. "He *says* he ain't been stealing lately, but he had enough blunt to keep Twitchell off him, so I'm not sure. I told him he wouldn't need to no more, but I don't know if he believes me."

"Have you found him some sort of employment, then? Or a school, perhaps? He and the others would do much better in school than on the streets, you know."

"I dunno much about schools, mum. Maybe I can make enough to pay for that, too. It's me what's getting a real job, you see." Polly pinkened as she spoke, however, and didn't meet Quinn's eye, which made her suspicious.

Tilting her head so that she could watch the girl's expression, Quinn asked, "What sort of job, Polly? Is it . . . respectable?"

Alarm flashed in the girl's eyes, and her cheeks turned even pinker. "I'm told it pays well," she said evasively.

Quinn's foreboding deepened. "Polly, look at me. What kind of employment are you talking about?"

But Polly still refused to meet her eyes. "I'd really rather not say, mum." She began to back away, but Quinn laid a gentle hand on her arm.

"Is it something illegal? You did say you wouldn't be stealing."

"No stealing, no, mum. I'm . . . I'm to be a fancy-girl. Mr. Twitchell says I've the face for it."

For a moment Quinn's mind balked. Surely— "You . . . you can't mean you would sell yourself— your body—to men? Is that what a fancy-girl does?"

Again Polly shrugged. "I guess you could say so, mum. I've talked to a couple o' girls what does it, and they say it brings in five times the brass any other job does."

"Oh, Polly, no! You mustn't, really." Her own horrifying experience with Sally at the Scarlet Hawk flashed through Quinn's mind. How much worse would it be for a child like this? "How old are you, anyway?"

" 'Most thirteen," she replied, standing up straighter. "Twitchell says I'm old enough." Despite her proud stance, however, fear lurked in her eyes. "How else can I take care of Gobby—and myself?"

Quinn made a sudden decision. "You probably don't know this, but I've just married. I'll need to hire a servant or two. I don't know whether it will pay so much, but I promise it will be far safer—and completely respectable. Would you like to work at that house there?" She pointed to Marcus's town house.

"Oh, mum! D'ye mean it?" There was no mistaking the girl's delight at the prospect.

Breathing a sigh of relief, Quinn nodded. "I certainly do, and I'd like you to start as soon as possible." If Marcus minded, he would simply have to get over it. "Where are you living now?"

"Twitchell's flash house in Seven Dials, with Gobby and the others."

"I take it you have no parents?"

She shook her head.

"Would Gobby want a position with us as well, do you think?" What could a boy of nine do? She'd ask the housekeeper.

"I'll ask him, mum. He won't want to leave his mates, but I think he'd be better away from there."

Quinn would have preferred to take them all in, but knew Marcus would never allow such a thing. "Yes, please try to convince him to come. That can't be a wholesome environment for a small boy."

"Aye, mum, I'll do that. Shall I come to you tomorrow?" Polly's demeanor had brightened considerably since Quinn's offer.

"Tomorrow will be perfect. I'll notify Mrs. Walsh, the housekeeper, to expect you first thing in the morning."

With profuse thanks and repeated promises to do her proud, Polly hurried away. Quinn watched her go, then turned thoughtfully back to the house.

It was a small start, but a start nonetheless. Perhaps she would not have time to make much of a difference before leaving England, but if she could salvage one or two young lives, she would at least feel her time had not been wasted.

Feeling more cheerful than she had in days, Quinn mounted the steps and reentered the house, which somehow seemed far less like a prison now.

Marcus scowled across Swallow Street at the narrow but well-kept house Gobby indicated. Not quite in Mayfair proper, it was on the fringes of the most fashionable part of London. "You can't tell me anything at all about this so-called gentleman who is holding Tig?" he asked again.

"He's tallish, with light hair. Never caught his name, though," Gobby replied. "Haven't had time to put a watch on the house, so I dunno if anyone else lives there with him or not."

The house was single-fronted, which meant it probably contained only two rooms, one behind the other, on each of its three floors, plus the attics. An upper window opened and a servant girl leaned out to shake a considerable amount of dirt from a small rug.

"We can't do much at the moment, with so many people about and all the servants awake, obviously," Marcus observed. "If you or any of the others can discover by nightfall which room Tig is being held in, however, I'll see what I can accomplish tonight."

"Aye, m'lord, we'll do that!" Gobby agreed enthusiastically. "Thank you, m'lord." Tugging the shock of red hair that hung over his eyes, the boy grinned his gratitude.

"Good lad. I'll be off home for now, then, but look for me here sometime around midnight." He started to walk away, then stopped, frowning down at the diminutive boy. "Perhaps one of the older lads should wait for me. You'll need your rest if you're to help me tomorrow."

In truth, he couldn't think it safe for a lad Gobby's size to be wandering the streets at night, though no doubt he did so all the time. Still, he felt a duty to do what he could to safeguard "his" boys—especially if this crimp had any cohorts about.

"You'll have something for me to do tomorrow, then?" As Marcus had hoped, Gobby fixed on the more exciting part of his comment.

He nodded. "Yes, but only if you're well rested and alert, mind you. It won't do to make careless mistakes." If the boy suspected for a moment that Marcus was coddling him, he would surely rebel. An idea suddenly occurred to him.

"What would you say to a real job, somewhere about my house? That way I could contact you whenever I needed to, and you could carry messages for me to the others."

"A job?" Gobby looked suspicious. "What sort of job?"

Marcus thought for a minute, taking Gobby's size and age into account. "Perhaps something in the stables? I'll talk to the head groom to see where he can use you. You'd have a warm place to sleep, as well—away from Mr. Twitchell."

Though he still looked doubtful, there was no mistaking the hope in the boy's eyes, and it tugged at Marcus's heart. "D'ye really think he'd have me? I've allus liked horses, though I ain't been around 'em much."

"I'm certain he can find work for you there. Report to the stables tomorrow, and after that we can discuss the next step in this current matter. Remember to tell Stilt or one of the others to meet me here tonight."

"I'll do that, m'lord. You can count on me!" Whistling cheerfully, Gobby headed back toward Seven Dials, presumably to recruit more lads to help in the reconnaissance of the crimp's town house and prepare for his new job.

Satisfied that he had done all he could for the moment, Marcus headed back to Grosvenor Street—and his new bride. He still had to show her that he was anything but stodgy . . .

But wait! The last thing he wanted was for her to guess his identity as Saint of Seven Dials. If she truly believed he was a thorough stick-in-the-mud, she would never suspect. But could he really act the part?

He grinned. He would simply take Robert, his stuffy eldest brother, as a model. If ever anyone merited the epithet "stodgy," Robert did. Meanwhile, would she have noticed that he'd left the house—assuming she hadn't taken this opportunity to flee? He spent the rest of the short walk concocting a reason for his absence, just in case.

"George, has there been any—" he began on entering the house, then broke off, catching a glimpse of a lilac skirt through an open door. "Never mind." He handed his hat to the footman and cautiously approached the drawing room.

Quinn looked up as he entered and startled him with a smile. "Good afternoon, my lord, er, Marcus. Would you care for some tea?"

"I, ah, yes. Of course." Nonplussed, he seated himself across the small table from her. "I'm, er, pleased to see you in better spirits," he ventured as she poured.

"Thank you. I fear I was rather overset earlier by the rapidity of events. A good cry has done me a world of good, however." She handed him his cup.

He blinked at her matter-of-fact tone. Taking the cup from her, he noticed that she was very careful not to touch him. He also noticed that her dusky curls looked remarkably fetching against the lilac gown she now wore. A very flattering gown.

"I've often heard that tears can be a sort of release for women," he commented inanely.

But she smiled again, as though he had said something perfectly reasonable. "I believe that may be true, though I am rarely given to weeping myself."

"No, I wouldn't imagine you are," he said truthfully. Diminutive she might be, but there was a strength about Quinn he had noticed from the first. "The week you have had would overset anyone, I should think. In fact, most women in your place would have taken to bed for days with the megrims."

"I rather doubt there are many other women in my precise position." For a moment her smile evinced actual amusement rather than mere politeness. "But I thank you for the compliment."

Marcus relaxed marginally. As she seemed willing to forget the angry words that had passed between them earlier, he was more than pleased to do likewise. Rather than allude to their unusual situation, therefore, he stuck to safer ground. "Did you find your room to your liking? It was Anthony's, as you may have guessed."

"I assumed it had been his or Lord Peter's."

He was almost sure he only imagined a slight wistfulness as she spoke Peter's name.

"Would it be permissible for me to have the hunting scene removed? I fear I may find it a bit unsettling to sleep beneath."

" 'Slife, I'd forgotten that painting! Anthony is mad for the hunt, of course. I'll have it sent on to him. And you're welcome to do anything you like to the room. Replace everything in it, if you wish. Indeed, I'd be amazed if your taste in any way resembles his. If there had been time—"

She held up a hand—a dainty, extremely feminine hand—to stem his babbling. "No, I realize there was no opportunity for redecorating, though I confess I was a bit startled at first." Her color deepened, and for a moment she did not meet his eyes. Had she thought it was *his* room, perhaps?

Suddenly Marcus was assailed by a vision of Quinn in his own bedchamber, lying upon his own bed, gazing up at him with those remarkable green eyes, her body—

He cleared his throat hastily. "I'll order dinner, and we can discuss whatever changes you'd like to make, both there and elsewhere in the house, over the meal. Is there any particular dish you favor?"

"I—well, you see . . ." She paused, appearing embarrassed. "I spoke with Mrs. Walsh a short time ago and took the liberty of ordering our dinner myself. She was kind enough to offer a suggestion or two as to what you might favor."

Marcus blinked, startled yet again. What a transformation from the railing termagent who had stormed up to her room earlier! "Well that's just capital, then," he said, fighting a distinct sense of unreality. "When is it to be served?"

"I asked her to have it ready an hour after your return, so that you would have time to change if you wished. I should have informed you at once." There was a question in her eyes, though she pointedly did not ask where he'd been.

"It will take me but a moment to change," he said, dismissing that concern before addressing the unspoken one. "Walking often settles my mind, and I felt the need for a good long one after—" He stopped, not wanting to bring up their earlier argument. "I should have left word, however, and for that I apologize."

Her smile did not quite reach her eyes, though it was pleasant enough. "You may come and go as you wish, of course. But I appreciate your apology."

Marcus distrusted this new side of Quinn, so different from what he had seen of her before. He stood, his tea untouched. "I'll just go up and change, then, and will see you shortly at dinner."

He bowed and left her, his head buzzing with the enigma that was his new bride. She was doubtless up to something, but until he knew what, he might as well enjoy this new civility between them. Perhaps he could even use it to get to know her better, even to win her trust—though he must be careful not to let down his own guard.

Still, if he could induce her to drop hers, to acknowledge the attraction that had more than once sizzled between them, it was just possible that this marriage could become quite tolerable. Quite tolerable indeed.

Chapter 9

⟨ ∞ ⟩

Quinn waited until Marcus's footsteps faded up the stairs, then hurried down to the kitchen to check on the progress of their dinner. So far, her plan of defusing her husband's antagonism and soothing him into complaisance seemed to be working. Now she was determined that the meal be perfect.

What she hadn't counted on was how pleasant—and attractive—Marcus could be when they weren't arguing.

"Mrs. MacKay, can dinner be served in half an hour?" Mrs. Walsh had introduced her to the kitchen staff at her request, during Marcus's absence.

"Aye, milady," the cook replied, wiping flour from her hands onto her broad apron. "Everything will be just as you asked."

A quick glance about the kitchen showed everything in order and progressing nicely, so Quinn thanked her and headed upstairs herself to touch up her own toilette before meeting Marcus again at the table.

One curl was unruly, refusing to cluster with its mates along the side of her neck. While Monette brushed it into submission, Quinn told herself that her appearance should not matter. She only wished to mollify her husband, not attract him. If she was to help Polly, and perhaps others like her, he needed to believe Quinn was satisfied with—or at least resigned to—her life here. That would also allay any suspicions he might have, making her eventual escape that much more likely to succeed.

Still, she couldn't suppress a feminine touch of pleasure at knowing she looked her best as she headed back downstairs.

Marcus was already in the dining room, looking outrageously handsome himself in a midnight blue coat and buff breeches, his dark hair falling rakishly across one eyebrow. "My lady." He greeted her with a formal bow, then held out a chair for her at one end of the long table.

He himself did not sit at the opposite end, however, but on the side, almost at her elbow. Her surprise must have shown, for he said, "This has been my accustomed seat for years. Besides, I thought conversation would be easier this way."

Quinn swallowed, finding his nearness oddly distracting. "Of course," she said, her voice higher than she'd expected. "And whose seat was this?" she asked then, in a more normal tone.

"No one's, unless we had guests," he replied. "Peter and Anthony generally sat across from me, on the rare occasions that we were all home for dinner at once. More often, whoever happened to be here had a tray in the library, the better to read while eating."

"I thought I was the only one who liked to do that," said Quinn, surprised again. He had not struck her as the reading sort. "My mother often admonished me for it."

"One must do something besides chewing to pass the time, if one is eating alone." Even by candlelight, his eyes were a remarkably bright blue, she noticed irrelevantly.

"That is what I told her—though I confess that my scoldings were occasionally for reading when others were present at the table, when I was younger."

"One assumes, then, that their conversation was not stimulating enough to hold your attention." His eyes held hers, a smile playing at the corner of his mouth.

She forced a lightness to her tone that she did not feel. "Only when I was too young to understand the business that my parents and brother discussed. Once I learned more, I was able to hold my own."

"You learned about the shipping business?" His surprise surprised her. "How little we know about each other. I would like to remedy that."

Again the look in his eyes unsettled her. She was relieved when a footman entered just then with the soup. Both fell silent while they were served, but when they were alone again, Marcus said, "You mentioned a brother—the one whose clothes you once borrowed, I presume? He is still in America?"

She nodded, taking a spoonful of soup. It was delicious. "Charles is to take over the business one day, and my father thought this would be a good opportunity for him to test his wings, so to speak."

"While the captain is away, you mean?" Marcus took his first taste of soup, and she tried not to focus on his well-shaped lips as he withdrew his spoon.

Dipping her own spoon again, she gave a small shrug. "Papa is away more often than not, but this is the first time Charles will have to deal with all of the business details unassisted."

"So you have actually been active in the running of a major shipping concern? How fascinating."

Quinn met his eyes again but saw no condescension there, only interest—perhaps even admiration? Flustered, she focused on her soup again. "My mother was, as well, before she died. It is a family business, you see, though it has grown remarkably over the past few years."

"Due in part to your own involvement?"

Shyly, she nodded. Admiration from a fine gentleman like Marcus was a novel experience, and not altogether unpleasant, she discovered. She debated telling him just how important her role in the business had been. Would it sound like bragging?

"Given the slipshod way I have managed my own finances, it appears I may have done myself a greater favor than I realized in marrying you—and I'm not talking about your dowry."

Raising startled eyes, she found him grinning, but not at all maliciously. "I . . . I do apologize for what I said earlier about that," she said quickly. "I was distraught, and—"

"And frightened, and looking for a way to strike back. I know, Quinn, and I don't blame you. Besides, you were quite right, in the sense that I have less to offer you—financially—than you have given me. I hope to make it up to you in other ways."

There was no denying the warmth in his eyes now, and it stirred an answering warmth inside her, even more disturbing—and pleasurable—than what she had felt at the docks, after he had rescued her. She swallowed, her soup momentarily forgotten. "Other ways?" she whispered.

"I'm sure there are things I can provide you. Introductions, tours of the city and country, new . . . experiences."

For a breathless moment, she was transfixed by an image of Marcus coatless, even shirtless, inviting her to explore, to touch, to experience—"I, ah, I should like to see more of London, yes," she forced herself to say, thrusting away such imaginings.

His smile made her wonder if he had guessed the direction of her thoughts, but he only said, "Then you will do so," and dipped his spoon again.

Over the main course of roast beef, Quinn managed to steer their conversation—and her unruly thoughts—into safer paths. In response to his questions, she told him in some detail about her part in the shipping business, and he regaled her with stories of himself and his brothers when they were younger.

By the time sweetmeats were brought for the close of the meal, she was feeling more comfortable with Marcus than she had imagined possible.

Whether that was a good thing or a bad thing, she had not yet decided.

"Would you like me to leave you to your brandy and cigars?" she asked, putting down her napkin. "Or do married couples dining alone do that?"

"I have no idea," he replied with a grin, "never having been part of a married couple dining alone. But I see no need for such ceremony—unless you do?" The question in his eyes was rather endearing, reminding her that he was as uncertain as she how to deal with their unusual situation.

She shook her head. "No, no need at all. I simply wished to do whatever was proper."

Proper. It was their wedding night, she remembered with a start that set her heart suddenly racing. The proper thing, the expected thing, would be to—

"Let's move back into the drawing room, then, where we can be more at ease," he suggested. "Or even the library."

She felt as though she'd been granted a welcome—it *was* welcome, wasn't it?—reprieve. "If the library is where you would normally sit after dinner, I have no objection to it."

"It's the most comfortable room, I think. You can tell me whether you agree." He stood, helped her to her feet, and extended an arm to escort her across the hall.

Such formality amused her, and that amusement steadied her nerves enough that she could place her hand on his arm without trembling at his nearness. Of course, he would not find formality amusing at all, traditionalist that he was—though the smile she saw playing about his lips when she dared to glance up at him made her wonder.

Quinn had only peeped into the library earlier, but now she was able to see that it was indeed furnished with deep leather armchairs, matching footrests, and conveniently placed small tables. In cooler weather, when a fire would be burning, it would be cozy and even more welcoming, she decided, as he went to the sideboard to pour two small measures of brandy.

"You're right. This is a more comfortable room," she said, taking the snifter he proffered. For the barest moment their fingers brushed, but she managed not to flinch or, she hoped, to betray by her expression that she had even noticed.

To cover her sudden confusion, she quickly moved to one of the chairs opposite the empty hearth.

Marcus hid a smile as he took the other chair. The girl was putting on a brave front, he had to admit. He'd caught more than one flicker of awareness from her during dinner, when he'd deliberately caught her eye or slipped a double entendre into the conversation. And just now, though she'd colored at his touch, she hadn't pulled away.

Looking at her now, he had to remind himself that she was a woman of twenty and not the sixteen she appeared. Still, though she was no child, she was clearly an innocent in matters of the flesh. If he wanted a marriage in more than name—and over the past hour he had become more convinced that he did—he would have to win her trust.

He was willing to be patient, however. Somehow he was certain the rewards would be worth any wait.

"Try the brandy," he suggested. "It's the best France has to offer—though I warn you that it has a bit more bite than sherry."

She took a sip before he finished speaking, and now she sputtered, glaring at him accusingly. "You did that on purpose," she gasped, her eyes tearing slightly from the strength of the liquor.

"I didn't, I swear it," he exclaimed, holding up a hand in self-defense. He couldn't suppress a chuckle, however, which no doubt undermined his show of sincerity. "I'm sorry, though. It's been a long time since I've offered brandy to a novice—not since my school days, in fact. You'll want to take very tiny sips until you're used to it."

It was dangerously reminiscent of their earlier conversation over the sherry, he realized belatedly, bracing himself for a similar ending. But though a delicately quirked eyebrow showed that she caught the similarity as well, she took another, very cautious sip, this time without coughing.

"You did promise me new experiences," she said with a half smile, "though I confess brandy wasn't what I expected." Then, suddenly conscious, she colored again and dropped her eyes.

Marcus took the chance to grin unseen, quickly schooling his face to a semblance of seriousness before she gathered her courage to look at him again. Perhaps he wouldn't have to be so very patient after all.

"What *did* you expect?" he asked, resisting the

urge to use a suggestive tone. He didn't want to frighten her back into her prickly shell.

But now she met his eye squarely. "Drives about London, a tour of the Tower, that sort of thing. I would love to see a balloon ascension, if they are performed at this time of year."

"Ah." His body had already responded to what he'd imagined, but he tried to quell it. "I'll do a bit of research and see what sorts of amusements are to be had about Town. Perhaps you would care to see other parts of England as well?" Traveling with her, staying overnight at quaint inns where they would be required to share a room, could be—

"Later, perhaps. For now, London will be sufficient. I'd prefer to learn more of it before . . . before the majority of Society returns in the autumn." Though she still faced him unflinchingly, he detected a tiny quaver in her voice.

"Society can't hurt you now, you know," he said gently. It seemed necessary to reassure her, to erase that quaver, to protect her. "You're a respectable married woman."

She gave a short, mirthless laugh. "Respectable? Surely, that is for others to decide—and pass judgment on? To listen to Lady Claridge, twenty-five years of marriage did not make my mother respectable. Not that respectability was ever a particular aim of mine, of course," she added, almost as an afterthought.

"No, you've made that quite clear," he said, smiling. The smile seemed to surprise her, and he suddenly remembered his plan to appear stuffy.

Forcing a more formal note into his voice, he continued. "If you can manage to refrain from doing anything shocking for a few months, the gossips will move on to other prey. When I offered you the protection of my name, it was more than a figure of speech, you know." Stodgy act aside, he meant that.

"And I've done little but rail against you for it. I'm sorry for that."

Marcus leaned forward, taking her hands in his. Her eyes went wide, a deep and mysterious green by the failing daylight filtering in through the long windows, but she did not pull away.

"I know this marriage was not what you wanted, Quinn, but I'm very much hoping you won't entirely regret it. I'll do what I can to ensure that."

What had come over him? No more than simple lust for this very attractive woman who was his wife, surely. That, and a perfectly human desire to protect someone he perceived as vulnerable, just as he would protect one of his street urchins. Yes, that must be it.

She smiled tremulously at him and that smile stirred strange longings that weren't precisely the same as lust, with which he was quite familiar.

"Thank you," she said with apparent sincerity. "And I will try not to make you regret your gallantry too terribly much, though, knowing myself as I do, I don't dare promise that you won't." Her smile was now self-deprecating, which somehow attracted him as much as her shy tentativeness had.

"If this past week is a fair measure, I can see your point." He smiled again, to take the sting from his words. "I'll simply have to make life interesting enough that you won't feel the need to go looking for adventure, I suppose."

"You see adventure as something to be avoided, then? Perhaps you will develop a taste for it over time," she said hopefully, even playfully.

"Perhaps," he responded, resisting the urge to contradict her. "But I trust you will not consider it your duty to instill in me a thirst for excitement." He fully expected to have plenty of adventure himself, given his new mission—but it was a mission Quinn mustn't suspect.

He thought she looked vaguely disappointed, but she only said, "Of course not, my lord. I realize that would go against your nature, and it is not for me to change your nature."

"Marcus, remember? And I can enjoy a balloon ascension with the best of them, I assure you. I'm not a complete dullard."

He still had no idea how she had formed that opinion of him, but it was clearly entrenched enough to work to his advantage, making her more unlikely to suspect the truth. A glance at the mantel-piece clock showed that he still had nearly four hours before his meeting at the crimp's house, but there were certain things he needed to do before returning there.

And other things he would like to do.

"It has been a full and rather trying day for you, I know. Perhaps you would care to retire early tonight?" he suggested.

Alarm flared in her eyes, then was quickly

shielded. "I, ah, yes, I am rather tired, I suppose. Nor have I yet become entirely used to London hours, I confess. At home I was used to an earlier start to each day, as well as an earlier end."

"Understandable." Marcus himself preferred Town hours, generally feeling far more alert at midnight than at noon, but did not say so. "Shall I escort you upstairs, then?"

"Escort—? I can find my—That is . . . If you wish." She alternately flushed scarlet, then went rather pale. Luckily, she didn't seem the fainting sort.

"It seems the, ah, polite thing to do, on your first night here." Polite was not at all what he wanted, but she was nervous enough already. And indeed, his choice of words did seem to calm her. Standing, he held out his arm and she rose to take it.

They mounted the stairs in a silence that was becoming awkward before she spoke again. "Which . . . which room is yours?"

He tried to take some hope from the question, though she could simply want to be forewarned, he supposed. "The next one along. Your room and mine are separated by a dressing room, but you can always lock that door from your side if you wish to."

He meant it as a jest, but she frowned. "I suppose that would be considered rather irregular, would it not? Not that I am afraid of you, of course," she added hastily.

"Irregular or not, I thought you might like to know." They had halted outside her door now, and he watched her, waiting for any sort of signal that she might welcome his company within.

"Thank you. You're . . . being very kind. I confess I did not expect that."

"Because you had convinced yourself I was some sort of ogre, apparently. I'm by no means perfect, but I'm not a bully."

She appeared fascinated by his shirtfront, not meeting his eyes. "I realize that now. I goaded you earlier with my foolish rantings, and it is not surprising that you lost patience with me. I'd have likely done the same in your place."

With one finger under her chin, he tipped her face up so that she had to look at him. "Don't try to take all of the blame yourself. I was rather insufferable myself, and did my own share of goading. Pax?"

Quinn nodded, almost imperceptibly. The tip of her tongue slipped out to wet her lips—a nervous gesture, but it sent fire straight to his vitals. Without thinking, prompted by instinct—or need—he lowered his own lips to hers.

Amazingly, she tilted her head back for his kiss, her eyes drifting closed as their lips touched. Drawing on reserves of self-control he hadn't known he possessed, Marcus lightly pressed his lips to hers, gentle rather than demanding, though he ached to clasp her to him, to take possession of her mouth, her body.

It was the sweetest kiss he had ever experienced.

And all too brief. He drew away before his body could rule his mind, desire already surging insistently through him despite the innocence of that kiss.

Quinn's eyes flew open, her expression startled and questioning. Then, tentatively, she reached up with one hand to touch his cheek, a tremulous smile playing about her lips.

His control broke. With an incoherent exclamation, he gathered her into his arms for another kiss. No pristine sealing of their marriage vows this time, but a claiming of rights, his need demanding an answering need from her.

And answer she did. Her arms went around his neck, drawing him closer, her whole length pressed against him as she returned his kiss with a passion he'd barely dared to guess she possessed. He slid his hands up and down her back, exploring her curves as he'd longed to do for hours. *Mine*, he exulted, the only thought to penetrate his swirling desire.

Moving his lips from her mouth to her throat, he tasted her skin, explored the mysterious hollow behind her ear. She responded with a tiny, throaty growl, her own lips fluttering at his temple, urging him on. With an answering growl, he brought his mouth back to hers, plundering it with his tongue, stroking, seeking. She pressed even tighter to him, her breasts firm against his chest, her hands massaging his back.

With one hand, he reached behind her for the door handle and turned it. He had a disorienting moment when the door swung open to reveal Anthony's room, its greens and browns somber by candlelight. Somehow, his mind had been primed for satin and lace. Not that it mattered.

Quinn felt the door open behind her with that one small part of her that was not totally immersed in Marcus, in her overwelming, unsuspected need for him. It seemed the most natural thing in the world that he would come in, join her on that big bed, and that they would become one in body as they had earlier become one in the eyes of the law and the world.

Why had she even questioned it?

Abruptly, her mind returned, battling with her body for supremacy. What was she doing? What was she allowing him to do? Was she mad? Though it took far more effort than she'd have thought possible, she pulled herself away from his intoxicating kiss.

In the dimness of the corridor, shadows emphasizing the planes of his face, he looked more handsome than ever—devilishly handsome, and not stodgy at all. His eyes were dark, smoky with a desire that nearly plunged her back into the madness with him. And it had to be madness!

"I— We—" she began, not at all sure what she meant to say, only certain that she needed to put things on a more rational footing before she was lost entirely.

"Yes, let's," he responded, his hands at her back moving again, threatening to snap her tenuous hold on reality. Then, in a deeper voice, "Quinn."

Though her name on his lips was incredibly erotic, it helped to remind her of who she was and how she came to be here. In sudden panic, afraid more of herself than of him, she backed away, shaking her head. "No! We . . . I can't . . . Good night, my lord."

Before she could weaken again and fling herself back into his arms, she took two quick steps backward and closed the door, then turned to lean against it—not to prevent his entry, but to lessen the temptation to open it again just as quickly. What had she done? *Almost* done . . .

Breathing heavily, her body still quivering its response to his touch, Quinn forced herself to calmness. She had *wanted* to let him make love to her! In fact, she still wanted it. Never in her imaginings of what marriage might be like had she expected that. Did that make her wicked?

But no, lovemaking between husband and wife was not sinful. Not even when they were virtual strangers? Marcus didn't feel quite like a stranger, though. Not any longer.

Thoroughly bewildered by her conflicting emotions, Quinn moved away from the door to advance into the room—alone. Had she perhaps been wicked to make him stop? After all, it was a husband's prerogative to— But no, that was merely an excuse. The truth was that she had wanted—still wanted—him as much as he wanted her. Perhaps more.

Impulsively, she turned back toward the door, only to hear a click that must surely be Marcus entering his own room, right next to hers. She stared at the dressing-room door, then took a step toward it. No, she didn't have the courage for that.

Her blood was slowly cooling, her capacity for thought returning. There was no rush. Marcus had said so himself after the wedding breakfast. She would do better to master this fever of the flesh until she decided what direction she wished her life to take. For her choice, once made, would be irrevocable.

With a sigh, she rang for her maid, who appeared a moment later to help her prepare for bed.

Alone again, between the sheets of the large, strange bed, regret still gnawed at her. Would there be another opportunity like that one? Marcus might interpret her panic as a rejection, a sign that she had no interest in him as a man. But—wasn't that what she wanted him to believe?

Remembering that last, fevered embrace, she had to smile to herself, even as the heat of embarrassment washed over her. He knew. Unless he was as innocent as she—which she very much doubted—he knew. But what would come next, she had no idea.

Chapter 10

Physically frustrated though he was at the moment, Marcus could not say he was completely disappointed. Quinn's response to him had been most gratifying, even if she had lost her nerve at the last. Still, he needed a distraction now, with her getting ready for bed only a few yards away. All too easy to imagine her maid helping her out of her gown, corset, shift . . .

With a mental shake, he moved to his desk and pulled out the stack of blank calling cards he had purchased several days earlier.

Working from memory, he inked a numeral seven in the center, then pulled out another pen and inkpot, this one filled with the gold ink normally reserved for the fanciest of invitations—again, bought solely for this purpose. With this, he drew an oval "halo" above the seven, then grinned at his handiwork. It was indistinguishable from the card Luke had given him on his wedding day two weeks before.

That memory stirred another, of his own thoughts about marriage such a short time ago. How his world had changed. Then, he'd had scarcely a care in the world, beyond what a given night's entertainments would hold. His life had been simple, unfettered . . . and empty.

No, he didn't wish to turn back the clock. His life had purpose now—more than one purpose, in fact. But with purpose came responsibility. And work.

Quickly, he inked several more cards, spreading them across his writing desk to dry, then pushed his chair back to consider the evening ahead as well as the tasks he had set himself for the days to come. His life wasn't empty anymore, but the things that filled it pulled his loyalties in different directions.

Shaking his head at such foolish philosophizing, he rose and stripped off his finery to don the subdued, nondescript clothing that was better suited to that night's activities.

It lacked only a few minutes to midnight when Marcus again stood opposite the narrow house on Swallow Street where Tig was being held. The first and second floors were dark, the only light emanating from the sunken kitchen windows and one attic window above. He hoped that meant the owner of the house was either out or already abed.

" 'Ere you are then, milord," came a voice at his elbow. Turning, he saw Renny, a painfully thin boy of eleven or twelve, second oldest in Stilt's gang and one of those Marcus had accosted that first day—the day he had first met Quinn.

He clasped the boy's grimy hand. "Well met, Renny. What can you tell me?"

"Gobby, Stilt, and me, we've took turns watching the house all day. Seems to be just the one bloke what lives there, and he's out now. Two other chaps dropped in a couple hours ago, and he left with 'em. Nobody home now but one manservant and two maids, from what we can tell."

"And Tig?"

"Up in the attics. He knows we're here—he came to the window after the swells left. We didn't dare shout, though, for fear of raising the alarm."

Marcus clapped him on the shoulder. "Good lad. That means he's probably not bound. That should make things a bit easier." Thoughtfully, he contemplated the house.

"There's another door in back," Renny told him, "but it leads to the kitchen, where the servants are like to be now. Windows are a good size, though."

"Yes, I was noticing that. Come on and show me which window is Tig's."

Crossing the street, they went to the end of the row of houses, to reach the alleyway running behind them. In a few moments, they joined Stilt in the tiny patch of garden behind Tig's prison, looking up at the narrow top window.

"That window's too small, even for Tig," Marcus commented softly. "Nothing for him to climb down by, anyway."

Stilt nodded. "He wanted to try, earlier. Just as well he couldn't squeeze through—he's not as sticky a climber as he claims. We'd have picked him up dead, I don't doubt."

Marcus had to agree. The upper walls were sheer, with no handholds visible, at least by the light of a half-moon. Below, however, a sturdy trellis and some ornamental brickwork might offer a way to a second-story window.

"Right then," he said in sudden decision. "If you two will keep watch, I'll see if I can spring him."

Already he was picking up their street cant, some of which he'd learned from Luke, he realized, back in their Oxford days. At the time, he'd assumed Luke had picked up the expressions abroad, he thought with amusement.

The trellis wasn't quite strong enough to bear his weight, but he was able to use it to steady himself as he slowly worked his way up the protruding bricks. It had been years since he'd done this sort of thing, but he soon discovered he still had the instincts that had aided him in many a prank on his brothers and Oxford classmates. In ten minutes, he had reached the darkened second-floor window that was his target.

As he'd hoped, no one had bothered to lock the upper window, and it yielded to his tug easily. No doubt it had stood open earlier, hot as the day had been. With a scramble that he hoped wouldn't be audible as far away as the kitchen, he hoisted himself over the sill and into a fair-sized bedchamber. He paused for a moment to listen, but heard no sounds from within the house. Good.

Quickly, he crossed the room and emerged into the short passage leading to the stairs at the side of the house. In a moment, he had climbed past the third story to the low door of the attic. "Tig?" he whispered. "Are you alone?"

A soft scuffling came from within, then a voice answered him. "Aye, guv, none but me here, but I can't reach the door. I'd a' picked the lock hours ago if I could."

Marcus smiled at Tig's cocky tone, glad that the boy hadn't had his spirit squelched. "I'll have you out of there in a trice."

Tig's captors had foolishly left the key in the lock, so there was no need to test his skill at picking it, rather to Marcus's disappointment. The attic was lit by a single guttering candle that showed the lad tied by a stout rope to a beam near the tiny window, his hands bound behind him.

Marcus refrained from asking how he'd have picked the lock—or scaled the wall—without use of his hands, and set about untying him. With the aid of his pocketknife, he soon had Tig free. "There we are, then. Follow me."

When Tig opened his mouth to thank him—or perhaps for more bluster—Marcus silenced him with a finger to his lips. "Later," he whispered. "Stay close."

Quietly, he led the boy down the stairs, pausing at the second floor, then proceeding down to the first.

Motioning Tig to wait, Marcus slipped into the small parlor, gazing about for anything he might—ah! On the mantel stood a pair of figurines that he was fairly sure were Chinese, and quite valuable. With a grin, he slipped both of them into his pockets and left a calling card in their place.

He then went to the small writing desk in the corner of the room. A quick search revealed a paper or two, and he added those to his pocket in hopes that in better light they might reveal more about Tig's captor.

"All right, let's go," he said, rejoining the boy on the stairs. They continued down to the ground floor, where they stopped again to listen. A murmur of voices came from the kitchen below, along with the sound of snoring—at least one of the servants was taking advantage of her master's absence for a nap.

Deciding it would be quieter than opening another window, Marcus boldly went to the front door, unlocked it, and led Tig down the front steps to the street. He waited until they'd walked a few houses down before speaking.

"Now, that wasn't so bad, was it? Were you able to discover anything about your captor or his friends?"

Tig gazed up at him in rapt adoration. "Gorblimey, guv, but you're slick as the Saint ever was. Taking over for him, are you?"

Marcus tousled his dark hair. "Helping him out, let's say. Look, here are the others." They had rounded the corner into the alley, surprising Stilt and Renny, who were still waiting behind the house.

"Mission accomplished," Marcus said. "Now get yourselves a good meal and a good night's rest. You've earned it." He flipped a shilling to Stilt, who caught it neatly. "I'll send Gobby to you tomorrow with further instructions."

The three boys nodded vigorously, all of them now regarding him with something like awe. With a chuckle and a wave of his hand, Marcus headed back to Grosvenor Street. Luke had pegged him, it seemed. Becoming the Saint of Seven Dials was just the change he'd been needing.

By morning, Quinn was able to congratulate herself on her narrow escape the night before. Had she given in to that flare of passion—surely temporary!— she would never be able to justify escaping England and her marriage, which she still intended to do. At least, she was *almost* certain she still intended it.

No, no, things had surely turned out for the best.

She went down to breakfast, still arguing with herself. Rather to her relief, Marcus was not in the dining room, so she took the opportunity to speak with Mrs. Walsh and arrange for Polly's placement among the lower servants, and to ask about possible positions for a young boy.

"Perhaps the stables, my lady," the housekeeper replied. "Would you like me to speak to the head groom about it?"

"Yes, please do," Quinn replied. "I'd like him to start immediately, if possible." She returned to the dining room, feeling pleased with herself, to find Marcus awaiting her.

At once, the feelings of the night before rushed back, and she felt her face coloring. Determined not to reveal more than she could help, she moved forward after only the slightest hesitation. "Good morning," she said, as brightly as she could.

Marcus returned her greeting blandly, adding, "I trust you slept well?" Perhaps she imagined the twinkle in his eye that accompanied the question.

"Yes, I thank you. Though the decor of my room is not to my taste, the bed itself is most comfortable." Mention of the bed threatened to make her blush again, so she quickly turned her attention to her plate.

"Will we be attending church this morning?" she asked then, to further distract herself from feelings best left unexamined.

Marcus looked up in evident surprise. "I haven't been in the habit of it, but, er, of course, if you think it best."

Quinn shrugged slightly. "I assumed it was customary."

"Yes, well . . . it is, I suppose. Why don't we, then? Start off on the right foot and all that." He seemed as relieved as she to have something specific to discuss—to do—on this first, awkward morning of their marriage.

Accordingly, they headed out right after breakfast and soon Quinn found herself in a small parish church much like the one she had attended with her father the morning after their arrival in London. The sermon itself was uninspiring, but she found a measure of comfort in the familiar rituals.

Upon leaving, a group of Evangelicals accosted them, handing out pamphlets. Not wanting to seem rude, she accepted a few and tucked them into her reticule. Perhaps she would glance at them later, if time hung heavy on her hands.

A light luncheon awaited them upon their return, as well as the Sunday newspapers—both most welcome diversions. After the closeness they had attained the previous night, awkwardness now erected a wall between them, allowing only the most inconsequential of small talk through.

Quinn knew she should be glad, but instead felt vaguely bereft—even lonely. With an inaudible sigh, she picked up one of the papers and began reading. The article on the effects of strengthened Corn Laws meant nothing to her, unfamiliar as she was with English politics, nor the items about various members of Parliament and their views.

Turning the page, she skimmed the society gossip with a sinking heart, thinking it was only a matter of time before she herself would be pilloried there—if she stayed. Then, on the opposite page, she found an article that caught her interest.

THE SAINT OF SEVEN DIALS STRIKES AGAIN! it began in bold letters, going on to describe a recent robbery by this apparently legendary thief. "For several years now, the audacious Saint has made a mockery of London's pitiful law officers, baffling beadles and magistrates and even the Bow Street Runners as he steals from the rich to give to the poor, like Robin Hood of old."

Fascinated, she read on as the article recounted a

few of the Saint's more daring exploits over the past few years. Sir Nathaniel Conant, Chief Magistrate of Bow Street, was quoted as saying, "A month ago we were sure we'd identified him, but these latest burglaries have set us back. Still, we are confident we will bring him to justice soon."

"Found something interesting, have you?" Marcus asked from across the table, making Quinn realize she must have made some sort of exclamation.

"Yes, this Saint of Seven Dials they write about," she responded with a smile, eager to return to a more comfortable footing with her new husband. "Quite the storybook hero, though your government officials don't see him in that light, as might be expected. Have you heard about him?"

To her disappointment, Marcus withdrew behind his own paper. "Oh, yes, we've all heard of him, of course," he said absently. "Fellow goes a-thieving every few months and suddenly he's a legend. Can't say I see what the fuss is about, myself. London is full of thieves, after all, and he is just one more."

"Oh, but he's not, if this article is to be believed!" Quinn exclaimed, puzzled and hurt by Marcus's withdrawal. "He gives what he steals to the poor, which I'm certain the average thief does not. And these calling cards he leaves, as though he is daring someone to catch him. He sounds rather extraordinary."

"Do you think so?" Marcus lowered his paper to regard her for a long moment. Then, his tone again bored, "The ladies all seem fascinated by him, now that I think on it. Personally, I believe the newspapers exaggerate the truth out of all reason to increase their sales. Legends make good reading, after all."

Quinn felt a stab of disappointment, but whether at Marcus's continued indifference or the idea of this Saint not being a hero after all, she wasn't sure. "Yes, I suppose that's likely, pity though it is," she admitted.

With another sigh, she leafed through the rest of the paper, finding nothing else of particular interest—until her eye fell upon a column on the last page, entitled "Shipping News." There were listed the departure dates and destinations of ships from each of London's docks, as well as other English ports.

A quick glance at Marcus showed him still apparently absorbed in his own reading, so she quickly scanned the listings. The only ship leaving for Baltimore this week appeared to be from Liverpool. There would be others, though. She'd check this column regularly, until she found one leaving from London. And perhaps she would leave with it.

With a simulated yawn, she rose. "If you don't mind, I believe I will go up to my room and attend to some correspondence. Perhaps I will give some thought to redecorating, as well."

"As you wish." He showed not the slightest reluctance to let her go. "I may go out for a bit, briefly. Dinner at six again tonight?"

"Six will be fine." She stood there for a moment, wondering whether she should say something, do something, to get him to really see her again. But no, things were safer this way.

Mounting the stairs to her room, she began to wonder if she had only dreamed the friendliness—and the passion—they had so briefly shared the night before.

Marcus waited until Quinn's footsteps receded up the stairs before reaching across the table for the paper she had been reading. He hoped he hadn't said anything to make her suspicious, but her mention of the Saint of Seven Dials had caught him rather off guard. Quickly, he located the article and read it through, chuckling when he came to Sir Nathaniel's quote.

"Well, it looks like I've about got Luke off the hook, then," he murmured to himself. "One or two more forays should clinch it." That thought reminded him that Gobby would be arriving shortly to take up his new job, and that he still had to speak with the head groom. He headed for the stables.

Thinking over what he had learned last night from Tig, he realized there was something else Gobby could do for him—something that might keep other boys from suffering the fate Tig nearly had. With a decisive nod, he strode through the kitchen garden and out the back gate, to speak with the groom.

"That's right," he said to Gobby a few minutes later. The boy had already been lurking in the mews, waiting for him, when he emerged from the stable. "You have yourself a job as a stableboy. It will be up to you to work your way up to groom."

Gobby grinned widely. "I'll do just that, milord, wait and see if I don't!"

Marcus nodded encouragingly. "I'm sure you will. Before you begin, though, I want you to ask the others to find out who this Mr. Jarrett's cohorts are, and where they live."

The papers he had taken Saturday night had revealed nothing but the name of Tig's captor, unfortunately.

"Aye, milord, I c'n do that," Gobby agreed enthusiastically. "They'll be able to tell you by tonight, I'll be bound."

Though he had to smile at the lad's eagerness, Marcus put a restraining hand on his shoulder. "There's no great rush, now that Tig is safe. Tell them not to let themselves be seen. Just follow him for a few days, find out his habits, his friends, and send us word. I'll take it from there."

Gobby nodded vigorously, a shock of red hair falling into his eyes. "I'll tell them, right enough, milord. They can get word to you through me."

"That's the idea. Off with you, then. Take this with you." Marcus handed him a meat pie he'd filched from the kitchen on his way through to the garden. "Report to Mr. Peters when you return, and he'll tell you what to do and where you'll sleep."

With a grin, the boy took a big bite of the pie and headed down the lane. Marcus gazed after him for a moment, hoping he wasn't putting any of the other boys in danger. But no, these lads faced terrible risks every day of their lives. He was simply trying to eliminate one of those risks. Once that was done, perhaps he'd tackle another. And Gobby should be safer, at least.

Turning back to the house, it hit him that he was planning to continue as Saint of Seven Dials even now that Luke's name was apparently cleared. But why not? Those boys clearly needed him, and so far, his marriage wasn't creating much in the way of an obstacle. Rather less than he'd hoped, in fact, though he fully intended that would change.

All things considered, he had to admit that his life had become far more interesting than it had been only a week earlier!

Quinn set down her pen with a sigh. She'd written a letter to her brother, advising him of her marriage and including some suggestions about changing their tea and spice routes, based on what she'd read in the London papers. Charles would likely ignore her advice, but she felt obligated to pass it along. It was all she could do now for the business that had consumed the past few years of her life.

"Blast!" The unladylike exclamation escaped her when a tear fell on her completed letter, smudging her signature. Quickly, she scattered sand across it, before the ink could run.

Folding up her letter, she set it aside for later posting, then cast about for something else to do, feeling unequal to facing Marcus again just yet. She pulled a handkerchief from her reticule, to dab nose and eyes, then noticed the pamphlets she had collected after church. The first was on temperance, the second a treatise on the necessity for daily Bible reading. The third, however, captured her attention.

A Mr. Throgmorton, a follower of the teachings of William Wilberforce and Hannah More, was soliciting funds for the establishment of a school for boys in London's slums. The pamphlet went on to press the advantages to the wealthy of getting homeless, wretched boys off the streets and trained for useful occupations, and ended with a direction for sending funds.

Taking up her pen again, Quinn began another letter.

Dear Mr. Throgmorton,   .

If you will consider establishing a school for girls, as well as boys, and placing it near the West End of London, I may be in a position to supply a large part of the necessary funding. I have observed that the lot of orphaned, homeless girls is at least as wretched as that of their brothers, and would do something to improve their lot.

Now, how to receive a reply, without betraying her identity? Ah!

You may leave word for me at Grillon's Hotel.

—A Sympathetic Lady

Before she could change her mind, she folded and addressed that letter as well, then rang for a maid.

"Have one of the footmen post these at once," she said. Taking the letters, the girl curtsied and left. Fortified by her renewed sense of purpose, Quinn headed downstairs to find her husband.

Marcus looked up from his book and smiled when Quinn appeared at the library door, the very sight of her quickening his pulse. "Come in, come in. No need to hover there—you're quite welcome to join me."

With an uncertain smile that tugged at his heart, she came into the room and sat down. "I'm not disturbing you?"

"Not at all. I was merely passing the time with reading, but conversation will do that far more enjoyably. Perhaps we can discuss what you'd like your first London amusement to be."

"Oh! You still mean to show me about, then?"

Her surprise surprised him. "Of course. Did you think I would go back on my word? Not my style, I assure you." In fact, the idea that she might think it bothered him more than he cared to admit.

"No, I . . . I suppose not. It was just— Never mind. What would you suggest I see first?"

Though he was curious about what she had left unsaid, he merely answered her question. "I saw in the papers that there is to be a balloon ascension on Wednesday, so I thought we should take that in. For tomorrow, our choices include a tour of the Tower and menagerie, a visit to the 'Change to see the tigers, viewing the Elgin Marbles, or perhaps a trip to the Egyptian Hall in Picadilly."

He was pleased to see her become more animated. "Oh, my! Every one of those sounds fascinating. What would you like to do?"

"This is for you, Quinn, not for me," he reminded her. "I told you that I plan to make your pleasure, the broadening of your experiences, my first object."

She blushed but did not answer, and he hid a smile. Clearly, she had no more been able to put their passionate good night out of her mind than he had.

"I have not visited the Egyptian Hall since Mr. Bullock acquired Napoleon's carriage and other trinkets," he continued. "Those may be worth seeing, along with the other exhibits there."

"Let's do that, then," she said, raising her chin, clearly determined to hide whatever confusion she felt at his earlier words. "Then perhaps the Tower on Tuesday."

Marcus relaxed, feeling the camaraderie they had briefly established last night creeping back. For a few hours he had wondered whether it had been an anomaly, but now—

"We have a few hours before dinner. Perhaps we might talk for a bit," he suggested.

"Yes, I'd like that," she replied. "Tell me more about the Saint of Seven Dials."

Chapter 11

Marcus started, all comfort fled. She couldn't possibly suspect, could she? "Why?" he asked cautiously.

"It seems an interesting tale to while away the time," she replied with a small shrug. "However, if you'd rather not—"

"No, no, I don't mind." How much should he tell her? Just what the general public knew . . . "You read the essentials in the newspaper, of course."

Her frown reminded him that she didn't know he'd read the article himself. "But surely there is more? Details they didn't have room to provide, the sorts of things that are known to most people I might meet."

She just wanted to be better informed before meeting more of the *ton*, he reminded himself. "Yes, yes, of course. Let me see. His notoriety began to grow some five years ago, I believe. Yes, it was

shortly after I left Oxford, now that I think on it."
That alone wouldn't implicate Luke—or himself.

"What set him apart from other thieves? His calling cards?"

"Those, and his methods. He became generally known for his audacity, striking in the midst of crowded parties, or in the dead of night when whole families were at home."

"How frightening for them!" she exclaimed, though she leaned forward with interest.

"He never hurt anyone," Marcus quickly assured her. "Was never even seen, in fact."

He recalled one of his favorite tales, from well before he knew who the Saint really was. "I remember once he stole a diamond parure, necklace, *and* earrings, while Lady Jersey was wearing them—at her very own ball! A fair amount of plate, more than I'd have thought one man could carry, vanished that same night. It was as though he were invisible, coming and going without a trace—except for his calling card, of course."

"And what are those like?"

He shifted uncomfortably. He had let his enthusiasm get the better of his judgment. If she were to somehow find the ones he kept in his desk upstairs . . . He must hide them better.

"I've never seen one, of course," he said evasively. "Something saying 'Saint of Seven Dials,' I presume. I fear I haven't read the stories all that closely."

Undaunted, she asked, "And his giving to the poor—is that true? How would the authorities know of that?"

"Those rumors started later, first among the lower classes, and then getting into the papers. I've heard beggars speak of him with reverence, so it may well be true." He winced, hoping he hadn't said too much.

She seemed not to notice, however. "To think he is living right here in London—perhaps even one of the nobility himself! Aren't you curious to discover who he really is?"

"Nobility? I seriously doubt it." He hoped his alarm wasn't visible.

"But to gain admission to society parties—" She stopped, regarding him curiously. "You don't approve of him?"

Belatedly, he remembered the role he'd decided to play with her. "Of course I don't approve of him. We pay taxes enough to help the poor. Far better that the upper classes contribute in that way, or through charitable donations if they are so inclined, than having it taken from them by force." He tried to mimic Robert's sententious tone.

She sat back, clearly disappointed in him, but he dared not recant. She was getting too close to the truth. "I see. Any deviation from propriety, from the established way of doing things, is to be condemned."

"I didn't say that, precisely." In fact, he disagreed violently, but she mustn't guess that. Especially not while they were on this particular topic.

"No, not precisely. But it is all of a piece with what I have observed of you thus far. I'm sorry I brought up the subject. I leave it to you to introduce the next one."

He wanted to erase the censure from her eyes, to make them sparkle again, as they had a few moments ago—as they had last night. "How experienced a rider are you? I thought perhaps you'd like a mount of your own, now that you are fixed in England."

Those last words had been a mistake, for she withdrew visibly. "Fixed. Yes, I suppose I am. But I would prefer to choose my own mount, if you don't mind."

"Not at all! In fact, I was going to suggest just that. It won't do for you to accompany me to Tattersall's, of course, but I can have a few suitable beasts brought round for your inspection."

Now she did brighten a bit. "That . . . would be nice. Would there be time tomorrow, after the Egyptian Hall, do you think?"

"I believe so. Have you a habit? You'll want to try their paces, I imagine."

Her face fell. He loved how her emotions flitted across her face. It meant he rarely had to guess how she felt. "Oh. No, I'm afraid I don't, not yet."

"No matter," he said briskly, eager to see the sunshine peek out of her eyes again. "For a trial run, any old gown will do. It's settled, then. I'll go to Tattersall's first thing in the morning and arrange to have a few bits of blood sent round at three o'clock."

To his delight, she smiled. "And I'll look over the gowns Lady Claridge declared too *outré* for Town wear and see if any might be converted to a passable habit. In fact, I'll set my abigail to the task at once, as she's had little to do thus far."

So saying, she rose and hurried from the room. Though he was sorry to see her go, Marcus was just as glad of the chance to gather his thoughts—and get his unruly body back under control. It was a tricky line he was walking, trying to win her trust and liking, while being careful not to disabuse her of the strange idea that he was stodgy.

He could not deny that the Saint's secret would be far safer if she thought him a thorough stick-in-the-mud. Quinn was clever, as well as unpredictable. If she were to discover his secret, she might well use it to force him to her will—even to take her to Baltimore. More fates than his could be at risk.

No, much as he might want to, he didn't dare let her know his true nature yet, while he also wore the mantle of the Saint. But how much longer that would be, he wasn't sure.

Quinn managed to putter about her room until dinnertime, making notes about a redecorating that she didn't necessarily plan to be here to complete. With pins and a few judicious stitches, Monette had already converted one of her gowns from home into a passable habit, fuming in mingled French and English about Lady Claridge's comments on a perfectly fashionable wardrobe.

Dressing for dinner with particular care, Quinn wondered why she bothered. Marcus was clearly the stuffy wet blanket she'd first thought him, despite his occasional moments of more interesting conversation. Still . . .

"Yes, bring that curl forward, so. Thank you, Monette." Confident that she looked her best, for all she would never be a Society beauty, she left the room—only to bump into Marcus himself in the hallway.

"Oh, excuse me!" she exclaimed. "I didn't mean—"

He steadied her with that smile she found so unsettling. "No harm done, my dear. And now I have the privilege of escorting you down to dinner. I wish I could claim that I hovered here in hopes of just that, but alas it was merely chance that brought us both to this particular square of carpet at the same moment."

Though his touch on her arm set her whole body to tingling, she met his eyes, which crinkled at the corners with amusement—and perhaps something more. "Surely you should have claimed it anyway? Perhaps you need lessons in flattery, my lord."

"Perhaps I do," he said with a grin, acknowledging her teasing. "Would you care to instruct me over dinner?"

"I?" She felt color creeping into her face. How could such a staid man have such an . . . *improper* effect on her? "I am no expert, I assure you. Social games have not risen to the same level of art in America as they have attained here."

"Then perhaps we can study the art together," he suggested, extending his arm to her.

She took it, determinedly ignoring the definite thrill that went through her at the contact. "What, shall we flatter one another while we eat? Surely that would soon become absurd."

He shrugged. "A bit of absurdity never hurt anyone."

Such a philosophy seemed at odds with what she knew of him, but she saw no sense in pointing that out. Perhaps he was trying to lighten his outlook, for her sake. "I happen to agree," she responded, as they descended to the dining room. "A sense of the ridiculous can be an asset at times, I have found."

"Have you indeed? Perhaps you can help me to acquire one, then."

Was he mocking her? Though his eyes still twinkled, she couldn't be sure. "I'm certain you would benefit thereby, so I will do my best." She smiled up at him as he seated her, so he would not take her words as criticism—though in fact they were.

Taking his own seat, Marcus motioned for the hovering footman to begin serving. "How do you propose to start? Shall I first learn to laugh at others, or at myself?"

"One must take whatever opportunities present themselves." She almost added "my lord" again, but stopped herself, fearing it might irritate him. "It is simply a matter of being on the alert for the absurdity that lurks in so many situations."

His eyes caught and held hers. "Such as our own?"

She nodded, though suddenly her heart had quickened its beat. "Prime fodder for a farce, don't you think? A man and woman bound for life who had not yet met a week before?"

"The possibilities are endless," he agreed, though from his expression she was not sure he alluded to farce. "You're right—we should explore them."

Somehow, he had done it again. A moment before she had felt in control of the conversation, but now she was out of her element. No, he needed no instruction in flirting, she decided. It was she who was ridiculously inexperienced at the game.

"This fish soup is excellent," she commented,

abruptly dropping the banter. "I must send my compliments to Mrs. MacKay."

One corner of his mouth quirked up, acknowledging her withdrawal from the sparring and claiming the victory. She found herself momentarily fascinated by that mouth, so mobile, yet so masculine. Then he spoke again.

"Curious, is it not, how people are prone to ignore the obvious while focusing on the inconsequential. Does that qualify as an absurdity, do you think?"

Gathering her courage again, she replied, "Oh, undoubtedly! As when a lady appears in a huge, ugly bonnet and all anyone mentions is how well the color of her gown becomes her."

"And the larger the 'bonnet' the greater the absurdity, I presume."

She knew he was referring to their own circumstances, and that her very refusal to acknowledge it was amusing him, but she only said, "Exactly. As though there were a cart horse in the drawing room that everyone is at pains to ignore."

"Yet what a relief when they finally acknowledge its existence, putting an end to ridiculous pretense! Or is that merely evidence of my lack of humor?"

"At . . . at some point, all hilarity has been squeezed from a situation," she confessed. "At that point, honest dealing is no doubt best."

He smiled into her eyes. "I'm pleased to hear you say so."

The footman entered again just then, to remove the soup and serve the roast pheasant, giving her a welcome opportunity to collect her scattered wits.

Attempting to move to safer ground, she asked what time he meant to go to Tattersall's on the morrow.

"Directly after breakfast, I think," he replied, apparently willing to suspend the word play. "Will you be ready to leave for the Egyptian Hall by noon, think you?"

For the remainder of the meal, they conversed safely on such topics as the amusements to be found in Town, and other parts of England he hoped to show her in the future. Though Quinn knew they were still studiously—absurdly—ignoring that cart horse in the drawing room, she decided that for the present she preferred it that way.

At least until she had decided what she truly wished to do about Marcus, about their marriage, and about her future.

When he again suggested she join him in the library at the conclusion of the meal, Quinn cravenly demurred, pleading a tiredness she by no means felt. Every moment in Marcus's presence seemed to play more strongly on her senses, dismantling the barriers she was trying to keep in place. She needed time alone—again—to repair them.

Though his smile was all too knowing, he accepted her excuse and bid her good night. "You'll wish to be well rested for our activities tomorrow, of course. I expect it will be a full day—and evening."

"Evening?" she almost squeaked. Yes, she needed to get away from him as quickly as possible.

"Did I not tell you? We have been invited to a card party at Lord and Lady Tinsdale's. Of course, we need not attend if you prefer not to."

"Oh!" She relaxed marginally. "I have no particular objection, though I have not been in the habit of playing cards much. Are the stakes likely to be high?" Might that be a way to raise funds for the girls' school she had in mind?

"It generally varies by table, so that one can find one's own level. And not everybody plays, of course. It will merely be a party with cards available. But you are tired, you said. We can discuss this tomorrow. Shall I see you up to your room?"

Last night's near disaster resonated through her, and she knew her color rose at the memory. "No! That is, there is no need. I . . . I will leave you to your brandy."

She could tell he was trying not to smile. "Very well, then. Till tomorrow, my dear." Raising her hand to his lips, he turned it over to press a lingering kiss to her wrist.

It was all she could do not to snatch it away, so intense were the sensations that swept through her at the touch of his lips to an area she had never realized was so sensitive. Then, as tendrils of fire swept outward to lick at other areas of her body, she had to fight the urge to move closer to him. When he finally released her hand, she was breathless.

"T-till tomorrow." Though she kept her head high and was careful not to walk away too quickly, she knew it was as obvious to him as it was to her that she was fleeing.

But whether from him or from her own desires, she was by no means certain.

* * *

Quinn was up early the next morning, for despite a restless night, she had gone to bed at a ridiculously early hour. Yet when she reached the dining room, she was told that Marcus had already eaten and gone, and would return for her by noon.

No doubt he was one of those "early to bed, early to rise" sorts that the moralists found so admirable, she thought, sitting down to her solitary breakfast. Just as well, she supposed, fighting a vague sense of disappointment. It wasn't as though she wished to keep late hours, mingling with the English *ton*.

She ate quickly, then went to find Polly, to see how she was settling into the household. The girl was scrubbing pots in the kitchen, looking more cheerful—and cleaner—than Quinn had yet seen her.

"Aye, it's a lot of work, milady," she confessed, in answer to Quinn's question, "but honest work, and fair wages. No one's like to beat me here—though I can't say as how I like the idea of takin' a bath so often as Mrs. Walsh says I must."

Quinn hid a grin. "You'll get used to that soon enough," she promised. "You may even grow to like being clean. If you do as Mrs. Walsh says, I've no doubt she'll find more agreeable chores for you. Perhaps you'll be promoted to chambermaid before long."

"D'ye really think so, milady?" Polly was clearly pleased by the idea. "It's a rare opportunity you've given me, and that's a fact. I wish Annie and the others could have such a chance."

"Is Annie another of Mr. Twitchell's . . . girls?" Quinn realized it was best to be vague about those girls' activities, with so many servants within earshot.

Polly nodded. "She's the one told me it weren't so bad, but I've seen her crying. And sometimes she comes back with bruises that Twitchell didn't give her."

Quinn's determination to do something for those unfortunate girls increased. "I can't believe there are so many men who would pay to abuse such young girls," she whispered, then remembered what that odious woman, Sally, had said on that subject during her own terrifying experience at the Scarlet Hawk.

"Oh, aye, there are, milady," Polly assured her as well. "Some what would surprise you—real swells and all."

"Gentlemen, do you mean?" She wasn't sure why that should seem so much worse, but it did.

Again, Polly nodded. "Some o' the girls, they've worked at being favorites with the nobs. They pay more, though they can be just as mean."

One or two of the kitchen staff appeared interested in the whispered exchange, so Quinn only sighed instead of speaking her mind. "Have you seen your brother?" she asked instead. "Mrs. Walsh was to look into a position in the stables for him."

"Oh, aye, milady! He started last night. Fair tickled he is, too—he's always been horse-mad."

"I'm pleased to hear that." And she was. Now two children were safe from the villainous Mr. Twitchell. "You'll let me, or Mrs. Walsh, know if either of you needs anything, won't you?"

"Aye, we will. And thank ye, milady." Polly bobbed a curtsy and turned back to her pots and pans.

Quinn left the kitchen thoughtfully, her relief at

rescuing Polly and Gobby tempered by her anger at the other things she'd learned. Yes it *was* worse for so-called gentlemen to patronize young girls—mere children. Those men, by virtue of their exalted positions in society, were supposed to be setting an example for the lower orders, as she understood the English social hierarchy.

Perhaps it was time someone reminded them of that. Mounting the steps to her room, she began formulating a plan—one that would put the fear of God into those depraved "gentlemen" while at the same time funding a school that would remove those poor girls from their clutches forever.

"That was most entertaining, and educational besides," said Quinn upon leaving the Egyptian Hall later that afternoon. "Thank you for bringing me . . . Marcus."

Marcus smiled down at his bride, pleased that she was calling him by his given name again. She had surprised him with her knowledge of the various artifacts they had seen. He had assumed an American education would be inferior to that of an Englishwoman of her class, but clearly that was not the case.

"You're quite welcome, of course, but I'm sure I enjoyed it as much as you did. Not having had opportunity to fight Napoleon's troops myself, I confess I developed rather a fascination for the Corsican from afar. That portion of the exhibit alone was worth the price of admission for me."

"I'm happy to know you do not feel you have wasted the afternoon, after spending your morning on my behalf as well." And she did look happy, he thought—as happy as he had seen her. He would love to see her even happier.

"This morning was no waste either, as I hope you'll agree when you see the cattle I've arranged to have sent round. We should get back, in fact, as they are to arrive at three o'clock, and it's nearly that now." He handed her up into his phaeton, sprang up beside her, and whipped up the horses to bear them home.

Home.

Odd, but the word seemed to fit better than it ever had during the years he'd shared that house with Peter and Anthony. Why was that? It wasn't as though Quinn had yet had time to stamp any sort of feminine touch upon it.

"Have you given any thought to how you'd like to redecorate your room?" he asked.

She seemed surprised by the question, but answered readily. "Yes, as it happens I made some notes on it yesterday."

"So that's what you were doing before dinner." He couldn't resist teasing her, fully aware that she'd stayed in her room to avoid him. At least she had put the time to good use. He'd half feared she might be planning another escape.

They passed Albemarle Street and Grillon's Hotel, where a pair of beggars was being shooed away from the entrance. "What think you of the state of the poor and homeless in London?" Quinn asked, abruptly changing the subject.

"I think—" Caught off guard, Marcus nearly blurted out the truth, that something needed to be done to help them, but caught himself in time. "That is, there are various societies trying to improve their lot. Certainly, I'd like to see fewer of them."

Quinn frowned at him. "The societies, or the poor?"

"The poor, of course. Can't say I've ever given them much thought, to tell the truth." He mimicked Robert's sententious tone.

"No, I suppose not," she said dryly. "One rarely sees them in Mayfair, after all. And when one does, they are doubtless rounded up and sent back to their accustomed haunts."

She was referring, he knew, to the day they'd met and the boys he had since befriended. This was dangerous ground, so he merely said, "They are safer there, surely. Less likely to attract the attention of the watchmen."

A glance showed her regarding him with distaste and disappointment, so he added, against his better judgment, "I'm not completely callous, you know. My taxes help the poor, and I've given to more than one charity in my time."

"Of course."

They turned onto Grosvenor Street then, so he returned to their prior topic, eager to abandon the riskier one. "You should just have time to change before the horses arrive. You did say your maid found something suitable?"

The irritation faded from her expressive face. "Yes, she was able to turn one of my gowns into a very passable habit. Will I try the mounts here, or will we go to the Park?"

"That will be entirely up to you." He breathed a

cautious sigh of relief that they were back to a safe subject, and one that animated her. Pulling the phaeton to a halt, he jumped down to assist her to the pavement.

"I'll take the phaeton round to the mews," he told her. "Meet me there, as that is where the horses are to be brought."

Nodding, she hurried into the house, her step light. Marcus watched her go, admiring her figure from the rear, before urging his pair forward again with a smile. If they could just avoid all topics to do with the Saint, he thought they would deal very well together. And perhaps tonight—

No, he would not think that far ahead. For now, it was enough simply to enjoy the moment.

Quinn arrived in the mews just as the men from Tattersall's appeared, leading four horses. "Excellent timing, my dear," Marcus greeted her, then turned back to regard the new arrivals with a frown. "Four? But I only selected three this morning."

"Aye," said the man he had dealt with earlier. "This one came in just after you'd left. Frisky, she is, but such a beauty I thought your lady might like to see her."

Indeed, the dainty chestnut mare had the cleanest lines and prettiest head Marcus had seen, but there was a fire in her liquid brown eye that bespoke unusual spirit. He turned to Quinn, to find her regarding the new mare with a rapt expression.

"She's lovely—remarkably like my Tempest back home. Though the others are quite nice as well, of course," she added, as though fearful of offending him.

He chuckled. "You never did tell me how experienced a rider you are, so I chose the gentlest mount they had"—he indicated the bay gelding—"as well as two others that seemed a bit livelier. Look them all over and decide which you'd like to try first."

Quinn obediently examined each horse in turn. The bay stood placidly as she stroked his flank, while the other gelding, a paler chestnut than the mare, snorted but did not shy. The gray mare Marcus had chosen merely nodded.

When Quinn approached the new chestnut mare, she skittered sideways a step, then threw up her head, tossing her golden mane. "Now, then," Quinn said firmly. Marcus's eyebrows rose with respect. She clearly knew what she was about.

The mare seemed to recognize the authority in her tone as well, calming noticeably, though her eyes were still wary. "Is she broken to sidesaddle?" Quinn asked the man holding her.

"Only just," he admitted. "There's no denying she'll need a bit of work, milady. We had a mite of trouble getting her here."

The mare's ears flattened as the man spoke, then she swung around and nipped at him.

"Here! None of that!" He brought up his crop to sting her sensitive nose, but Quinn grabbed his arm before the blow fell.

"No, don't!" she cried. "It's clear she's been mistreated. More of the same will only make her more skittish. Has she a name?"

The man shook his head. "The gent what sold her to us only called her Trouble, but I think that was because she wouldn't take to his wife."

"I'll call her Tempest, then, in memory of home."

Marcus stepped forward, startled by her decisive tone. "Hadn't you better try her—and perhaps one of the others—before naming her?" He'd known difficult horses before, and this one would be a handful, no doubt about it.

But Quinn only smiled at him. "If you insist." Once the chestnut mare was saddled, Marcus tossed Quinn to her back, bracing himself to catch her if the mare pitched her off. But though she sidled a bit, she didn't buck or rear.

"If you'd care to join me, my lord, I suggest we take her to the Park to try her paces."

Over the next half hour, Quinn showed herself to be an excellent rider—one of the best Marcus had seen, in fact. Whenever the spunky mare threatened to misbehave, she was able to bring her into line with a word and a touch, never once resorting to crop or heels. It was as though she spoke the horse's language.

He watched appreciatively as Quinn put the mare through her paces, making what he knew was quite difficult look easy. Would his bride never cease to amaze him? He rather hoped not.

When they returned home he purchased the mare for her without question, then congratulated her on her choice once the men from Tattersall's had gone.

"I admit I was skeptical, but you and Tempest seem made for each other," he said, as they entered the house, she having reluctantly left her new mount in the stables. "I hope she will make London a happier place for you."

Quinn was still flushed with triumph and exertion, looking positively beautiful, he thought—so vibrant and alive. "I believe she will. Thank you."

The gratitude shining in her eyes seemed genuine. It stirred his blood unexpectedly, and far more profoundly than the past half hour's appreciative observation of her form while riding.

"You're more than welcome, of course. I only wish I knew of more ways to make you happy," he said, drawing closer to her.

She gazed up at him, her green eyes going wide. "If I think of any, I shall be sure to let you know." Her voice sounded rather breathless. Then she blinked, glancing about the hall. The footman who had opened the door to them still stood there, only a few yards away.

"Shall we go up to change before dinner?" Marcus suggested, not taking his eyes from hers. At her nod, he extended his arm and she took it, still bemusedly watching him.

As they mounted the stairs, he could see understanding of what was to come dawning in her eyes. He saw no fear there, only anticipation of another new experience.

He was determined not to disappoint her.

Chapter 12

By the time they reached the upper hallway, Quinn felt lost in a dizzying haze. It was as though the exhilaration of riding again had swept away rational thought, leaving only sensation—and she wanted more. Caught in a current she hadn't known was there, she was now powerless to resist it, or even to want to.

"It occurs to me that you have not yet seen my chamber," Marcus said huskily, as they drew level with hers. "Would you care to?"

She could only nod, her brain apparently having abdicated, leaving her wayward body in charge.

Her hand still on his arm, Marcus opened the next door and escorted her inside. The room was similar to her own only in its masculine tone. Furnished in deep blue and pale gray, it welcomed her, from the overstuffed chairs to the exquisite landscapes on the walls . . . to the large four-poster bed near the window.

"Perhaps this is more to your taste than Anthony's decor?" he murmured, watching her.

"Yes. Yes, it is," she responded, her voice like a sigh. Somehow she couldn't seem to tear her gaze away from the bed. Would he—? Would they—?

Softly he closed the door, then turned to face her. "I'd love to share yet another remarkable experience with you," he said, reaching up to trace one finger down her cheek. "I believe you will find it most pleasant."

She pulled her attention away from the bed to meet his eyes, and was immediately lost in their deep blue depths. "Like the brandy?" she whispered.

His smile was tender, making her feel oddly cherished. "Better than brandy." He made it a promise.

With a sense of inevitability that she couldn't seem to want to fight, she took what she knew was an irrevocable step, beyond which there would be no returning. "Show me."

A flame kindled behind his eyes, and he lowered his mouth to hers, pulling her gently against him. She responded instantly, aware that she had been living for this moment since she had broken away from him two nights ago. No, since that moment at the docks. Now it was as though the intervening days had never happened, the same madness that had seized her then back in full force.

This time, when her mind tried to warn her of folly, she ruthlessly silenced it. She didn't care. Nothing else mattered. Nothing but this.

His hands were moving up her back now, unfastening the hooks of her gown one by one. For an instant she faltered, nearly retreating from his kiss, but he sensed it at once. His hands stopped and he plundered her mouth more deeply, exploring her depths with his tongue. She melted against him again, and when his fingers resumed their work, she made no protest.

He drew back then, but only slightly, kissing her temples, her ears, her throat, as he deftly worked her dress down her shoulders. She shifted slightly to help him, only then realizing that her arms had somehow found their way around his broad back.

She had to release him long enough to extricate herself from her sleeves, and then her hands were free again, to do some exploring of their own. His coat was fashionably tight-fitting, but she was able to peel him out of it, even as he went to work on her corset laces. His cravat was a puzzle, however, threatening to delay her long enough for her brain to start functioning again.

Once that happened, she feared she would never go through with this—and at this moment she desperately wanted to continue.

He chuckled, deep in his throat, at her fumbling efforts, and the sound resonated through her, stimulating already-sensitive nerve endings to a higher pitch. "Allow me," he murmured against her lips, and skillfully divested himself of both cravat and shirt, seemingly without effort.

Never before had she had opportunity to skim her hands over a bare male torso, and she took full advantage of the chance, delighting in the smooth hardness of his chest, shoulders, and arms, roughened in spots by crisp, dark hair. Suddenly she understood what inspired artists and sculptors to reproduce the male form. "You're beautiful," she whispered.

He chuckled again. "Surely, that was my line?" he asked. "But I thank you. I'm not sure anyone has ever told me that before."

Though she felt herself blushing, Quinn smiled up at him, amazed by her own audacity. "Then they should have, for it's quite true." The concept of male beauty was new to her, but she found herself embracing it fully.

To her surprise, Marcus seemed to color slightly himself. "I'd like to appreciate you as thoroughly. It is time we came to know each other completely."

His words almost—almost—frightened her, but she found herself agreeing completely. She helped him to finish unlacing her corset, to remove her shift. Her fingers faltered at the fastening of his trousers, but then he helped her again, divesting himself of the last remnant of clothing, all concealment gone. Finally, they stood before each other as nature had made them.

"Now I can say with heartfelt sincerity that you are quite beautiful yourself, my wife."

The possession in his eyes should have disturbed her, but instead she reveled in it. "And you, even more than I realized, my—my husband."

Her tongue stumbled over the word, but it was true, of course. He *was* her husband, and it was wrong to deny him—to deny the physical completion of their marriage. Still, the sight of him, freed of his nether clothing, startled her. Somehow, she hadn't realized . . .

Before she could complete the nervous thought, he moved to her, took her in his arms, and lifted her.

She felt suddenly tiny, encompassed by his strength, which somehow aroused her further, and then he laid her on the very bed that had so fascinated her.

"I want you to be my wife in truth, as well as in name," he whispered. "But I will do nothing you do not want. Tell me what you want, Quinn."

"You," she responded, her voice strange and wild in her ears. "You . . . promised me new experiences."

"And you shall have them."

He knelt beside her on the bed and, hands on her shoulders, gently coaxed her to lie on her back. Quinn felt vulnerable in such a position, but excitedly expectant. She gazed up at him, watching his expression, trying to guess what he would do next.

His eyes swept over her, as though exploring every detail of her body by the golden afternoon light from the windows. She had never felt more exposed, but though she knew she was blushing, she made no move to cover herself. It was as though his gaze was a physical thing, caressing where it touched, stimulating and soothing simultaneously.

Then his eyes met hers, and he smiled, a slow, lazy smile with a power behind it that she didn't understand—but wanted to. She smiled back, certain now that she must be mad. Just as she began to wonder what sort of spell he had cast over her, he leaned down and kissed her, sending her mind back to whatever region it had retreated to before, leaving her body again in ascendancy.

Her eyes drifted closed and she relaxed, molding to the feathered mounds beneath her. Softly, he touched her cheek then, his fingers featherlike, caressed her throat, her shoulder, her breastbone. When his hand finally came to rest upon her breast, she breathed deeply, arching her back slightly to intensify the pleasurable contact.

Now his lips began to move as well, first exploring the edges of her mouth, then the curves of her face, nuzzling her neck, sweeping back up to tease her earlobe, and then her lips again—but only briefly. He began to trace the path his hand had followed, nipping at her collarbone, making her twitch, while his thumb traced circles around her breast, ever-smaller circles that centered on her sensitive nipple.

Again she caught her breath, startled by the intensity of the sensations he was producing. His mouth continued its exploration, kissing, nibbling, until his tongue took over his thumb's activity. She arched further, thrusting her breasts shamelessly up at him, reveling in the way he captured one in his mouth, suckling her, massaging her with his tongue. His left hand slid lower, while the right now cupped her other breast, teasing it as he had the left one.

At first his left hand, trailing fire down her rib cage toward her belly, was a mere distraction, her senses focused on what he was doing to her breasts. Never had she realized her body was capable of such sensory abandon, such wanton pleasure! Then his hand moved lower still, tracing her navel, brushing the top of the curls below.

Quinn shuddered, but it was a shudder of delight, though mingled with vague alarm. For a fire was growing, an inch or two lower than his questing fingers—a hungry fire that clamored for feeding. Though her breasts still strained toward his touch, his tongue, now she pressed upward with her hips, urging on the progress of his hand.

Heedless of her urging, he took his time, burying his fingers in her curls, inching toward the goal that cried out for his touch. She felt as though every nerve in her body was alight, alive, almost—but not quite—overwhelmed. She wanted to be overwhelmed. A faint whimpering distracted her, then she realized with a small shock that it had come from her own throat.

He lifted his head, releasing her breast, and she had to fight the urge to cry out in protest before he shifted his attention to her other breast, renewing the exquisite sensations there even as his left hand moved lower still.

Quinn swallowed convulsively, not sure how much more of this sweet torture she could endure. She clasped his head to her breast, twining her fingers through his hair, though her focus was more on his hand than his head, the hunger for his touch reaching unbearable heights.

Then, one quick finger stroked the cleft, the heart of her desire, making her gasp aloud. Releasing her breast again, he covered her mouth with his own, even as he stroked again. And again.

Each touch intensified her pleasure, her longing, to previously unimaginable levels. Was there a limit to how much pleasure a person could experience? She hoped not, even as she suspected she might die of it. Thrusting her hips higher, she opened herself to his touch, inviting him to do whatever he wished, to take her to whatever brink awaited.

She felt him shifting above her, moving into a position that gave him better access, and she welcomed it. Then, still stroking with a rhythm that sent flame licking all the way to her toes, he slipped one finger inside of her, then withdrew it. Then again, and again, while he mimicked the rhythm below with his kiss.

Arching ever upward, she felt something hard between their bodies, something hot and smooth. Sliding her arms around his back, she pulled Marcus down to her, encouraging him to press his whole length against her, wanting to feel more of him against more of her. Lifting his head, he smiled down at her, his eyes dark and smoky. She suspected hers were the same.

"Enjoying your new experiences so far?" he murmured, never stopping his rhythmic stroking.

The power of speech completely beyond her, she nodded. His smile broadened for an instant, and he was kissing her again, his body moving with the same rhythm his hand had established.

His shaft, which had seemed impossibly large when she first beheld it, now slid along her belly, teasing and tormenting her while his fingers continued to spur on her desire. Wriggling a bit, she shifted under his warm weight until his shaft pressed against her cleft, nudging his hand out of the way, its tip moving against her most sensitive spot.

She opened to him, and gradually, gradually, he moved lower, until he was entering her, barely entering her. She wanted more. Breaking her own mouth free of his, she frantically covered his face with kisses, pulling him tight against her, trying to show him with her body what she needed, though she herself wasn't entirely sure what that was.

But he seemed to know. Growling deep in his throat, he drove deeper and deeper into her, though she could tell that he was still holding back. She wanted all of him. *Now.*

Wrapping her legs around him, she drove him home, deep, deep into her depths. Her body protested with a slight stretching, pulling ache, but it was nothing to the triumph she felt at engulfing him fully, taking him completely into herself. He plunged ahead, needing no more urging, taking what he needed from her even as she took what she needed from him.

Just when Quinn was sure her body could take no more of this ecstasy without exploding or dissolving, she reached a new pinnacle, and all thought was left behind, drowned in a wave of pure sensation that tossed her in its mighty grip. As if from a distance, she heard her own voice and his, crying out in unison.

He thrust once, twice more, then lay still atop her, while she felt as though her body had turned to liquid—warm, sweet liquid, like the sherry she had drunk on her wedding day. Never had she felt more fulfilled, more physically sated.

Gradually her body stopped thrumming, allowing thought back in. Slowly her mind regained control, analyzing what had just happened in a sort of surprise. Who could have guessed she possessed such wanton desires? That she could abandon herself to them so completely? Had such wickedness always been a part of her?

It hadn't felt wicked, however. Nor could she bring herself to regret what had been the most intense experience of her life—though what it might mean for her future she had not yet had time to contemplate.

Above her, Marcus stirred.

Belatedly realizing that his full weight lay on Quinn's small frame, he propped himself up on his arms, gazing down at her beneath him. Her eyes drifted open to meet his, passion still visible in their green depths, though now a question flickered there as well.

"That was . . . remarkable," he whispered. "Thank you."

Now her eyes widened, one eyebrow quirking upward. "Surely that was my line?"

He chuckled, relieved. Though she had clearly enjoyed his lovemaking, he hadn't been at all sure how she would react once it was over. Their budding friendship still seemed to be intact—a fact that mattered far more to him than he'd expected.

"That's two experiences I've shared with you today," he said, managing a teasing tone despite the emotions that threatened to overwhelm him.

"Three, if we count riding in the Park." Though still slightly breathless, her own voice was light as well. "I can't help but wonder what else you may have in store for me."

Unable to help himself, he captured her lips, still swollen and ripe, for a quick kiss before replying.

"Even a balloon ascension will seem tame after this. At least, I hope it will."

"Do you mean this wasn't the balloon ascension?" she teased. "I could have sworn I was high in the air a moment ago." Then she blushed deeply, as though suddenly realizing what she'd said.

Laughing again, he rolled off her, though he'd have preferred to lie there with her—in her—for hours. He felt a sudden need to distance himself, emotionally as well as physically. To figure out just what this was she was doing to him. Facing away from her, he sat on the edge of the bed.

"I suppose we should dress for dinner soon—unless you would prefer to have it sent up to us here?" He glanced over his shoulder at her and winked.

She stared at him for a moment, then frowned. "That's tempting, but I suppose we should go down—particularly if we mean to attend that card party afterward."

Marcus bit back an oath. He'd forgotten all about the invitation to the Tinsdales' house. "It will be an opportunity to show the world that all is well—and perfectly respectable—with our marriage," he said. "Advisable, therefore, for the sake of your reputation."

Just now, however, he'd have preferred to spend the evening alone with her, just as they were now—which was dangerous for reasons having nothing to do with her reputation.

"If you think it advisable, then I suppose we should go—though I confess I feel anything but respectable at the moment." She smiled up at him, glorious in her nudity, and he felt his heart twist within him. How had she become so precious to him so quickly?

Clearing his throat, he stood and reached for his clothing. "You can go through the dressing room to your own chamber if you'd prefer. Then you won't have to dress to go out into the hallway."

He heard her sitting up behind him, but didn't turn, afraid that one more glimpse of her luscious body would catapult him right back into bed with her.

"Yes. Yes, I'll do that." Her voice sounded odd, so he risked a glance over his shoulder. She had retrieved her gown from the floor and now held it before her, screening her dainty charms from his view. Such belated modesty should have been funny, but he felt no inclination to laugh.

She slipped from the bed and gathered up the rest of her things, then, with a last, tentative smile, disappeared through the dressing-room door. A few moments later he heard her ringing for her maid, and he belatedly rang for his own valet.

No doubt he would feel more like himself once he was dressed, once he'd had a chance to consider everything rationally. But as Clarence appeared to help him into his evening clothes, he suspected he would never be quite the same again.

Dinner was a strange meal. Oh, the fillet of sole was light and flaky and the pheasant done to a turn, doing great credit to Mrs. McKay's skill. But what on earth did one talk about after a passionate bout of lovemaking with a husband one scarcely knew?

Quinn was only slightly comforted by the observation that Marcus seemed nearly as awkward as she in finding suitable topics of conversation. She was certain this had not been his first experience with a woman, as it had hers with a man—but perhaps he had not been in the habit of dining with his paramours afterward?

"What time are we expected at the Tinsdales'?" she asked, realizing even as the words left her mouth that she had asked the same question not five minutes earlier—not that she had attended to Marcus's reply.

"People will be arriving throughout the evening," he responded, reminding her why she hadn't recalled his previous answer. There hadn't really been one. "We can arrive when we choose, and leave when we choose, except in the very unlikely event that one of the royal dukes should make an appearance."

"Of course." Already his words faded from her mind, as she watched his hand move from his plate to his mouth. What remarkable hands he had . . .

"Would you care for more turnips?" he asked then, apparently noting her interest in the motions of his eating. "Not one of my favorite vegetables, but McKay makes them quite edible."

She blinked, focusing again on her own plate, trying not to dwell on how those remarkable hands had made her feel. "I . . . I seem to have plenty still, but thank you." She was not overfond of turnips herself, so she cut a small piece of pheasant and brought it to her lips.

Glancing up, she saw him watching her lips with an odd half smile before he noticed her gaze and attended again to his food. Now she was able to watch his lips, as remarkable as his hands, envying his fork with each bite he took.

But this was absurd! She could not let mere animal passions—for surely, that was all this could be—overset her reason and subvert her goals.

Could she?

"What games do you think will likely be played tonight?" she asked, in another attempt to divert her mind from the rebellious channels it persisted in taking.

He blinked, then frowned slightly, his eyes losing the oddly distant expression they'd held for much of the meal. "Whist, of course, and likely a table or two of piquet and perhaps vingt-et-un. It will depend on what the guests fancy. If you've a particular favorite, I've no doubt you'll find others to make up a table. Have you?"

"Have I what?" She'd been watching his lips again, losing track of what they were saying.

"A favorite game."

Oh. "A, er, a card game? No, not really." Had she left all of her wits upstairs in his bedchamber? It seemed so. "I do know how to play whist a little, though."

He was regarding her rather strangely, she thought, and no wonder. "Well. That's good, then." For a moment he looked as though he were about to say something more, but then his eyes seemed to lose focus again, and he absentmindedly took another bite of pheasant.

A very sensual bite.

Oh, stop it! she scolded herself. Determinedly, she turned her full attention to her own plate. If he felt the need for any more conversation, he could select a topic. She refused to make a fool of herself by opening her mouth again until she had herself firmly in hand.

He appeared to feel no burning need to chat, however, so they passed the remainder of the meal in awkward silence. "Shall we go, then?" Marcus asked, rising as the last course was finally removed.

Quinn stood, relieved to be finished with what had surely been the longest meal of her life. "Certainly. Let me just ring for my maid to bring down my spencer and bonnet."

Her abigail brought the lightweight short jacket of salmon cambric to wear over her pale peach evening gown—all she would need, as the evening was yet warm. When Monette would have slipped it over Quinn's shoulders, however, Marcus stepped forward and took the spencer from her to do that office himself.

The light brush of his hands on her upper arms sent a most outrageous thrill through her—one she tried unsuccessfully to subdue, though she was fairly certain she hid it well. "Thank you, my lord," she said lightly, flashing him a quick, bright smile.

He smiled back, a vague puzzlement in his eyes, and extended his arm to lead her to their waiting carriage.

The crowd at the Tinsdales' was not large, as the Season was essentially over, but still there were more people there than Marcus would have preferred. Odd, considering that he'd always felt perfectly at home in social situations. Looking about at the assemblage, some of whom were already congregating at the tables scattered about the small ballroom and anterooms, he wished for nothing more than to be back home—with Quinn.

"Marcus! I confess, I didn't expect to see you here, after reading word of your marriage mere days ago!" Lord Fernworth, with a few others of his social set converged upon him. "This is our new Lady Marcus, I perceive?"

His grin was not quite a leer, but Marcus felt an irrational urge to plant him a facer nonetheless. As usual, Ferny had quite clearly been drinking more than was good for him.

"My lady, may I present Lord Fernworth." The introduction was stiff, so he attempted a lighter tone as he turned to the others. "I believe you met Sir Cyril Weathers at the Trumballs' last week, and this is Mr. Thatcher. Is Peter about, Harry?"

Harry Thatcher made a show of kissing Quinn's hand—probably because he'd noticed Marcus's reaction to Ferny's words—then shook his head. "He may turn up later on, but he had some business or other to attend to first. But you know me—I hate to be late to a party."

"Hate to miss any chance of someone else's wine," Marcus retorted, but then he grinned, taking the edge from his words. Harry could keep pace with Ferny and then some, and often did, but he was Peter's closest friend—and he himself had always liked the fellow. Why was he so touchy this evening?

"Oh, almost forgot," Lord Fernworth said then. "Here's a fellow who particularly wanted to make your acquaintance. His father and mine were friends, though I haven't seen much of him since our school days. Been in the country the past year or two, ain't you, Noel? Lord Marcus Northrup, Lady Marcus, let me make known to you Mr. Noel Paxton."

The gentleman named stepped forward with a pleasant smile that nevertheless hinted at a steely purpose. "Delighted to make your acquaintance, my lord, my lady," he said, bowing. "I hadn't realized you were newly wed when I asked Lord Fernworth to introduce me. I've no wish to intrude, of course."

"No intrusion, Mr. Paxton," said Quinn graciously, offering her hand. "We are here to socialize, after all."

Marcus nodded. "Always delighted to meet a friend of Ferny's, of course."

"I'm glad to hear that," Mr. Paxton replied. "At some point, when it is convenient for you, of course, I'd like to have a private word with you, Lord Marcus."

Fernworth chuckled. "Oh, yes, I should have mentioned that Noel is come to Town at Sir Nathaniel's request to act as a sort of special consultant for the Bow Street Runners. He spent some time during the war gathering intelligence, and the Runners thought to put his skills to peacetime use."

Marcus managed to look only mildly interested. "Oh?"

Mr. Paxton nodded. "With the war over, I confess I've rather missed a challenge. But now I believe I may have found a fresh one in this legendary Saint of Seven Dials."

Chapter 13

~~~⌒◯◯⌒~~~

Quinn smiled up at the newcomer, though she wondered at Marcus's sudden stillness beside her. "An admirable pursuit no doubt, Mr. Paxton, but I'm not sure I can bring myself to wish you luck," she said. "I only became aware of the Saint's existence yesterday, upon reading about him in the paper, but he seems quite a heroic figure to me."

"To you and to most other ladies, from what I have heard," Mr. Paxton replied. "But there is no denying that the man is a thief, and one of the most worthy adversaries I've faced. I'll pursue him with proper respect for his prowess, if that is of any comfort to you."

The gentlemen all chuckled, though Quinn thought Marcus's laugh sounded rather forced. Clearly his disapproval of the Saint went even deeper than she had realized.

"But why would you wish to talk to me about him?" Marcus asked then. "I certainly know no more of the man than anyone here—perhaps less than most."

Mr. Paxton's smile never wavered, but there was something in his expression that made Quinn shiver. "Perhaps you know more than you realize. At least, that is my hope. But enough of that for now. If you will send word when you have a free hour, I'll call on you at your convenience."

Marcus shrugged. "As you wish. But now, I have promised to show my wife how some of our English games are played. If you will excuse me?"

Mr. Paxton and the others repeated their felicitations on their marriage, and Marcus led Quinn away from the group toward one of the tables just forming.

"You won't help that man catch the Saint of Seven Dials, will you?" she asked him once they were out of earshot.

"As I said, I can't imagine how I could. If I had the means, however, I wouldn't hesitate to assist in the fellow's capture—if only to remove him as competition." He punctuated his words with a wink.

Quinn felt warmed by such evidence of his regard, even if he was only teasing. Memories of what had passed between them only a few hours ago made her color and look away, driving all thought of the Saint of Seven Dials from her mind—for the moment.

Marcus shook his head in wonderment as Quinn took her fourth hand of whist. Either his bride had been less than honest about her experience with the game, or she was a natural at cards. It was almost a shame the stakes were so low.

"You're quite the quick study, I must say, my dear," he told her as the points were tallied up. "Shall we try something else and give others a chance here?"

Quinn rose with no show of reluctance. "Yes, I would like to learn the other fashionable games as well—if you don't mind?"

"Not at all." He managed not to grin, helped by the sense of foreboding that had hung over him since meeting Mr. Paxton. The man must have questions about Luke, and he hoped he would be able to answer them without putting his friend in any danger.

"Thank you both," Quinn said to the others at the table. "This has been most instructive."

Mr. and Mrs. Heatherton, who had agreed to help in Quinn's instruction, responded graciously, though if their words had a slightly sour edge, Marcus could hardly blame them.

"What would you care to try next?" he asked as they moved among the other widely scattered tables. "Euchre, perhaps? Piquet I can show you at home, as it allows but two players."

"Euchre would be fine," she replied, "though I've played it before, both three- and four-handed. I would like to learn piquet, I confess."

He glanced down, but her eyes were averted, her cheeks a shade pinker than normal. Was she suggesting she'd like to go home? To be alone with him? Certainly he had no objection. He was finding it difficult to focus on the games anyway, between his awareness of Quinn and the looming interview with Mr. Paxton.

"I'd like to teach you," he said after only a slight hesitation. "Shall we take leave of our hosts, then?"

Her color deepened further, but she smiled. "I have no objection if you do not, my lord."

"No. No objection whatsoever." In fact, he preferred to leave before Peter could put in an appearance. And Quinn—Quinn was more alluring than ever, her dusky curls offering a sensual contrast to her creamy throat and pale peach gown.

With a start, he realized that he was in grave danger of becoming besotted with his own wife. Worse, at the moment he didn't much care, as long as he could have her in his arms, in his bed, again. "Let's find Lord and Lady Tinsdale, then, shall we?"

"No need to apologize for your early departure," Lady Tinsdale assured them a few moments later. "I am flattered that you came at all, so soon after your wedding. What a surprise that announcement was to us all! But an agreeable one, of course."

Her eyes betrayed her curiosity to know the details behind such a hasty wedding, but she was too well bred to ask awkward questions. Marcus was exceedingly grateful that Lady Mountheath was not in attendance that night, however.

"You are too kind, my lady."

"Indeed," Quinn agreed. "We look forward to seeing you again soon." And on that amiable note, they left for the short carriage ride back to Grosvenor Street.

"That was pleasant," Quinn remarked as she took her place beside him on the seat. "Thank you for suggesting it."

"You are more than welcome, of course. I'm pleased you enjoyed it." Marcus was glad the ride *was* short. The dark, intimate confines of the carriage made him all the more eager to resume Quinn's introduction to new delights. So eager, in fact, that he found it difficult to sustain a coherent conversation, while her frequent silences made him wonder whether she was similarly preoccupied.

Helping her from the carriage a few minutes later, Marcus was startled at the effect the mere touch of her hand had upon him. He'd been infatuated before in his youth. If that was all this was, he knew only one certain cure—to get his fill of her. A most appealing notion, on several levels.

"Did you wish to play at piquet now, or would you prefer to learn when you are fresh from a night's sleep?" he asked, as they entered the house.

Her glance was mischievous. "Well, since you put it that way, I suppose I would learn more quickly when my wits are sharper."

"I was rather hoping you would say that." Already his body was anticipating hers, chafing at any delay.

"I thought perhaps you were."

Absentmindedly handing his hat and coat to a hovering footman, he held her eyes with his and watched as her smile slowly faded, to be replaced by an urgent question, a hunger nearly matching his own. His impatience increased.

"Come. An early night will do us both good."

She swallowed visibly, but nodded, pausing only to put off her bonnet before allowing him to escort her up the stairs. At the door to her chamber, she hesitated. "Should I—?"

"I can help you undress for the night. If that would be—"

"Yes," she said breathlessly. "That would be most . . . kind of you."

He opened the door and with a glance—echoed by a nod from Quinn—dismissed her waiting abigail, who disappeared with a knowing smile. For an instant, Quinn frowned, as though having second thoughts.

"She's French," Marcus reminded her. "I'm sure she approves thoroughly—and will be quite discreet."

Quinn's frown disappeared, and she swayed closer to him. "I suppose so. And even if she is not, we are married."

"Precisely." A week ago, those words would have been profoundly disturbing to him, but now he found them strangely erotic. "Here, let me help you out of your things."

She turned obediently and, slipping his hands beneath her spencer, he stripped it from her, caressing her shoulders and bare arms as he divested her of the thin jacket. "You'll be warm enough without that, I think."

"Yes. I'm feeling . . . very warm indeed. Perhaps too warm."

He needed no further encouragement. "I'll soon remedy that—though perhaps only briefly." Turning her so that she faced away from him, he went to work on the row of tiny buttons down the back of her gown. As the dress parted, inch by inch, he couldn't resist leaning forward to kiss the creamy flesh now revealed above her stays and shift.

She inhaled sharply at the first touch of his lips, but did not protest, and he continued until she was able to step free of the gown. Carefully, just as though he were her servant, he gathered up the peach fabric and laid it across the chest at the foot of the bed. Then he turned back to her with a wink.

"I want to stay in your abigail's good graces, you see. Otherwise, she might be unwilling to let me take over her duties again."

Quinn's eyes widened. "Again?"

"One never knows. Now, let's see." Her corset laced down the back, so he again turned her away from him, this time nuzzling her neck while he worked. Her dark curls tickled his nose, tantalizing him with a faint scent of roses.

Once her stays were removed, he knelt to remove her shoes and stockings, one by one. She stood mesmerized, obediently lifting each foot for him. He hadn't had a chance to explore her legs earlier, but now he ran his hands from knee to ankle, appreciating their slim strength. A sudden urgency seized him, to have those legs again wrapped around him as he buried himself in her.

Standing, he glanced around the room. "I hadn't realized just how oppressive Anthony's tastes are. Would you care to accompany me to my room?"

She nodded. "I like your room better—at least until I can redecorate." Clad only in her shift, her hair about her shoulders, she looked younger than her twenty years, but he knew that the body—and desires—of a woman lay beneath the thin cotton.

"So do I. Come, then."

He led her through the dressing room and into his own chamber, where candles had been newly lit and a decanter and pair of glasses stood ready on his desk. It appeared Quinn's abigail had tipped off his valet— or perhaps Clarence had acted on his own initiative.

The candlelight warmed the blues and grays, casting flickering shadows across the beckoning bed. "As I stood in for your maid, perhaps you would care to assist in my valet's absence?" suggested Marcus, turning to Quinn with a smile.

"That seems only fair." With an answering smile, she moved to strip him of his coat, then his waistcoat and shirt, skimming her hands down his arms as he had done, then sliding her palms across his bare chest. "Mmm," she murmured appreciatively.

Did she know what she was doing to him? "I'm still half-dressed," he reminded her hoarsely.

Her brows rose in mock surprise. "So you are. How negligent of me." Kneeling, she removed his shoes and stockings, even as he had removed hers, lingering over his legs and feet. Her position put the top of her head in close proximity to the bulge in his breeches, arousing him further, though she seemed oblivious.

When she stood again, they were very close, her breasts nearly brushing against him. She hesitated for a long moment before reaching to unfasten his breeches, now straining over his arousal. When it sprang free, she stepped back, glancing down and then averting her eyes. Nervously, she licked her lips, and he felt it as intensely as though her mouth were upon him.

Visibly summoning her courage, she stepped forward again to peel his fashionably tight-fitting knee breeches from his legs, unable to keep her eyes from his erection, only inches away from her face. When she stood again, he was naked as the day he was born, his whole body on fire for this remarkable woman he had married against his will.

"Now you are the one who is overdressed," he told her.

"And whose fault is that?" she whispered.

"Allow me to rectify the matter." In one swift motion, he lifted her shift over her head and tossed it over the back of his desk chair. "Now we are equals."

She blinked at him. "What an extraordinary statement. I like it."

He hadn't really intended a broader meaning than their mutual nudity, but Marcus decided he could live with it. In almost every way except in the eyes of the law, they *were* equals. And he liked that, too.

"Equal, but still different, of course," he clarified.

She grinned up at him, delighting him with her lack of fear, or even diffidence. "*Vive la différence*," she said, a wicked glint in her eye.

Then she was in his arms, though he wasn't sure which of them had moved first. He found her mouth with his, probing deeply, claiming and possessing her. She felt so right, molded against him like this. Her arms came around him, smoothing up his back, massaging his shoulders.

In return, he skimmed his hands down to her tiny waist, stroking the feminine swell of her bottom, pulling her more tightly to him. Her smallness made him feel fiercely protective and powerful at the same time. To think that he'd once said he preferred statuesque women . . .

She tangled her fingers in his hair, standing on her tiptoes to deepen the kiss, pressing her belly more firmly against his arousal. He slipped a hand between them to explore her cleft with one finger and found her slick and ready for him. She tightened convulsively around his finger, nearly making him climax on the spot.

With a groan, he grabbed her bottom with both hands and hoisted her up to impale her on his swollen shaft. Instinctively, she wrapped her legs around him, his body mostly supporting her. She seemed to weigh nothing at all. Reveling in their size difference, he lifted her up, then lowered her, rhythmically.

When she tightened again, this time around something far more sensitive than his finger, his knees nearly gave way. He took two quick steps and sat on the edge of the bed, still buried deep inside her. Now she had some leverage of her own and moved atop him, while at the same time moving her lips across his jaw to nibble at his earlobe.

"I never guessed England would hold such incredible experiences for me," she breathed, then caught her breath in a gasp as he drove upward. She caught the rhythm at once, rocking on his lap, driving him to the very edge of his tenuous control.

Again he slid a hand between them, wanting her pleasure to equal his own. He found her nubbin with his thumb and stroked in tempo with his thrusts, with her rocking rhythm. Throwing back her head so that her hair streamed down her bare back, she gasped again, gripping him, releasing him, faster and faster.

Against his chest, her nipples went suddenly hard, and she cried out, then quickly muffled the sound against his shoulder. Freed by her release, he gave himself over to the glory of passion, pounding into her two, three more times, before the world exploded around him and he heard his own voice panting her name.

She collapsed against him, as spent as he, and he lay back until he was cradling her in his arms, sideways across the wide bed. He felt dazed. Even this afternoon, as far beyond any previous experience as it had been, was nothing to this. He felt as though he had emptied his very soul into her.

It was a long time before either of them spoke, and he wondered whether she had been as shattered by the experience as he. Finally she stirred, tilting her head back to look at him in the flickering candlelight.

"Will our next conversation be as awkward as the one over dinner, do you think?"

He nearly choked on a laugh at such an unexpected question. "Surely not. We can talk about whist now. Or piquet, once I've taught you."

She giggled. "Or horses. Why didn't we think of that at dinner?"

"Distracted, perhaps?" Marcus gave her a squeeze. Far from getting her out of his system, at the moment she felt delicious against him, and completely necessary. He supposed he should hope that the feeling would fade with the afterglow of lovemaking, but he didn't. How could one wish away happiness?

"Mmm. Perhaps." She nuzzled his neck, and he

felt himself growing hard again inside her. "You're surprisingly distracting, my lord."

"I'll take that as a compliment, and must say that the same is true of you, my lady."

She must have noticed his arousal, for she squeezed him playfully. "I'm flattered."

Slowly, he began moving within her, savoring every languorous sensation. He took his time, exploring her body with his hands, enjoying her doing the same with his.

"Has anyone ever told you you have beautiful legs?" he asked, stroking her from hip to calf.

"No—but then, I've never bared them to anyone but you." Ducking her head, she experimentally licked one of his nipples, sending unexpected sensations straight to his groin. He moved faster inside her.

"Well, you do. And I'm glad."

"That I have beautiful legs?" She licked the other nipple, seeming pleased with the result of her first trial.

He kissed the top of her head. "No, that only I have seen them. Did you never go swimming back in Baltimore?"

"I . . . no. I never had a chance to learn, as there was no suitable place nearby." There were odd pauses between her words, as though she was finding it hard to concentrate. He grinned.

"Then that is something else I will teach you— though not here in London."

"I look forward to it—oh!" He had slid his hand between them to stroke her again, and she responded as eagerly as he'd hoped.

In no hurry, since they had the whole night before them, Marcus set about pleasuring his lady as thoroughly as the hours ahead would allow.

Quinn stirred and stretched, a feeling of well-being permeating her. Her arm touched something solid and warm. Startled, she opened her eyes, to see blue bed hangings in the early-morning light. Memory rushed back, both sweet and alarming. Had she really done all those things? Had he?

Roused by her touch, Marcus rolled over and greeted her with a sleepy smile, his eyes as blue as the draperies. "Good morning, my lady."

Yes, they really had. Quinn felt herself blushing, though she knew it was rather late for modesty—or regret. "Good morning, my lord," she replied, confused by her conflicting feelings. "I . . . I suppose I should return to my room, to dress. My abigail—"

"Your clothes are there, at any rate. But don't worry about what your maid may think. As you pointed out last night, we are married, after all." His wink unsettled her further.

Everything that had seemed so right, so natural, so . . . necessary last night seemed a species of madness today. How could she have been so very wanton—and enjoyed it so? Even now, his smile had the power to stir her. She sat up, her back to him.

"Yes, you're right of course. I'm being foolish." An understatement, surely! "I'll see you downstairs for breakfast shortly."

Slipping from the bed, she snatched her shift from the back of his desk chair and pulled it over her head before turning to face him, only to find him frowning questioningly.

"There's no hurry, you know. But if you are hungry—"

"Famished," she declared, oddly anxious to remove herself from his influence before she could be sucked back into the magic of the night. She needed to find herself again, to separate what was real from the delusions of fantasy.

"I'll see you downstairs, then."

The question remained in his eyes, but she couldn't answer it just then. Not until she had answered it for herself. With a cheery wave, she headed through the dressing room to her own chamber. There, after a quick wash with the cold water in her basin, she rang for her abigail.

Monette appeared, her expression carefully blank. "Yes, milady. You wish to dress, or would you prefer a tray brought up first?"

"Actually," she said on sudden decision, "I would like a bath before anything else. Pray have hot water brought up at once."

Though the bath eased the lingering soreness between her legs and washed away all physical signs of her passionate night, it did nothing to cleanse her thoughts of their wanton leanings. Toweling her hair dry while Monette laced up her corset, Quinn admitted she wanted nothing more than another night like the one just past.

Laying aside the towel, she seated herself at her dressing table so that Monette could brush out her damp curls and stared at her reflection in the glass.

Her face, her green eyes, looked no different than they had yesterday morning, but she knew she had changed irretrievably. She was truly a woman now, and . . .

Dear Lord, she was in love. In love with her husband. Stodgy as he was—everywhere but the bedroom—antithesis of everything she was herself, representative of the very sort of people who had cast off her mother, Quinn had fallen head over heels in love with Marcus.

In a daze, she allowed Monette to dress her in a fetching pink day dress, wondering what she should do with her shattering discovery. She mustn't let Marcus guess, of course. In all of his endearments by candlelight, he had never spoken of love—and it would be absurd to expect it, as they still scarcely knew each other, except physically.

No, she would keep this knowledge to herself until such time as she had reason to believe her feelings were returned. Or until they faded on their own, which was surely just as likely. After all, what did she and Marcus have in common, besides mutual lust? She could afford to wait.

But meanwhile, there could be no thought of leaving, of attempting to return to America. To do so would be to rip her heart from her breast, and for what? For the sake of a family business that would continue profitably without her? She had found work at least as important here, she realized, remembering her idea for a girls' school.

"Thank you, Monette." Her toilette complete, she headed downstairs, wondering whether Marcus would have finished eating by now, as she had taken such a long time in her chamber. Even so, she risked a detour to the kitchens before joining him in the dining room.

"Mrs. McKay, may I borrow Polly from you for an errand?" she asked when the cook greeted her in surprise.

"Why of course, my lady. But wouldn't one of the footmen—?"

Quinn shook her head. "Not for this particular errand, but thank you. Polly?"

The girl hurried over to her, while the cook discreetly moved out of earshot. "Yes, milady?" Already the girl's accent had lost a trace of its rough edge.

"I'd like you to go to Grillon's Hotel and ask whether there is a message for 'A Sympathetic Lady.' If there is not, I'll need you to check tomorrow, as well. Or—do you suppose your brother would be willing to do so? I would pay him, of course."

"Oh, aye, milady! I'll go today, and ask Gobby to go tomorrow, if need be."

"Perfect. Thank you, Polly. Bring any message to me privately."

The girl bobbed a curtsy and promised to do as asked, betraying not the slightest curiosity. Quinn smiled and left her, hurrying now to the dining room.

"I was wondering whether you had fallen asleep again," Marcus exclaimed, rising to help her to a chair. "A bath?" He touched a damp tendril of her hair with an intimate smile that made her toes curl.

"Yes. I'm sorry I took so long. And I really am famished!"

At his signal, a footman brought her a plate loaded with ham, toast and shirred eggs, as well as a steaming pot of chocolate. She tucked into it eagerly, for her overnight exertions had indeed stimulated a prodigious appetite.

"You weren't exaggerating, I see," said Marcus with a grin. "As soon as you finish, I was wondering if—" But at that moment, a loud knock sounded at the front door.

They glanced at each other curiously, then turned at the heavy sound of approaching footsteps. James appeared in the dining-room doorway, looking rather flustered. "Captain Peverill," he announced.

Before Quinn or Marcus could rise, the captain pushed past the footman, into the dining room. "Sorry to intrude so early," he said gruffly, "but I haven't much time. My ship sails on the afternoon tide, and I have a lot to do before then."

Chapter 14

Quinn stared. "You are leaving, Papa? Aboard what ship?" None had been listed as leaving for Baltimore in the shipping news she had perused yesterday.

"One of our own, of course—the *Atalanta*. She's to take on barrels of wine in Lisbon and Madeira before heading home."

Which meant its destination had been listed as Portugal rather than Baltimore, of course. Taken completely off guard by this development, she protested, "But the *Atalanta* was not to sail for two more weeks—I remember the schedule clearly."

"Shipping schedules change constantly, you know that, Quinn. We're taking advantage of the weather, as well as news of an exceptional new winery in Lisbon. I'm hoping to be one of the first to bring their wares to America."

Quinn had to nod—she'd likely have recommended the same course had she still had a hand in the business. Which she never would again, it appeared. This sudden departure left her no chance even to consider accompanying him—as he'd doubtless intended.

When she did not respond, Marcus rose and bowed. "I'm certain you will wish to say your farewells in private. As I've finished my meal, I will leave you to do so and attend to some business of my own."

The captain watched him go, then smiled at Quinn. "Such a fine young man, Quinnling. Again, I congratulate you. I can depart secure in the knowledge that I'm leaving you in good hands."

The resentment Quinn had felt on her wedding day came flooding back, making her momentarily forget what had passed since. "Is that why you forced me into marriage? To relieve you of responsibility for me?"

Her father helped himself to coffee and some pastries from the sideboard, then seated himself across the table from her, his eyes shadowed. "I hope you're saying that to relieve your understandable irritation with me, and don't really believe it. You've never been a burden to me, Quinnling. Never."

She knew it was true. She'd more than pulled her weight at home, particularly since her mother's death. "Then why? So that you could point to me and say that your daughter married the son of a duke?"

"I can't deny I'll enjoy that," he replied, his expression showing more self-knowledge than she'd have credited him with. "But my main concern was always your welfare. After—"

His voice broke, and he cleared his throat noisily before continuing. "After your mother died, you changed. Distanced yourself from me, Charles, all of your friends, and flung yourself into the business. I can't deny it was good for the business, but I knew it wasn't good for you. A young woman needs friends, parties, admirers—and a husband and children of her own."

"So that's why you brought me to England? To force me back into the world and separate me from the business?" Quinn didn't know whether to resent him even more or forgive him on the spot.

He nodded, his rough face still pink with emotion. "Lord Marcus seemed like an answer to prayer, the very thing to set you on the proper path—to happiness. Do you not think he'll make you happy Quinn? Truthfully?"

The events of the night before came rushing back. "Perhaps marriage will not be so bad as I feared, after all." She fought to keep from blushing.

"But will you be happy?" her father pressed her. "I hate to leave without feeling I've done my best for you. If now, knowing Lord Marcus better, you'd honestly prefer an annulment—"

Quinn lost her battle, the color rushing to her face. "I, er, no. I think that probably isn't an option."

The captain raised an eyebrow. "Ah. Like that, is it?"

Quinn could not answer, not even with a nod, but her silence was apparently enough answer in itself.

Her father's face relaxed into a tender smile that yet held a trace of sadness.

"Are you in love with him, Quinnling?" he asked gently.

"No! That is, I don't know. I mean, I've only known him a week. But . . . we do seem to deal well together, so far."

Rising, her father came around the table to kiss her cheek, then enfold her in a gentle bear hug. "I'd say you're off to an excellent start then. Lord Marcus is a good man, and you are a treasure, of course. I'd say the two of you have a better shot at happiness than most."

"I hope you're right, Papa," said Quinn, returning his embrace. And she meant it. After this conversation, there could be no question of her returning home to Baltimore. Ever.

She walked the captain to his waiting carriage, her emotions a confused tangle of hope and regret. *Could* she make this marriage work? She supposed she would have to try.

"Oh! I nearly forgot." Her father paused even as he leaned down to give her a farewell kiss. "Lord and Lady Claridge have invited you and your husband to accompany them to the theater later this week. I imagine you'll be receiving a visit or note from them shortly."

"How . . . how nice." A final effort of her father's, or a real attempt at reconciliation, she wondered? She'd be able to tell when she saw them again, she supposed. "Have a safe voyage, Papa! Give my love to Charles, and write to me often."

Though he'd never been much of a correspondent, the captain nodded. "I'll do that. And I'll look forward to your letters, as well. Have a wonderful life, my Quinnling." And with that, he climbed into the carriage and was gone.

Quinn watched him drive away, feeling as though her last link with home had just been broken. A tear slid down her cheek.

"My lady! There you are."

Dashing away the tear, she turned to see Polly at the front door, holding a letter.

"You have something for me, then?" Shaking off her melancholy, she walked up the steps and took it. "Thank you, Polly, you have done very well indeed. Go on back to the kitchen now. If I need you again, I will let you know."

Conscious of the footman in the hallway, Quinn returned to the dining room and her unfinished breakfast before opening her letter. Addressed to A Sympathetic Lady, it read:

Dear Madam,

I received your kind offer with all gratitude, and am most willing to consider an adjunct school for unfortunate girls, agreeing with your esteemed self that they, too, often find themselves forced by poverty into depraved and immoral circumstances. The expense will not be inconsiderable, but I will trust to your kindness to allay that concern. I have enlisted the help of Mrs. Hounslow of the Bettering Society for this project, upon whose discretion and sincere charity you can rely. I have enclosed her direction, that you may wait upon her to discuss the particulars. Yours in gratitude,

—M. Throgmorton

Quinn refolded the letter and tucked it into her sleeve just as a footman appeared with a fresh pot of chocolate to replace the one that had cooled. She thanked him absently, already considering when she might safely—and secretly—call on Mrs. Hounslow.

It appeared she was now irrevocably fixed in this country—and in her marriage—for good or ill. Marriage, however, had never been an end in itself for her. She needed real purpose in life. This new project would have to serve.

And while she strove to untangle her conflicting feelings about her husband, and to decipher his toward her, it would act as a welcome distraction, as well.

"Excellent work, lad!" Marcus exclaimed at the end of Gobby's lengthy report. He had nearly forgotten his promise to meet with the boy that morning, behind the stables. "I had no idea their operation was so extensive. Five of them, you say?"

Gobby nodded. "That we knows of so far, anyway. Stilt—he can write the best of us—put down here where they all live." He handed Marcus a torn sheet of paper with a list of names and addresses, all in or near Mayfair.

Marcus's eyebrows rose as he recognized two of

the names, men who moved among the better circles, though he didn't know them well. "And all of these are actually involved, not just friends of our Mr. Jarrett?"

"Aye, we think so, guv—er, milord. Talked to other lads from other flash houses and found out they've took a fair number off the streets, like what they did to Tig. And Tig says he heard Mr. Jarrett talking to the two what visited about selling him."

"And which two were those?" Marcus held out the list.

Gobby squinted at the names. "They was Mr. Hill and Captain McCarty. Would that be these here?" He pointed.

"Yes, thank you." McCarty was a half-pay Army captain and Mr. Hill was cousin to Sir Gregory Dobson, if he recalled correctly. Both in need of additional funds, no doubt, though that in no way excused their dabbling in what was essentially slavery.

"I'll take it from here." At the sight of the boy's crestfallen face, he added, "It may be I'll need a look-out tonight, however. Can you or one of the others meet me at the corner of Duke Street and Chandler at ten o'clock?"

Gobby's grin returned instantly. "I'll be there, milord! And maybe one o' the other lads, too. We all want to help, you know."

Marcus gripped his shoulder affectionately, wishing he could take in all of his friends as well, giving them food, schooling, and employment. Someday he would, he vowed. "I know you do, and I appreciate it. Thank the others for me as well, all right?"

"Aye, milord. I'll see you tonight!" With a cheery wave, Gobby disappeared into the stables.

Walking back to the house, Marcus suddenly realized that leaving might not be so simple a matter as it had been before. Somehow, he'd have to dissuade Quinn from staying overnight in his room—not at all a task he relished, particularly as they were finally establishing a rapport.

He sighed. Legendary thief and attentive husband weren't exactly complementary roles. Somehow he'd just have to learn to integrate the two—at least until he'd put this ring of crimps out of business and thrown the Runners completely off of Luke's scent.

Reentering the house, he found Quinn just leaving the dining room. "Has your father gone already?" he asked in surprise. "I had hoped to wish him good passage."

"I extended your good wishes," she replied with a nervous laugh, though he couldn't think why she would be nervous. "He had much to do before sailing."

Marcus nodded. "I'm sorry he had to leave England so soon. No doubt you will miss him."

"He promised to write." Quinn's eyes met his, and for a moment the night came rushing back. He took a step toward her, his body already responding to her nearness. Her eyes widened, her lips parting as if in anticipation. But then she spoke.

"I, er—I thought perhaps I would begin making the changes to my room today. I have some notes upstairs I'd like to show you. It will only take me a moment to fetch them."

"Oh. Of course." He blinked, wondering what madness had nearly overtaken him. It was broad daylight, with servants all about, for heaven's sake. "I have some correspondence to attend to. I'll be in the library."

With a last, uncertain smile, she hurried upstairs, and he headed to the library. Pulling out a sheet of paper, he penned a note to Mr. Paxton, suggesting a meeting that afternoon. He might as well get that over with, as delay could only serve to arouse the man's suspicions.

Dispatching the note with a footman, he wondered how he would manage to slip away from Quinn that night without arousing *her* suspicions.

Quinn pulled Mr. Throgmorton's letter from her sleeve and hid it in the drawer of her writing desk, under the stationery. That had been close! She had nearly moved into Marcus's arms when he had looked at her so smolderingly—and he would almost certainly have heard the letter crackle if she had.

"Foolishness," she said aloud. Surely she had only imagined that he was about to embrace her downstairs, in full view of the servants. Marcus was far too proper to do such a thing.

Wasn't he?

Yes, she was simply letting her memories of the night influence her perceptions. That was all. He surely knew how to separate proper daytime behavior from private nighttime pleasures. She had best learn how to do so, too, or she would risk embarrassing him.

Checking her appearance in the glass, she headed to the door, only remembering as she stepped into the hallway that she had supposedly come upstairs for her decorating notes. With an exasperated sigh, she went back to the desk and snatched them up, then hurried downstairs.

Marcus was in the library, as he had said, sorting through a small stack of letters.

"Ah, there you are, my dear. There are not many invitations, as most people are leaving or have left for the country, but I have found one or two we might want to consider." He handed them to her. "Did you bring your notes?"

"Yes." She exchanged them for the invitations, and they both read in silence. "A Venetian breakfast? What is that?"

"An *al fresco* party, or fancy picnic, if you will. I thought it might be fun. You've done more planning than I realized," he added, indicating her notes. "There is little left to do but choose fabrics and commission the changes. *Brava*, my dear."

She felt herself pinkening with pleasure at his praise. "I'm rather anxious to brighten up my chamber, I confess. And yes, the Venetian breakfast does sound entertaining, and perfect for this time of year. I'd like to attend."

"Then that's what we'll do on Thursday. Would you care to pen our acceptance, or would you prefer that I do so?"

"Oh. Which is proper?" She really would try to learn the proprieties and abide by them whenever she reasonably could.

"Wives generally handle such social correspondence, I believe—at least, my mother always has."

"Then I'll write it. Was there nothing for tonight?" The other invitation was for a ball on Friday.

He gave her a grin that was part grimace. "A rout at Lord and Lady Mountheath's. I assumed you'd prefer to forgo that one."

"You assumed correctly," she said with a shudder, remembering that lady's nasty barbs. "Though I do wonder how she reacted to the news of our marriage, since she so obviously did not believe we were betrothed."

Now Marcus laughed. "I fear neither of us was particularly convincing that evening. It's a good thing I never attempted to earn a living treading the boards."

"Nor I." Quinn recalled the shock and dismay she had felt when her father had manufactured their betrothal and Marcus had confirmed it. "But . . . we do seem to be making the best of things, do we not?"

His smile grew tender, making her heart race. "We do indeed. Did I not tell you that we would deal quite comfortably together?"

It was hardly a declaration of affection, and she felt a small knot of disappointment in her breast. "Yes, you did."

And she had thrown the words in his face, she recalled. To change the subject, she asked, "Are we to go out this afternoon? You mentioned something yesterday about the Tower."

"I did, didn't I? And we will go, if there is time. I fear I must meet with Mr. Paxton first, however."

"That man we met at the Tinsdales'? Does he really think you can help him to catch the Saint of Seven Dials?" The idea of proper Marcus being in even the slightest way associated with such a dashing, daring figure seemed rather comical.

"He seems to, though I can't conceive why. I'm curious, so I sent word that I would speak with him this afternoon. I doubt I will be gone long. We are to meet at White's."

Struck with a sudden idea, she said, "Oh, do not rush through what is likely to be an interesting interview on my account. We can always visit the Tower another day. In fact, I believe I may take the opportunity to run an errand or two myself, if I may have the carriage."

"Certainly. I can take the phaeton, or ride. But what sorts of errands?"

She was reminded of her father questioning her the day she attempted to take ship and fell into such trouble at the docks. But of course she planned nothing so risky today—just a visit to Mrs. Hounslow, in a perfectly respectable part of London.

"Shopping, of course," she said innocently. "I will need a new parasol if we are to attend that Venetian breakfast."

"Very well, I won't worry if I should run into friends at White's, then, which is not unlikely. I will be home in time for dinner though, certainly."

"As will I. Perhaps I will speak to a draper about fabrics for my bedchamber, as well. You approve my ideas?"

They fell to discussing her redecorating plans

then, and if Marcus seemed distracted, Quinn attributed it to the usual male disinterest in such matters.

Not until he handed his horse to one of the grooms at White's did Marcus think to wonder whether Noel Paxton could get in. A member himself since leaving Oxford, he tended to forget that the requirements were fairly stringent. There was no sign of the fellow loitering outside, however, so he determined to wait inside, keeping an eye on the street from the bow window.

He'd only taken a few steps into the main room, however, when he saw Mr. Paxton motioning to him from a table in the corner.

"I hope my choice of meeting place is amenable?" he asked, joining Paxton at the table.

"Perfectly," the other man replied. "Newly wed as you are, I understand your preference to meet here rather than at your home. I daresay your wife is still settling in. I recall the fuss my sister made over her first establishment after she married."

"I'm glad you understand." Marcus found himself liking the fellow and caught himself, realizing how dangerous that could be. "Some port, perhaps?" He signaled a passing waiter.

Once he had gone, Paxton said, "I won't keep you long. I'm sure you are eager to return to your bride."

There was no point delaying the inevitable, Marcus decided. "You wished to speak with me about the Saint of Seven Dials?"

"Yes. I had a most curious tale from the Marquess

of Ribbleton a week or two since. It involved a duel, in which you and he acted as seconds."

Marcus thought quickly. Luke had been engaged to duel Lord Bellowsworth over Lady Pearl's honor, but had ended up fighting—and killing—his own uncle instead. According to Luke, the man who had passed himself off as Lord Hardwyck for years had been a murderer, and well deserving of his fate, and the Duke of Oakshire had apparently agreed, for he had ensured that the details never became public.

"I was there, yes," he replied after what he hoped was no more than a reasonable hesitation.

"Then you know that it was a most irregular proceeding, quite apart from the fact that duels are illegal in England."

Though Paxton was watching him narrowly, Marcus merely shrugged. "Do you mean to set the Runners on the lot of us for taking part? Can't see how that would help your case."

"No, of course not," replied Paxton with a smile. "My concern is not with the irregularities—I believe a man was killed? But more particularly with something Lord Ribbleton told me that man said before Lord Hardwyck ran him through."

It took an effort to keep his expression pleasant and unruffled, but Marcus had long years of experience at inquisitions by his tutors, father, and older brothers when he'd landed in various scrapes.

"Ribbleton and I were at the far side of the field. I can't recall anything that was said with any clarity, and am rather surprised that he claims to do so. I do know Lord Hardwyck acted in self-defense," he said earnestly, as though that must be the main concern. "Knox threatened the lady who is now Luke's wife."

"Yes, I have spoken—briefly—with the Duke of Oakshire, and he tells me there was no question of a murder charge. Knox was apparently quite deserving of his fate."

"There you are, then." Marcus sat back with a smile, as though the interview must now be at an end.

But Paxton shook his head, tenacious as a dog with a bone. "Ribbleton claims that Knox identified Lord Hardwyck as the Saint of Seven Dials just before he died. That Hardwyck killed him for it, in fact, though the Duke does not appear to share that view."

Marcus managed a credible laugh. "Luke? The Saint? I'm not surprised the Duke of Oakshire won't credit such a theory. Why, he wasn't even in London for most of the Saint's career, nor has he the temperament for it." He was confident that if Paxton ever had opportunity to interview Luke himself, his friend could portray himself in whatever light he chose.

"As I said last night, I simply wish to follow every lead. If it were only Ribbleton's word, I might have discounted it, but one of the Runners claims that a boy known to fence for the Saint is now in Lord Hardwyck's employ. Do you know anything about that?"

That would be Flute, Marcus realized, a lad Luke had rescued from the streets once he came into his title. "I know he took in a street urchin or two at the instigation of his wife, who has long been known for her acts of charity."

Paxton frowned. "I didn't know that. Lady Hardwyck was doing this sort of thing even before her marriage, then?"

"Yes, quite the crusader, Lady Pearl. You must be new to Town not to know that. I'm sure Luke will have his hands full trying to keep up with her reforming and such."

"I see." Paxton was clearly disappointed. "As Hardwyck is reportedly still on his wedding trip to the North, I would have found it difficult to link him with the Saint's most recent theft, in any event. Still, I felt obliged—"

"Of course," Marcus agreed, feeling almost weak with relief. "Such thoroughness is admirable. Sir Nathaniel is fortunate to have you on the hunt."

Paxton grinned at him, relaxing a bit now that the inquisition was over. "I was recommended to him by the Foreign Office, now the war is over. I was offered a diplomatic position, but it wasn't my cup of tea."

Marcus's curiosity was piqued. Had the man acted as some sort of spy, then? But it would be tactless to ask, apart from the fact that too much conversation with the fellow could be risky. "Prefer more of a challenge, do you?" he contented himself with asking.

"You could say that. And the Saint is presenting the finest I've had since Waterloo. I've barely started my investigation, but I hope you'll alert me should you hear of anything that might be helpful."

"Of course," Marcus assured him. Finishing his port, he rose to go.

Mr. Paxton stood as well. "Once your friend Lord Hardwyck returns to London, I'll have a word with that street urchin of his. Perhaps he can provide the scent I'll need to bring this fox to ground."

Marcus felt a sudden thrill of alarm. Flute had been friends with Gobby, Stilt, and the others. Suppose— But no. If Luke trusted the lad, then he would trust him as well. And if Luke thought there was any risk to him, he wouldn't bring the boy back to London. Still, a discreet letter north might be in order.

"Excellent plan," he agreed, as he and Paxton headed toward the door. "He may well know something, if he actually sold goods for the Saint at one time."

They reached the street a moment later, and Marcus waited impatiently for his horse. As pleasant a fellow as Noel Paxton seemed, he felt more than ready to be away from him.

"Of course, the Saint must have another fence working for him now," said Paxton as Marcus mounted. "I have someone on the street who can keep me apprised. The Saint may be a hero to the poor, but loyalties can be bought, as I've discovered time and again. Good day to you, and my apologies for taking you away from your bride."

Marcus bid the man farewell and headed home, wondering just how deep the loyalty of "his" lads actually ran.

Chapter 15

"**M**rs. Hounslow?" Quinn asked as she was shown into the small but very clean parlor of a small but very clean house on Gracechurch Street. "I am . . . A Sympathetic Lady."

"Welcome! Welcome indeed!" Mrs. Hounslow, a tiny, active woman with iron gray hair and very bright gray eyes, hurried forward to clasp both of Quinn's hands in her own. "I have been hoping you might call. If you had sent word in advance, I would have arranged a nice tea, of course, but I'm sure Maggie can find us something."

The middle-aged maid who had answered the door nodded and bustled off, as energetic as her mistress.

"Now, my dear, pray have a seat so that we can discuss how best to help those poor, poor girls. I have been after Mr. Throgmorton for a year and more to include them in his plans, but he seems to feel that whatever funds he can scare up are put to better use on the boys, which is rubbish, of course, but men can be so muleheaded, don't you agree?"

Quinn took the indicated chair, feeling almost breathless herself just from listening to the birdlike woman's rapid speech. "Yes, they certainly can be," she assented. "In fact, the reason I have chosen to use an alias for my help is that I am uncertain of my husband's support in this endeavor."

"Ah! No doubt a wise precaution, my dear. One never knows how men will react to such things. Even the most charitably minded among them can become rather peculiar when it comes to their own wives participating in a project, particularly a project that has the potential to bring her into contact with the less fortunate—some might say, the less desirable—elements of society."

Mrs. Hounslow seated herself across from Quinn, but immediately jumped back up. "Ah! Here is our tea. Let me help you place the table, Maggie. Yes, thank you. I'll pour out, there's a dear. I know you want to get back to your baking."

She turned back to Quinn with a bright smile, speaking as she poured. "Maggie fills a multitude of roles for me, so I hate to demand too much of her in any one of them. Now, where were we?"

"We were going to discuss how I might best aid your plans for a girls' school," Quinn replied, trying to hide her amusement at the woman's manner. "I am prepared to contribute generously, provided I can do so discreetly."

"Bless you! Bless you indeed, my dear!" her hostess exclaimed, proferring a plate of tiny tea cakes.

"The situation of some of the poor girls in this city is fouler than you can imagine. My heart has ached for them, simply ached."

Quinn nodded. "Yes, I agree. I've come to know one girl, have taken her into my employ, in fact, to prevent her turning to an extremely dangerous and immoral line of work."

Tears started to Mrs. Hounslow's gray eyes. "You are charity itself, ma'am. So many girls forced into that line of work. Would I could rescue them all. Maggie is the only servant I can afford to keep on, or I'd have some of them here with me, as well. I do what I can, however, with what I can spare from my jointure. We'll get that school now, though, you mark my words, and those poor, dear girls will be prepared for fitting employment." She nodded vigorously and took a sip of tea.

"What will it cost, do you think, to set up a proper boarding school for, say, thirty or forty girls?" Quinn asked, thinking that Mrs. Hounslow more accurately typified Charity than she herself, who was doing this as much for distraction as for the sake of the girls. "I'm particularly concerned for those in and around the Seven Dials area."

Mrs. Hounslow nodded again, her pristine white cap bobbing on her gray curls. "So Mr. Throgmorton said, and quite understandable, as the girls near the West End will be the ones you have opportunity to observe and feel such commendable sympathy toward. My dream is to see several such schools about London someday, serving all of the nastiest rookeries. Oh, another word for thief dens, my dear. I presume from your accent that you are American, and may not be familiar with our local terms—which makes your charity all the more admirable, in my eyes."

Quinn wasn't sure why that should be the case, but she smiled. "You were going to give me an idea of how much money might be required?" she prompted.

"Oh! Yes, yes of course. Thirty or forty girls, you say? And a boarding school? Dear me . . ."

"I rather fear a day school would give those currently employing these girls too much opportunity to impose upon them during their free hours."

The little woman's eyes widened. "Why of course, how clever of you! And you are quite right. In that case—" She named a sum that made Quinn's eyes widen in turn. How would she ever manage to contribute so much without Marcus's knowledge?

Mrs. Hounslow must have noticed her hesitation, for she hurried on into speech. "Yes, it is a lot of money, I know, but for a boarding school one must consider meals and dormitories, for teachers as well as pupils, as the teachers would have to live at the school as well. Then there is the building itself. Mr. Throgmorton, I know, has investigated various possibilities for the boys' schools, so he likely would have suggestions for us."

Quinn nodded. Somehow she would come up with the money, even if it meant asking Marcus to release her own dowry to her—a humiliating prospect. "And how soon do you think we might hope to have such a school in operation?"

"Oh, I will have to ask Mr. Throgmorton about that, but if an existing building can be used, I should think fairly soon, if the funds are forthcoming. I realize it is likely far more than—"

"Speak to Mr. Throgmorton," Quinn told her. "I'll send the first few hundred pounds to you by the end of the week, so that he can secure us a building. I'll want regular progress reports, of course. They can be sent to Grillon's Hotel, as before, and I will call here when I can."

Mrs. Hounslow's eyes overflowed again. "What a saint you are, ma'am! The girls are fortunate indeed to have such an advocate."

"Hardly a saint, Mrs. Hounslow, but I would like to make a difference." Reference to a saint had set her thoughts along a new and interesting path. She rose. "I must go, but I will return when I can. Thank you so much for your assistance in this matter, for I had no notion where to begin."

With mutual expressions of gratitude, she and Mrs. Hounslow embraced, and Quinn left for Bond Street to do a quick bit of shopping to justify her long absence. While looking over a selection of lacy white parasols, she mused over the idea that had struck her just before leaving Gracechurch Street.

The Saint of Seven Dials was known for helping the less fortunate. If she could find a way to contact him, might he be persuaded to contribute some of his spoils to her cause? Certainly, it seemed worth the attempt.

Marcus was home when Quinn returned. As she entered the house, her abigail in tow, he emerged from the library with a smile that held no hint of suspicion. "I trust your shopping expedition was productive, my dear?"

"I'll let you judge," she replied with an answering smile, stifling an unexpected twinge of guilt for keeping the true purpose of her outing from him. Turning to Monette, she opened one of the parcels, to display a pretty, ruffled parasol.

Before he could comment, she rushed into nervous speech. "It was my first foray onto Bond Street, you know, so it took me a bit longer than I expected. So many shops concentrated into one area! Baltimore has nothing like it."

He raised a brow at her babbling, but only said, "A lovely trinket, and quite appropriate for a Venetian breakfast. I'm pleased you have returned, however, as ladies generally aren't seen in Bond Street this late in the day."

"Yes, I noticed that," she replied, biting her lip at the implied rebuke. "By the time we left, it was nearly all gentlemen on the street. I hope I haven't done something improper again?"

"Nothing that can't be excused in someone so new to Town. I must remember to warn you about such customs before you go out on your own again. But come, show me what else you have bought, that I may exclaim over it."

Feeling rather foolish and guiltier than ever, she opened the other packages. If not for her visit to Mrs. Hounslow, she would never have strayed beyond the "proper" Bond Street hours.

"Only a few other things, really. This bonnet, and some ribbon to match my green morning dress. I—I thought I might wear it in my hair." He had moved closer to inspect the items, and his nearness was making it hard to concentrate.

"Very pretty." He was looking at her, however, and not her purchases. She felt her color rise, as it did all too often in his presence. Surely by now she should be getting over this schoolgirl foolishness?

"I'm glad you approve," she said, making a job of rewrapping the items before handing them to Monette, to take upstairs.

When she would have followed her maid, he said, "I had thought we might go for a ride in the Park before dinner, but perhaps you would prefer to rest?"

"Oh! I'm not at all tired," she declared, turning back to him. "I'd love a chance to get to know Tempest better." *And you, too,* she added silently. Though she was coming to know his body well, she still knew little of the man within it.

"I'll call for our mounts, then, while you change into your 'new' habit."

She chuckled. "I'll have to have a proper one made up soon. I won't be a moment." She ran lightly up the stairs, guilt and embarrassment forgotten in her eagerness to ride again.

Refusing to allow Monette to fuss with her hair, she was ready quickly and went down to find the horses already at the front door. The groom holding Tempest looked wary, as though the mare had already attempted to either bite or kick him.

"Mind this 'un, milady. She's a bit snappish," he said, confirming her guess. "Needs to learn her manners, she does."

"We'll learn our Society manners together, Tempest and I," Quinn replied, nodding to Marcus that she was ready to be tossed into the saddle.

As she had yesterday, Tempest quieted at once the moment Quinn settled into proper riding posture and took up the reins. It was clear the mare had originally been well trained, even if recent poor handling had made her temperamental. Rather like Quinn herself, perhaps? She grinned at the thought.

"You do like to ride, don't you?" Marcus commented, mounting his own horse with an answering grin. "There's something else we have in common."

Together, they started off in the direction of Hyde Park at a gentle trot. "Something else?" Quinn echoed, riding easily at his side. "What was the first?"

He slanted a look at her that made her face heat. "We both enjoyed the Egyptian Hall, did we not? But I confess I was thinking of more—active—pursuits."

Eyes resolutely ahead, she tried to speak lightly. "Perhaps we can discover other, ah, amusements we both like. Or more intellectual pursuits. You like to read, I believe you said?"

"Of course. Books are a suitably safe topic." There was a hint of laughter in his deep voice that stirred her blood even as she tried to calm her body to a more proper state. "I can't claim to be a great reader, but I'm fond of Shakespeare and Milton, as well as several modern novelists whom most would call frivolous."

That *did* surprise her. She'd have expected him to limit his reading to political or historical treatises, more in keeping with his sober bent.

They reached the Park gates and turned in, to find the paths fairly crowded, as it was the fashionable hour. For a moment or two, Quinn had to focus her attention on Tempest, who was inclined to take exception to the other horses, sidestepping and trying to fling up her head. Keeping a firm grip on the reins without pulling, she spoke soothingly yet firmly, and the mare soon settled down again, allowing them to proceed.

"My compliments on your horsemanship," Marcus said as they turned onto a less crowded path. "You handle her superbly."

"She simply needs a light but firm hand." Again Quinn wondered if there was a parallel to her own situation. This time the thought did not amuse her particularly. "Harshness will spoil a horse as quickly as coddling will, I've found."

"I agree."

Glancing quickly at him, she wondered if he was drawing parallels of his own. Nettled, she changed the subject. "Look, here is a fairly deserted path, off to the right. Shall we try a canter?" Without waiting for his response, she set Tempest down the path at a near gallop, delighting in the smoothness of her paces, her brief irritation evaporating.

"Hold up, hold up!" he called out, as she neared a turning in the path.

Though she slowed her mare, she glanced at him quizzically. "Too fast for you?" she asked teasingly.

"Not for me, but anything faster than a hand canter is frowned on in the Park, particularly at this time of day. Not all riders are as skilled as you are."

So she had unwittingly broken yet another rule, she thought with a resigned sigh. "It appears that Tempest is learning her Society manners more quickly than I am. I'm sorry."

He shook his head. "My fault—I should have warned you. I keep forgetting that you haven't been accustomed to all of these silly strictures."

"This one isn't silly," she admitted. "It makes sense from the standpoint of safety. Perhaps many of the other rules Society imposes have valid reasons as well, and I simply don't know what they are." Somehow she doubted that, however.

"You— Hm. Perhaps."

She wondered what he had started to say. Something critical of her, most likely, which he had broken off rather than risk an argument . . . or rather than risk hurting her feelings? Either way, she was grateful.

"It's getting late," she said. "I suppose we should be getting back?"

"Yes, let's. I'm famished." He seemed as desirous of dropping the discussion of rules as she.

They had nearly reached the Park gates when a familiar blue phaeton entered, its lovely driver spotting them at once. She nudged the equally pretty girl at her side before trilling out a greeting.

"Lord Marcus! Fancy you still in Town, when I read of your wedding only yesterday! Cecy and I were quite in the dismals at the prospect of losing you, and yet here you are. How delightful!"

As before, her eyes were all for Marcus, Quinn noticed sourly, and the other lady was gazing at him just as dotingly. It was as though she wasn't even present.

"Good afternoon, Lady Regina, Lady Cecily." Marcus swept an elegant half bow from the saddle. "Allow me to present my new bride, Lady Marcus. My lady, you remember Lady Regina Prescott, and this is her sister, Lady Cecily Prescott."

"Dear, dear friends of your husband's," Lady Cecily added. "Delighted to meet you, Lady Marcus. What a lovely, er, habit." Both sisters tittered, staring at Quinn's modified gown before again gazing up at Marcus from under their lashes.

His jaw tightened, Quinn noticed. "We are but acquaintances," he said dampeningly, his sensibilities no doubt offended by the ladies' blatant flirting.

Quinn was more amused than jealous, though the comment about her habit stung a bit. A real shopping excursion was definitely in order—and the sooner, the better.

Lady Regina's next words distracted her from such plans. "That's not what you told Cecily last spring, when you stole a kiss from her at the Heathertons' ball. We were both rather hoping to discover whether you would live up to your reputation, but alas! It appears we shall not have the chance." She shot Quinn a glance of dislike. "Come, Cecy."

They drove on, leaving Marcus to frown after them while Quinn regarded him curiously. Becoming aware of her gaze, he turned back to her with a shrug. "Lord Knottsford should keep a tighter rein on his daughters. Pray pay them no mind, my dear. They delight in stirring up trouble."

Quinn managed a smile and nod, her momentary shock fading somewhat. "I suspected as much. They

both seem quite as high-spirited as Tempest here."
She did not add that it was patently absurd to imagine staid Marcus doing something as scandalous as stealing a kiss at a ball—not to mention having a "reputation"!

But then, how well did she know him, really?

By the time they finished dinner, speaking primarily of their plans for the balloon ascension on the morrow, Marcus was fairly certain that Quinn had not taken the Prescott sisters' comments to heart. Who would have guessed that Cecily had told her sister of their tryst at that ball, or that her sister would mention it publicly? Brazen hussies, both of them.

He had once found them both alluring, odd as that seemed to him now. Neither had affected him remotely the way Quinn did, however, for all that they were more classically beautiful. They lacked her wit, as well as her . . . he could only call it authenticity. There was something refreshingly *real* about Quinn.

While he had to maintain this facade of propriety for now, he hoped she wouldn't take his hypocritical comments about Society rules too much to heart. It would be a shame if she were to become conventional.

"Will you join me for a brandy again?" he asked, as the last course was removed. "It shouldn't make you cough this time, as you are no longer precisely a novice."

She regarded him suspiciously, as though uncertain whether he referred only to the brandy. "Very well, I'll give it another try," she said after a slight hesitation.

Preceding him into the library, she seated herself while he poured. She took one cautious sip, then another. No coughing.

"Much more enjoyable, now that you've had some experience, is it not?" he asked with a grin, pulling the opposite chair close.

Her glance showed that she definitely caught his double meaning this time. "Yes, it's actually rather pleasant. I could easily grow to look forward to it, I think." She took another tiny sip, then met his eyes, her own twinkling.

"I'm delighted to hear it." He held her eyes, his pulse quickening, his body looking forward to pleasures other than brandy. Her expression changed from playful to aware, her lips parting slightly as her eyes turned smoky.

"Are you?" The question escaped her like a sigh.

"I am indeed." He scarcely recalled what they were talking about. Thoroughly aroused, he leaned forward until his knee grazed hers. "In fact, everything about you delights me, Quinn. Though we've known each other such a short time, you've become very dear to me."

A flicker of surprised stirred in her eyes, but she smiled. "That sounds dangerously like a declaration, my lord."

Startled, he realized it did. Even more surprising, he felt no desire to retract it. Still, caution prevented him making it irrevocable. "I still have some work to do on this flirtation business, it seems. You did promise to help me."

"I never claimed to be an expert. But since I already have you leg-shackled, surely you need not fear raising unreasonable expectations in my breast?" she said playfully.

"And just what *are* you expecting in that lovely breast of yours?" he asked, moving even closer.

She pinkened, but met his eye without flinching. "All of the experiences you promised me, my lord—and more. What less?"

Taking her hand, he stood. "Come then. It is time we continued your education—or would that be entertainment?"

"Both, I think." She rose, leaving her brandy nearly untouched, as was his. Her eyes strayed to his breeches, where his arousal must be quite apparent, then smiled, her color deepening further.

He found her mix of confusion and boldness adorable—and irresistible. Taking her by the hand, he led her up to his chamber, his anticipation growing. Drawing her into the room, he closed the door. "Now, what new experience did you have in mind?"

With a throaty chuckle that inflamed him even further, she tipped her face up for his kiss. "How would I know, if it is new? I depend upon you to enlighten me."

Over the next few hours, they mutually explored some of the variety possible in the marriage bed. Experienced though Marcus was, the enthusiasm of his partner was a novelty, and one that added enormously to his own enjoyment, he found.

Tasting, touching, moving from bed to chair to floor, Quinn was willing to follow his lead, trusting him to show her the heights of pleasure and to show her how to please him as well. That very trust disturbed him now, as they lay entwined on the bed, resting from their exertions.

Why could he not trust her as completely?

Because he had secrets beyond his own to keep, he answered himself, and much as he wanted to tell her everything, he couldn't risk Luke, or the lads on the street, to the chance of an indiscreet word she might let fall to the wrong ears. In fact, she herself could be in danger should that happen.

He looked down at her as she dozed, remarkably innocent in sleep, and smiled. No, he couldn't believe she would deliberately hurt him or the others, but discretion had not so far proved to be Quinn's strongest suit. Which meant he would have to slip away from the house that night without her knowledge.

Leaning down, he kissed her gently on the brow and watched as her eyes fluttered open.

"Mmm. Are you not tired?" she murmured with a sleepy smile.

"Indeed, you have quite worn me out, little vixen," he replied with a grin. "But having you here is so tempting, I fear I will get no sleep at all if you stay."

She struggled to sit up, looking charmingly confused. "Oh. Do you wish me to return to my own room for the night, then?"

"Perhaps it would be best, if we are to be well rested for the balloon ascension tomorrow."

He held his breath. If she wanted to stay, he'd simply have to get word to Gobby somehow, for he'd never find the willpower to leave her here, naked, in his bed.

"Yes, I suppose you are right," she said reluctantly, and her very reluctance was another temptation. He forced himself not to respond, not to touch her again, as he longed to. Instead, he helped her out of bed and into her shift before accompanying her to the dressing room door.

"We'll have tomorrow night—and every night after," he reminded her—and himself—as she put a hand on the doorknob. "Until then—"

The kiss nearly broke his hard-won control, but he managed to keep his hands from straying, difficult as that was. Finally, with a little sigh, she pulled away from him.

"If I am going to sleep in my own bed, I'd best go now. Good night, Marcus."

"Good night, Quinn." He almost added, *I love you,* but caught himself, aghast, before the words could escape his lips. Shaken, he watched her disappear through the door, wondering how he could have come so close to saying such a thing.

Could it, just possibly, be true?

But then he glanced at the clock on his mantelpiece. He'd have to consider that unsettling question later. If he was going to make his promised meeting by ten o'clock, he needed to leave immediately.

Letting himself softly out of the house a few minutes later, he finally understood why Luke had given up his calling as Saint once he'd married.

Chapter 16

∽◇◇◇∼

Tired as she was, Quinn had a difficult time falling asleep. Monette had magically appeared to brush out her hair and help her into her nightgown, then had faded away again, leaving her alone with her thoughts in the big four-poster bed.

Rolling onto her side, Quinn reflected again on the contrast Marcus presented. His concern for propriety had been evident when he cautioned her against staying too late in Bond Street, and again when she had foolishly galloped in the Park. But in the bedchamber, he seemed to have no such worries. There, he had appeared to throw caution to the winds—until now.

She'd been embarrassed and hurt when he'd suggested she return to her room, but she'd been careful not to show it. Now she tried to convince herself she should be flattered that he found her such a distraction that she would keep him from much-needed sleep. But—

A creak outside her door made her sit up, listening. Had that been a footstep? After a tense, silent moment, she lay back down. If so, it was doubtless Marcus's valet, leaving him for the night, or one of the maids, snuffing the candles in the hallway sconces. Nothing for her to worry about.

Only one night in his bed, and now she couldn't sleep in her own? She chided herself, wondering if she were really as smitten as all that. If so, it would be too bad, since he could clearly do without her for a night.

With a sigh, she reminded herself that she had always valued independence, that she had goals of her own, unconnected with Marcus. If she was wise, she would do well to guard her heart. But as she finally drifted off to sleep, she still hadn't suppressed the longing she felt for his touch, dangerous as she knew that could be to her future peace of mind.

Immediately upon returning from his meeting with Mr. Paxton, Marcus had written and posted a letter warning Luke. Walking briskly toward Duke Street, he remembered that with satisfaction. Now his friend would not return to Town unaware of the investigation, at least.

Still, if he was going to do what he'd planned to overset the crimps' operation, he needed to work quickly, before Paxton had time to begin questioning more of the Seven Dials street urchins. He'd also need to alert his own group to the danger. If one of "his" lads was arrested as a result of his own activities, he would never forgive himself.

Gobby, Stilt, and Tig awaited him at the corner he'd designated, looking rather pleased with themselves.

"Gent's gone out, milord," Stilt whispered as soon as he reached them. "Two of the others on that list was with 'im, too. Renny's the best of us at tailing, so he's gone after 'em to see what they're up to."

"I'm just as good," Tig protested, puffing out his thin chest. "But I was hoping I could help you here, like I did before at that other house."

Marcus valiantly kept his expression serious. "And I appreciate that. I appreciate what all of you have done, in fact." Quickly, he told them the gist of his conversation with Mr. Paxton that afternoon, including the man's plan for catching the Saint through his cohorts.

Gobby snorted indignantly. "There's some things brass can't buy, milord." The others nodded fiercely. "There are lads on the street who'd sell their own mothers for a few shillings, but the Saint always knew better than to trust 'em."

"That's right, milord," Stilt agreed. "Still, it's good you warned us. It won't do for anyone to boast we've been helping the Saint through you, where the wrong ears might hear." He looked pointedly at Tig, who pretended not to notice.

"That was my primary concern," Marcus told them. "I know how word can get around, and it would only take one lad putting profit over principle to land us all—and the Saint as well—in prison."

They all nodded again, faces set and serious. Yes, he could trust them, Marcus thought with relief.

"Now, on to tonight's work," he said then, and at

once their eyes brightened. "We'll start here, at Captain McCarty's lodgings, but I hope to hit at least one of the others tonight as well." The sooner he could put a stop to this operation, the better. "You say he's gone out. How many servants?"

"He just seems to have the one manservant, and he's gone out as well. His rooms are on the second story, left-hand side," Stilt told him.

"Excellent work! So those windows, there, would be his?" Marcus asked, pointing. The boys nodded.

He considered the house for a moment. The front door might well be unlocked for the convenience of other lodgers, but then it might not. It would be awkward if someone came along while he attempted to pick it, not to mention any explanations he'd have to give if he were seen inside the house and possibly recognized.

Luke's primary strengths had been his ability to disguise himself as anything from beggar to bishop, and sleight of hand. Marcus's own specialty was getting in and out of rooms undetected. So, the window it was.

Telling the boys to stand guard, he set to work. This window was lower than the one he'd breached two nights since, and the wall far easier to climb. In moments he was inside, with none the wiser.

A quick search showed Captain McCarty's lodging to consist of only two rooms, a bedchamber and small parlor. Marcus turned his attention to the writing desk, as before, and this time was better rewarded. A book of accounts appeared to list money paid and owed to McCarty, though he couldn't read it clearly by only the light from the windows. He pocketed it to peruse later and continued his search.

He took a few more papers that looked as though they might be useful, then discovered a secret drawer. When opened, it proved to contain a sheaf of banknotes and a small pile of golden guineas. With a grin, he took it all, leaving a card in its place. Money needed no fencing, and therefore wouldn't put his lads at risk.

Satisfied, he left the way he had come, latching the window behind him with a variation on the same trick he'd used at Lord Hightower's house. The whole operation had taken no more than fifteen minutes.

"That's done," he said to the waiting trio. "Let's see if we can find Renny near one of the other gents' houses. It's early yet, so I'm hoping to accomplish a bit more before bedtime."

Quinn was up early the next morning; she had bathed and eaten breakfast before eight o'clock. Marcus had not yet come down, so she took the opportunity for another private word with Polly under the pretense of showing her which brasses needed polishing.

"I've spoken with a lady who wishes to establish a school for girls in London, not far from here. Tell me, if such a school existed, and you and other girls you know were allowed to attend for free, would you want to do so?"

Polly frowned at her, as though not quite understanding. "A school? To teach us ciphering and geography and such? What good would that do the likes of us? And what would we live on?"

Quinn had anticipated just those questions, and had her answers ready. "Yes, you would learn arithmetic, and to read and write. But you would also receive training that would fit you for employment in a shop, or a higher position in a household. Your meals and lodging would be provided as long as you were in the school, and you'd be protected from your old master."

Now, Polly nodded slowly. "I'd like that, I think, meaning no disrespect for what you've done for me already, milady. And I knows some other girls what would jump at the chance. Just yesterday I had a quick word with poor Annie, her face all black-and-blue. She's wanting to quit as a fancy-girl, but Twitchell won't let her."

"Do you mean Twitchell beat her for trying to leave?" Quinn asked angrily. "I really must—"

But Polly shook her head. "No, mum, it weren't Twitchell. It was the swell what paid her. Some likes it rough, she says, and she wants out. She's afeared next time the gent might kill her."

Quinn's eyes narrowed. "Gent? Might you know the man's name?"

"No, milady, but I could probably find out. Why?"

"Don't worry about the why just now. See if you can get me his name, as well as the names of any other *gentlemen* patronizing your young friends. I may be able to, ah, protect the girls somewhat. I won't let them know you told me."

"Aye, milady, I'll try, then. I'm that worried about Annie, and some of the others, too."

"You have a good heart," Quinn told her. "And

now, one more question before you get back to your work. What do you know about the Saint of Seven Dials?"

Polly's eyes widened. "I've had nothin' to do with him, milady, I give you my word! And Gobby, he don't mean no harm, I know he don't. He—"

"Wait, Polly, I'm not accusing you of anything, or Gobby either. But—do you mean that Gobby has had some sort of contact with him?"

Though she looked as though she wished she hadn't said anything, Polly answered slowly. "He *says* so, but you know how boys like to brag. Could be it's just so much moonshine."

Her heart beating faster, Quinn tried not to let her excitement show. "Do—do you think Gobby might be willing to send a note to him? I'm hoping he might be convinced to help support the school I mentioned."

"Oh!" Polly's eyes went round with surprise. "I can ask him, milady."

"Thank you. I'll get a note to you later today. Mind, though, that Gobby is not to say where it came from. Not even a hint!"

The girl nodded vigorously, clearly delighted to be involved in the excitement of a secret scheme. Quinn left her to her polishing then, her mind full of plans.

If the Saint could be persuaded to help, she wouldn't have to approach Marcus about money at all. She trusted her husband, of course, but he might be so scandalized on learning about those poor street girls—and more, her own involvement—that he would have them arrested, when they were no more than victims of circumstance. She didn't dare risk that.

And even if the Saint wouldn't help—or Gobby couldn't contact him—she might now have the means to implement her original plan to raise funds. Who better to underwrite their redemption, after all, than the very gentlemen who were debasing those poor girls? Once she had their names, she was confident that she could find a way to induce them to pay.

Quite pleased with her morning's work, she headed up the stairs to pen the note she had promised to Polly—her first contact, she hoped, with the legendary Saint of Seven Dials.

"Thank you, Clarence," said Marcus with a yawn as his valet finished tying his cravat. He'd been out later last night than planned, but it had been worth it. He now had written evidence of the involvement of four of the five men in the kidnapping ring.

Now he just had to decide what to do with that evidence.

Would Captain McCarty or Mr. Hill report the theft of their ill-gotten gains, now that they must be aware that incriminating documents had been stolen as well? If they did, he would be hard-pressed to turn over those documents to the authorities without implicating himself. Perhaps he shouldn't have left the Saint's calling cards after all.

But no. This sort of work was right up the Saint's alley, in his opinion. The idea of filth like those men quaking in fear of the Saint's retribution amused him mightily, in fact. Somehow, he'd find a way to put those documents to use without giving himself away.

Finishing his ruminations as Clarence finished with his boots, he stood and left the room, wondering whether Quinn would have eaten yet.

On discovering that she had, he ate quickly, then sent a servant to ask her to join him in the library. A minute or two later, she appeared in the doorway.

"You wished to see me?" She seemed somehow remote, though lovely, in a dove gray round dress. More like the Quinn of a week ago than the passionate woman of the past two nights.

"We'll want to leave within the hour if we're to catch the beginning of the balloon ascension," he said. "I think you'll find the preparations interesting."

She nodded. "I'm certain I will. I must speak with Mrs. Walsh for a moment, and then I will be ready to go—if that is acceptable?"

Why was she being so tentative? He must have hurt her feelings last night, though she had pretended otherwise. He wanted to apologize again for sending her from his room, but feared he'd be tempted into unwise explanations if he did. He'd simply have to cajole her into better humor over the course of the day—without dropping his guard.

"Certainly. Do whatever you need to do, and I'll arrange to have the carriage ready in half an hour."

With another quiet nod, she left him. Just as well, he told himself. Clearly he needed to rein in his feelings for Quinn, or he might do something foolish, like tell her everything. Far safer for both of them that they maintain an emotional distance for the present, much as he might wish otherwise. *Act like Robert would*, he reminded himself.

Though they were early, a fair crowd had already gathered in Green Park to watch the brightly colored silk balloon fill slowly with heated air. As this entertainment cost nothing, the lower orders jostled with the upper classes for a better view.

Marcus took the opportunity to strengthen Quinn's false impression of him. "Perhaps we should stay in the phaeton to watch. Some of this crowd looks as though they haven't bathed in weeks," he said pompously. "They should be cordoned off in a separate area from the rest of us."

As he'd expected, she frowned at him. "They have as much right to see the spectacle as we have, surely, my lord?" But then she paused, biting her lip. "I . . . do see your point, however. I have no wish to have my reticule snatched by pickpockets, who no doubt abound at such events."

"No doubt," he agreed, though he regarded her curiously. "Unattended children, particularly, are like to be thieves."

She turned her head to watch the slowly inflating balloon, so that he could not see her expression. "So I have heard. Why do not the officers of the law do something about them? People should be protected from such activity."

This was a change, but he did not dare point that out—or mention how he really felt about the plight of those poor children. "London needs more police officers, no doubt of that. Law enforcement in the city is a disgrace, giving criminals far too much leeway. My father has been attempting to change that."

In fact, the duke was a proponent of much harsher penalties as well as an expanded police force, and while Marcus agreed in principle with the latter, he could not approve the former. Not now that he knew what drove so many lads to thievery.

"Good . . . good for him," Quinn said, her face still averted. Then, in a completely different tone, "Oh, there is your brother Lord Peter!"

Sure enough, Peter was making his way through the crowd toward them, smiling broadly. "Delighted to see you both here!" he exclaimed as he drew near. "I haven't quite dared to call, so soon after the wedding, but I've been eaten up with curiosity to know how you are adjusting to married life. May I?"

Though Marcus cursed Peter's timing in appearing just then, while he was intentionally keeping Quinn at arm's length, he reached down a hand to help his brother into the phaeton.

"Quinn, you are lovelier than ever. A good omen, I hope?" Peter asked as he settled himself on the high seat behind them.

She dimpled up at him, looking more animated than she had yet today, Marcus thought irritably. "Why thank you, Lord Peter. I have . . . little to complain of, thus far." She glanced quickly at Marcus, then away.

"We're rubbing along quite well," Marcus said in response to his brother's questioning look, trying to stifle the sudden resentment he felt. It was none of Peter's concern, after all. And why did Quinn have to sound as though she had reservations?

"So this brother of mine has done nothing to embarrass you yet?" Though Peter's tone was teasing, Marcus felt an irrational desire to push him to the ground six feet below.

Still smiling, Quinn shook her head. "Not at all, though I fear he cannot claim the same of me. Just yesterday he had to scold me for galloping in the Park. I'm trying to reform my madcap ways, however."

Scolded! He had not scolded her! Marcus opened his mouth to say so, but Peter was already speaking again, damn him.

"Pray don't change a thing, my dear. You are perfectly charming as you are. Is she not, Marcus?" His tone held a hint of rebuke now.

"I tell her so constantly," Marcus said as blandly as he could manage.

Peter regarded him narrowly. "I hope that's true. Mutual respect and kindness are essential to a happy marriage, while constant criticism is likely to injure it ultimately."

"Speaking from your years of experience, are you?" Marcus snapped, finally goaded into losing his temper.

But Peter was impossible to provoke. He merely put up a hand as though defending himself, and said, "I'm only sharing what I've observed in the marriages of friends."

"If I wish for your counsel, I will request it." Even marriage, it appeared, was not enough to render him an adult in his brother's eyes, insufferable mother hen that he was.

Some measure of his anger must have penetrated,

for Peter finally said, "Of course, dear boy. I had no wish to meddle. I'll leave you two lovebirds alone, then."

With an agility at odds with his dandified appearance, Peter sprang lightly down from the phaeton, then swept Quinn a parting bow. "May all your days be happy ones, my lady. And yours too, of course, Marcus."

"Thank you, Lord Peter," Quinn responded, with a curious frown at Marcus. "I hope to see you again soon."

"Feel free to call on me at any time. I am staying at Marland House until September. I would offer to drop by, but I believe I'd best wait until my brother issues an invitation." With a jaunty wink that only irritated Marcus further, he sauntered off.

Quinn rounded on Marcus at once. "You were abominably rude to Lord Peter, when he was only trying to be kind. Why?"

"Kind?" Marcus echoed sourly. "He was meddling where he had no business meddling, and he knew it. And I'll thank you not to air our private concerns before my family."

"Air—I did no such thing! I was simply being polite—something you cannot claim, my lord."

"Perhaps you'd do better to be less *polite* to other men in public, then." Even to his own ears, his words sounded unreasonable, but the sight of her smiling at Peter after her earlier coolness toward himself had stirred up feelings he didn't care to define.

Quinn was glaring at him, her green eyes fairly ablaze. "Are you accusing me of *flirting* with your own brother? It seems nothing I do can please you. I should have gone back to Baltimore after all."

Marcus wanted to tell her that she pleased him very much, more than any woman had ever pleased him, but instead he pointed across the field. "The balloon is beginning to rise. I know you don't want to miss it."

She stared at him disbelievingly for a moment, then turned away to focus on the brightly colored balloon, her back rigid. He wanted to touch her, to twine her dark curls around his fingers, to pull her against him, but he couldn't do any of those things in this setting. And he had no words to explain the jumble of feelings that were fighting for supremacy in his breast. He would try to explain later, when he was calmer, he told himself.

As the balloon rose slowly into the sky, Marcus guiltily realized that his foolish jealousy—for that was what it must be—had spoiled much of Quinn's pleasure at the novelty.

"I'm sorry," he said quietly, watching her tense profile.

She shifted slightly, but did not look at him. "Is that an apology, or are you saying you are sorry you married me?" Her voice was muffled, as though she was fighting back tears.

"The former, of course. How can you ask?" Now he did touch her, a tentative hand on her shoulder.

She shrugged it off. "Then I accept your apology. And now, my lord, I wish to watch the ascension."

His hand hovered near her curls, then he dropped it into his lap. Damn Peter, anyway! They had been getting along so well until he came along with his impertinent questions.

But no. Quinn had been withdrawn all morning, doubtless because he had sent her from his bed last night with no better explanation than wanting sleep. Peter had simply pointed up the problem that already existed—the problem of trust.

He didn't dare trust Quinn with the truth about the Saint of Seven Dials, and now he'd implied that he didn't trust her near other men, either—which he had to admit wasn't true. And she, apparently, couldn't trust him to accept her as she was, but felt she had to change to please him.

That was absurd, of course. She must see that. He had apologized, hadn't he? And she had shrugged it off, along with his touch, as though it meant nothing.

Reluctantly, he realized that he would be wiser to leave this little estrangement in place until his business with the crimps was finished. He wouldn't have to make excuses to keep her from his bed if she avoided it on her own. That wasn't at all what he wanted, however.

Wrapped in his warring thoughts, Marcus was surprised when the crowd began to disperse, the excitement over. He'd missed it entirely. Not that it mattered much—to him.

"What did you think?" he asked Quinn, picking up the reins and urging the pair forward. "Did it live up to your expectations?"

She glanced at him, a sad smile curving her mouth. "Does anything, ever?"

He had no answer for that, and they drove back to Grosvenor Street in silence.

"I believe I'll rest until dinner," Quinn told him, as they entered the house.

"Of course," he said, still uncertain how to breach the wall she had erected between them, and even less certain that he should try.

With a distant nod of her head, she moved to the stairs. He started to go after her, his heart urging him to take her in his arms and prove to her with his body how he felt, but then he stopped. As he stood irresolute in the hallway, reason again warring with passion, he noticed a crudely addressed letter amid the elegant invitations and cards on the hall table.

Mindful of the footman at his post by the front door, he picked up the entire stack of letters and retreated to the library with them, momentarily distracted from his dilemma over Quinn. A sheet of paper, addressed to him in Gobby's unschooled hand, was wrapped around another letter whose direction had been much more neatly penned: *The Saint of Seven Dials*, it read.

He would have to have a stern talk with Gobby, he realized with a sense of foreboding. This could easily be a trap set by Paxton or someone else who had somehow linked the boy to the Saint. Suppose one of the servants had become suspicious and opened the outer paper?

Curiosity quickly overcame dismay, however, and he broke the inner seal. The letter was written in the same firm but distinctly feminine hand as the direction.

> *Dear Sir, whoever you may be,*
>
> *Knowing of your concern for the unfortunate poor of this city, I wish to petition you on behalf of some of the most unfortunate of all—the girls of the street. I am attempting to fund a school for their benefit, and would be most appreciative of any assistance you can offer. Donations may be made to Mrs. Hounslow in Gracechurch Street, as she is to organize the school with the assistance of Mr. M. Throgmorton and the Bettering Society. Thanking you in advance for your charity,*
>
> *—A Sympathetic Lady*

Marcus read through the letter three times, committing it to memory, then carefully burned it in the grate and scattered the ashes. Assuming the letter writer was genuine, he was inclined to do as she requested. He still had the money he had taken from two of the crimps, and this seemed a worthy cause.

More than a little bit curious about this "Sympathetic Lady," he headed for the stables to speak with Gobby, in hopes of discovering more about her.

Chapter 17

"A girl gave it to you, you say?" Marcus kept his voice low, though he and Gobby were well out of earshot of the other stable hands. "Someone you know?"

He thought Gobby hesitated before nodding. "I knowed her from Twitchell's. She asked me not to tell her name, but I trust her."

"And she said a woman gave her the letter. Did she tell you what sort of woman? Was it a lady, or a commoner?"

"She wouldn't say, milord. Should I not have passed it along, then?"

Though frustrated, Marcus shook his head. "No, no, it's fine. I just wanted to discover the details, lest it was some sort of scheme to discover the identity of the Saint. It seems to be legitimate enough, however, so I'll see that he gets it."

"Aye, milord, I figured you would." Gobby's grin

told him what he'd already suspected—that the lads were on to him. But it seemed they were willing to keep that knowledge to themselves, not even admitting it to him. That was fine.

"Do keep your eyes open for any suspicious activity, however. Should you see anyone watching the house or trailing any of the servants, I want you to notify me immediately."

The boy nodded. "I'll do that, milord, and I'll alert the others, too." Then he gazed up at Marcus speculatively. "Will you be needin' any of us again tonight, think you? Last night went a treat."

But Marcus shook his head. He was very much hoping to get Quinn back into his bed in the evening, and once he had her there, he wouldn't let her go again.

"Probably not. If I should change my mind, I'll send word." Quinn might refuse, after all, in which case he'd prefer to be out accomplishing something rather than nursing his wounded pride.

Dressing for dinner, he urged Clarence to hurry with his cravat and was rewarded by seeing Quinn emerge into the hallway just as he stepped from his own room.

"How fortuitous," he said, stepping to her side. "I was hoping I might have the honor of escorting you down to dinner."

She started slightly, but then looked up at him with a cool smile. "I would not wish to deny you any honor, my lord." Taking his extended arm, she paced decorously down the hall with him.

Despite her coolness, his body responded powerfully to her touch. "Again, I wish to apologize for my ill temper earlier today. I hope I did not spoil the ascension for you."

"You apologized already, or had you forgotten?" She did not look at him, instead concentrating on the steps as they descended.

"No, I hadn't forgotten, but . . . I didn't have the impression you truly forgave me." They reached the ground floor and he paused, making her face him. "Will you? Please?"

She frowned slightly, but met his eyes readily enough. "I cannot hold you responsible for your upbringing or your world, my lord. In truth, you have been less critical of my behavior than perhaps I deserve. But I still do not understand the hostility you displayed toward your brother."

He led her forward again, into the dining room. "I suppose I should try to explain, though I'm not sure I understand it completely myself." Once they were both seated, he continued. "You have an older brother, do you not? Have you never felt resentment toward him for telling you what to do?"

"Charles has rarely tried to tell me what to do," she said, picking up her spoon. "If anything, the reverse has been true, particularly when he returned home after college and had to relearn much about the business."

She took a mouthful of soup and Marcus watched the spoon enter and leave her mouth, nearly losing the thread of their conversation in his fascination. "I see. Well, it was not that way with me and Peter—or my other brothers. As the youngest, they've all had a tendency to advise, scold, even coddle me. Siblings can be worse than parents in that regard." Certainly no one could accuse his father of coddling!

"So you felt that today Lord Peter was attempting to do that, to advise, scold, and coddle?" She seemed doubtful.

"Wasn't he? Prying into the details of our marriage, offering advice on how I should go on. Did it not seem so to you?"

She shook her head. "I thought he was simply being kind, and showing the sort of interest one might expect from a close family member. Of course, he did say something about *you* embarrassing *me*, rather than the other way around. Clearly it was intended to amuse me, but I suppose I can see where you might take it amiss."

So she still thought him too prosaic to be capable of anything remotely embarrassing, Marcus thought, amused himself. If she only knew the truth. Just as well, however. "No, that didn't offend me, particularly," he said truthfully. "It was his platitudes on mutual respect and such, and the implication that I don't appreciate you properly. Because I do, I assure you."

Just now he was appreciating her rather too much, in fact, as the tightness of his breeches could attest.

"True respect and appreciation extend beyond the bedchamber," she said, as though she could see his lap through the table. He shifted uncomfortably.

"Yes, of course," he agreed quickly. "Do you feel that I have shown you a lack of respect? It has not been intentional, if so."

She regarded him almost sadly, he thought. "No,

I'm sure it hasn't been. No doubt you are treating me with all of the respect most wives can expect of their husbands, and perhaps even more."

"And you wish for something beyond that?" He truly did want to understand, but felt increasingly at a loss.

"I am quite capable, you know," she said, as though that were some sort of answer. "But I feel as though my abilities may wither away from lack of use. I . . . should like to be more useful."

Marcus smiled in relief. "Is that all? That is easily remedied, then. Feel free to take over all management of the household, to redecorate the entire house instead of just your room, whatever you like. I'll put no obstacle in your way. I'm sure you can find enough to do to keep you from boredom."

She stared at him, the delight he'd hoped his words would produce distinctly lacking. "Boredom? I never said—" But then she stopped with a sigh. "Thank you, my lord. I'm certain I can."

"Marcus, remember?" he reminded her gently, wondering what he'd said wrong. If she did what he suggested, she'd be more useful than he himself had ever been—well, until his recent forays as the Saint of Seven Dials.

"Of course. Marcus." She set down her spoon, though her soup was but half-finished. "I find I am not particularly hungry after all. In fact, I have a bit of a headache. If you will excuse me?"

He took her hand in sudden concern. "Are you unwell?" That would explain her moodiness. "Should I call for a physician?"

"No, no, I am only a trifle indisposed. I'm certain I'll feel quite myself in the morning." Gently, she pulled her hand from his grasp and stood. "Pray finish your own dinner, Marcus. I'm quite able to make it upstairs on my own."

He had stood when she did, but now he reluctantly sat back down, since she so clearly wished it. "Very well. But do not hesitate to ring if you should need anything—anything at all."

"Thank you. I won't." Then, with that same sad smile, she left him.

Frowning after her, Marcus finally admitted what he'd been trying to deny since his near declaration the previous night. He'd fallen completely, desperately, head over heels in love with his wife. Even if it risked his secret, he was no longer going to attempt to keep her at a distance.

No, come morning, assuming Quinn was feeling better, he planned to launch an all-out assault on her heart. He would not give up until she loved him as desperately as he loved her. Then he'd show Peter, show the whole world, what a happy marriage was!

"You're certain you feel completely recovered?" The tenderness in Marcus's voice threatened to undermine Quinn's resolve to keep him at a distance, as he helped her from the carriage upon their arrival at Lord and Lady Jeller's Venetian breakfast.

"Yes, I told you it was merely a passing indisposition. I'm perfectly well today," she replied, stepping onto the wide sweep of lawn surrounding the house.

She would *not* let him cajole her into renewed intimacy. The risk of further hurt was too great.

The Jeller home was in Chelsea, just beyond Mayfair on the outskirts of London, making it a perfect setting for an outdoor entertainment. Quinn wished she still possessed the innocence to enjoy it. Marcus had taken that from her, along with her sense of purpose. But while the former was gone forever, the latter was being renewed. Polly had promised to have those names for her by dinnertime.

"This is lovely," she said in spite of herself. She hadn't realized such pastoral beauty existed so near to London.

"Lord Marcus! Lady Marcus! How delightful of you to come," exclaimed Miss Melks, hurrying forward with her sister Augusta in tow. "The most romantic tales have been circulating, and we were so hoping you would tell us the truth of them."

"Girls, girls!" Lady Jeller followed her daughters at a more decorous pace. "Let them get fairly out of their carriage before pelting them with questions, do. Welcome, Lord Marcus. I am pleased you were able to attend, and your new bride."

Marcus swept Lady Jeller a bow and made the appropriate introductions. "I don't know what stories you have heard," he said then, "but I like to think ours is a romantic one."

He put an arm about Quinn's waist, making her rebellious body thrill with remembered pleasure. She felt herself blushing and realized that would only lend credence to his words.

"I'm most happy to meet you, Lady Jeller," she said. "I must number your daughters among my first friends in England, as they were so kind to me at my first Society function."

Lucinda and Augusta smiled and tittered, then converged on her again. "A secret engagement was romantic enough, but a surprise wedding, only days after it came out!" Augusta exclaimed. "You must be very in love." Both girls sighed melodramatically.

Quinn did not dare meet Marcus's eye, though she felt him looking at her. "We, ah—"

"Yes, we certainly are," he responded firmly, pulling her close against his side. "And the beauty of such a quick wedding is that now I have the pleasure of paying court to my own wife, to make up for the lack of time I had to do so before our marriage. This way is far more satisfying, as you may imagine."

The Misses Melks' eyes grew round, and they both blushed, then tittered. "Why, you haven't changed a bit, Lord Marcus," Lucinda scolded him teasingly. "Still such a rogue! You're a very lucky woman, Lady Marcus, you are indeed." She then nudged her sister and led her away, leaving them alone.

Quinn looked up at Marcus doubtfully. "Did you not admonish me only yesterday for speaking of our private concerns to your brother?" Marcus, a *rogue*?

He met her eyes, his own twinkling very much as a rogue's might. "I already admitted I was wrong in what I said yesterday. Did you have any other fault to find in what I told the Misses Melks?"

"Other than the fact that it was a complete falsehood?" What had he meant by saying they were in love? She couldn't bring herself to ask directly, so added, "Or have you been courting me without my realizing it?"

"Not properly," he said, his blue eyes warm on hers. "But I mean to begin—and I hope that you will very much realize it."

She felt herself pinkening, and could not blame the warmth of the sun, shielded as she was by her new parasol. "You do?" she asked in a small voice, trying to fight the absurd pleasure that welled up in her at the very thought.

Instead of answering, he led her toward the tents that had been erected over the buffet tables. "Come, my lady. Let us see what dainties I can tempt you with. We'll fill our plates, then find a secluded spot for tender flirtation."

Quinn had never seen him in this mood outside of his bedchamber, but she could not seem to protest. Smiling and nodding at those people she had already met, Marcus making introductions to those she had not, they proceeded to the tables, where he loaded a tray with generous amounts of food and drink.

"Hmm. That arbor near the pond looks promising," he said then. "Let's see if it is still unoccupied."

It was. Grapes nearing ripeness hung in clusters above their heads, thick green leaves screening them from every direction but that of the pond, which stretched before them in idyllic stillness, a single swan gliding across its surface.

"This is lovely," Quinn said. *And romantic,* her rebellious heart added. Dangerously so, in fact.

"It is." Marcus set the tray at one end of the wooden bench beneath the arch of grapevines. "If we should buy an estate of our own, perhaps we can have something similar built." Taking her hand, he sat next to the tray and pulled her down to sit on his other side.

"Per—perhaps we can." An estate of their own? Quinn had not allowed herself to think seriously of any future they might have together, but suddenly the idea held a powerful appeal. A house in the country, with horses, dogs—perhaps children . . .

Marcus picked a strawberry from his tray and held it out with a smile. "May I tempt you, my lady?"

She reached for it, but he shook his head. "No hands. For today, I am your slave. Let me feed you as though you were an Egyptian queen."

Remembering the friezes they had seen at the Egyptian Hall, Quinn giggled, then, feeling a bit foolish, opened her mouth for the strawberry. He placed it on her tongue, firm and cool, and she bit into it, releasing its sweetness. Holding it by the stem, he brought the remaining half to his own mouth and bit off the rest. The intimacy of sharing the fruit sent an unexpected sizzle of desire through her.

Already, he was plucking something else from the tray—this time a small bunch of hothouse grapes. "One for you, one for me," he said, alternately popping one into her mouth and then his own. The sweet coolness of the grapes burst in her mouth as she chewed. Quinn had never realized fruit could be so . . . erotic.

Next he held up a thin slice of melon. "You eat from that end, and I'll eat from this," he suggested. Her eyes locked with his, she obeyed, their faces, their lips, drawing closer and closer as the melon disappeared. He took the last bite himself, then with a quick flick of his tongue, caught a drop of juice that had escaped the corner of her mouth.

A jolt went through her, and she tried to prepare herself for the assault on her senses his kiss would be—but he was already turning back to the tray. "Ah! A nice counterpoint." He proferred a peeled section of grapefruit, again holding it so that they could eat from either end, though their noses nearly touched.

After the sweetness of the melon, the tart grapefruit was almost a shock—but not an unpleasant one. This time when they met in the middle he licked the tangy juice from her very lips, his tongue exploring their outline. Quinn's eyes drifted closed from the sheer sensuality of it.

When he turned away again, still without kissing her, she found her voice. "Is this a courtship, my lord, or a seduction?"

He looked back at her, a smoky glimmer in his blue eyes. "Which would you prefer?" He held up another strawberry.

"Never having experienced either, I will reserve judgment," she replied, opening her mouth for the fruit. This time he treated the strawberry as he had the melon and grapefruit, dangling it between them so that they could bite from opposite sides.

Quinn chewed and swallowed, her lips a mere

hair breadth from his. His masculine scent seemed to surround her, mingling with the sweetness of the fruit. Unthinkingly, she parted her lips slightly, and he accepted her unspoken invitation, closing the minuscule gap between them.

Quinn felt as though it had been months since he had kissed her, instead of barely more than a day. She drank in the sensations as one perishing, slaking her thirst. His arms went about her, and she slid her own around his back, fruit and scenery alike forgotten in the passion of their embrace.

With sudden certainty, she knew that this was right, that the completeness she had missed was to be found only here, in Marcus's arms. And with that certainty came surrender—to him, and to her own feelings, which she had tried so hard to deny.

He must have felt it, for he deepened the kiss, his hands roaming up and down her back. But when he began to unfasten her gown, sanity abruptly returned.

"We—we mustn't," she breathed against his still-questing lips. "Not here."

Raising his head, he glanced around. "No one is watching," he assured her with a grin, and undid another hook at the nape of her neck.

"Marcus!" she exclaimed, laughing and pulling away. "I begin to think you really are a rogue after all."

He pulled a tragic face. "Alas, I am discovered at last. But I have heard it said that reformed rogues make the best lovers."

She stared at him, still doubting. Her staid, stodgy

Marcus, a rogue? Truly? She remembered comments from his brother, from those spiteful ladies in the Park, and today from the Misses Melks. Could it be that he was only stodgy around *her*? Not that he was being the least bit stodgy now . . .

"From what I have experienced so far, if you truly were a rogue, then that saying is quite accurate," she said, a smile tugging at her lips.

"I thank you for the compliment," he replied, lifting her hand to his lips. "Are you sure you don't want another demonstration right now?" He waggled his eyebrows at her.

She was far too tempted, actually, but this time it was her own sense of propriety that won out, rather than his. "I will defer it till this evening, when we can truly be alone."

"Very well. Now I've a reputation to live up to, I'd best fortify myself. Cheese?" He handed her a slice and took one himself.

His grin made her suspect he'd been bluffing about making love to her right there, where they might be discovered, and for a moment she wished she had put him to the test. *Had* she been wrong about him all along, or did he merely wish her to think so? Now she wasn't sure at all.

There was no denying the chemistry between them, however. It fairly hummed in the air as they finished their repast, exchanging lingering looks, if no more food. All too soon, they were done. Quinn took a last, longing look around their hideaway, resolving that she really would try to re-create it if she ever had the chance, then rose.

"Should we not rejoin the party? Our absence may be noticed."

"No matter if it is. We are newlyweds," he replied, but stood with her, leaving the empty tray. "Still, I can't resist the chance to show you off a bit. Come."

Though she knew she should feel offended at the idea of being displayed like an ornament, the idea that he was proud enough of her to show her off gratified her, nearly making up for the night before last, when he had sent her away. Perhaps he really had been tired . . .

"Lady Mountheath! How pleasant to see you again so soon."

Quinn turned at Marcus's greeting to see the woman she had most dreaded meeting again. Telling herself there was nothing more to fear from her, she forced a polite smile to her face.

"I was so delighted to learn that your betrothal was a true one after all," she said, showing far too many teeth as her eyes raked over Quinn, lingering meaningfully on her midsection. "The announcement of your wedding, however, took us all by surprise yet again, I confess."

With a smile as determined as Lady Mountheath's, Quinn responded, "We wished to be married before my father left England. Business required him to ship out earlier than planned, so we decided not to wait."

It was a perfectly plausible explanation, and Lady Mountheath's smile sagged a bit in disappointment. "Of course. Very practical. I wish you both every happiness."

They moved on, leaving her to hunt for gossip elsewhere. A few other acquaintances greeted Marcus. He introduced Quinn to those she had not met, then fell into a discussion on the burning of a notorious gaming hell. While they talked, Quinn looked about her, nodding a greeting to Miss Chalmers before her eye fell upon Mr. Paxton, determinedly heading their way.

"Lady Marcus!" he exclaimed as he reached them. "I trust you are beginning to feel more at home in England? Lord Marcus." With a nod he greeted her husband as well. Marcus returned the nod before turning his attention back to the animated description of the fire Mr. Thatcher was providing.

"Good day, Mr. Paxton. Yes, I'm settling in, I believe," Quinn responded with a smile. "How goes the thief-catching business?" With her new connection to the Saint, she found herself more curious than before—and a tiny bit nervous.

"Slowly, I fear, but I've by no means given up hope. Sooner or later he will make a mistake, and then I shall have him—though no doubt I will incur the enmity of innumerable ladies when that happens."

He was handsome, she supposed, with his chestnut curls and hazel eyes, but he held not a tenth of the attraction for her that Marcus did. She saw him only as a threat to her plans for the girls' school—but of course he must not suspect that.

"Surely you cannot think us as shallow as that, Mr. Paxton," she said teasingly. "Romantic as the Saint may seem in stories, I'm sure most of us prefer law and order in our heads, if not our hearts."

Though he still smiled, his eyes were shrewd, she thought, as he lowered his voice. "I do hope so, Lady Marcus. I understand that you have hired a child or two from off the streets since your marriage?"

Polly and Gobby. He'd somehow learned of their passing her note to the Saint! Fighting to let no trace of panic show on her face, she shrugged. "Our housekeeper handles the hirings, but it seems a charitable thing to do; there are so many unfortunates."

"Of course. But should one of these new servants have any information about the Saint's activities, you will send me word, will you not?"

The intensity of his gaze compelled honesty, so she chose her words carefully, sensing that he would spot a lie. "You can trust me to do the right thing, Mr. Paxton," she said firmly. "That is a promise."

Chapter 18

The small group around Harry Thatcher burst into laughter at his description of a young buck with his breeches afire. Marcus forced a chuckle, but in fact his attention was given solely to Paxton's conversation with his wife. Quinn had just promised to help the man catch the Saint of Seven Dials!

Did she know about Gobby? Clearly Paxton did. He would warn the boy when they returned home—against Paxton, and perhaps against Quinn, as well.

He now turned to Paxton himself, smiling as though he'd been listening to Harry instead of to him. "Did I hear you say you've made progress in your investigation?"

But Paxton shook his head. "No real progress, no. I'm merely trying to pursue all leads, however slight, until your friend, Lord Hardwyck, returns."

Marcus relaxed marginally. Still, someone must have informed him about Gobby coming to work in the stables. One of the other boys in the group, perhaps?

Just as well he'd brought only Gobby as lookout when he'd delivered the donation to Mrs. Hounslow. He'd had to be exceedingly quick to avoid the alert maidservant's eye as he left the money just inside the kitchen door, with a note attached.

"How very energetic of you," he responded now with a feigned yawn. "I'm glad to see you are able to take *some* time off for pleasure."

"I suppose my work ethic does border on the *bourgeoise*." Paxton grinned, appearing completely at ease now. "But it requires no more energy than a devotion to the hunt, or the gaming tables. Perhaps less."

"And is far more useful," Marcus agreed, relaxing further. "*Touché*." Again, he found himself almost liking the fellow, blast it. He turned to Quinn. "Did you say you wished another glass of lemonade, my dear?"

Though she'd claimed no such thing previously, she nodded. "Indeed, I am quite parched, my lord. If you will excuse us, Mr. Paxton?"

Once they were out of earshot, she asked, "How long are we expected to stay?"

"Dare I hope that means you are eager to be alone with me?" In truth, he was more than ready to leave, and not just because he wanted to resume his seduction of his wife.

"Am I so obvious?" Her smile made his other concerns fade to the background, his heart quickening its beat.

"Let us make our excuses to our host and hostess, then," he suggested. Accordingly, they sought out Lord and Lady Jeller, in conversation with a group of people near a charming folly not far from the tents, and bid them farewell.

A few of those standing by cast knowing glances his way, but Marcus didn't care. They were quite right in their suppositions, in any event. Glancing down at Quinn by his side, he marveled again at how petite she was, how innocent she appeared in her confection of white lace and muslin. He knew what passion lurked beneath that angelic exterior, however, and he was eager to release it.

"We have no plans for the rest of the day, have we?" he asked as he handed her into the carriage. Given an entire evening alone with Quinn, surely he could—

"I received a note this morning from the Claridges," she replied, "inviting us to join them at the theater tonight. We needn't go if you do not wish to, of course."

"I'd rather like to take you to the theater, I believe." They'd have plenty of time together beforehand—enough time, he hoped, for what he had planned.

But then his thoughts returned to his earlier concern. "Did I hear you promising Paxton you'd help him in his investigations?" The words were out before he could prevent them.

She glance at him, clearly startled. "Not in any active way." A rather evasive answer, he thought. "Since I can't imagine what help I could possibly be, it was surely an empty promise in any event."

"No doubt." He wanted to ask her about Gobby, but realized that would only arouse her suspicions if she were yet unaware that he'd been hired. "I agree, of course, that it would be our duty to report anything we might learn, from whatever source—however unlikely that seems."

"I am relieved that we are of one mind on the matter."

As she seemed no more inclined to discuss it further than he was, he changed the subject. "What production are we to see tonight? I presume it is at one of the smaller theaters, as the larger ones have concluded their seasons until October."

"Yes, the Lyceum. An operatic comedy, I believe my uncle said."

They lightly discussed theater in general—he was surprised to learn she had attended often in Baltimore—until they reached home. "I find I am already hungry again," Marcus said teasingly as he led Quinn into the house. "Perhaps we should ask Cook to prepare us a tray?"

The look she slanted up at him showed she caught his meaning. "Shall we take it in the library, or upstairs, do you think?"

"Oh, upstairs, definitely. The chairs in the library are so inconveniently placed for sharing a meal, you know."

That wasn't true, but if she noticed she didn't comment upon it, agreeing that his was an excellent plan. Sending a footman to request that a repast of assorted meats, bread, cheeses, and fruit be sent up, they mounted the stairs together.

On reaching his chamber, Quinn turned to him with a wicked smile that made his pulse race. "I believe you said something about a demonstration, my lord?"

"Shall I begin it now, or wait until the food arrives?" he asked, stroking her cheek with the back of one hand. Indeed, he was burning to resume his interrupted seduction.

"Oh. I suppose you should wait," she said with a little pout that required him to kiss her. She responded eagerly, and it was only with great difficulty that he restrained himself from undressing her at once.

Her own hands worked at his cravat, then his shirt fastenings, until he was bare to the waist. "Unfair," he murmured, and began undoing the hooks down her back, delighting in the smoothness of her skin as it was revealed, inch by delicious inch. He was just easing her dress over her shoulders, still kissing her deeply, when a discreet tap sounded at the door.

They broke apart, and Quinn glanced down at herself, and then at him. "Oops." She sounded contrite, but her eyes danced with mischief.

"Vixen. Into the dressing room with you, while the tray is brought in."

Obediently, she disappeared and Marcus, flinging a dressing gown about his bare torso, opened the door. The footman wisely did not notice anything amiss as he placed the tray as directed on a low table and bowed out of the room.

"You may come out now," Marcus called, and at

once Quinn reappeared, pulling her gown back up over her shoulders. "No need for that," he said, throwing off his dressing gown and meeting her halfway. "Now, where were we?" Lowering his lips to hers, he eased the dress back down to her waist.

Soon they were both stripped to the skin, but when she glanced toward the bed, Marcus shook his head. "Not yet. I have more seducing to do first."

He might not be ready to tell her the truth about the Saint, but he was still determined to disabuse her of the notion that he was some sort of stickler for propriety. Taking her by the hand, he led her to the waiting tray and seated himself on the thick carpet, pulling her down beside him.

His hand hovered over the assortment. "Now, my lady, what is your pleasure?"

"Hmm. One of those pastries, perhaps. I'll work my way up to the meat."

"Very well, my naughty wife," he said with a low chuckle. Picking up a triangular pastry, he held it to her lips, taking a bite from his end as she took a bite from hers. Flakes of buttery crust drifted to settle on her breasts. When their lips met in the middle, he flicked a drop of the sweet filling from the corner of her mouth with his tongue before going after the errant crumbs.

One flake teetered on her right nipple, and he took it into his mouth rather than risk losing it. She gave a little gasp, and he smiled up at her. "Much neater if we clean up as we go, don't you agree?"

Moistening his lips, he plucked the remaining crumbs from her chest, then sat up again, his arousal more than evident. That she noticed was equally clear, from the darting glances she sent, as well as her heightened color.

"I'll choose next," he said, picking up a particularly juicy-looking peach. Holding it between them, they again ate from opposite sides, their gazes locked and smoldering. Marcus had used food as a seduction device once or twice before, but never had he been so profoundly affected himself.

Juice from the peach ran down his chin and dripped, and he jumped when its coolness landed squarely on his erection.

"My turn to tidy up, my lord." She bent down, her curls brushing his thighs, and took his shaft into her mouth as he had done with her breast.

Now it was his turn to gasp at the astonishingly exquisite sensations her tongue produced. When he bucked, she responded with a throaty laugh, then sat up just before he could lose control completely. "More peach, my lord?" she asked innocently.

He could not immediately speak, so he held up the fruit again, his body chafing for more of her. This time he angled the peach so that the juice ran down her side, pooling on her belly before a rivulet escaped to disappear into the curls below.

With a wink, he handed her what was left of the peach and kissed his way from just beneath her breasts to her navel, where he licked up the sweet juice there before following its trail lower. Her sweet, musty scent inflamed him further, and it was sheer delight when she cried out as he flicked his tongue into her cleft.

"Ready for the meat now?" he asked, lifting his head.

Her lips were slightly parted, her eyes bright with desire. "Yes," she whispered. "I'm ready."

Though her meaning was clear, he plucked a slice of roast beef from the tray. "Here you are," he said, holding it out with a grin.

She took it from him, her eyes on his, then deliberately rolled it into a cylinder. Smiling wickedly, she licked the end of the roll before taking it into her mouth to suck on it. His body reacted powerfully, as though her mouth were upon him instead of the roll of beef—as she clearly intended.

"You hussy," he growled, then leaned forward and bit off the other end of the roll, ready to move to the next level. "Wine?" he asked, turning to fill the glasses on the tray from the decanter.

"Just enough to wash this down," she replied, finishing her share of the beef, then licking her lips seductively.

Marcus handed her a glass, taking a sip from his own. "If I didn't know better, I'd almost suspect you'd had instruction at this sort of thing," he told her.

Her eyes went wide and innocent. "But I have, my lord."

"What?" He nearly spilled his wine.

"Was that not a lesson you gave me earlier today, in the arbor? I was merely embellishing upon your teaching. I take it I have been an apt pupil?" Though she kept her expression innocent, her lips quivered with suppressed laughter.

"Devastatingly so." Tossing off the remainder of his glass with a single gulp, he set it down and reached for her hand. "Time for the next course. No, I don't mean food," he added, when she glanced at the tray.

Setting aside her own glass, she slid closer, moving easily, naturally into his arms. He lowered his mouth to hers, tasting the tang of the wine on her lips as he caressed her bare back. Her hands slowly glided from his shoulders to his waist, as though savoring the shape of him, arousing him further.

Deepening the kiss, he lowered her gently onto the plush carpet with one arm, running his other palm down her body, from shoulder to knee, delighting in her feminine curves. Then back up, along her inner thigh, where he paused, his hand cupping her curls, his fingers barely brushing what lay beneath.

She arched, a faint moan vibrating against his lips. Exploring with one finger, he found her moist, ready, but still he delayed, savoring her arousal, though his own clamored for completion. Slowly, slowly, he stretched his length beside her, until he lay on his side, facing her, his hand gently teasing her the while.

She broke the kiss to look at him, her green eyes glinting with mingled mischief and desire. Then, without warning, she pushed him onto his back and climbed astride him. "Don't toy with a starving woman," she scolded with a grin, sliding her mound along the length of his shaft, making him gasp at the exquisite sensation.

Lowering her head until her hair fell about his face in dusky profusion, she kissed him again, still pressing herself to him below, sliding forward and back in an ever-quickening rhythm. Just as he felt he might explode, she raised herself slightly and impaled herself on him, tightening about him like a glove.

Instantly they climaxed together, with long, shuddering sighs, as he expended himself into her depths and she received him. She collapsed atop him, and he held her close, breathing in the scent of her as his heartbeat slowly returned to normal.

Again he felt an almost overwhelming urge to tell her he loved her. This time it was not shock that prevented him, but prudence.

As his senses returned, so did the knowledge that he could not completely trust her, dear as she was to him. And until he could do so, he dared not give her that much power over him—or, at least, he dared not let her know how much power she already had. Not while he was yet unsure whether his feelings were returned.

"More wine?" he asked, when she finally stirred. "The rest of our dinner awaits."

Half an hour later, finishing their repast to the accompaniment of light banter about the events of the day, Quinn sighed inwardly. Though her body was sated and relaxed, her heart was less than satisfied. She and Marcus had reestablished physical intimacy, but they seemed no closer than they'd been before—perhaps less.

She couldn't help feeling that Marcus kept a part of himself from her, nor could she deny that she was doing the same. To surrender herself to him completely, to let him know how much he meant to her, would be to lose the last of her freedom. Irrational as it was, she feared to take that final step.

"I suppose we'd both best dress, if we are to go to the theater," she suggested, as Marcus set their empty plates and glasses back on the tray. She remembered that Polly had promised those names to her this evening. Would she have them already?

"Yes, I suppose you're right." Though he spoke as though he were reluctant to let her go, he stood at once, helping her to her feet. "You'll want these, I suppose, in case your abigail is lurking in your chamber," he said, picking up her chemise and gown. "Here, I'll help you into them."

Quickly and competently, he helped her back into her clothes, making her wonder afresh how much experience he'd had with such things before. More than she'd originally credited him with, obviously. The thought brought with it a pang of something beyond simple surprise, but she refused to dwell on it.

"Thank you. Shall we meet downstairs later?"

He nodded. "We needn't leave for nearly two hours, so you've time for a bath, if you'd like. I have a few things to do as well."

With a light kiss that seemed almost to make a mockery of the passion they had so recently shared, he opened the dressing-room door and saw her back to her room.

Instead of the bath she'd have preferred, Quinn

had only a quick wash before dressing, so that she would have time to speak with Polly before meeting Marcus again. When she reached the kitchen, the staff was just finishing their own dinner at the long wooden table, Polly at the end nearest the back door.

Catching the girl's eye, Quinn gave a few instructions for the next day's meals to Mrs. McKay, then said, "I wish to take a look at the garden before it grows dark. If we can find seeds or seedlings locally, there are one or two American vegetables I'd like to attempt here."

She motioned for Polly to follow her, and at a nod from the cook, the girl accompanied her out into the garden.

"It's that lucky you came by now, milady," Polly said softly as they moved among the rows of greens, ostensibly looking for a suitable spot for additions. "Annie should be by anytime."

Even as she spoke, the gate creaked. Looking up, Quinn saw a girl in faded blue silk standing frozen in surprise at the sight of her. She turned as though to flee, but Quinn called out, "Please don't go, Annie. I'd like to speak with you."

Hesitantly, the girl stepped into the garden, looking to Polly for reassurance.

"It's all right, Annie. Her Ladyship wants to help, the way she's helped me."

"Truly, milady?"

The girl, only a year or two older than Polly, with wide blue eyes and pale curls, was quite lovely—or would have been, if not for the ugly purple bruise that spread across one cheek. Anger boiled up in Quinn at the sight of it.

"I do indeed, Annie. Can you stay to talk for a moment, while Polly fetches you something to eat from the kitchen?"

Annie nodded. "Mr. Twitchell won't let me work until this fades." She indicated the bruise. "Leastways, not where I usually work, and the lower sorts don't start their carousing till later in the evening."

Quinn's mind shied away from the particulars of what this girl's life must be like, but her resolve to help stiffened. "And where do you usually work, Annie? No, you won't get into any trouble," she promised when the girl looked wary. "But to help you, I'll need some information. Polly says you'd like to leave this line of work?"

Now the girl smiled at last, making her appear even lovelier. "Oh, yes, milady! I've a cousin who's an actress at one of the theaters, and she says I'd be a natural there, but Mr. Twitchell, he won't hear of it. I even offered to pay him part of my wages if they hire me, but he says it won't be enough."

"How much . . . are you earning now?"

"I don't rightly know, milady. The gentlemen, they pays Mr. Twitchell direct. He don't trust us girls with that kind of money. Prob'ly figures we'd run off with it."

As they'd be quite justified in doing, of course, Quinn thought. This Mr. Twitchell was no fool, apparently, for all he was evil. She wondered whether Mr. Paxton might be willing to do something about him.

"Annie, will you tell me who gave you this bruise?" Quinn gently touched the girl's discolored cheek.

She bit her lip, then nodded. " 'Twas Lord Pynchton," she admitted. "He gets a bit rough sometimes. None of us girls like to go to him, so Twitchell makes us take turns."

Quinn didn't think she'd met the man in question, but the very idea of someone who wielded the power of a peer doing something like this to a helpless girl appalled her. "Are there any others like him? To truly help, I need as many names as you can give me."

"He's the worst," Annie said, "but Lord Ribbleton once blacked Maisie's eye when she took too long getting undressed. Most of the others aren't too bad—not scary-like, anyway."

Quinn made a mental note of the two names she had so far. "And who are some of those others?"

"There's a fair number, milady. Some of my own regulars are Sir Hadley Leverton, old Lord Simcox and Mr. Hill."

Under continued, gentle questioning, Quinn was able to elicit another dozen names of gentlemen who patronized Annie's friends, under the auspices of the enterprising Mr. Twitchell. Polly returned with a pair of meat pies as she finished.

"Thank you, Annie, you've been most helpful. I intend to assist as many of your friends as I can. But please, don't let anyone know what you've told me. It could put you at risk, as well as making it more difficult for me to help you."

Both girls promised fervently to keep her secret, and Quinn waited until they left—Polly back to the kitchen and Annie through the gate—to pull out the small notebook she'd brought along. Quickly, she wrote down all of the names before she could forget them.

Then, finally, she was able to give way to the shock and dismay she felt, which she'd carefully concealed before, not wanting Annie to construe her reaction as blame. Looking down at her list, she shook her head, fighting a wave of queasiness.

Several of the names were familiar to her. In fact, she had met two of the men—and their wives—at the Claridges' house. What would her aunt and uncle—and others—say if they discovered the truth about those so-called gentlemen?

And what might those gentlemen pay to avoid such discovery? Enough to fund her school for girls, she hoped. She just needed a suitable—and anonymous—way to put the choice before them.

Reluctantly, she skimmed to the bottom of the list. Surely, Lord Fernworth was a friend of her husband's? If members of Marcus's own circle patronized these poor girls, did that mean that he was aware of it, and did not care? Or worse . . . No, she would not even consider that possibility.

She started to head for the house, then paused. On sudden decision, she turned again and instead went through the gate and around to the mews. There was a fair amount of activity in the stables as a carriage was readied for their trip to the theater. Farther along, other carriages were being made ready for other residents of Grosvenor Street as the fashionable hour approached.

Then Quinn saw what she was looking for—a shock of hair as red as Polly's. "Gobby!" she called softly. "I need to speak with you."

Putting down the pail he carried, he came forward, respectfully tugging his forelock. "Aye, milady?"

"Is . . . is your job here to your liking?"

"Oh, aye, milady! I thank ye kindly for taking me on, and His Lordship, too."

Quinn bit her lip. "Has His Lordship spoken with you since you began working here? Has he . . . seemed to notice you?"

She thought the boy looked confused for a moment, but then he shook his head. "A great lord like that wouldn't speak with the likes of me, milady."

"No, no, I suppose not. Then we'll hope he doesn't remember you from that day on the street more than a week ago."

Gobby's eyes widened, and Quinn could see he had just realized that she was the girl who had been dressed as a boy that day. He opened his mouth as though to ask a question, then closed it, apparently recalling their comparative stations.

Quinn smiled. "Yes, that was me. The workings of fate are strange, are they not? But I hope in this instance it has worked to your advantage, and to Polly's." She hesitated for a moment, but then her curiosity won out over caution. "Gobby, what can you tell me about the Saint of Seven Dials? What sort of man is he?"

Instantly, his smile disappeared. "I dunno what you mean, milady, and that's a fact. If Polly told you I know anything, she's wrong. I've heard tell of him, that's all, like everyone else."

"Of course, of course. I'm sorry." She should have known he'd never betray the Saint to someone of her class! "I was simply curious. Now, I have a favor to ask of you."

"Yes, milady?" He still looked suspicious.

"I'd like you to run over to Grillon's Hotel when you get an opportunity and ask if any message has been left for A Sympathetic Lady. If there is one, bring it back here and have Polly give it to me. It's for a friend of mine."

She was prepared to elaborate on her fictitious friend should he ask questions, but he only nodded. "Aye, milady, I'll go tonight. Will there be anything else?"

"No, Gobby, thank you. Do let me know—through Polly if you prefer—if you need anything. And if His Lorship *should* question you, please don't mention any of this."

She headed back to the house then, slipping back upstairs to her room, where she again pondered her list of names until a tap at her door interrupted her plotting. Fearing that it might be Marcus, she quickly tucked the notebook into the drawer of her writing desk before rising to answer. "Yes?"

One of the housemaids opened the door with a curtsy. "Begging your pardon, but His Lordship says to tell you he's in the library, whenever you wish to join him."

"Thank you." Checking her hair in the glass, she followed the girl downstairs, her mind still occupied with her plans for the coming days.

Chapter 19

I f Quinn seemed preoccupied on the way to the theater, Marcus scarcely noticed. He'd found a letter from Luke awaiting him when he went downstairs earlier, informing him that his friend would be returning to London by the first of August, less than two weeks hence. After his conversations with Paxton, he felt it was more important than ever to establish that Luke could not possibly be the Saint of Seven Dials—which meant he had work to do tonight.

The Lyceum was relatively crowded when they arrived, a testament to how few theaters were open in late July. Lord Claridge spotted them at once, however, hurrying over to greet Quinn warmly.

"How lovely to see you again, my dear. It appears that married life agrees with you. Does it not, ladies?" He turned to his wife and daughter, who had followed more slowly.

Lady Claridge smiled—a less artificial smile than Marcus had yet seen her wear, though he could not have called it warm. "You are looking well indeed, Lady Marcus."

"Yes, cousin, you are. And what a scrumptious gown!" exclaimed Lady Constance, her enthusiasm apparently genuine. "Lord Marcus, we are cousins now, as well." She extended her hand with only a hint of a simper.

Marcus greeted them all warmly, feeling far better disposed toward the people who had helped to force him into marriage than he had the last time he'd seen them.

"I am honored by the connection, I assure you, Lady Constance," he said, bowing over her hand, then her mother's.

"I must warn you, Lord Marcus, that I promised my brother-in-law, before he left, that I would stand in his office by making certain our Quinn is happy."

Though the marquess spoke with his usual mildness, there was an underlying seriousness to his tone. For the first time, Marcus noticed that his eyes were much like Quinn's. "Are you, my dear?" Lord Claridge asked then, turning to his niece.

Smiling, she nodded. "It seems Papa was right about Lord Marcus. He's showing himself to be quite passable as a husband." She slanted a mischievous glance up at Marcus, making him remember rather too vividly their afternoon tryst in his bedchamber.

"I trust you can say the same of your bride?" Lady Claridge asked then, one eyebrow raised skeptically.

"More than passable, madam, I assure you," he replied.

"Lord Marcus is most kind," Quinn said. "I fear I've been a bit of a trial to him, with my unfamiliarity with English ways."

"Not a bit of it," he retorted at once, determined to put her concerns on that score to rest—as he should have done before. "I find her most refreshing, and no more prone to error than any girl raised in the country might be."

Lord Claridge nodded affably. "Quinn has no doubt been accustomed to more independence than is usual here, between my dear sister's influence and her American upbringing. I've never felt that was altogether a bad thing, and I'm happy to hear it has caused no problems between you."

Lady Claridge sniffed, but did not contradict her husband, rather to Marcus's surprise. It appeared that the balance of power there had shifted subtly, and he suspected that Quinn and her father were somehow responsible. Curiously, Lady Claridge and Lady Constance appeared happier than before, if anything.

They all moved toward the gallery as they spoke. This theater did not have the private boxes that the larger, more fashionable ones did.

"My dear, you already know Lord Fernworth and Sir Cyril Weathers," Marcus said, when two of his formerly closest friends approached. He wondered now that he had ever found pleasure in their dissipated society.

Ferny bent over Quinn's hand. "Delighted to see you again, Lady Marcus," he said, with slightly less slurring than he'd used at the Tinsdale do. "Just as charming as before."

Quinn all but snatched her hand away, and it appeared to Marcus that she had all she could do to cling to her smile. "Too kind," she murmured, then turned to greet Sir Cyril with only slightly more warmth.

Had Ferny done something to offend her? He would have to find out—and give the fellow a friendly thrashing, if he deserved it. Every now and then Ferny needed a reminder that everyone didn't value the pursuit of pleasure above all else, as he did.

That thought made Marcus wonder again at the change that had occurred in himself over the past few weeks, as undeniable as it was profound. He hoped he wasn't turning into a crashing bore.

"It's been ages since we've had a good carouse," Ferny said to him then, echoing his thoughts. "Realize there are some pleasures you've likely sworn off—" he winked at Quinn, who stiffened and looked pointedly away—"but a night out gaming might do you good. What say you to a stop in at Boodle's later?"

Marcus had to grin in spite of himself. The fellow really was incorrigible. "I think not, though I thank you for the offer. My gaming days are behind me as well. But perhaps I'll see you tomorrow night, at the Wittington do?"

"Oh, aye, I'll be there. But how you can live without—" Catching Quinn's eye again, Lord Fernworth broke off. "See you then," he finished lamely, and he and Sir Cyril went off to find their seats.

"Don't mind Ferny," he said to Quinn, as her expression still seemed strained. "He's a nodcock, of course, but not a bad sort for all that."

She looked at him doubtfully. "You don't think so?"

He shook his head. "If he doesn't cut back on the spirits, he may find himself permanently dicked in the nob, but most of his vices are cheerful ones. Still, if he says or does anything to offend you, you must let me know."

"Of course," she replied, allaying his earlier worry somewhat, though she still looked rather perturbed. Likely she didn't care for Ferny's innuendoes in front of her relations. He'd see it didn't happen again.

Marcus, Quinn, and the Claridges moved on to take their seats at the front of the gallery, which offered an excellent view of the stage as well as the promenade below. His mind still puzzling over his new reaction to Ferny's old habits, he almost didn't notice one of the crimps he'd been tormenting.

Mr. Hill, the most highly placed of the group, was taking his seat on the lower level, deep in conversation with Lord Ribbleton. Could there be a connection there? It seemed unlikely. Ribbleton, a marquess, had no need of funds, to the best of his knowledge, and surely wouldn't risk his standing in Society by becoming involved in criminal activity.

Still, that matter of his carrying tales about Luke

to Mr. Paxton. Perhaps a visit to Lord Ribbleton's study—and valuables—would not be out of order.

Tonight, however, if he could slip away from Quinn, he intended to conduct some Saintly business at the home of Sir Gregory Dobson, Mr. Hill's cousin. Even if he had no knowledge of the crimps' activities, his wealth was helping to support them. Besides, Marcus had never cared for the fellow.

"What's the matter, cousin?" Lady Constance whispered as the curtain rose. "You look as though you have swallowed a fly."

Realizing she had allowed her false smile to slip, Quinn hurriedly pulled it back into place. "I was simply lost in thought. It . . . seemed that those gentlemen had been drinking."

In fact, it was Marcus's very friendliness toward Lord Fernworth that had soured her mood. The thought that Marcus might ever have been involved in the things she knew his friend to be guilty of made her almost physically ill.

Lord Claridge, who was seated between his daughter and Quinn, overheard her. "Now, dear, pray don't judge your husband by his friends," he murmured, as though reading her mind. "Single gentlemen often behave less than circumspectly, but marriage generally sets them right." He smiled fondly at his wife, who, surprisingly enough, smiled back.

"Yes, my lord, I'm certain you are right."

The comedy began, the music and singing raucous enough that only Quinn could hear her uncle's next comment. "Take your father, for example. He was quite the rebel in his youth, as I recall, encouraging poor Glynna to leave all she'd been raised to, to join him in the former colonies."

Quinn stared at him, the mediocre performance quite forgotten, trying to imagine her father as a rebel. "Is . . . is that why your father cast her off?"

He nodded, sadly. "I never blamed her for cutting all ties with her family. Father was really quite harsh. But he is gone now, and I'm delighted at this chance to mend old breaches." He patted Quinn's hand.

Involuntarily, Quinn glanced past him to Lady Claridge.

"Yes, even Lenore now admits that the scandal my father kept alive for so long is dead at last, and that the family reputation is in no danger from you. It is my hope that we will see much of you, and that you and Constance might become friends."

Lady Constance apparently heard that final remark, for she turned, her eyes meeting Quinn's for an awkward moment. But then she smiled tentatively, and Quinn smiled back. It was a beginning.

Turning back to the play, Quinn realized that her father's wishes had been answered—she truly had been reconciled to her mother's family. Had her own marriage been a necessary means to that end, however? And even if it were not, did she truly regret it now? She honestly didn't know.

Quinn was unusually quiet during the drive home from the theater, but as on the drive there, Marcus was too wrapped up in his own plans to pay much attention. Not until they were inside the house did he rouse himself to his surroundings, asking if she'd like to join him in the library for a brandy.

He wouldn't risk hurting her again by pleading weariness, he'd already decided that. But perhaps if he could convince her to drink more than one glass—

"No, I don't think so tonight," she said then, spoiling that plan. "In fact, I believe I will go up to my bed at once, as I find myself quite tired. If you will excuse me?"

Though it solved his problem handily, Marcus could not help feeling a trifle disappointed himself. He took care not to show it, however. "Certainly, my dear. Are you feeling indisposed again, as you did last night?"

"No, no, merely tired. Good night, Marcus."

He leaned over to kiss her good night, but she had already turned away. Surely this was more than mere tiredness? He remembered how she had acted just before the play, after Ferny's foolishness. "Quinn—" he began.

She turned, questioningly, but he remembered in time that he had work to do tonight. He could unravel this mystery tomorrow. "Sleep well," he said.

"Thank you. I'll try." Without a backward glance, she mounted the stairs, leaving him to frown after her.

If he could finish his business with the crimps, once Luke was back in Town he'd have no pressing reason to play the Saint again. That excitement had already paled in comparison to what he was finding with Quinn, in any event. He looked forward to a time when he could safely tell her everything.

That reminded him that he had yet to warn Gobby about Paxton's suspicions. He'd need the boy to act as lookout for him tonight, as well. Brandy forgotten, he headed for the mews.

Gobby popped out from behind the stables as he approached, clearly waiting for him. "I'm that glad to see you, milord!" he exclaimed as soon as they'd gone a discreet distance from the other stable hands. "Something havey-cavey going on."

"Oh?" It appeared his worries had been well-founded. "Are you being watched?"

But Gobby shook his head. "Not so's I've noticed, and I've kept my eyes peeled. But something's up, word getting around somehow. Your missus was out here earlier asking about the Saint."

"Lady Marcus came out to the stables to speak with you specifically?"

The lad nodded emphatically. "Aye, that she did. I didn't think much of it, till she mentioned the Saint. After all—" But he broke off whatever he'd been about to say, and concluded, "I didn't tell her nothing, of course."

Marcus briefly wondered why Gobby wouldn't have thought her very presence here odd. Did she perhaps come frequently to visit her new mount, Tempest? Not that it mattered just now.

"Good lad. It's especially important now that you not let on—to anyone—that you've ever had any dealings with the Saint. That investigator I told you about appears to be suspicious already, and he's likely enlisted others—possibly even my wife—to help him dig up information."

"Suspicious about *me*, milord?" Rather than look frightened, Gobby grinned and puffed out his chest. "I ain't never been specifickly investigated. Can I tell Stilt an' all? Tig'll be—"

"You can warn them, but be careful. Someone has clearly tipped Paxton off about your working here, and it may well be one of the lads you trust. We don't dare trust anyone too far." And that included Quinn, unfortunately.

Gobby's eyes widened. "One of me mates? I don't believe it! More like it was one of the other stable lads here, or one of Ickle's lads."

"Ickle?" Marcus hadn't heard that name before.

"He heads up another bunch of pickpockets and such. Him and Twitchell are always trying to steal the best lads from each other. Kind of competitive, like."

A rival gang, then, Marcus thought. He'd known that there were many more thief-masters than Mr. Twitchell about, of course, but he could only deal with one threat at a time.

"Yes, that's a possibility, I suppose," he admitted. Surely a more likely one than that Quinn had tipped off Paxton? "Still, for now we'd best operate on the assumption that anyone may be an enemy. It should only be for another week or so, at any rate."

Gobby stared up at him. "Why's that, milord?"

"Because the Saint will be retiring—for good."

"That'll be a sore blow to . . . to lots of folks." The boy looked stricken, in fact.

Marcus laid a hand on his shoulder. "I know, but it will be for the best. And in the meantime, I'll need you as lookout again tonight, if you're willing."

Though he still looked disappointed at the news of the Saint's retirement, Gobby nodded eagerly. "Willing and able, milord! Right now?"

"I need to change my clothing first. Then we'd best wait another hour or so, to increase the likelihood that the household in question will be abed. I'll be back for you then."

Walking back to the house, he considered what Gobby had told him about Quinn. It was possible, of course, that she was simply curious about the Saint—as so many ladies seemed to be—and was asking all of the servants about him. Or, if she'd learned that Gobby was recently hired—perhaps from Mrs. Walsh—she might have been fulfilling her promise to Paxton.

Either way, it was dangerous. Clearly, his instincts had been sound to keep the truth from her, much as he hated doing so.

The moment she reached her room, Quinn sent for bathwater to be brought. She hadn't had time for a real bath earlier, and now she felt far more in need of one—not that mere water could wash away the taint she imagined.

Remembering Marcus's conversation with Lord Fernworth, she took what comfort she could from the fact that Marcus had refused to meet him tonight. But what of Fernworth's comment about Marcus "swearing off" certain pleasures, implying women were involved?

Had Marcus consorted with fancy-girls, as Polly called them? Quinn had not led a particularly sheltered life. She knew that unmarried men—and some married ones—kept mistresses. Adult mistresses. To know that Marcus had done so would not upset her. Or, well, not horribly, at any rate. Perhaps that was all Lord Fernworth had meant.

A tap at the door heralded the arrival of her bathwater. She waited while the maids poured kettle after kettle of steaming water into the tub, then dismissed them all, her abigail included. She needed to be alone.

The hot water seemed to clear her mind as well as cleanse her body. As she soaked, her nebulous plans took shape. Lord Fernworth had said he would be at the Wittington's ball tomorrow night. Knowing that, she could make certain he was the first to be given an opportunity to contribute to her school fund.

As they were such close friends, Fernworth would likely tell Marcus of the potential threat. She would then be able to judge by Marcus's demeanor whether he feared similar extortion. If he remained calm, she would consider him innocent. If he grew nervous, however . . .

"I pray he will not," she murmured aloud, scrubbing her arms with the washcloth. In truth, she was unsure if even certain knowledge of past atrocities could extinguish her love for him now. And what did that say about her?

She scrubbed harder.

As she was toweling herself dry, another, tentative tap came at the door. Throwing on a wrapper, she opened it to find Polly, an envelope in her hand.

"Ah. From Gobby, I presume?"

Polly nodded. "He brought it to me while you were out, but this was my first chance to slip away from the kitchen without anyone asking questions. Gobby had enough questions of his own, the meddling little worm." Her freckled face primmed up with disapproval.

Frowning, Quinn ushered the girl into her room and closed the door. "Questions? What sort of questions?"

Now Polly flushed, as though belatedly realizing what she'd said. "He didn't mean no harm, milady, I'm sure of it. But you know how curious young boys can be."

"I do indeed, and I'm not angry at Gobby. Please, though, tell me what questions he asked."

"He started off accusing me of telling you about him knowing the Saint and all. Said you asked him questions—"

"Yes, I'm afraid I did," said Quinn, interrupting her. "I shouldn't have done so, for of course he would assume you were involved. I'm sorry. Was that all?"

Polly shook her head. "He wanted to know about this letter, too—who this Sympathetic Lady is, and what she's up to. Likely the Saint asked him to find out. Or maybe His Lordship. I saw him talking to Gobby not ten minutes ago, though they didn't see me."

"His Lordship? Lord Marcus, you mean?" Quinn asked in astonishment. He must know Quinn had hired Gobby as well as Polly, then. He had overheard her speaking with Mr. Paxton earlier today, and must have known she was being less than truthful. Why had he not mentioned anything to her afterward?

"Aye, milady. Will he be angry that me and Gobby have been sending notes for you? Will he turn us off?" Polly's eyes were large and worried.

"Absolutely not." Quinn put all the conviction into her tone she could muster. "You were acting under my orders, and I certainly won't allow either of you to suffer for that. Nor can I imagine Lord Marcus seeking to punish you in any way."

Whatever faults she might imagine him to possess, vindictiveness did not seem to be one of them. Of course, she'd known him less than two weeks, amazing as that seemed . . .

"Thank you, milady!" Relief shone from Polly's face, the worry gone. She turned to go.

"Just a moment." Going to her writing desk, Quinn pulled out two silver shillings, then came back and dropped them into Polly's hand. "One is for you, and one for Gobby. Thank him again for me."

"Aye, milady, I'll do that. And thank *you*!" With a grateful curtsy, Polly hurried out.

Quinn smiled after her for a moment. It was so easy to give pleasure, sometimes. If only everything could be so simple. Then, closing the door, she turned her attention to the letter.

It was from Mrs. Hounslow, not the mysterious Saint of Seven Dials, she saw with a tiny pang of disappointment. The contents, however, quickly revived her spirits. A small square of paper fluttered out when she broke the seal, which she ignored while she read the letter.

My Dear Sympathetic Lady,

I cannot thank you enough for your intervention on behalf of the school we discussed. Though normally I would prefer to operate strictly within the bounds of the law, for the sakes of those poor unfortunate girls, I must gratefully accept the generous donation, in the sum of one thousand, two hundred pounds, from that remarkable gentleman known only as the Saint of Seven Dials. I have enclosed the note he left with his donation for your perusal. This sum will allow the immediate purchase of a suitable building near the area discussed, as well as most of the necessary furnishings. I should say that as much again would allow the hiring of as many teachers as we need, as well as board for students and teachers for the first year. In other words, we are halfway there! Should you somehow be able to prevail upon the Saint to duplicate his generosity, or should you otherwise procure the remainder of the funds needed, you will have made a lasting difference in the lives of those unfortunate girls we discussed, as well as making a very real investment in our country's future. Pray accept my gratitude, from the bottom of my heart.

—E. Hounslow

Quinn read through the letter with delight and amazement, then bent to snatch up the paper that had fallen. It was a card, inked on one side with a numeral seven, surmounted by a golden oval. On the reverse, in print rather than script, so as to make the hand unrecognizable, were these words:

Mrs. Hounslow,

Enclosed please find a donation for your girls' school, submitted at the request of A Sympathetic Lady.

> *Your servant,*
> *The Saint of Seven Dials*

Halfway there! Clutching the letter and card to her breast, Quinn twirled about the room, feeling even more pleased with herself than she had the time she had saved her father's business fifteen thousand dollars with her accounting skills and suggestions. That had only brought her family more wealth, when they already had enough and to spare. But this! This would transform lives, bringing the possibility of a secure future within reach of girls who previously had no such hope at all.

Even her lingering doubts about Marcus could not dampen her euphoria. Seized with sudden determination to raise the remainder of the money at once, she went to her desk and cut a sheet of heavy, pressed paper into six squares, discarding the portion with the crest. On these squares, she wrote identical notes, taking her cue from the Saint and disguising her handwriting by printing:

*Your lewd activities with girls below the age of con-
sent have been documented. To avoid general expo-
sure and the censure of the world, leave two hundred
pounds, in notes, at Grillon's Hotel, wrapped in an
envelope and addressed to A Sympathetic Lady.*

Once finished, she regarded her handiwork with
satisfaction. Now she had only to deliver these notes
to six of the gentlemen Annie had named. If all of
them complied with her terms, the school would be
completely funded.

The only problem was delivery. The first note
would somehow find its way into Lord Fernworth's
pocket at the Wittingtons' ball the next night, but
what of the others? She would simply have to keep
the cards with her and wait on chance—at least until
she could form a better plan.

Accordingly, she tucked them into the lining of
the reticule she meant to carry to the ball, then hid
the notes from Mrs. Hounslow and the Saint at the
back of her desk drawer, next to her list of potential
contributors and her original letter from Mr. Throgmorton. So light was her heart, she felt disinclined
for sleep.

Only one thing remained to mar her peace of
mind. On sudden decision, she rose, pulling her
wrapper more tightly about her. She would confront
Marcus now, this very night. She would ask him
what Lord Fernworth had meant, and allow him to
clear himself of her suspicions. Then she would confess that she had hired Polly and Gobby, for charitable reasons.

Depending on his reaction, she might even tell him the truth about A Sympathetic Lady and enlist his help in her scheme.

Knowing that she was letting her heart rule her head, but at the moment caring not a whit, Quinn passed through the dressing room and cautiously opened the door to Marcus's chamber. At once his valet came forward.

"Yes, my lady?"

She swept the room with a glance, ascertaining that Clarence was its sole occupant. "Where is Lord Marcus?" she asked, attempting an authoritative tone fitting to the lady of the house.

"Out, my lady."

Her composure slipped. "Out? He has gone out? Did he say when he planned to return?"

"Not for two or three hours, I should say, my lady. He asked me not to wait up for him."

Quinn swallowed. Had he decided to join Lord Fernworth and his set at Boodle's after all? What might their evening entail, besides gaming? She couldn't bear to think about it.

"Thank you," she belatedly said to his valet, then retreated to her own chamber, feeling both foolish and angry.

Why had he not told her he would be going out? It must be because he intended to do things of which he knew she could not approve. And all, perhaps, because she had pleaded weariness, leaving him to his own devices.

No! She would not accept the blame for this. Marcus was a man grown, and his choices were his own responsibility. She only hoped that she was mistaken in her guess at what those choices might be.

Her earlier exhilaration gone, a wave of weariness washed over her. With trembling fingers, she removed her wrapper and prepared for bed.

She would carry through with her plans for raising the remainder of the money. Until she did, it would doubtless be best if she could contrive to spend as little time in Marcus's company as possible.

Her heart would be safer that way.

Chapter 20

Breaking into Sir Gregory's house had been more of a challenge than Marcus had expected. When he had arrived servants had still been very much awake, one in the kitchen and another moving about the house. He'd had to enter through the coal bin, then dart from room to room to avoid detection.

Finally, however, all was quiet, and he was able to set to work. His first goal was Sir Gregory's study, a small room adjacent to the parlor on the first floor. A quick but thorough search turned up no evidence that the man was involved in any way with the crimps—not that Marcus had particularly suspected he might be. He therefore pocketed the fifty or sixty pounds in notes that had been hidden in the desk and moved on.

Mindful of the girls' school that doubtless needed more funding, he took a candle from one of the hallway sconces and headed for the plate closet on the ground floor. It was locked but unguarded. He'd been practicing his lockpicking, and had the door open in the space of two or three minutes. Raising his candle, he surveyed the silver stored there.

Quickly, he made his choices—flatware and a few silver plates that would be difficult to trace, as they bore no crests or other identifying marks. Wrapping the pieces in cloth to prevent their clanking, he filled the small sack he'd brought, then, with a flourish, placed a card in the empty space remaining. Finally, he left the closet door ajar, so that the theft would be sure to be noticed on the morrow.

Carefully, he made his way to a window that provided an easier exit than the coal cellar and opened it—then froze at the sound of a low growl. Turning, he saw moonlight glinting from the bared teeth of a large Irish setter.

Frantically, he racked his brain for the dog's name, certain that he'd heard Sir Gregory mention it during one of his interminable stories. It was something to do with Irish legend, he recalled . . . Sidhe? Tara? Ah!

"Banshee. Hello, Banshee," he said in as natural a tone as he could manage. "That's a good dog, then."

The beast stopped growling, its tail moving uncertainly from side to side as it approached to sniff the intruder. Marcus wished he'd brought something—anything—that a dog might eat, but he had nothing.

"Yes, you're a fine lass, you are. A credit to your breed, I don't doubt." He managed to inject some enthusiasm into his voice, and the setter responded at once, rearing up to place her big red paws on his shoulders and lick his face. Marcus chuckled.

"Sorry excuse for a watchdog, that's what you are, Banshee. But I won't tell your master if you won't." He stroked her silky ears for a moment, then gave her a final pat on the head before vaulting through the window.

He was turning back to close it when the bitch suddenly lived up to her name, splitting the night with an ear-piercing howl. For a horrified instant Marcus tried to hush the dog, then realized she'd likely already awakened the household—and any nearby neighbors in residence, as well. Tucking the sack of purloined silver under his arm, he turned and fled.

He'd wanted his last exploit noticed and credited to the Saint of Seven Dials, he reflected as he turned a corner and sprinted along a narrow lane between larger streets. He supposed he should be grateful to Banshee for serving his purpose so well.

Quinn took a breakfast tray in her room, unwilling to face Marcus until she had decided whether or not to question him about his absence last night. As she ate, she realized that her original plan of the night before might serve her best. She would observe Marcus's reaction once Lord Fernworth received her note and adjust her own actions to his.

That settled, she considered how she might avoid her husband until tonight's ball. Gazing around the room for inspiration, her eye fell upon that dreadful hunting scene. Of course! She would immerse herself in redecorating her chamber. He could have no reason to find that suspicious in the least.

Accordingly, as soon as she was dressed, she set out for the drapers, leaving word with a footman for Marcus, telling him of her plans. The morning was spent selecting fabric in shades of lilac and cream, and the afternoon, back in her chamber, in consultations with decorators and upholsterers.

By evening all had been settled, with work scheduled to begin on Monday. The hunting scene had already been removed, to be shipped to Anthony's hunting lodge.

Only once during the afternoon had Marcus peeped into her room, but upon her asking him which of two striped patterns he preferred for the walls, he had retreated at once. Quinn told herself it was just what she had intended, but now, finishing a solitary dinner in her room, she felt a pang of loneliness.

Strange how dependent she had become on Marcus's company after a bare week of marriage. She had always despised women who clung to their husbands, unable to carve out lives of their own. It was something she had admired in her own mother, that she had interests and activities unrelated to Papa's, as well as an active hand in the family business.

Shaking off her foolish melancholy, she rose and rang for Monette. She did have interests of her own, and a worthwhile project to pursue, she reminded herself. At the ball, she would be conducting business far more important than decorating a room, even if no one knew of it but herself.

Despite her determination to remain aloof from Marcus until she knew more about his vices, past and present, Quinn could not suppress a thrill of satisfaction at the obvious admiration in his eyes as she descended the stairs. As this was to be her first real ball in England, she had taken pains to look her best. If his greeting was any indication, she had succeeded.

"You are breathtaking, my lady. I was ready to complain of your long seclusion, but now I see it was time well spent." He took her hand as she reached the bottom step and lifted it to his lips for a lingering kiss.

"You look exceedingly fine yourself, my lord," she responded with a smile. It was true. Dressed in deep blue superfine with silver in his waistcoat and a blindingly white cravat, he looked as handsome as she had ever seen him.

He returned her smile, and her heart turned over. "And you told me you were no expert at flattery," he teased.

"I seem to recall that you told me the same thing," she countered, still smiling in spite of herself. How could he so thoroughly undermine her defenses with only a few words? "Is the carriage ready?" she asked, to distract herself from her body's reaction to his nearness.

"It should be at the door in a moment. Were you able to decide between those two patterns? Lilac suits you, by the bye." His eyes twinkled appreciatively as he surveyed her from head to toe, lingering on her bosom and then her face, which she felt heating in response.

"Thank you. It's always been a favorite color of

mine. And yes, I chose the narrower stripe for the walls, and two shades of solid lilac for the bed hangings."

He nodded, though she had the feeling he was not taking in the meaning of her words, despite the intensity of his eyes on hers. "Bed hangings," he echoed. "It sounds lovely."

"We shall see." She strove for a brisk tone, but feared she failed to achieve it. "By Thursday, all should be completed."

"I look forward to seeing the results of your efforts. Of course, you will not wish to sleep in that room while it is in the disarray of transformation. Luckily, I do not mind sharing."

"Too kind," she murmured, her heart accelerating. No, she *must* not let him charm her—not yet. "It won't become an issue until Monday, however."

He shrugged. "The invitation is open at any time, regardless. Ah, here is the carriage." Extending his arm, he escorted her out to the conveyance. She resolutely tried to ignore the effect even such casual contact had on her senses.

The Wittington house, on Curzon Street, was larger than their own, though not so grand as the Tinsdales', and boasted a fair-sized ballroom, which took up much of the first floor. Examining the layout of the room as they advanced into it after greeting their hosts, Quinn realized that movable walls must divide the ballroom into two or three smaller rooms for daily use. Very clever, she thought, wondering whether extensive remodeling might allow anything similar at their house on Grosvenor Street.

"Marcus, old fellow! Delighted to see you again so soon." Lord Fernworth's voice pulled her abruptly back from such musings, reminding her forcefully of her plans for the evening.

"You're out early, Ferny," Marcus replied easily to his friend. "Got in enough gaming last night that you didn't need more this afternoon?"

Had Marcus met him at Boodle's? Quinn wondered.

Lord Fernworth grinned and shrugged. "Wittington keeps a good cellar, so I thought it prudent to be prompt tonight, that I might take fullest advantage." He turned then to Quinn, who determinedly kept a smile on her lips, mindful of her plan. "Dare I hope that Lady Marcus yet has a dance or two free?"

"As we have but just arrived, none has yet been spoken for, my lord," she responded. The idea of dancing with Lord Fernworth repelled her, knowing what she did of him. But a dance would give her the perfect opportunity to slip one of her notes into his pocket.

"I do insist that you save me the supper dance, my dear, as well as any waltzes," Marcus said before Lord Fernworth could reply. "Perhaps the first dance, as well?"

She wondered why he was regarding her so curiously. "Of course, my lord." Surely he couldn't suspect—

"The second set then, my lady?" Lord Fernworth asked, with a gallant bow. His attempt at charm seemed clumsy after Marcus, but Quinn inclined her head.

"Very well, my lord."

As soon as Fernworth left them, Marcus turned to her, his expression concerned. "It didn't occur to me until just now to ask whether you dance. My abject apologies for not inquiring sooner."

So that was what he'd been curious about! Relieved, she laughed aloud. "Yes, my lord, even in the wilds of Baltimore, people dance. In fact, one of the benefits of involvement in a shipping concern is the opportunity to gain early intelligence of new trends in Europe. I'd wager I waltz as well as you do."

"Indeed?" His eyes were twinkling again, looking almost impossibly blue. "Perhaps I'll accept that wager, if we can agree upon the terms. Let's see . . . If I lose, you may share my bed. If you lose, I share yours."

She smacked his arm with her folded fan. "You are incorrigible, my lord! I was not speaking of an actual wager, and well you know it."

"Pity," he said with an exaggerated sigh. The small orchestra signaled the start of the first dance then, and he led her onto the floor for the traditional minuet.

Privately, Quinn was more than a bit relieved to discover that her dancing skills had not deteriorated noticeably from disuse. It had been a over year since she'd attended a ball, she realized, what with her mother's death, her immersion in the business, preparations for her absence, and her journey to England.

At the close of the minuet, Marcus bowed. "Pray forgive me for doubting you, my lady. I see you are as naturally gifted at the dance as in all other things." A quirk of one eyebrow gave his words a meaning that made her blush.

"You flatter me, my lord."

"I am working on my skills in that area—but stating a simple truth hardly counts, I fear."

Before she could respond, Lord Fernworth appeared at her elbow to claim his dance. Swallowing her distaste for the man, she accompanied him to the floor. The country dance did not allow for much conversation, for which she was grateful—but it also did not allow her easy access to his pockets.

As she moved up the line for the second time, she took advantage of a movement of the dance where her back was to the set to slip a note from her reticule into her left glove. Passing from hand to hand along the line, she met up with Lord Fernworth again at the top, where he was to swing her about before their promenade back to the bottom.

Linking arms as the dance required, she found her right hand close enough to his coat pocket that she was able to touch it. They then reversed, linking opposite arms. Smiling brilliantly at him the while, she managed to slip the note into his other pocket just before they joined both hands for the promenade.

Quinn was pleased enough with herself that she did not need to feign her smile for the remainder of the set. When Lord Fernworth discovered that note, he would have no way of linking it to her. Any woman—or even any man—in the set could have planted it, and he likely would dance more sets before he found it.

Thanking Lord Fernworth with every appearance of sincerity, she returned to Marcus, who had partnered Miss Chalmers in a set on the other side of the floor.

"I'm pleased to see you are no longer irked at Ferny," he commented once his friend was out of earshot. "I know he's a complete fribble, but there's no real harm in him."

Quinn opened her mouth to refute his claim, but realized she could not without revealing more than she was ready to. Luckily, Miss Chalmers spoke before her hesitation could be noticed.

"Lady Marcus, have you heard the gossip of the day? The Saint of Seven Dials was nearly caught last night!"

"Indeed?" Quinn tried to disguise her alarm. If he were caught, he could be of no more help to her school.

Marcus nodded. "Miss Chalmers was telling me the tale as we danced. It appears he made the mistake of burgling a house that boasts a watchdog."

Miss Augusta Melks, standing nearby, overheard them and moved to join the conversation. "Sir Gregory says that one of his servants actually caught a glimpse of the Saint as he fled. He described him as tall, young, and vigorous." She giggled, covering her mouth with her fan.

"Could there be any doubt of that?" asked Miss Chalmers with a sigh. "Even my mother agrees 'twould be a shame if he were caught." She nodded toward Lady Wittington, who was deep in conversation with a pair of dowagers.

"He'd be wise not to take such chances then, I should think," said Marcus, though Quinn thought he appeared rather bored by the topic. "If you'll excuse us, ladies, there are a few people to whom I have yet to introduce my wife."

Quinn was just as glad to leave the conversation, fearful that she might give something away if she joined in. Still, she could not deny her curiosity to know more of the mysterious Saint. Tall, young, and vigorous—and perhaps a gentleman in disguise, as well? She knew there was no point in quizzing Marcus about him, however, as he had shown a disinclination for the subject.

A moment later she was effectively distracted by a series of introductions, some of which were accompanied by solicitations to dance. She graciously agreed to partner several gentlemen, two of whom happened to be on the list of names Annie had given her.

When the next set began, she found herself facing a Mr. Hill, of whom Marcus had seemed to disapprove, she'd noted with some satisfaction. Indeed, he seemed almost out of place at this gathering, his clothing less than expertly tailored and his expression both sly and discontented. She would never have agreed to partner him but for the chance to further her goal.

"I understand you are cousin to Sir Gregory, the man who so nearly apprehended the Saint of Seven Dials last night," she said as the dance opened.

Mr. Hill nodded, nearly treading on her foot as he executed the first steps. "My cousin doubtless exaggerates the matter," he said with an unpleasant laugh, "though I confess I'd have been delighted to hear the scoundrel was in custody at last."

"You do not ascribe to the notion of his heroism, then?" she asked, not particularly surprised. This man likely had no notion at all of what true heroism was.

"Heroism! Pah!" he exclaimed rudely, earning a glare from two other ladies in their set. "I've had valuables of my own stolen by this so-called Saint. The Runners can't catch him soon enough for my liking."

"My sympathies, Mr. Hill," said Quinn, neatly sliding a note into his pocket. "I did not realize you were one of his victims." The movements of the dance parted them then, and she was just as glad. He was the most unpleasant man she'd ever met in a ballroom.

Two dances later, she was able to slip another note into the pocket of Sir Hadley Leverton, then the orchestra struck up a waltz.

"My dance, I believe, my lady?" Marcus materialized in front of her as she left the floor with Sir Hadley.

With a smile of appreciation for his vast superiority over her recent partners, Quinn willingly accompanied him back to the floor. When he placed a hand at her waist, the familiar tingle helped to erase less pleasant memories.

"I confess you have surprised me in your choice of partners this evening," he said as the music began. "Some of them make Ferny appear positively distinguished."

She forced a laugh, though his perceptiveness alarmed her. "Oh, we Americans are not so discriminating as you English, you know. I assumed that anyone you were willing to introduce to me must be worthy of my notice."

A slight frown marred his handsome brow. "Then why—? No matter. But pray rest assured that you are well within your rights to refuse anyone, whether I introduce him to you or not."

"Thank you, my lord, I shall keep that in mind in future." And indeed, she had no intention of dancing with any other disagreeable men—ever—if she could avoid it. None of the others on her list had asked her, in any event.

They danced in silence for a few moments, and then Marcus said, "A pity you did not take me up on my wager earlier. You would have won it easily."

She flushed with pleasure at the compliment, for he was no mean dancer himself. In fact, his skill was one more bit of evidence that he had never been so stodgy as she had once imagined. "I cannot agree, but I thank you," she said, dimpling up at him.

He held her gaze with his own for a long moment, and she felt the beginnings of desire stir within her. Had Lord Fernworth found his note yet, she wondered? Would he mention it to Marcus—and how would Marcus respond?

And why on earth had she decided on such a silly test when she knew in her heart that Marcus was incapable of the same level of depravity as his friend?

Just as the thought crossed her mind, she caught sight of Lord Ribbleton across the room. She had met him briefly yesterday at the Jellers' picnic, but had not yet known that he was one of the nastier patrons Annie and her fellows had to suffer. He—and Lord Pynchton, who had caused Annie's injury—must both receive notes somehow. If not here, then at their homes.

"Do you agree with what some are saying, that the Saint of Seven Dials is growing careless?" she asked Marcus, an idea occurring to her.

He gave a slight shrug and twirled her expertly before replying. "I suppose it's possible. He seems to grow ever bolder, and if he continues so, he is bound to be caught. Mr. Paxton seems the sort to take advantage of any slip he might make."

"So I had thought," she agreed, then fell silent again, thinking. What if there were two housebreakers for Paxton and the Runners to pursue? Surely that would dilute their resources and make the Saint more difficult to catch.

Perhaps A Sympathetic Lady should mimic his exploits in the course of delivering her ultimatums. Her imagination fired by the idea, she scarcely noticed the remainder of the dance, smiling absently as Marcus released her to her next partner.

By the time her reel with Mr. Pottinger ended, she had determined to attempt an assault on Lord Pynchton's house that very night, if she could slip away from Grosvenor Street without being discovered. She would enlist Polly's help, if the girl was still awake on their return.

Marcus partnered her again for the supper dance, and paid her some small compliment as the dance brought them together. She responded automatically, wondering whether she was truly capable of breaking into a house and escaping again undetected, as the Saint so frequently did.

There was only one way to find out.

Chapter 21

Marcus led Quinn in to supper, wondering at her abstraction during their last two dances. Something was clearly preying on her mind, but what?

"Penny for your thoughts," he whispered, bending close to her ear as he pulled out a chair for her.

She froze in the act of sitting down, her head snapping up. "What? I . . . I was just thinking how long it's been since I attended a ball." Her smile was no more convincing than her words.

Seating himself beside her, Marcus took her hand. "Come now, my dear, I can tell something is bothering you tonight. Can you not tell me what it is?" If Paxton were here tonight, he might suspect it had something to do with her questioning of Gobby, but he hadn't seen the man all evening.

She hesitated for so long that he thought she might not answer. Finally, she said, "Much as I hate to admit it, I suppose I am a bit shocked by some of the people who are considered *haut ton*. From things I have, ah, overheard, it sounds as though some of them indulge in rather shocking vices. Perhaps I was more sheltered in Baltimore than I realized."

Marcus relaxed. "I'm surprised that anything can shock you in a ballroom after your experience at the Scarlet Hawk."

Though she blushed charmingly, she shook her head. "That was different. The people there—Well, they weren't the sorts from whom one would necessarily expect the highest standards of behavior."

"Whereas the people here should be above the baser sins of the flesh?" He chuckled. "Sheltered indeed. But I do understand what you mean. Some of the men here have seats in Parliament. I suppose, at least in theory, we *should* expect better of those who make our laws."

"Exactly. But you think that's foolish, don't you?" Her green gaze was doubtful, as though she expected a rebuke from him.

They were interrupted briefly as another couple took their places just across the table. After nodding a greeting with barely concealed impatience, Marcus turned back to Quinn, his voice low and serious.

"No, it's not foolish at all. If more thought that way, I have no doubt this country would be the better for it. Don't let anything my frivolous friends say—or that I say myself—make you compromise your ideals."

She regarded him for a long moment, as though trying to divine exactly what he meant, then nodded. "Thank you. I won't."

"Good girl. Now, what can I get you from the buffet?"

As he filled their plates a moment later, he wondered why it had seemed so very important that she realize he meant what he said, and whether his words signaled yet another change in him.

The remainder of supper was conducted on a lighter note, trading quips and gossip with Mr. and Mrs. Beckhaven, the couple opposite them. They were pleasant people, and both Marcus and Quinn warmed to them as they talked.

They rose from the table as the orchestra resumed its labors, and Quinn concealed a yawn behind her hand. "How late is this ball likely to last, do you think?" she asked.

He smiled down at her, a protective fondness that could only be love welling up within him. "We can leave at any time, if you are tired. The orchestra will likely play on until two or three."

Her answering smile did indeed show signs of weariness. "I fear I may never get used to Town hours," she said apologetically.

"Come, let's make our excuses to our hosts, then. I had forgotten what a long day you have already put in with the decorators."

By the time they reached Grosvenor Street, it was clear to Marcus that Quinn's tiredness had not merely been a ruse to be alone with him, as he'd hoped it might be. Therefore, he offered no objection when she apologetically headed straight for her bed.

Feeling disinclined for sleep himself, he went to the library for a brandy. He couldn't deny he'd enjoyed all the talk of the Saint's exploits, exaggerated though they were by late in the evening. It was amusing to listen, knowing they were actually discussing him—to be a secret celebrity of sorts.

Still, he intended to give it up. Not only for Quinn's sake, but for his own. Already he was growing hardened to the idea of stealing, and he didn't care to think where that might lead. Luke had stolen from necessity and a thirst for vengeance, but he himself, while using the proceeds charitably, was primarily in it for the thrill. Not a particularly noble motive.

He glanced at the clock on the mantelpiece. Half past one. Perhaps he would attempt his final foray, to Lord Ribbleton's house, tonight, and get it over. Draining his glass, he stood, only to be startled by the sound of the front door knocker. He emerged into the hall just as the door was opened by a sleepy footman to reveal Lord Fernworth.

"I need to speak to Lord Marcus," he said in agitated tones. "It's rather important. Pray tell him— Ah! Good, you're still up." Spotting Marcus near the library door, he came forward eagerly.

"A bit late for a social call, Ferny," Marcus commented, wondering whether his friend was even drunker than usual.

But Fernworth shook his head. "Not a social call, not exactly. I need to ask your advice."

Marcus stood aside to allow his friend to precede him into the library, then closed the door. "Well? What is it?"

Fernworth paced back and forth for a moment before dropping heavily into one of the soft leather chairs. "Perhaps it's just a prank. I'm hoping that's all it is. But if it ain't, I'll need to decide what to do."

"What sort of prank?" Marcus asked patiently. "Has someone filled all of your wine decanters with water?"

"No, no, nothing so harmless. Here, see for yourself." Ferny pulled a scrap of paper from his pocket and handed it to Marcus, who read it through, then looked his friend in the eye.

"So? Is it true? Have you been engaging in"—he glanced down at the note—"in 'lewd activities with girls below the age of consent'?"

"That's the devil of it," said Ferny, running a hand through his fair hair. "I don't ask for a wench's age, as long as she's willing. But it's possible."

Marcus felt a twist of revulsion. The age of consent was only twelve, though laws had been proposed to raise it. "If you think it's possible, you'd be wise to pay the lady, I should think, rather than risk running afoul of the law—not to mention social censure." Quite an enterprising woman, this Sympathetic Lady!

"Give in to extortion? That's your advice?" Ferny looked disappointed. "I thought you'd have a better plan. And suppose this woman, whoever she is—assuming it really *is* a woman—is preying upon others as well?"

"Presumably, if they are innocent, they will ignore her warnings, fearing no reprisals. If they are not . . ." He shrugged. He could feel no sympathy for men who would use mere children—not even for Ferny, if it were true.

But now another thought occurred to him. "Where did you come by this note?" he asked.

"Found it in my pocket. Someone at the Wittington do must have put it there, but I've no idea who."

"Indeed?" Now Marcus's interest was well and truly caught. So this Sympathetic Lady had been present at the ball, had she? That narrowed down the possibilities considerably, unless—"Could a servant have done it, think you?"

Lord Fernworth shook his head. "Don't see how. The only ones I recall being close enough were the footmen serving drinks, and one of them could hardly have slipped anything into my pocket without dropping his tray. No, it must have been during a dance, or at supper."

A woman of quality, then. He'd suspected it from first reading her note to the Saint. Ingenious of her to go after the very men who made her proposed school so necessary. He was glad he'd done his bit to contribute.

"Pay it," he advised Ferny now. "What is two hundred pounds, after all? And stick to the older wenches when you go carousing from now on."

His friend nodded fervently. "I'll do that, right enough. Two hundred pounds ain't a small sum for me, but I can call it the price of a lesson, I suppose. What will this Sympathetic Lady do with the money, do you think?"

Marcus shrugged, hiding a smile. "Perhaps something charitable. Believing so should soothe your conscience, as well as ease the sting of payment."

That sum would have been significant for Marcus as well, before his marriage to Quinn, he realized.

Ferny snorted. "First the Saint, and now this mysterious lady. As if taxes weren't steep enough without such vigilante philanthropists." Rising, he poured himself a generous measure of brandy and tossed it down so quickly that Marcus winced. "Here's hoping Paxton can catch them both. But for now I suppose you're right, and I'd best pay."

With that, he took his leave, Marcus staring after him thoughtfully. Ferny was right. This Sympathetic Lady and the Saint did have much in common, at least on the surface. He found himself more and more curious about her true identity.

Tomorrow, he decided, he would take steps to discover it, if only so that he could warn her about Paxton. In any event, he planned to send what he'd stolen from Sir Gregory to Mrs. Hounslow, as well as whatever he picked up at Ribbleton's house. He'd have to go there tomorrow night, as it was too late now to ask Gobby to play lookout.

Looking forward more than ever to the time when he could tell the entire story to Quinn, he extinguished the candles and headed up to bed.

"Oh, do be careful, milady!" Polly whispered, as Quinn headed around to the back of Lord Pynchton's town house. Looking over her shoulder at the girl, she put a finger to her lips and nodded.

Getting here had been tricky enough. On reaching her room at home, she had sent Monette to bring

Polly to her, then had dressed once again in Charles's clothes. But as they had tiptoed down the back stairs, someone had knocked at the front door, nearly scaring her to death. She had listened long enough to discover that it was Lord Fernworth before slipping out through the garden.

As she'd hoped, Polly knew where Lord Pynchton lived, and had been quite willing to accompany her to his house on Mount Street once Quinn explained her purpose. Now, however, faced with the reality of housebreaking, Quinn had to confess she was as nervous as Polly appeared to be. She had come this far, though, and had no intention of turning back.

The back of the house looked much like their own. The kitchen and back doors would doubtless be locked. She tried them anyway, and discovered to her intense relief that the door leading to the ground floor had not been latched properly. Softly, she pushed it open and crept into the back hall.

A moment later, she understood why the door was unlocked, for she heard the unmistakable sounds of a man in the throes of sexual excitement coming from behind what must be the parlor door. Lord Pynchton must be engaged with one of those poor girls of the street at this very moment!

Incensed, Quinn took two quick steps toward the parlor, then stopped. How would she explain her own presence in her current attire, even if her intervention might spare the girl a bruising like Annie's? No, she would do better to stick to her original plan, much as she itched to punish Lord Pynchton more directly.

Reining in her fury, she moved to the card tray in the front hall and deposited her note. Even if he paid, she was determined to report Pynchton to the authorities—not that she knew how to go about it. Perhaps Mr. Paxton could be of help.

Her task complete, she tiptoed back through the house, steeling herself against the faint whimpers coming from the parlor. In a moment she was in the garden, hurrying back to where she'd left Polly as a lookout.

"Let's go," she said, belatedly realizing that she was trembling. This had been far more upsetting than she had expected. Weariness overwhelmed her as fear and anger receded, and she was stumbling with it by the time they returned to Grosvenor Street.

How did the Saint manage such activity night after night? Her admiration for the mysterious hero rose even higher. She was glad she herself intended only one more such foray. After visiting Lord Ribbleton's house the next night, she hoped to have enough money for the school. Then A Sympathetic Lady could retire, secure in the knowledge that she'd made a difference.

As she and Polly neared the house, she recalled Lord Fernworth's visit. Could it be that he had discovered her note and had come to tell Marcus about it this very night? If so, what did that mean? And was he still there?

She hesitated, but then saw that the library window was dark, as was the window of Marcus's bedchamber above. Creeping back into the house as quietly as she'd left it, she secured the door behind her.

Whispering her thanks to Polly, she made her weary way up to her bed. Even dismay at the possible implications of Lord Fernworth's visit couldn't keep sleep at bay, and her last thought was to wonder whether the Saint felt this tired after every caper.

Rather to Marcus's surprise, he was up before Quinn the next morning, though it lacked only a few minutes to noon. When he had finished his breakfast without her appearing, and ascertained that she had not rung for a tray in her room, he wondered with concern whether she might indeed be ill, despite her earlier denials.

Unwilling to wake her, he decided to spend an hour or two at White's, in hopes of hearing something of the progress of Paxton's investigation. Perhaps a few discreet questions might elicit some clue as to the identity of the elusive Sympathetic Lady as well.

White's was rather thin so early in the day, but Marcus spotted Sir Cyril Weathers at a table with two or three other men of his acquaintance, all equally dissolute and brainless. He approached them, however, as they were all associates of Ferny's.

"—overheard Leverton saying he discovered one in his pocket as well," Sir Cyril was saying as he reached the table. "A dull stick like that, can you imagine? Oh, hello, Marcus. Care to join us?"

"For a bit," Marcus replied, pulling up a chair and

signaling for a glass, that he might partake of the bottle of claret on the table. "What news?"

"Bit of extortion, it seems," replied Lord Pynchton sourly. Marcus had never cared for the man, ever since seeing him viciously beating his mount in the Park once, for shying at a particularly loud carriage.

"Indeed? Have you informed the authorities?" he asked, filling his glass and taking a judicious sip.

Sir Cyril leaned forward. "That's the problem, you see," he said earnestly. Clearly this was not the first bottle the group had shared today. "This person threatens to go to the authorities herself, if her terms aren't met."

Marcus feigned surprise. "*Her?* Never say any of you are engaged in illegal activities! I'll not credit it."

Lord Pynchton waved a dismissive hand. "Illegal. Pah! As though anyone cares about what one does with street whores. I'll not pay a groat myself, I can tell you that."

Marcus's attention sharpened. To the best of his knowledge, Pynchton had not been at the Wittington ball last night. "So you've received some sort of threat yourself?"

He nodded, though he looked more angry than distressed. "Right in my own home. If I can find out who this Sympathetic Lady is, she'll be up on charges of housebreaking. Now *that's* a crime."

A chorus of agreement greeted his declaration, and Marcus listened as they continued to discuss the outrage. It appeared that Sir Hadley Leverton, among others, had discovered a note like Ferny's in his pocket last night. They knew of no one but Lord

Pynchton who had received one at his home, however.

This new topic crowded out all others, including any news of the Saint or the Runners' investigation.

Finishing his glass of claret, Marcus rose. "I'll give you good day, gentlemen, and wish you luck in unraveling the mystery. Should I hear anything to the point, I'll let you know."

He returned home to find a message from Quinn stating that she had gone out shopping with Lady Constance, and might spend the afternoon with her as well. She must not be ill, then, he thought, relief mingling with disappointment at missing her.

Over a solitary light luncheon, he thought over the women who had been present at the Wittingtons' last night, trying to guess who this Sympathetic Lady might be. Not Miss Chalmers, surely? She was high-spirited, but didn't appear to have the intelligence for such a scheme. Nor did either of the Misses Melks . . .

By the time Quinn returned for dinner, he had narrowed the likely suspects to three or four ladies, all known for their outspokenness on political matters. He still had trouble imagining any of them actually breaking into Pynchton's house, however.

"Well met at last, my dear." He greeted her at the door with a kiss, unconcerned by the footman's presence. "I presume you are feeling much more the thing after a good night's sleep and a day of shopping?"

"More—? Yes, thank you," she responded with a bright smile that held a trace of something almost like guilt. "The outing cleared the last of the cobwebs, I believe. I was clearly more unused to the exercise of dancing than I realized."

Marcus couldn't deny that some of the country dances, in particular, were quite physically demanding—and Quinn had danced almost every one. His worries about her health dissolved, to be replaced with other, vaguer ones. "Your lack of recent practice was not evident, I assure you." In fact, she had put half the English ladies to shame.

"You are too kind. But now, I hope you will excuse me. I wish to have a word with Mrs. McKay before I go up to dress for dinner." With another falsely sunny smile, she eluded his grasp and headed for the kitchen.

He stared after her, frowning. What the devil was the matter with her? Had he offended her in some way? Her demeanor reminded him of the first day or two of their marriage, when she had still been so wary of him. But why should she be so now?

A sudden chill swept through him. She had spent the day with her cousin, likely talking about home and family. Was she considering a return to Baltimore after all?

He almost asked her over dinner, but realized how such a question might sound if she was planning no such thing. And if she was, did he really have any right to stop her? Oh, he had a legal right, of course, as her husband, but he couldn't be easy at the idea of ordering another person's life to suit his own.

"Had a nice long chat with Lady Constance, I suppose?" he asked instead, watching her closely, counting on her inability to hide her emotions to give him a clue to her plans.

Indeed, she started slightly, and her eyes avoided his as she responded. "Yes, it was pleasant to get to know her better. Will you have a bit more of this haunch? It's remarkably tasty."

She clearly wished to drop the subject, so he followed her lead and moved the conversation to more general topics, though his fears were by no means allayed. Her refusal to join him in the library after dinner, on the grounds of having correspondence to attend to, only lent more weight to those fears—but still he could not bring himself to ask her directly.

"I'll see you in the morning, then." He tried not to make it a question, but it came out that way.

"Of course." With no more assurance than those two cool words, she left him and headed upstairs.

Marcus tried to settle himself in the library with a brandy, but his mind was focused wholly on Quinn. What might she really be doing, thinking, planning? How cowardly of him not to come right out and ask her.

Abruptly, he stood, his brandy scarcely touched. He would not wait until midnight to visit Lord Ribbleton's house after all. The marquess was known as an upright sort, so tonight being Saturday, he likely wouldn't be out past that hour in any event. No, this would be the best time to catch him away from home.

Besides, Marcus felt he might go mad if he sat there thinking any longer!

* * *

"Is all of my hair concealed?" Quinn asked, turning from the glass so that Polly could check the back of her head. "You're certain it won't be dangerous to attempt this so early?"

Polly shrugged. "All's I know is, this is the time of night servants most often slip away, knowing their masters and mistresses are out for the evening. Then they make sure to be back by midnight, so's they won't be missed."

"Very well, then." Quinn had to admit that she'd prefer to get this over with while she was still relatively alert. It was amazing sheer sleepiness hadn't caused her to do something foolish at Lord Pynchton's house the night before. "Let's go."

As before, they used the servants' staircase, Polly going first to make certain Quinn wasn't seen in her odd attire. The kitchen servants were yet about, so they exited through the ground-floor entrance to the garden, though the chance of being spotted by Marcus was greater. Quinn was fairly certain she had heard him go into his room earlier. She hoped he wouldn't take it into his head to check on her. Not tonight.

Safely out of the house, they quickly walked the short distance to Lord Ribbleton's imposing house on Grosvenor Square, directly opposite the Duke of Marland's mansion. Quinn stared at it doubtfully, wondering if she had the courage for this after all. It was a far grander house than Lord Pynchton's and would doubtless have more servants about, even if Lord Ribbleton was out—which she had no real way of knowing.

"Let's go around to the back," she suggested to Polly. "Perhaps I'll be able to peep through a window or two to determine whether it is safe."

They had to go all the way to the end of the square, then back through the alleyway behind, where the mews were located. Though a few stable hands were about, no one paid them any notice. Lord Ribbleton's gardens were far grander than their own, with ornamental plantings and raked paths between the shrubbery—which offered an ideal place for Polly to hide while keeping lookout.

Cautiously, Quinn approached the house, every sense alert so that she could hide if anyone came to a door or window. There was a light in the sunken kitchen windows, as she'd expected, so she went to the door leading from the main floor to the gardens, as she had at Lord Pynchton's last night. Here, however, the door was firmly locked.

Bending, she examined the lock, wondering if she might be able to pick it somehow, as the Saint apparently did on a regular basis. Five minutes probing with a hairpin, however, produced nothing but a few scratches on the door and one rather painful one on her hand. With a disgusted sigh, she gave it up and moved to inspect the lower windows.

She would *not* give up on her plan. The afternoon with her cousin had shown her that she could, indeed, fit into English Society, with a bit of effort. Her existence for so many years had revolved around the family business that even after achieving a degree of understanding with Marcus, she'd believed, deep down, that she must one day return to it.

Today had brought home to her that that chapter of her life was truly closed. Which meant she needed a new purpose, a permanent purpose—and this must be it. Last night she'd told herself that after leaving Ribbleton's note she would be done, but now she knew she could not walk away and leave everything else to Mrs. Hounslow.

No, A Sympathetic Lady would continue her crusade, one way or another.

Ah! The tall window on the corner farthest from the kitchen seemed be unlocked. Peering inside, she saw what appeared to be a music room, deserted and lit only by the window and faint candlelight from the hallway beyond.

With a quick glance to be certain no one was watching, she tugged at the window sash. It was heavy, and took all of her strength to budge, but when it finally did it moved soundlessly, its casement clearly well tended. Her heart pounding, she took a deep breath and stepped over the low sill, then pulled the window almost closed behind her.

From just inside the garden gate, Marcus surveyed the back of Ribbleton's ostentatious mansion. Upright or not, the man clearly wasn't above flaunting his not-inconsiderable wealth. "Wait here," he cautioned Gobby, and made his way silently through the elegant but deserted ornamental garden to the house.

He was nearly there when he heard a sudden rustling and what sounded like a gasp from a nearby stand of shrubbery. Frowning, he took a step toward it, only to startle a pair of ring doves into the air with a clap of wings that made him jump.

Shaking his head, he turned back to the house with a rueful smile. Just as well he was planning to retire. This business was starting to make his nerves jittery. First dogs, and now doves. What next? Mice?

Unerringly, he went to the window he'd already noticed was slightly ajar. It opened easily enough, into a deserted music room. As he crossed it, he caught up a golden ornament perched on the pianoforte and pocketed it, then went on to peer into the hall beyond. Would Ribbleton's study be on this floor, or the one above, he wondered?

Across the way, double doors stood wide, leading to a large parlor of some sort, also dark, lit only by the sconces in the hallway. Marcus moved softly in that direction, intending only to glance within for any sign of a desk before continuing in search of a study or library.

As he reached the double doors, however, a movement near the fireplace sent his pulse racing. Blast! Was some maid in there, dusting in the dark? But no. Looking closer, he saw that the slim figure was in breeches, and moving furtively. Some scullery or stable lad, looking to line his pockets illegitimately?

The figure turned his head, and something about him suddenly struck Marcus as familiar. The cap, the coat, the build—he had met this lad before. Was it one of his own group? Too tall for Tig, too short for Stilt, but—

With a shock that nearly knocked him reeling, he

suddenly remembered where he'd seen this "lad" before. His heart pounding again, but with a completely different sort of fear, he moved softly into the room.

Chapter 22

There! Lord Ribbleton could not miss her note, propped right against the clock on the mantelpiece like that, Quinn thought with satisfaction. She only wished she'd asked for more money, as the man could clearly afford it. Too late to change the note now, but perhaps she might steal something?

With an eye to small valuables, she turned—only to discover the large shape of a man looming between her and the hallway.

She nearly screamed, but clamped a hand to her mouth so that only a squeaky gasp escaped. The man stood still, his back to the dim light, watching her, his face obscured in shadow. "What . . . what do you want?" she managed to whisper, realizing as she said it what a stupid question it was.

He must assume she was a thief, a housebreaker— and he was not far wrong. What would Marcus say if she were arrested? How would it affect his reputation, his standing in Society? And why had she not considered that particular pitfall before?

When the man did not answer, and made no move to detain her, a thread of hope tempered her fear and despair. Perhaps this was a dull-witted servant that she could talk her way around, one who had no more business in this room than she did.

"I was just . . . bringing some coal for the grate," she explained lamely, gesturing toward the hod. Perhaps in the dark he would not notice it was empty. "His Lordship likes to have it ready, even in summer."

Finally, the imposing figure stirred, then spoke. "Does he? You must be quite useful to him, then."

Quinn felt her mouth fall open. "M-Marcus?" It came out as a strangled whisper. "What are you doing here?" Before he could answer her question, she did so herself. "You followed me!" She wasn't sure if she was outraged or touched by his concern.

He shook his head, but she grasped him by the arm. "Come, we must leave at once! It would never do for us to be caught here."

"I tend to agree." His voice was cool, with so little inflection that she could not tell whether he was angry or not. "Follow me."

"But—" He shook his head again, silencing her, then took her by the hand to lead her to the very room where she had entered. He must have seen her climbing through the window, she realized. Why had Polly not warned her?

He paused for a moment, one hand in his pocket, staring at the pianoforte, but then shrugged and continued on toward the window. "You first," he whispered. "I'll follow and close it behind us."

He seemed remarkably calm, she thought—far calmer than she felt, and he was the one who should be most rattled, discovering his wife in breeches, in another man's house. Wondering how she could best explain her actions to him, she stepped through the window, to the terrace outside.

Marcus followed her, then turned to pull the window nearly to. Then, as she watched in mounting amazement, he pulled some sort of wire from his pocket, looped it around the latch inside, closed the window and neatly dropped the latch into place before extracting the wire.

"Where on earth—?" she began, but her question was cut off by another voice, from a few feet away.

"Now this is a surprise. I had always believed the Saint to work alone."

Quinn whirled, her heart again in her throat, to see Noel Paxton coming up the steps of the terrace toward them.

"I confess, I had begun to have some sympathy for your cause, if not your methods," he continued amiably, as though conversing over tea in a drawing room. "But now that I find you are teaching your young apprentices to housebreak, my duty is clear."

With a shock as great as the one she'd experienced inside, Quinn realized that Mr. Paxton believed Marcus to be the Saint of Seven Dials. Though the idea was laughable, she could not allow it to persist, not when it was in her power to set him straight—no matter what it might mean for her own future.

"I fear you have mistaken the matter, Mr. Paxton," she said, and felt a spurt of amusement when he started visibly at the sound of her voice. "Lord Marcus is here because of me, not the other way around. He followed me, to keep me from coming to harm."

Paxton stared at her, then back at Marcus, then at her again. "But . . . but *you* cannot be the Saint, Lady Marcus. You have only been in England a few weeks, and the Saint has been operating for several years."

Quinn forced a smile to her lips. Where was Polly during all of this? she wondered. She hoped the girl had the sense to remain hidden. "I never claimed to be, Mr. Paxton. I am simply A Sympathetic Lady."

A long silence greeted her words. Marcus was staring at her, apparently as astounded as Mr. Paxton. Finally, the latter found his voice. "Perhaps we should move farther from the house before discussing this, if we are to avoid alarming those within."

"We can return to my house, if you'd like," Marcus suggested. "I should like to get to the bottom of this as well." His tone made Quinn shiver.

But no! She was not sorry for what she had done. Head high, she accompanied the two men from the garden, through the alleyway, and down the street. From the corner of her eye, she saw two smaller shapes following them. A glance behind revealed Polly and Gobby, their heads close together as though deep in an argument. It appeared that Polly had some explaining to do as well.

Ten minutes later, they were all seated in the library of Marcus's house, Quinn feeling more than a little bit self-conscious in her breeches. Not for the world would she go change, however, and give the two men the opportunity to decide her fate in her absence.

"Now, perhaps you can tell me how breaking into Lord Ribbleton's house denotes any sort of 'sympathy,' Lady Marcus?" Mr. Paxton began, taking a sip of the brandy Marcus had poured him. "Sympathy for whom?"

Quinn lifted her chin and met his gaze unflinchingly. "For the unfortunate young girls Lord Ribbleton has abused. He, and others like him, deserve to be exposed for the depraved monsters they are."

Paxton nodded, patronizingly, she thought. "I agree that prostitution is a grave evil, and far too prevalent in London. However, if I were to try to bring all of their patrons to justice, I fear half the male population would have to be taken into custody."

"I am not stupid, Mr. Paxton. I realize that the general problem is too large for me, or you, or anyone, to remedy. My concern is with the youngest girls forced to this life, before they are even aware of other options. And with those so-called gentlemen who not only use them sexually, but injure them in the process. Lord Ribbleton is one of those, as is Lord Pynchton. Both have recently beaten young girls in the course of pursuing their . . . pleasures." She felt her mouth twisting with disgust.

"I see." To her relief, the patronizing tone had disappeared. "That *is* a bit more serious, and something

I believe I must look into. Thank you for bringing it to my attention, Lady Marcus."

Quinn inclined her head graciously, aware how absurd she must look, but relieved that he now understood. His next question, however, brought her up short.

"But where does the Saint come into this?" He turned to regard Marcus narrowly. "Are you helping your wife in this crusade?"

"The Saint has helped me, yes," Quinn replied, though the question had been directed at Marcus. "He has contributed money toward a school I am attempting to establish for those unfortunate girls, with the help of Mrs. Hounslow of the Bettering Society, to give them alternatives to the life they now live. But Lord Marcus knew nothing about any of it until tonight."

Mr. Paxton never took his eyes from Marcus, however. "Indeed?" he asked. "I rather doubt that, since his movements over the past week have dovetailed remarkably well with the Saint's activities. He was even seen leaving a package at Mrs. Hounslow's house on Gracechurch Street a few nights ago. Perhaps the donation you spoke of?"

Quinn turned to stare at her husband. Surely, Paxton couldn't really believe—

"I'll have to have a word with Gobby," Marcus said then. "I thought he was a better lookout than that."

Paxton smiled. "He's very clever, actually. I was forced to rely on boys of a similar age from a rival flash house to avert his suspicions—which unfortunately makes their testimony suspect. And some of your targets have been rather unusual, I confess, if they are to be believed. Or perhaps there is more to this than simply the amassing of charitable funds?"

Quinn felt the blood drain from her face as she stared from one man to the other in complete shock. *Could* it be true? She could draw no other conclusion. Marcus—*Marcus*—was the Saint of Seven Dials!

"In fact, there is. I'm surprised your own spy never mentioned the kidnapping of some of his fellows by a ring of crimps operating right out of Mayfair."

Mr. Paxton frowned. "In fact, he did. He feared I was one of them when I first approached him. I had no leads to pursue, however, as he could give me no names or descriptions."

"Then you may be interested to know that I have all the proof you'll need to bring those men to justice—written proof. It's yours, on condition my wife is kept entirely out of this."

Quinn gazed at Marcus gratefully, though her head still swam at the enormity of her discovery. And she had never suspected a thing! How could she have been so blind? To think that, even now, he could be more concerned about her than about himself humbled her further.

Paxton shrugged. "Housebreaking would be the most I could charge her with, and there is no indication that anything was stolen. Besides, I cannot fault her reasons." He paused. "Or the Saint's."

"Then—?"

"I'd still like to speak with your friend, Lord Hardwyck, when he returns to town," said Paxton, rising. "But I've begun to believe that the Saint of Seven Dials may be legendary after all, as no *one* man seems to fit all of the facts I've gathered."

Grinning, Marcus rose to shake the other man's hand. "Perhaps he is," he said. "In any event, I believe London has seen the last of him."

Paxton shrugged, his expression enigmatic. "Perhaps—for the present. But if a future need for him should arise, who knows?"

With that cryptic comment, he bowed and took his leave. Marcus saw him to the door, then returned to the library. "It appears we both have some explaining to do," he said.

Rising, Quinn put both of her hands in his, wondering how she could ever have considered this man the least bit stodgy. "We do. But first, I should like to get out of these clothes. Perhaps . . . perhaps you would be willing to help me?"

"More than willing." The worry that had lurked in his eyes since their meeting at Ribbleton's—nay, since before dinnertime—melted away, and he smiled, extending his arm to escort her upstairs.

Once in his chamber, he took her in his arms for a long, passionate kiss. Finally, when she was breathless with desire, he raised his head to look deep into her eyes. "I love you, Quinn. And after tonight, I hope we never feel the need to keep secrets from each other again."

Quinn felt as though something inside her was unfolding, blossoming, filling her whole being with new hope and life. "I love you, too, Marcus. I have from the start, though I tried to convince myself otherwise." She sighed happily, resting her head against his broad chest. "And now, I can't wait to hear all about the Saint, who you so cleverly pretended to disdain."

"Are you sure you can't wait?" he asked, leaning in for another kiss.

"On second thought, I suppose I can."

"Yes, Paxton and I had a long talk." Luke sat at his ease in the library of Hardwyck Hall, a room nearly three times the size of Marcus's library.

It was now two weeks since Marcus and Quinn had achieved perfect understanding. Marcus glanced over to where she sat talking with Lady Pearl, Luke's wife, a fresh wave of love and desire pervading him sweetly. Life was exceedingly good.

"Do you think he suspects?" Marcus asked, turning back to Luke. "What about Flute?"

Luke shrugged. "He suspects, that's obvious, but he has no proof, particularly with Flute still at Knoll Grange, two hours away. Oddly, I didn't get the feeling he was really trying to force me to admit anything. He seemed more interested in what I could tell him about the Saint's history and methods."

"Perhaps he means to write a book about him," suggested Marcus with a chuckle.

"Perhaps. I'm hopeful he'll put Twitchell out of business, at the very least. But tell me, have you given any more thought to purchasing that estate we spoke of yesterday? The one adjacent to Knoll Grange? Pearl and I would spend more time there if we had agreeable neighbors."

"Among your dozens of estates? I'm honored." Marcus grinned. "And yes, Quinn and I discussed it last night. She feels we could open a sort of boarding school for street urchins at Bloomfield Manor, though of course we'll have to take a look at the house, farm, and buildings before deciding."

Luke glanced over at their wives, in animated conversation. "Then I can guarantee Pearl—and I—will want to be a part of it. And I don't doubt Flute would be willing to help fill it with students. His knowledge of Seven Dials and its denizens is formidable."

Quinn and Pearl joined their conversation then, and the four of them discussed at some length the logistics of setting up such a place. Quinn then went on to describe the progress being made with her school for girls here in London.

"Already, Mrs. Hounslow has hired several teachers, as well as a housemother. If all goes as planned, we will be able to open the school in September with fifty or sixty girls, with room to triple or quadruple that number over time."

As she elaborated on her plans, Quinn sparkled with excitement, alive with purpose and enthusiasm. Marcus realized anew how trammeled she must have felt with only the circumscribed role of Society matron to fill. Her talents would have been wasted running a single small household, planning nothing more challenging than balls and teas.

Driving home to Grosvenor Street an hour or so later, he said casually, "Luke tells me that Bloomfield contains an ironworks as well as a farm that was once far more productive than it is now. He thinks that with a bit of good management, it could easily become self-supporting again."

Quinn looked up at him, her interest clearly caught. "Might it support the school we discussed—perhaps with enough left over to send periodically to Mrs. Hounslow here in London?"

Marcus shrugged. "I have no notion of how to make a profit from iron, wool, or produce. A steward, perhaps—"

"Let me try!" she exclaimed, her eyes shining. "I'll hire a steward, too, of course, but I can research the markets, transport, price margins . . ." she trailed off, frowning. "But I suppose ladies—especially conventional English ladies—don't involve themselves in such things."

He pulled her against him, to nuzzle the top of her head. "One of the things I love most about you is the fact that you're anything but a conventional English lady. I'd be delighted for you to try your hand at running our new 'family business.' "

Her smile returned, lighting up her face—and his heart. "I do love you, Marcus." The emotion shining out of her green eyes made him hard with desire, even as it sparked an answering wave of tenderness within him.

"And I love you, my enterprising wife. Who would have guessed that my rebellious bride would become a prize worthy of a king?"

"Or worthy of a Saint, better than any mere king, and far more deserving." She snuggled against him, her smile promising yet more rewards to come.

*The weather is getting warmer, and things
at Avon romance are getting hotter!
Next month, don't miss these
spectacularly sizzling stories . . .*

MARRY ME by Susan Kay Law
An Avon Romantic Treasure

Emily Bright has found a place to call her home, but imagine her shock when she is awakened in the middle of the night to discover a tall stranger who claims she is sleeping in *his* bed! Should she marry Jake Sullivan and make this claim come true?

MY ONE AND ONLY by MacKenzie Taylor
An Avon Contemporary Romance

When Abby Lee strides into the office of Ethan Maddux and begs for his help, he barely agrees to give her ten minutes out of his busy day. So how *dare* he ask her to spend time with him at night? Abby knows that when business and pleasure mix—look out!

A NECESSARY HUSBAND by Debra Mullins
An Avon Romance

He's the long-lost heir of the Duke of Raynewood . . . she's a delectable society lady who learns it's her role to turn him into a proper Englishman. Of course, there are rules about these things . . . but sometimes the rules of society are meant to be broken.

HIS SCANDAL by Gayle Callen
An Avon Romance

Sir Alexander Thornton has a reputation as the most dashing— and incorrigible—man in England. He wagers he can win a kiss from any lady in the land . . . but that's before he meets proper Lady Emmeline Prescott.

REL 0402